1st Edition
autographed

ROXANA

Marian Castle

Books by Marian Castle

DEBORAH

THE GOLDEN FURY

ROXANA

BY

MARIAN CASTLE

WILLIAM MORROW & COMPANY

NEW YORK

1955

To Carrick

ROXANA

Chapter I

ROXANA HAD TO wake up. Some insistent, recurring sound had pried her out of her slumber. She frowned sleepily, rolled over, and drew her slim young legs up until she was a tight little ball of resistance. But it was no use; she was awake.

She lay there in the dark tentatively exploring her own identity, trying to place herself in time and space. She could not be back home in the Iowa farmhouse because no rain thrummed on the roof, threatening to wash the land away like so much brown sugar under a boiling teakettle's spout. She knew she was not in the covered wagon, drawn up somewhere alongside the trail because, when she stretched out her hand, she encountered no rough board sides.

As she waited for the strange, impending sound to repeat itself, she was aware of the faint dissonances of the night outside: the pounding of distant machinery, the vacuous bray of a burro, the far-off barking of dogs, and the steady chucking noise of axles as ore wagons jolted downward.

Now she knew where she was: she was Out West. She was lying beside her little sister Avis on a hard pallet in one corner of an abandoned shaft house in the mining town of Central City, Colorado. Across the room slept her father and mother.

Then she heard it again, the sound. It was her mother's

sobbing, coming with the dreary, hiccuping regularity of sobs that have started up, and died down, and started up again at intervals all night long. Her mother, Eunice Renner of the straight delicate lips, the neat drab bun of hair on the exact top of her head, and the quick competent movements, was crying in a lost, bitter way.

Roxana was shocked. Never before in her sixteen years of life had she heard either of her parents weep. It was upsetting. Parents ought not to cry, or be afraid, or act uncertain and forlorn.

Why didn't her father say something? Why didn't he try to comfort her mother? But Roxana knew why; when it came to words, her mother could always best him. Roxana sensed that he was lying there stiffly awake, but keeping up the pretense of sleep so that he need not have to use the weapon of words with which he was so clumsy. She knew that her mother knew he was awake, too, and that she was baffled and enraged by it.

For the first time, Roxana was aware of the secret life of her parents, unshared by their children. Abruptly she thought of them as people, instead of merely as a handy backdrop for her own living.

So her mother really and truly hated it Out West. Hated it as grimly as she had hated the neighbor Jim Lake, who returned from Colorado full of wild tales which set Dan Renner's feet a-twitching; so that when the bank began to threaten, he was only too glad to pull up stakes. Roxana realized that nothing would ever win her mother over; she was determined to make Dan Renner pay for bringing them out here, and pay for his own happiness in being here.

Roxana thought back to their hasty flight two months before. Even at the time, she had known it was more than the June floods of 1879 that were driving them out of Iowa just when the corn reached to her shoe tops; and that it was more than the bank's threats to take everything, including the team. It was an urgency in her father's voice and an eagerness in his eyes as he grabbed things from his wife's grasp and hurled them into the covered wagon backed up to the kitchen steps.

"You got enough stuff, Eunice. Come along! We'll buy new Out West. Don't fret—we ain't leaving much. Only this old house, a few sticks of furniture and a little farm machinery. Let the bank have 'em if they're so set. But, by God, they ain't going to get my team!"

Her mother's agreement had been biting.

"Sure, hang on to your team, but let the bank take the farm—and my parlor organ and your new reaper rusting out in the yard. Everything I've saved toward, these seventeen years. It's like the banker said, 'A man would have to *work* at being shiftless, to reach such a pass in seventeen years!'"

Roxana's father had tightened his lips and moved out of lashing distance of his wife's tongue. He lacked the words or the will or the meanness to lash back.

Roxana remembered her mother carrying a last load across the splintery kitchen floor that she had scrubbed with wood ashes until it was as white and frayed as an old rope. Her mother would leave a clean house behind even when she was fleeing from it between two suns.

Somehow Eunice Renner had managed to stow the family of four and their most cherished belongings in the big farm wagon that Dan had fitted with arching bows and canvas cover. Her caster set with the shining glass cruets was wrapped in her best chemise in the round-topped trunk. Dan Renner's black fiddle case was fastened up under the concave wooden ribs of the wagon. Eleven-year-old Avis' doll dishes were buried in the sack of corn meal. Even Roxana's freckle lotion was there, although she carefully hid from her mother six pictures of famous actresses and her dried rabbit's foot. Real actresses, Roxana had read, used a rabbit's foot to spread paint on with; but it could not have been the sinewy foot of a jack rabbit, because this one scratched when she dusted cornstarch over her cheeks with it.

[3]

Silently each of the four had stopped to take one last look at the sway-backed old house and the tipsy-looking barn, outlined against the greenish pallor that preceded dawn. The place looked secret and withdrawn, like the corpse of an old tramp shrouded in the specious dignity of death.

Her mother was the last to climb into the wagon.

"Movers!" she sniffed. "Sneaking off in the night—setting out for nobody knows where."

"We know where, don't we, Roxy?" inquired her father with forced cheer. "Coloraydo—we're on our way!"

Roxana and her father had enjoyed that westward journey across a prairie sea under a sky too vast for it. As they left the long-grass regions east of Kearney, with the occasional slough guarded by a gray heron on stilts, and reached the dry short-grass country of the grama and buffalo grasses, Dan Renner expanded. He and Roxana winked often at each other and cracked foolish little jokes and sang loud duets like "Sweet Betsy from Pike," their heads back, their mouths wide.

But Avis and her mother hated every mile. Avis, solemn as a trout, grew peaked, drinking water from the creeks. Her mother kneaded her side where the jolting of the lumber wagon had started up her old pain.

With a certain callous need for joy, Roxana and her father had refused to let those two spoil things for them.

"Ah," her father would say, breathing deep. "Out West, a man can stretch to his full height." The sun would fairly crackle on his wavy black hair and glance off the smiling whiteness of his teeth.

Even hunting fuel was a game for Roxana, with Boots their farm dog scampering along beside her, chasing real and mythical prey. But it was never any game for Avis. As they put behind them the last of the groves, and then the tree claims, and finally even the dry farms, fuel grew so scarce that the girls had to resort to cow chips. Avis would give a little scream when she picked up a "green one," moist under-

[4]

neath, with bent-over bleached grass blades and repulsive scurrying insects. Roxana learned to pick only the old dry clods. At first she carried them fastidiously in her finger tips to the fire where her mother was cooking. But by the time they reached Denver, she was stacking them chin-high in her apron.

Would she ever forget those nights along the trail, camped near the shallow sweep of the Platte? Roxana loved to lie looking out the open flap of the wagon, lining up the Dipper with the North Star and listening to the after-dark sounds: the velvet thump of a horse's hoof, the cry of a night bird, the sibilance of the breeze as it stroked the prairie grasses.

When she had her first view of the mountains—or were they only low-lying clouds?—she felt an awed thickening in her throat. Mountains! Always she had wanted to see mountains. But these looked too faintly, gauzily blue to be made of granite and pine trees. All the way across the intervening miles until they reached Denver she watched them grow larger and more beautiful.

When the wagon actually entered the mountains through a cleft outside Golden, she looked up at the frankly frowning canyon walls and felt transported. It was Avis who crowded against her mother and whimpered as if she felt a menace in that frown.

"I don't like it down in here—I want to be where I can see out. Let's go home."

"We haven't got any home now, Avis," her mother said with acid resignation. "Your father says he's bringing us Out West to make our fortunes."

Dan Renner had only slapped the lines sharply against the tired horses' backs. How could a man answer a woman who talked past him to their children?

Roxana was suddenly back in the shaft house in Central City as she felt Boots' wet muzzle nudging her outflung hand on the floor. She wound her fingers in his silky ears. Beside her, Avis grunted and flounced over on the thin pallet

[5]

through which every ridge of the warped planks jutted. Even in her sleep, Avis could complain.

"Feather beds—pshaw!" her father had scoffed yesterday afternoon as they neared this Central City, high in the front range of mountains. Her mother had not wanted to leave Denver, with its coal heaters and gas lights and soft beds. "In Central City," her father assured them, "we'll sleep on 'Irish feathers.' That's a fine soft bed made of little pine-bough tips. If we expect to make our fortune, we got to hit for the mining towns. And Jim Lake says the mine diggin's at Central are thicker'n holes in a pepper pot."

The diggings were thick, but dwelling places were scarce, at least for people who could not afford the high-toned Teller House or one of the numerous boarding houses. And there were no trees left on the once-wooded hillsides to strip boughs from to make fine soft beds; there was not even a roof to put between them and the sky. They were tired and hungry and cold as the wagon wound its way up the steep gulch street from Black Hawk to Central City, stopping here and there so Dan could ask about lodgings.

The three womenfolk huddled in the wagon while Dan made inquiries inside a saloon. How cold it was for mid-summer, Roxana had thought. The minute the sun fell behind the jagged hills, their teeth had begun to chatter.

A miner walked past on the high board sidewalk with a rollicking swagger, swerving close to the wagon to give Roxana a confiding wink. She flushed and looked straight ahead. But all of a sudden she did not feel the cold; she felt only pleasantly tingly instead. She thought she might find this Central City interesting.

They could tell, when Dan came out of the saloon, that he had had luck. He dangled a key attached to a foot-long piece of wood while he talked to an old man who was pointing and giving directions. They watched the old fellow set off up the hillside, the copper toes of his high boots clinking against the stones, his wiry body bent against the grade.

All the tiredness had slid off Dan Renner's shoulders as he climbed back into the wagon.

"Didn't I tell you?" he boasted. "First fella I met in the saloon was this old Steve—has charge of a closed-down mine, the Blue Bottle up on Mammoth Hill." He gestured with his whip. "Says we can use the shaft house free of charge till we find something better. He'll meet us there—it's only half the distance by path as by road. We're fixed finer than silk, Eunice. Old Steve says you can see the whole range from up there."

Eunice was silent. The road up to the mine was steep and rocky and took all of Dan's skill. Avis was whimpering softly.

The old man panted into view just as they reached the shaft house. Roxana stared curiously at the unpainted shed-like building. The door in the middle was flanked on either side by a small high window, and a faded sign above it weakly warned trespassers to keep out or they would be prosecuted.

As the hinges squeaked open, the old man told them proudly that the mine had once been a paying vein till she faulted. Inside, in the middle of the room, rose the frame-work of a windlass; a "windle" he called it. Under it on the floor was a trap door of warped planks.

"She goes straight down a hundred foot, that there shaft," he boasted, pointing to the insecure-looking trap door.

The family instinctively shrank back from it.

They could cook on the old forge, their host explained, and bed down in the corners where the roof didn't leak so bad. Lovingly he hefted what he called "hand-swedging" tools beside the anvil and took a fond inventory of the clutter of rope and rusty mine buckets and broken lanterns. The inside walls had been papered with newspapers, now stained and hanging in ribbons. At shoulder height around the shack ran a two-by-four shelf on which sat a dusty array of cans of nails and grease, and a straggling line of ore speci-mens. It was Roxana's first glimpse of an ore specimen; it

[7]

was the first time she had seen a man pick up a chunk of rock, lick it with his tongue to bring out the metallic shine, and proffer it with proud confidence to prove its richness.

When the old man had gone they ate a cold supper by the light of the lantern, which cast an uneasy network of shadows on the roof. As the mountain chill penetrated their bones, and as a pack rat scampered off with a clatter in one corner, they tried to swallow the dry, crumbling corn bread, but it stuck to the roofs of their mouths. For once neither Dan Renner nor Roxana had enough lift to their own spirits to prop up the sagging mood of those other two.

Roxana came back to the present with a start, as her mother gave a sharper sob from her pallet in the far corner of the shaft house. It was too loud even for Dan to continue his pretense of sleep. Roxana heard a rustle of bedclothes and a creak of floor planks as her father rolled over.

"Better get your sleep, Eunice. We got a long trip ahead to Leadville."

"I'm not going."

"Sure you are. There's nothing here. I asked all over, last night."

"I'm not going, Dan. Not that I think much of this Central City. Ugliest place I ever set eyes on. No trees—just a big gulley with a lot of gravel piles. And houses propped up on stilts to keep from falling face down in the filthy creek. Creek! When I dumped my wash water at home, it made a better creek than this one. But at least there's a school and churches here. And I saw a yellow rosebush like my mother used to have, hanging down over a wall. If this is an 'old camp,' God forbid that I should have to see a new one like Leadville!"

"I've tried to tell you, Eunice," said the voice, with thinning patience, "the easy gold has all been skimmed off the creek bars here long ago. At Leadville there's silver under every boulder."

"I won't go."

"You're a setting hen about being moved! We'll strike it rich in Leadville, I tell you."

"You're always telling me, always promising—and never making good. You could get work here if you wanted to. Teaming, or in the mines."

"Day wages! Haven't you any ambition? There's still a fortune to be dug out of the ground."

"But not by you, Dan. You'd get taken in by a no-good mine. Or sell out just before you struck the vein. Or fritter away what you did get in buying more claims. I know you. And day wages would be so nice and regular."

"I should have come alone!"

There was the angry, hopeless silence of a man and woman lying close together in body and far apart in spirit. Then the sobs took up again with fresh intensity.

Roxana heard her father turn over. His voice was still impatient, yet with a certain male tenderness in it, too.

"Now, Eunice girl, it's going to be all right." The words were muffled, muffled in bedclothes or in his wife's hair. "Now, now, Eunice girl." There was the kindly rhythm of patting in his words, as if he knew no better method of persuading his wife. The sobs lessened, diminished to a sniff.

For the first time this night Roxana realized that she was eavesdropping—on a husband and wife—in bed. Her cheeks scorched. If hearing her mother cry had made her aware of her parents as people, hearing their softened voices in the dark made her aware of them for the first time as possible lovers.

Against her will, she remembered those horrid things the older Bixby girl had told her at school. At first Roxana had refused to believe them. Not that she hadn't seen plenty of animals. Animals, on a farm, were always up to queer capers. Even when her mother had talked fast and breathily, pointing in the opposite direction, Roxana could not help seeing. Yet she had never minded; they were only animals. But her father and mother! It had been unthinkable; it had been revolting; it had been fascinating. And after a while she supposed it was true. But the trueness had had only a remote and unreal quality until now. It had had none of the dreadful actuality of this wheedling note in her father's voice, and her mother's sighs. Fear and horror froze her into rigid awareness.

And then her mother said with plaintive, bartering stubbornness, "You will settle down here then, Dan? You will try for day wages?"

Roxana heard an expletive as her father knocked over something in the dark reaching for his boots.

"Might as well get up and start a fire!" he snorted.

Roxana relaxed like a snapped bowstring. The light was beginning to come grayly through the two small windows. She shivered and crept closer to Avis' sleeping warmth.

Dan Renner nurtured no grudges. He had never been more inventive and helpful than he was that day. He found some old charcoal to start a fire in the forge. He laid planks from one rusted mine bucket to another to make a table. He pounded nails. He turned a box into a cupboard.

"No harm trying to be comfortable," he said. Or in trying to look on the brighter side, his tone implied.

He returned with an empty bucket from a trip outside to report that there were no public hydrants or wells in Central City. People bought water by the barrel and stored it in tanks in their houses. It was forty cents a barrel.

"You can't tell me folks take enough baths Out West!" sniffed Eunice. She turned flapjacks with one hand while her other fist worked at her side. Worry-pains, the doctor at home called them. There seemed scant likelihood that she would ever be free of either the worry or the pains in this raw new land so ill-suited to a woman who liked a cozy, well-lined, predictable life that she could draw around her like a warm garment against the winds of fate.

Roxana's father made one trip downtown for supplies, another trip for water, and another to ask about a job. Roxana suspected that his forays were chiefly to get away from his wife.

On the morning of the second day he decided righteously that he had better do something about his wagon brakes. He would go down and hunt up a blacksmith. He eased out the door.

Eunice did not object; she scarcely heard him. She was attacking the dusty old shed with a duck-tailed broom, beating it, pummeling it, punishing it. Every gouge of her broom was a dig at her husband for bringing her to such a place.

Eunice Renner's sole talent lay in making over and in doing without. She could sponge and turn and stitch an old coat into a respectable garment; she could achieve a lily-white soap out of grayish drippings; she could slip some goose eggs under a hen and end up with the softest featherbeds in the county; yet she did it all with an air of martyrdom. Never had she faced the fact that a life of luxury would have denied her the expression of her only talent—making-do.

She set the two girls to work. It was time they stopped dawdling and mooning. This corner seemed fairly dry; Roxy could hang their clothes over here. Avis could wash and wipe the dishes and put them in this dry-goods box-cupboard. Roxy had better air the bedding in this brisk wind. How did a body wash sheets in a place where you had to buy water by the barrel?

Two hours went by before Roxana saw any hope of release.

"I guess you might as well put on your bonnet and go downtown for me, Roxy," said her mother grudgingly. "Your father spends enough time down there to 'tend to all my errands, but he's never around so as I can tell him what I want. I need five cents' worth of saleratus, and Avis' shoe-laces have been knotted twice. Now mind, no loitering!"

Eunice dug deep into her petticoat pocket for her coin purse.

Roxana felt as if the door of her cage had suddenly swung wide. Swiftly she furbished up her toilet. Sixteen was plenty old enough to wear a boughten wire bustle instead of this contraption made of wadded-up newspapers, she thought resentfully, as she tied the hump under her petticoats. She could still blanch at the possibilities implied in the folk tale about the woman who wore a similar makeshift bustle under her thin dimity, with the words *Cedar Falls Bugle* showing through for all to read.

She looked at herself in the cracked mirror, frizzed out her dark bangs, batted her sooty lashes, and set out the door with a leggy leap, wearing her youth like a feather in her hair.

On the eminence of the mine dump she paused in the sharp dazzle of sunshine. It was a high bright world, with a chill under the brightness. Rimming the horizon were the white peaks. Nearer were the barren hillsides. Down below straggled the building-lined Gregory Gulch up which they had driven day before yesterday. Already she could see that what their worn guide book called "The Richest Square Mile on Earth" was really just a lot of giant gopher holes in the hillsides and four tatterdemalion settlements strung like clumps of broken beads along the dirty thread of the creeks.

Sure, it was ugly, just as her mother had said, but it was so alive. Far below, buglike teams pulled tiny loads, and little black ants of men scurried in and out of toy buildings and along crooked toy streets.

Down at her right, beyond the railroad trestle that spanned the road, she could see Black Hawk, the first of the towns they had come through. Above it, with no line to separate it, was Mountain City where, her father said, they first discovered lode gold. At her feet, Central City clambered up the steep slopes, each line of rooftops on a level with the street above, and each street a rocky shelf. It had much the handsomest business buildings, made of brick, and much the fanciest wooden houses, hanging like bird cages to the cliffs and flaunting their cupolas and bay windows and lace-edged eaves. The fourth town, Nevada City, was up another gulch to her left. In all four towns, she knew, there was scarcely a tree. So this was the Richest Square Mile on Earth!

Her mother was right; yet her glance was indulgent as it swept the mine-pocked hills, studded with old stumps. Her father had explained that they had had to use all the trees to timber the mines and fire the engines at the mills. She guessed Central City was like the small boy who grew so fast he couldn't stop to tie his shoes. No one had time here to think about trees; everyone was too busy making money.

She could smell it; she could hear it everywhere—this making money. The fumes from the many smokestacks made her nose wrinkle. Staccato sounds beat on her ears: the metallic *thump-thump-thump* of stamp mills crushing ore, the creaking axles of strings of quartz wagons jolting toward the mills, the shouting of men to horses or mules or burros or to other men. It had a sharp, exciting, clangorous sound. The clangor of riches. Roxana savored it all—the town below, the tiered mountains, the barren gulch and the rough jostle of life.

She took a headlong slanting downward course, skittering over the mine dumps that her mother called gravel piles, until she reached Main Street that joined at an angle the long winding gulch road. As she hurried along the boot-chewed wooden sidewalks, bending forward to lean on the wind, her eagerness whipped the color into her cheeks until they were the pink of half-ripe cherries. She wanted to see what was around the corner; she had always wanted to see what was around the corner.

What lots of saloons! But it was a dry-goods store she was looking for. She chuckled at how many more stores sold

[13]

wet goods than dry. The crowds made her slow her gait. At this time of day housewives were doing their marketing, eyes averted from the saloons' swinging doors, behind which business was always good; for men were always off shift, and every pocket clinked with coins.

And what handsome brick buildings too; she could count a dozen or more. She stood on a corner and stared. From a heavy dray two grunting men were unloading a square rosewood piano at the foot of a steep flight of stone steps. Another man hurried along the street with an open tray of newspaper type in his hands. From the bank behind her men hurtled in and out the doors quite as fast and as drunkenly as they did from the saloons. She dodged out of their way. There was something drunken, too, she sensed, about the atmosphere inside those walnut-paneled bank rooms. She caught meaningless yet heady snatches of talk about "dust" and "blossom rock" and Eastern Capital.

Bemused, she moved on until she came to a general store, where she made her purchases. As she rejoined the throng on the sidewalk, she gave a little squeak of pleasure. A few doors down the street her father was just putting his boot sole up on the hub of his wagon, which was drawn up at the curb. She ran toward him with a quick lifting of the heart.

"Pa!" she sang out.

Dan Renner saw her with a start. He glanced uneasily from her to the wagon.

"I got a chance to freight a load. It's good pay, Roxy, and we need it."

"Freighting to where?"

"To Leadville."

Leadville! She remembered the talk in the night. So he had found an excuse to go to Leadville after all.

"When are you leaving?"

"Right now. Here, take what money I've got and give it to your mother. I was going to stop by." He emptied his pockets. Then he caught hold of her arm and bent as if to kiss her. But malelike, he drew back and contented himself with giving her arm an affectionate shake.

"Be a good girl, Roxy. I'll send money as fast as I can."

"You mean you're going to *stay?*"

"Only till I make a strike. Don't you fret, and don't let your mother fret." (As if that last were possible.)

"Aren't you going to say good-by to her? Aren't you going to tell her about the new job?"

"I'm getting such a late start. If I don't have time, you tell her. On my next trip, you can go along, rabbit." It was an ancient joke, the "rabbit." He used to tease Roxana, who always wanted to go along, at any hour to any place, that she was just like a jack rabbit—born running. He smiled at her again, and after he stopped, there remained the fond tracks of the smile around his eyes. It was always like this when he looked at Roxana.

He climbed into the wagon. Roxana noted that it was filled to the endgate with bulging gunny sacks. She watched it set off up steep Spring Street that wound over the hill and out of sight. The wagon never even swerved as it passed the side road that led to the shaft house where her mother was sweeping in the corners. She might have known; her father had not had the slightest intention of going back for that final tongue-lashing.

She saw the sun glint on the straining horses' backs; she saw Boots' tail waving happily over the edge of the seat; she saw the canvas cover bob and sway. He was going to Leadville without her. She began to run.

"Pa!" she cried. "Take me with you!"

But already the wagon was far ahead, and her cry was drowned in the creak of axles and the harsh rattle of iron tires on flinty rocks.

She came to a stop and stood there staring. There was something sobering about even a little parting. Yet it was only to Leadville, she told herself, and he had promised to take her along next time. She was envious of him because

[15]

he had got away—and under the dutiful cloak of earning money for them.

Quivering, rebellious, every nerve and tendon straining after him, she was like a colt plunging against a high fence. She wanted to go too; now, today, not next time.

Chapter II

HEAD DOWN, Roxana rushed across the street, directly in front of a heavy quartz wagon with screeching brakes. The driver strained back on his lines, cursing both team and girl. She made a leap for the high sidewalk beyond, too agitated to care. It wasn't fair for her father to escape so easily, she thought; she wanted to escape, too.

She must vent her frustration upon someone. Her father had removed himself. There remained only her mother. She left the street and began to climb, skirting the gravelly mine dumps. Once she jumped back to avoid being showered with waste rock as an ore car spewed its contents down the face of the dump. A flying chip of rock bit her cheek. She rubbed at it, unheeding.

Not that she actually planned to hurt her mother. But because she felt misused herself, she experienced a rough satisfaction, a feeling of reprisal against life, in being the bearer of unpleasant news. She paused dramatically in the doorway of the shaft house.

"Pa's gone! He went to Leadville. He took Boots with him. Last I saw, his wagon was heading over the hill."

She was sorry the instant she saw the effect of her words. Her mother sank down on an upended box, her hand at her stomach, her face contorted.

Avis threw her sister a reproachful (and slightly superior)

[17]

glance and hurried to mix a dose of soda. Eunice Renner drank it between gasps, with Avis watching and unconsciously mirroring her mother's look of pain.

Roxana fluttered near, garrulous with apology.

"He got a chance to freight a load over. He had to leave in a hurry or he would have stopped to say good-by."

Her mother's lips tightened with her hurts from within and her hurts from without.

"He turned over all the money he had to you. He said it wasn't much, but he'd send more soon. He said his one aim was to try to make you comfortable—he wants to buy you a fine feather tick, not one made of 'Irish feathers,'" Roxana rushed on, embroidering her father's remarks because of her sense of guilt and because she could not help it. "He said he'd rent us a house with a yellow rosebush hanging over the wall. Oh, he'll be sending back money the minute he makes a strike."

"He'll never make a strike," said her mother drearily. "He'll mean to send us money, but he won't. We better hang on to what we got. Women don't need much."

Perhaps her mother didn't need much. Probably Avis didn't need much either, for already Avis was a "regular little woman" who could do without quite as well as any grownup could. But Roxana was always hungry. Here it wasn't even noon, and her stomach was scraping her backbone.

"Maybe I could get a job," she suggested, brightening. A job would take her away from this gnawing, ladylike penury.

"What on earth could you do, Roxy?" belittled her mother. "You aren't trained. Working out is all you could do, and you'd hate that. Besides, nobody but your own mother would put up with your moony, unreliable ways—working yourself into a sweat if it's something you like to do, and then forgetting all about the bread dough you'd set to raise behind the stove, until it had run all over the kitchen."

Roxana's lips tightened. How her mother could rub things in. Just because she forgot that once. Besides, she had no intention of working out, which meant working in somebody else's kitchen. Not that she had any exact idea of how she could earn a living. But there must be ways. She had seen pictures in *Leslie's* of women with chignons firmly netted and with ruffled aprons over their draped skirts, working at a contraption called a "typewriter." And she knew that nice women nursed and taught school, although she was not fitted to do either. And one could always color photographs, she had been told. Surely there were "positions" where she could wear her good dress and be admired by gentlemen— at a respectful distance, of course.

"I'll find something. My one hope is to make you comfortable—" She stopped, halted by the bitter tightness of her mother's face. Yet she was quite unaware that she was parroting her father's supposed farewells, or that she looked all too like him at the moment, with that prancing eager look and a quivering at the corner of the mouth as if she were already tasting her freedom.

But for several days Roxana was forced to stay close at home because of her mother's relapse. She blamed herself for it. In her contrition she was a model of filial industry. She swept the rough plank floors and aired the quilts and made gruel and rubbed her mother's back and tried to keep the shaft house tidy.

She made occasional overtures to her little sister, but the skeptical blue eyes under the arched childish brows fended her off. Avis suspected any soft gestures from Roxana, just as she suspected and feared this strange new world, called Out West, that her father had brought them to. She was frightened by everything in it, from this horrid shed with the covered-over bottomless pit in the middle, to the ugly town below from whence came those crunching, pounding, booming noises from mines and ore mills.

With the fierce envy of eleven for sixteen she disapproved of Roxana's maturing young body and flighty ways. She disapproved and was fascinated.

Roxana discerned only the disapproval. It seemed to her that everything she really wanted to do was improper, whereas everything Avis liked to do was commendable. Avis was the sort who *liked* to clean erasers for the teacher, who *liked* to help her mother about the house. When her mother crocheted, Avis hooked yarn over a knitting spool, making long colored angleworms of yarn which she coiled around and sewed into circular mats. No one knew what to do with the mats, but there was something admirable about a prim little girl sitting beside her mother at Ladies' Aid hooking yarn over a spool.

Roxana was secretly glad that Avis was too young to be sent alone on errands down into the beckoning hubbub of Central City's business district. When at last her mother was well enough for her to leave, she tied the coins doled out to her in one corner of her handkerchief, completely closing her ears to the admonitions doled out at the same time. Like her father, she possessed the happy gift of deafness when she willed it.

"Yes, yes," she murmured absently. "Potatoes, buttons, beans, thread."

At last she was free. But when she reached Main Street, she found she could not enjoy the store windows after all, for they held such handsome hams and sides of bacon, such beautiful embroidered cloth-topped shoes and lengths of flowered percale. It was terrible to be young and hungry and always wanting things—and then to be only a woman who must make do with what a male provider happened to send. She shut the eyes of her mind tight against certain memories. The day, for instance, that the banker had come out to the farm to see about the overdue loan, and her father had been away. Her mother had tried to argue with the man, but you could see she did not believe in Dan Renner's hopes and schemes either.

"Your husband's a good enough promoter," the banker had said with a stiff smile, teetering on the shaky top step of the porch, "but a poor provider, I fear." And her mother had not disputed him.

Roxana's head went up. My father is wonderful, she thought. There's no one like Pa. Just wait till he makes a strike. But at the post office she could not control the sharp, "Oh, no!" of disappointment when she found there was no letter for them.

It was a week since her father had left. There had been plenty of time for him to get a letter back to them with money in it. He must have been well paid for freighting that load over. But still she shied away from her mother's verdict that he was a do-less man whose promises meant no more than his name on a note.

She tightened her mouth and walked on. Presently the tight look relaxed into a half-smile as she was swept along by the afternoon crowds whose feet thudded hollowly on the high mud-spattered wooden sidewalks.

Mine shifts had just changed. There was a feeling of gaiety and ease in the air. Tired, dirty-faced men stopped in at the saloons, carrying lunch buckets shaped to hold their half-moons of meat pasties. Miners' buxom wives called out to each other in their strange Cornish dialect. Ladies, obviously wives of mine superintendents or lawyers or doctors, minced along holding up their skirts in one hand to keep from snagging them on the wooden sidewalks and also to show off ankles as shapely as goblet stems. Roxana noted that the pudgy ones whose legs were probably shaped like butter churns did not worry about snags but just let their skirts drag.

Now that she had the chance, there was something she must see. She climbed the steep grade past the impressive hotel, the Teller House. Her father had told them it contained a Knabe square grand piano and a kitchen range that was as long as a locomotive. And that once, a few years back, they had paved the way up to the front door from the street with silver bricks for President Grant to walk upon. Silver bricks! It sounded splendid and slightly insane. Roxana was glad she had come to such a country. Nobody back in Iowa paved sidewalks with silver bricks.

The new stone opera house was her goal. She stared up at it with probing yearning. She even cautiously tried each of the front doors. But they yielded nothing. The boards in front contained no pictures of actors and actresses, only tatters of torn paper.

Well, it was something just to see a real opera house where they gave plays on the stage with casts that came all the way from Chicago and New York.

Glancing around to see if anyone was looking, she made her way along the side of the building, where the little trash-filled creek ran under both the opera house and the hotel. What would her mother think of *that?* A stream running under a building because there wasn't any other place for it. As it was, the buildings had to push their haunches back into the rocky hillsides in order to have room in front to plant their feet.

Again she found only a locked door. But she stood and stared up at it with painful intentness. Through this door went actors and actresses. Some day she was going to get inside a real theater. She was going to see a real stage play. She was going—on the stage—herself! She had never said it before, and the saying of it brought a dappling of color to her cheeks.

But obviously this was not her day to start. She dawdled back along Eureka Street and turned on to Main. Suddenly a horseback rider caught her eye. A petite blonde girl, plump and compact as a dove, who looked as if she had been lovingly stuffed into her tight riding habit, rode sidesaddle along the wheel-torn street. She held her reins correctly high in her left hand and kept her eyes correctly straight ahead. Oh, but the girl knew, Roxana sensed, knew every admiring or envious glance that followed her.

At the foot of the hill the rider turned around and rode

slowly back, head still held disdainfully high. So she wasn't really out for a ride, thought Roxana, who loved to gallop their farm horses across an open pasture. This other girl was just showing off because she was lonesome, she surmised with quick sympathy.

At that point the rider tried to halt her horse in front of a brick building with a flight of wooden steps hanging to the outside wall. But the horse side-stepped and circled and jerked its head up and down in a threatening fashion.

Roxana moved forward, caught hold of the bridle and held it while the girl slid to the ground.

"Thank you. Horrid beast; a mouth like iron."

"I think maybe your cinch has loosened and let your saddle slide," Roxana offered.

"No, it's the horse. Crowbait!"

"He looks like a pretty good animal to me; you should see what I used to ride on the farm," Roxana defended, as she expertly tightened the cinch. "I've always thought a side-saddle must be uncomfortable for a horse, with the weight all on one side."

"When you're used to your own fine saddle horse, these livery-stable animals are worse than mine mules. But going riding is something to do," said the other plaintively. "And I had to stop in here on business."

For the first time Roxana paid attention to the brick building with the broad flight of outside steps leading to a door above, and noted the gaudy cloth sign along the second-story level, "Shoo Fly Variety Theater."

Theater! She was electrified.

"You're an actress?" she asked.

"Well, not exactly. Not yet."

"I want to be one dreadfully. I think about it all the time. For years and years—ever since I was fourteen—I've been collecting pictures of actresses. I've got six now. I have to keep them hidden from my mother, because she disapproves of play-acting. My name is Roxana Renner, and my family call me Roxy," she ended with a rush.

"I used to act in home-talent plays back in Oshkosh, Wisconsin," said the other a little wistfully. "I'm really very light on my feet; I won several prizes for figure-skating. My name is Lizzie—Mrs. Harvey Doe—they call me Baby Doe."

The two girls measured each other. Roxana gazed in patent admiration. Baby Doe, she said to herself. It had a pretty sound, like a young fawn. Such a beautiful riding habit, the finest broadcloth, and what a lovely plume sweeping down over her cheek. Her hair is pure gold; how I wish I had gold hair. Her eyes are blue as Avis' china doll's eyes, and her mouth dents in at the corner with a dimple that sort of comes and goes.

The young woman known as Baby Doe returned the inspection with equal intentness. Leggy as a colt, she thought. Bet she isn't a day over sixteen. You can fairly see through her skin. And what odd greenish eyes—the color of . . . of peeled grapes. And with a perfect *mat* of eyelashes. How tall she holds her head on her neck; nobody will ever nickname *her* Baby.

Roxana turned at last to glance up at the sign on the brick building. "Shoo Fly Variety Theater—Ten Acts—Fourteen lovely Young Ladies—Professor Jay, the World-Famed Magician—the La Verne Family Contortionists, Limp as Boned Chickens."

Roxana spoke tensely. "My father's gone to Leadville, and my mother's sick. I've simply got to have work. I wonder how you get to be an actress."

"I have to find something to do, too. Anything that will get me away from this smug hole. You haven't any idea how mean people can be—mean and jealous, if you so much as—"

If she so much as what? Roxana wondered with kindling curiosity.

"But your husband?" she asked. "Would he let you go on the stage?"

The young woman flushed. "I'm . . . alone in the world."

So she was a widow! But anyone who could rent a horse and own a black broadcloth riding habit must be pretty well off. With the callousness of the very young who have known neither love nor grief, Roxana thought it might not be at all bad to be a rich and beautiful young widow.

"I was stopping in here to see about a job. I've got a friend in the show business," Mrs. Doe volunteered.

Roxana mustered all her courage.

"I wonder—would you ask about a job for me, too?"

"Sure. He's going to give me a try-out. I'll ask for you, too."

"Oh, thank you." Roxana was tremulous with gratitude. "I sang in a cantata once. Tell him that."

The other girl's attention had strayed. Two men were stopping in front of the steps leading up to the Shoo Fly. Roxana gave only a fleeting glance at the thick-set older one, whose jowls were padded and shiny and red from good living. It was the thinner, younger one with the jaunty chestnut sideburns who caught her attention. He carried himself with such a cocksure air; he had such lively brown eyes, with a sardonic droop to the left lid, in a face that was tanned as leather. His brown bowler hat was tilted at an angle; his waistcoat was palest fawn; in his necktie glittered a jeweled horseshoe.

Roxana was dumb with admiration. She was seeing a real member of the theatrical profession at last.

Neither man seemed to notice her, standing there wide-eyed and gawky. Each gallantly crooked an elbow for pretty Mrs. Doe, who bridled and blushed, pausing only long enough to thrust the reins into Roxana's hands before she set off up the steps between the two gentlemen.

Roxana was only too glad to serve. Hadn't Mrs. Doe offered to speak to her friend about her?

She busied herself making friends with the horse, talking

[25]

to it companionably while she waited for the girl to come back down.

It was some time before the latter reappeared on the stairs, alone. She seemed to be having a little trouble tucking her gold locks up under her hat and straightening the hat itself so that the plume did not tickle her eye. Her smile was wide and bright and aimless.

"Did you ask him?" Roxana could not wait.

"Ask him?" the other said vaguely.

"You know—your friend in the show business—did you ask him about me?"

"I'm to have a try-out tomorrow night. I guess you could come, too."

"What time did he say?"

"About seven. They don't open till rather late; then they stay open nearly all night. They serve a kind of a lunch and drinks during the performances."

Roxana's words of thanks got all tangled up, in her excitement. But already the blonde girl's attention had wandered. Roxana was used to that by now. She saw that Baby Doe had begun to sparkle again. Roxana suspected that only gentlemen could bring out that look, both dewy and luminous. Her own glance followed the other's and there, indeed, across the street from them was a gentleman lifting his hat and bowing in their direction; in Mrs. Doe's direction of course.

Somehow she was not surprised when the older girl said pleadingly, "Do you mind leading this nag back to the livery stable? I'm tired of riding." She did not wait for Roxana to consent.

Roxana watched her pick her way across the ridgy road in her high-heeled riding boots and then she turned her attention back to the horse. She looked longingly up at the saddle. She had never sat on a true sidesaddle in her life. At home she either rode astride in the back pasture where no one could see her, or else she draped one knee around the saddle horn and pretended she was on a lady's saddle.

She glanced down now at her full calico skirts and back at the horse. The temptation was too great. Lifting one foot to the stirrup, she swung herself effortlessly up. The horse did a skittish side step or two and sprang forward in a long lope that jolted her hair loose and sent her cotton skirts ballooning. But she was enjoying it too much to hold the animal in.

For a brief two blocks she raced, and then the horse turned in sedately at a stable door. She slid to the plank floor amid the startled and amused glances of the livery stable hangers-on. She explained that she was returning the horse for Mrs. Doe and then turned and rushed out of the ammonic gloom, her cheeks flushed with embarrassment and delight.

As she walked back along the street, tucking up her hair and straightening her twisted basque, she thought how immensely exciting life had suddenly become. She had just ridden horseback; she had met a rich and beautiful young widow called Baby Doe; she had seen a gentleman in the show business; and she was to go for a try-out tomorrow night. She gave an ungrown-up skip. If she could only manage her mother.

At the thought of her mother she remembered her errand. Her mother was probably already put out at her lateness. If she forgot the errand too—! She turned in at the first general store she came to, her eyes roving swiftly over the cluttered interior. There were several clerks, all male of course; only occasionally did a daring woman stand behind a store counter.

Roxana was attracted, as always, by the pyramid of ribbons where each shining color was rolled on its white paper cylinder and the cylinders stacked in a pyramid five feet high. Charmed, she watched the hands of a clerk rewind a satiny length; the rest of him was obscured by the pyramid. How she loved ribbons! Just a few folds of that pink shimmer tucked in the back of her navy blue chip bonnet, with maybe a rosebud or two, and the old thing would be transformed.

Even her mother admitted that she had a way with bonnets. With her very first money as an actress (she drew a deep breath), she would buy new ribbons.

A voice said, "Can I do something for you, miss?" and she found herself looking up into the face of the ribbon-measurer. She was startled to find him young and tall and fresh-cheeked. All the clerks she had ever seen had been terribly old, forty or so, and sort of dusty-gray, as if they had lost all their own gloss to their satins and ribbons.

"Why, yes, I came in to buy—let's see—potatoes and buttons and beans and thread," she recited, looking up into his friendly eyes.

He repeated the words after her gravely, as if she had said pearls and ivory fans and Malaga grapes and attar of roses.

When he had stacked the parcels in her arms, he asked with concern, "Do you think you can carry all this? Where do you live?"

"Up on the hill." She flushed. "Not the high-toned one, but the mine dump one. It was all we could get—the shaft house of the old Blue Bottle Mine. My father went to Leadville a week ago to try his luck. We ought to be hearing from him any minute and then we'll move into something decent." She smiled confidingly. "He says the mines here are playing out, but he can't get my mother to budge. She thinks this place is awful enough, but that Leadville would be worse."

"But your father is right. My uncle and I came to prospect, too, and we found out the same thing—that Central's big boom is over. So we're just working here till we can save up a grubstake. We've got wind of something really good." He looked mysterious, and his eyes grew bright with plans. "When we hit it rich, we're going back home to Kaw Center and buy a general store. I've got a lot of ideas I want to try out. You know—things arranged in departments—" He gestured disapprovingly at the clutter around him.

"That will be fine," she said vaguely, wondering why anyone should want to keep a general store, or go back to Kaw Center.

"You say you just got here," he said. "I wonder if you're interested in singing?"

Her eyes sparkled. This was back to the pleasantly specific and personal.

"How did you guess? I sang in a cantata once at home. In *Pharaoh's Court* it was."

"We've got a singing society that meets in the church. This is a mighty lively town. All winter they have speakers on the Lyceum—the men call it 'The Spout Shop.' " He grinned at her. "We younger fellows belong to the volunteer fire companies and have cotillions. But what about the singing society tomorrow night? If you'd like to go—I mean, I'd like to take you."

Tomorrow night! Her heart plummeted.

"Oh, dear, not tomorrow night, I can't. I'm to have a try-out—an interview about a position. I've got to find something to do until my father gets back." She must make him know that if her father were here, naturally he would not permit his daughter to soil her hands with work (paid work, that is).

Regret clouded his eyes.

"I'm certainly sorry. Perhaps another time."

"Rob. Rob Evans!" shouted an exasperated voice. "Give me a lift with this barrel of sugar. And where did you put that sowbelly that was starting to turn green?"

Rob Evans turned away with reluctance.

"Rob!" repeated the harassed proprietor, waddling down the aisle, his paunch bulging precariously over the top of his trousers. Obviously his young clerk was dallying long after a sale was made.

"Yes, some other time!" Roxana finished daringly and ran out of the store before he could think her forward.

Later she explained guardedly to her mother about the try-out—or rather, interview—she was to have tomorrow evening with the manager of the—ah—Shoo Fly Restaurant. Yes, it was a queer name for a restaurant, and she guessed the reason for all their trade being in the evening was because the miners came off shift late, or something.

"I'll tell you more about it after I've talked to the man. I'll likely have to wait on tables. I don't know if I could stand up under carrying all those heavy trays," she suggested craftily.

"Fiddlesticks! If the rest can, you can. Hard work never hurt anyone," snapped her mother weakly, just as Roxana had counted that she would. "And don't let that fellow be deceived by the pindling look of you. I could tell him you're strong as a yearling mule and twice as stubborn."

Roxana hid her elation.

"I'd better wash my dress."

She heard her mother ruminating aloud. "So long as it isn't play-acting and showing yourself off," she murmured. "You know I don't hold with either play-acting or dancing, Roxy. Look what dancing did in the case of Herod's step-daughter and John the Baptist."

Roxana had never quite seen the connection between that good man's fate and her learning to dance, but she did not argue. All she asked was a chance to get even the smallest part at the Shoo Fly Variety Theater. The very word sent delicious, shuddering waves through her. Theater!

Chapter III

THAT NIGHT the lantern light cast goblin shadows up on the roof of the shaft house as Roxana ironed her dress on a plank stretched between the anvil and the forge. Such an ugly dress, she thought, sort of brindle-colored. When she became an actress— She was too excited to go to bed. She felt alone with the shadows in the dim old building. Her mother was asleep on her bed in the far corner. Avis was curled up like a garden snail under the covers.

Roxana mended the crocheted lace on her best petticoat. She tried her hair a new way with a waterfall effect, which she frankly admired in the cracked mirror hanging from a post.

Alone with her glittering plans, she tilted her head back, parted her lips in a smile of pure coquetry, and widened her greenish eyes. Suddenly she bent forward anxiously to study a spot on her chin that might, just might, turn into a pimple. But it was only a shadow from the smoky lantern. She arched her neck and tossed her head with a ponylike curveting. Leaning closer, she bared her teeth to inspect them. Teeth were so important. But hers were as small and even and white as kernels of Iowa sweet corn.

She held out her hand with a languishing smile to an invisible companion. Silently her lips formed a syllable, *Rob.* What a lovely name. *Rob Evans.* I'm so sorry about the singing society, Rob. But I'd just love to go to the cotillion, now that you ask me.

She widened her eyes. She had read about starry eyes. She was sure her eyes were starry. Now he was lifting her hand to his lips. Slowly she withdrew the hand, dropping her lashes over her starry eyes.

"Oh, for lan's sake, Roxy, stop making faces and come to bed. You make me sick to my stummick!" declared a voice sharp with childish disgust.

Roxana landed back on hard reality. Flushing, she buttoned the top button of her high-necked nightgown, blew out the lantern, and crawled into bed beside Avis. But she did not nestle close to her sister, spoon-fashion, as was their wont on chilly nights. Avis was always spoiling things! Roxana remembered how, when she was rehearsing for the cantata, she had rubbed buttermilk on her skin each night until Avis complained to their mother that Roxy stank like a sour churn.

In the morning she had forgotten her affronted dignity. Her excitement frothed up again. She daubed her shoes with blackening and washed her hair in some of the hoarded forty-cent water. She dried it outside, sitting on a boulder overlooking the town, the midday sun shining hotly. She tousled her hair with flirts of the towel, spraying it out into a dark fan that gave off iridescent splinters of light.

As the day wore on her tension increased. Her heart beat in great gallops as she dressed and slipped on her mother's worn dolman and bade the two at home good-by.

It was mountain dusk as she made her way down into the gulch. The bottom was already in shadow. Days were short down in gulches, she mused with pleasantly morbid relish. Maybe life was short here, too. You were always hearing about mine accidents and runaway teams and shootings.

The Shoo Fly at the hour of seven still wore the closed and sleeping look of all night-blooming things. The second-story windows were dark. She climbed the long flight of steps and rapped on the door at the top. There was no answer, although she thought she heard sounds of activity within. She rapped again.

At last she tried the door, and it opened readily. She peered around the shadowy hallway. Nobody was in sight. She edged inside. Where was everyone, and where was the theater part where they served the lunch and drinks while the acts were going on?

She was standing there uncertainly when a door beside her burst open, and framed in the light was the resplendent young man of the bowler hat and the fawn waistcoat. Only now he was without both hat and waistcoat; his shirt sleeves were rolled up, and his hair was untidy. He studied her in the half-dark.

"So, the young lady on horseback! Understudying Miss Fanny Louise Buckingham in *Mazeppa*, eh? You were certainly a sight—hanging on for dear life, your skirts flying, and the old nag running like a race horse."

"I was *not* hanging on, and it wasn't an old nag. That's a good horse, not over four years old."

"I beg your pardon. What can I do for you?"

"I'm looking for—are you the manager?"

"Of what?"

"Of this theater. Are you the one that hires people? Mrs. Doe promised she'd speak to you about a job for me. She said to come back tonight for a try-out at seven."

"Hmm. Baby Doe told you that? You think you want to work here? Better step inside and talk it over."

He opened the door upon an office that contained an oak desk, a sagging horsehair sofa, and two hard kitchen chairs. He motioned her to one of the chairs and seated himself behind the desk. For a moment he contemplated both her diffidence and her assurance.

"Any experience?"

"I . . . I sang in a cantata back home. *Pharaoh's Court,* it

[33]

was. I took the part of the princess." Even to her own ears, it lacked a certain authority.

"Church cantata, huh? Not exactly the Shoo Fly. I guess you haven't been in town long. What does your father think about your working here?"

"He's in Leadville. He wouldn't dream of letting me work, of course. But we—my mother and sister—we haven't heard from him since he left eight days ago, and we've got to eat—I mean, I simply must find a position."

"Well, if it's work you want, why don't you apply for a job at the Teller House? I saw a sign in the window, 'Chambermaid wanted.' "

Roxana's head went up furiously. He was insulting. Chambermaid! How dared he? (To Roxana, the word "chamber" did not connote a bedroom.)

He shrugged. "Well, you said you wanted work. And you look mighty young for the Shoo Fly. How old are you anyway?"

She said icily, "I'm plenty old enough, and I intend to go on the stage. I've always wanted to go on the stage."

He continued to study her.

"Ever see the cancan? Ever seen a variety theater show?"

She squirmed.

One corner of his mouth dented knowingly.

"I'll bet you've never seen a real stage show in your life."

She did not answer. What if she hadn't? She had loved being in the cantata. She had thirsted over stories about the stage. She had gone to infinite pains to collect her six pictures of actresses.

"Well, let me tell you a variety theater isn't what you think it is. Most of them are only thinly disguised—" He stopped, fumbling for words; then he shook his head and started over again patiently. "It's just a long hall full of tables with usually a balcony of curtained boxes around three sides." He made a circular gesture to show her. "There's an apron-sized stage at the end. Audience mostly males that eat and drink straight through the show. Food bad—liquor worse. Why, I've seen a drop of whiskey spilled on the table eat its way clean through the wood in ten minutes and fall to the floor."

She batted her eyes in doubt. Was he telling the truth? She wasn't used to this solemn, yet half-teasing tone in a man's voice. Nervously she fingered a specimen of ore, used as a paper weight, that was lying on the desk in front of her.

"But the stage shows are even worse than the liquor and food," he went on scoldingly. "They wouldn't fit into your cantata. Most of them would make a cigar-store Indian blush."

Still Roxana stared at him and said nothing, the slim black feathers of her brows arched defiantly.

"And on top of everything else," he finished in triumph, "the show girls have to take turns 'working the boxes.' "

"Well, I'm not afraid of *work*," she said with dignity.

"Work! Work!" He ran his lean brown fingers through his already untidy chestnut hair. "Can't you understand it means selling champagne inside the curtained boxes, with the curtains drawn, and the gentlemen behaving—not like gentlemen?"

Roxana said plaintively, "But I want to go on the stage," as if that answered everything. Still with her happy deafness; still with her stubborn deafness.

He muttered something unintelligible.

"I'd just like to be your father for five minutes, and you know what I'd do?" He opened and shut his hands and slid his chair closer.

She sat back from him as far as she could get. There was something definitely alarming about this young man.

"Then—then do I get the job?"

He exhaled a breath so sharply that it had a whistling sound.

"All right. You begged for this. Pull up your skirts."
She blanched.

[35]

"Do what!"

"Pull up your skirts so I can see your legs. I've been trying to tell you the kind of place this is. Our show girls don't wear enough clothes to wad a gun. I have to see what kind of legs you've got."

Roxana was almost paralyzed with shock. Show off her *legs?* No man, not even her father, had seen her legs above the ankles since she had put on long skirts two years ago. Perhaps he was a white slaver. She had read tracts about white slavers. She was suddenly afraid. She wanted to go home to her mother.

But she wanted to go on the stage.

He continued to watch her from under level brows, his carnelian-brown eyes unblinking.

Surely Godiva, with her long hair to shield her, suffered no more than did Roxana as she stood up at last, eyes averted, and gingerly raised her skirts above her ankles.

"Your legs. I've got to see your legs," he said grimly.

She lifted her skirts knee-high and waited. Now her eyes sought his face for his answer.

He gave her knees, which were knocking together in fright, a thorough scrutiny. Then he put his head back and let out a laugh. A horrid, sneering, making-fun laugh, she thought.

She dropped her skirts with a swish. Her cheeks flamed.

"I'm sorry, but you won't do, my dear," he said. "Our customers like a girl with meat on her—white meat as well as dark, to put it delicately. Not a skinny little plucked pullet."

She was blinking with rage and humiliation as she fumbled for her reticule. Skinny little plucked pullet indeed! White meat—dark meat.

"You're . . . you're— Just because I haven't quite filled out yet. My mother says if I'll drink more milk—" Badgered and beset as she was by him, she still refused to retreat. "I'll be back—I'll be back in a month to ask for a job again."

[36]

"After what I've said you'd come back *here?*" He shook his head as if to get a ringing out of his ears.

"How else am I going to get on the stage?"

His eyes narrowed, and he seemed to be biting the inside of his cheek. Then his glance dropped suddenly to her skirt hem. With a hawk-swift movement he swooped and caught hold of a raveling from the lace flounce of her best crochet-edged petticoat. She jumped back, but he would not let go. Horror-frozen, she watched him pull on that raveling, and pull and pull, even while he decorously held her skirts down.

"You mustn't do that—it's my very best—" She backed into the wall. "Stop it!" She tried to defend her pear-shaped skirts by cupping her hands down around her knees.

"But you had a thread dangling," he explained with hurt innocence, as he stood up. "You wouldn't want to walk along the street with a raveling hanging down?"

He pointed with benevolent satisfaction to the airy pile of thread on his desk.

"Now I guess you won't trip over a dangling thread. Though you may find, when you get home, that you haven't got very much on, under your dress." His mouth twitched slightly and his drooping eyelid almost winked at her.

She glared at him, shaken with suspicion. *Was* he laughing at her?

"Oh, you . . . you . . . you—"

"Just call me dearest, if it will make it any easier."

"I think you're despise . . . despisable!" She turned to run.

"Not so fast, young lady, not so fast. That's a real gold nugget you're making off with. Worth money."

She halted, completely undone by this dreadful young man as she watched him, right in front of her very eyes, reach inside her reticule and extract the gold-ore paper weight she had been fingering a little while before. In her absent-minded frenzy she must have dropped it there. She was al-

[37]

most in tears now, but she swallowed them back, as she stood there, shaken and scarlet, her breasts rising and falling, her heart plunging wildly. Then she caught her underlip in her teeth and flung her head back. Her eyes glittered through her tears.

"You haven't answered me yet. If I drink milk—if I come back in a month—?"

Now his laughter was gone. He was glowering at her incredulously.

"No!" he shouted. "You little mule, you!" He grabbed her by the arm. "Not next month, not next year, not ever." He gave her arm a yank that spun her around like the last one in the line of crack-the-whip and hauled her toward him.

Both were breathing fast, both were glaring. She found herself drawn steadily closer until she was staring straight up into those blazing eyes with the red-brown fire far back in them. She could feel the sinews in his forearm. Suddenly she was afraid and not afraid. She was meltingly weak and surging with triumph. She had no fight left in her, only this warm lovely weakness. Why, he was going to kiss her, and she had never been kissed before.

And then he spun her away from him, still holding her with that tough brown hand of his.

"Hah!" he laughed harshly. "Who'd ever have thought I'd be cast in the role of Galahad—with a little plucked pullet?" And then—oh, final indignity of a humiliating, insulting, maddening hour—he reached down and gave her a whack. Not a push, not a pat, but a good hard spank with the flat of his hand just where her newspaper bustle ended.

"Now git! And don't you ever show your face inside this dive again!"

She got. His door slammed shut behind her.

She almost fell down the long flight of steps in the darkness. She was glad it was dark, so no one would see her bawling angrily as she made her way toward a side street. She had never been treated so in her life. Skinny little plucked pullet! She rubbed her wrist where he had held her with that awful grip. She reached back and rubbed the place below her bustle.

She stopped in front of an unlighted shop window to give way to her rage. She clenched her fists and bit at her knuckles. Oh, to show that dreadful man! Oh, to get even with him! Oh, to punish him!

When at last she could take in her surroundings, she found that she was staring through the window at a display of coffins, eerie in the moonlight. She gazed at them with actual relish, inspecting their shirred and padded interiors. A nice pretty coffin like that was much too good for some people. Even the sight of the baby coffin all in white left her unmoved. After all, some things in life were worse than death.

The sign on the window said, "Gilbert Anker, Coffins."

She was still standing there, drawing jerky little breaths, when a pleased and surprised masculine voice behind her made her whirl.

"Miss Roxana! It's Rob Evans. The singing society let out early. Did you get your position?"

Roxana's head went up; she smiled and gave a little shrug. Gone were all traces of tears and anger. She was an actress.

"It turned out to be quite impossible. I had no idea. We'd only just got here and naturally I'd never been inside such a place before—"

"What place?"

"The Shoo Fly Variety Theater."

He muttered a shocked expletive. His face set into sternness in the bluish moonlight as he looked down at her.

"Whatever made you go there? Who put such an idea in your head?"

"A lady I met. She was so kind; she told me they had an opening and to come at seven for a try-out if I wanted to go on the stage."

"But that's not the stage. That's not even a theater, as a nice girl thinks of one. That's just a . . . a den of vice—with terrible goings-on." He was beside himself with memories that could not have been entirely secondhand. Then he stiffened. "What *lady* told you to go there?"

"A pretty Mrs. Doe—Mrs. Harvey Doe. I helped her yesterday with her horse."

"Not Baby Doe! Why, she's separated from her husband and is the talk of Eureka Street! Runs around with other men and goes to the Shoo Fly at night for *wine suppers*." His voice lowered.

"I can't believe—she's so pretty—"

"Ask any man on Eureka Street. Great Moses! If only you'd told me yesterday what you were planning to do, I could have stopped you." (How little did he know Roxana.) He helped her over the rough crossing and Roxana felt suddenly fragile and cared for and feminine. The very tensing of his arm under her fingers was flattering.

"I could hardly get out of the dreadful place fast enough when I found out what it was like," she said piously. "Of course, I probably wouldn't have suited them anyhow. I guess I'm not their type. I'm perhaps a little on the thin side."

"You are not! You're just right. No, you certainly wouldn't suit the Shoo Fly, where they only want big bouncing cows. A graceful, beautiful, ladylike girl like you would certainly be out of place there."

Roxana was anointed with the healing unguent of adulation. She stepped more daintily; she held her head higher; she sparkled with smiles as she held to the crook of his elbow with two fingers. What a gentleman he was. How infinitely finer than that detestable man at the Shoo Fly with the diamond stickpin and the rolled-up sleeves and the haystack hair. She'd bet he *was* a white slaver. As she thought of how much she hated him, she began to shake again.

"What's the matter?" Rob inquired solicitously.

"I . . . I was thinking what a narrow escape I had, and how glad I am that I happened to run into you."

"Me, too. A little thing like you out all alone at night. You need someone to take care of you." He squeezed her hand between his arm and his ribs so tight that her finger tips grew numb, but the pain both comforted and appeased Roxana.

He would have kept her talking in front of the shaft house in the moonlight, but Roxana's mother called out almost at once, "Roxy? That you? Will you come and mix me a dose of soda?" And Roxana had to leave a dazed young man to stumble down the path in the moonlight.

It was not until Roxana was undressing and untying the tapes around her waist that held up her four petticoats that she remembered and looked down at her quite intact crocheted flounce. Not a thread was missing. Not a single crocheted daisy had been unraveled.

The truth broke upon her. There had never been any dangling raveling. And the nugget in her reticule was just a trick, too. She recalled the sign outside the Shoo Fly: "Professor Jay, World-famed Magician." She'd been the butt of Professor Jay's insane humor. First he had insulted her; then he had played tricks on her; and finally he had turned her down for a job. Of course he wasn't the manager of the Shoo Fly at all. He was only one of the acts. Now she recalled the older man who had accompanied him up the steps. *That* was the manager; *he* was the one Baby Doe had said to talk to. This Professor Jay, World-famed Magician, had merely happened to be there in the office and had made sport of her. Just wait till morning!

All night she tossed, until again Avis complained in her sleep.

The next day, on her trip to the post office, she flounced angrily up the walk to the Shoo Fly. This time she would not be put off; she would demand an interview with the manager. She would give him a piece of her mind about that impudent blatherskite of a Professor Jay who insulted young ladies applying for work.

[41]

On the door of the Shoo Fly was posted a sign, "Closed for Repairs. Will Open Later Under New Management."

Her anger drained from her. Slowly she retraced her steps to the post office. She forgot even to glance in through the window of the store where Rob Evans worked. An undelivered piece of one's mind rests heavily on the spirit.

Chapter IV

ANOTHER DAY PASSED, and another. There was scarcely a mittenful of meal left. You could stretch beans and prunes just so far. Roxana strained the last of the boiled beans to make a weak gruel for her mother. She and Avis could eat the solid mush. But the gruel only made her mother retch and throw up. She could no longer lift her head from her hard pallet on the floor; even the doses of baking soda failed to help.

Roxana longed for their old family doctor. She longed for some older person to ask advice of, but she knew none. She found something vaguely comforting about Avis' shadow-like presence following her about, whereas, a week ago she would have shrugged it off impatiently. Impulsively she put her arm around the child's shoulders and surprised a look of rapt adoration before the little girl could hide it under her usual air of prim skepticism.

"When Pa gets back, we'll get a nice hen to make broth out of," Roxana told her mother. "It's strengthening. You'll be up in no time. The man at the pharmacy said lots of people had mountain sickness when they first got here."

Her mother brightened.

"He did? I thought it was just my old pains at first, but I guess this is different. Did you tell him how the pain kind of starts here in my stomach and runs out my back? Did you ask him if that's how mountain sickness is?"

"He said it affected everyone different," evaded Roxana. For the first time in her life she was consciously sparing her mother, shielding her. "Pa will know what to do. When Pa gets back—"

"Yes, when he gets back." Her mother ran a tired hand over her forehead.

How thin the hand was, Roxana thought; bluish, with corded tendons standing out. How sick her mother's hair looked; hair could look sicker than anything else about a person. For the first time, also, she faced the fact that parents were not guaranteed to be permanent, that "things" could happen to them. She sponged her mother's face in the hoarded water. Her father simply *had* to come back—and soon.

Her steps lagged that afternoon as she walked down to the post office on her daily trip. She did not know that a constant faint hunger is more exhausting than hard labor. She had to force herself to take the extra steps over to the curb to ask the driver of a freight wagon if he knew anything about a Dan Renner who had started off to Leadville ten days before with a load of stuff. The man shook his head. He was sorry, but he was on the Caribou haul himself.

As usual, there was nothing at the post office for them. She was just stepping down the high step to the sidewalk when her heart gave a leap, a great physical leap like a fish flopping over inside her chest.

A friendly little black-and-white dog was absorbedly following, nose down, a fresh scent along the sidewalk. She shrieked with joy.

"Boots! Why, it's Boots. Where's Pa?"

At her cry, the dog lifted his head, turned and raced toward her, hurling himself straight at her—a loving canine missile. She caught him up in her arms and had to hold her head back out of reach of his lapping pink tongue. She squeezed so hard he yelped.

"Was I ever so glad to see anybody! Where's Pa, Boots? Let's go find him. Where's Pa?"

Looking over the head of the squirming, wriggling, licking dog, she found herself gazing at a stooped, saturnine man who watched her with a startled expression. She noted how thin his shoulders were, making peaks under his shabby overcoat. He attempted to speak, swallowed a couple of times, and moistened his lips.

Boots was still having dog hysterics in Roxana's arms. She smiled over his head at the dour stranger, unable to keep from sharing her happiness.

When he spoke at last, it was in a rapid rattling whisper. His hand went up to his throat with a gesture of apology. So that was it; he had some kind of throat trouble.

"I guess you know this dog?" he said.

"I should say I do! He's our dog Boots. My father took him to Leadville on a freighting trip. It means Pa's back. He must be right close by. You'd never get Boots to leave him."

The man remained unaccountably sober. Something in his lined face quenched her joy a little. He did not turn away from her but continued to watch the dog in her arms —wriggling body, waving tail, lapping tongue.

"No, I reckon that little dog wouldn't leave him—willingly," came the reply in the whisper that was like dry leaves in a wind. "I had quite a time—"

It took a minute for the words to pierce the thick layer of her joy and her expectancy. Roxana tightened her arms defensively around the dog as if to ward off the news. Her eyes were wide, the pupils black and staring in their green irises.

"What are you trying to tell me?"

"I picked up your dog on the road back from Leadville."

She began to shake.

"But where was Pa?"

He did not answer, but took her by the arm and led her over to a bench beside the hotel.

He had been on his way back from the western slope with a load of lumber for his shop, he told her. Gil Anker, his name was. Shop—Gil Anker, she thought dully. Where had she seen that name?

The road over the Mosquito range was bad, he said, little more than a trail that had to be gouged out and propped up every so often by the freighters using it.

"Your father was traveling alone. I guess his brakes—"

"He didn't have any. He was going to get them fixed." Her teeth were chattering with a chill.

"The road, one place, was nothing but a narrow shelf coming straight down the side of a canyon. I had to rough-lock my wheels together with a chain. I reckon your father didn't know to do that."

"He . . . he never drove in the mountains before—except to come to Central."

"I saw marks, like as if wheels had slewed over the edge. There was a couple of wagons stopped just beyond. The drivers were down below in the gulch." Angry pity filled his face.

Roxana waited, not breathing, just waiting for the raspy voice to go on.

"They were burying a man," he said.

The girl's face was set, stunned into disbelief. This hasn't anything to do with Pa, she told herself. It can't be Pa.

"Seems one of the men was the owner of the load that went over—he'd hired the driver. The team was dead, and there was no getting the wagon out. All we could do was pile rocks on the mound. The owner said so far as he knew, the man didn't have any family, but he'd notify the authorities in Leadville anyhow." The husky whisper that made her want to clear her own throat in order to help him stopped bleakly.

Great silent tears were streaming unheeded down Roxana's face. She was staring at him in naked anguish.

"They had to tie up the little dog before they could get him away. I tried to touch him but he snapped at me, weak as he was. I offered to take him along with me. He fought me, but I finally got him into my wagon. It was hours before I could coax him to eat. I'm sorry, miss."

Roxana's desolation was so vast that she could not speak for a while. When at last her words came they were choked and thick.

"My mother's sick. She's just waiting till Pa gets back. Our food is gone. We're living in the shaft house of the old Blue Bottle Mine. I'll have to tell her lies; I'll have to say Pa is staying on in Leadville." Her voice broke into little shards of grief. "I'll say he sent the dog back by another freighter and that . . . and that he won't be coming back right away."

She let out a long shuddering sob as she got to her feet. She could not bear to put the dog down. He was a link with her father, with his gaiety, with his wandering feet, with his smiling good humor, with his warmth and love. She turned and stumbled away from the man, her head buried in the dog's silky ears.

Climbing the gravelly slope, she felt Boots licking the salt tears off her hands.

Chapter V

ORPHANS. The word was new. Roxana tried it over silently with swollen tongue. Her eyes were swollen; her throat was swollen. She could feel Avis shivering against her. Her arm stole around the child. Just the two of them now.

A little wind fingered the wispy black veil on her hat. There was always this little wind up here; even now in late summer, there was this faint chill under the warmth. It lifted the hair on the back of her neck and tightened the skin of her cheeks and made her breasts grow taut under her high-buttoned basque.

Her eyes were bent on the ground, and she noticed the stalk of a mountain flower crushed under her foot. With the scuffed toe of her shoe she carefully righted the delicate row of dangling scarlet bugles. It seemed suddenly terribly important to prop up that single trampled flower on a hillside already dappled with flowers.

While her attention was concentrated on the slanting stem, she need not look down into the raw ragged hole, its sides all lumpy with pebbles. Yet she could not keep from looking. She wondered if the men who had dug her mother's grave had watched for gold as they worked. There was a macabre story out of Leadville about a gravedigger who had struck it rich and forgotten to bury the corpse.

[48]

Corpse! She blanched, and her arm tightened convulsively around Avis. They were orphans now. But orphans were a species, like widows. Widows 'n' orphans. She had heard the words thus, all her life. But orphans had always meant other people, not the Renner girls, not Avis and Roxana.

What would become of them? Last night, to quiet Avis' sobs, she had gathered the eleven-year-old on to her lap—surprisingly heavy, Avis was, with her bones pressing sharply —and assured her over and over, "We'll stick together, Avis. We'll never let anyone separate us."

"You promise not to leave me? Not to let them 'put me somewhere'?" The sobs were panicky.

"We're sisters, Avis. Sisters stick together."

Avis relaxed then, and Roxana experienced both the sober satisfaction and the burden of being leaned upon.

Her red-rimmed eyes roved over the flinty cemetery hill. Everything out here was like that—flinty. Just a few inches under the mountain flowers was that harsh, rocky ground. Just above the rim of the bare hills was the hostile line of snowcaps. And even in the midday brilliance there was this faintly moving chill straight off the ice fields.

The preacher's troubled voice went on. She saw the single bouquet of fluttery, tissue-petaled mountain poppies. The preacher's wife had stripped her neglected garden this morning and thrust the flowers into her hand.

"I'd go, if I could," she assured Roxana, wet-eyed. "If it wasn't for the boy."

Roxana had nodded. A month ago her own world had been secure and changeless and immortal. Now nothing was secure. Now she was frightened by the dreadful perishability of human beings. Her father had died. Her mother had died. The minister's little boy was slowly dying of a failing heart.

She saw the preacher's bony wrists jutting from his coat sleeves as he held his worn little black book with the scuffed brownish corners. Beyond him stood Gil Anker, his deeply lined face an engraving of anger—anger at life and at death. It was Gil Anker's coffin shop she had cried in front of; it was Gil who had brought the news of her father's death, who had provided her mother's coffin, and who would now see to filling in the grave after they were gone.

How kind they had all been. For the first time in her self-centered life Roxana saw herself in relation to others, rather than as the shining hub of a nebulously expanding universe. For, meager as the setting of her old life might have looked to others, it had at least been hers by right. She had not needed to know the uneasy feeling of gratitude. Now she had no rights; she must feel grateful for everything. Being an orphan was humbling.

It was exactly a week since she had run into Boots and Gil Anker on the street. She had not been able to keep the news of her father's death from her mother, and Eunice had grown steadily worse.

When Gil Anker came up the path one morning, Roxana had greeted him with despairing relief.

"Oh, I'm glad, Mr. . . . Mr. Anker. I need to ask some-body—"

"That's what I thought," he whispered. "And 'Gil' is what I answer to. My shop is straight down below. From the edge of your dump, you could spit down my chimney if you took a notion."

"I stopped in front of your shop once," said Roxana.

"I make coffins," he said as calmly as if he had said shoes. "And grateful I am to the dead for keeping me alive. Came west years ago for lung trouble—settled in my throat. I started dealing faro. Regular, steady work it is, in a boom camp like this where every young sprig thinks he has to raise hell and prop it up. Well, what with the smoke and night hours, the doc says, 'Get outdoors or die.' So now I make coffins in the yard behind my shop—and live."

He waved a tattered cheroot, more chewed than smoked. He looked down at it bitterly.

"No, I'm not supposed to have even this, but a man's got to have something to remind him he's a man, don't he?" All the while he was eying Roxana as if giving her time to get hold of herself.

"Do you know anything about sickness?"

He frowned. "Too much."

"Would you take a look at my mother? I'm afraid—"

She led him inside, past the anvil and the forge, to the corner where her mother lay. Eunice was too weak to open her eyes. When the man felt her pulse, she relaxed a little.

"Oh, Doctor, my worry-pains are killing me," she sighed.

"I know," he whispered. "Worry-pains do." He laid the veined yellow wrist back on the quilt after a while and got to his feet.

Outside, he looked at the girl steadily.

"She ought to have a real doctor."

She twisted the long muslin string of her apron into a narrow rope.

"We haven't any money. We were just making out till . . . my father—" The stinging in her eyes and her throat was too sharp for her to go on.

His brows met fiercely.

"It's a damn shame—pardon me, miss. Being poor is sure tough gristle to chew! Mining towns are geared to them that strike it rich. There's no place for us that are still living on hope." He turned to go; then he looked back. "I'll be watching up this way. If you need anybody sudden-like, hang a towel on that boulder."

By morning she hung the towel out. If only Gil Anker would see it.

He saw it. He was there in a few minutes. One look at her mother, and he turned to Avis. Roxana could almost see his thoughts darting about. Avis was too young to be sent downtown alone, yet he had to get rid of her somehow.

"Here, child, your mother's pretty sick, and some sage tea might help. It's a low gray-green plant—there's some outside the door—you scamper up the hill and find me an apronful. A big apronful."

Avis had rushed out obediently. She liked being told what to do. She was lost and forlorn without her mother's tartly loving orders.

It was none too soon. For right after that came the retching and the blood. Roxana longed to be a little girl, too, sent away on an errand. She wanted to be spared. Until that minute she had yearned with all her tense young body and soul to be grown-up. But while Gil Anker was saying, "Here, hold this basin. . . . Try this cold cloth. . . . Better prop her head up. . . ." Roxana was sensing that one paid high for grown-upness, for long skirts and bustles and chignons and independence.

Her mother had died, and she had watched her die. She felt that she had put away childish things forever.

Gil Anker had flagged a passing miner and sent for the preacher. Then he gently led Roxana away from the terrible quiet of the pallet in the corner. He made her sit down. He talked in his dry-leaf whisper. Roxana sensed the kindness in him.

"Time was when Reveren' Starbuck and me was enemies. He said I could tear down on Saturday night all he could build up during the week. Though, just the same, he brought me a can of hot soup when I got sick. And now, since I've changed my occupation, we're almost friends. We're often on the same case—"

He halted abruptly; then went on, as if he must fill in the gaps of waiting.

"He's one of them crazy-good young fools, the preacher is. The night the bawdy—I mean, Millie Sower's place burned, he worked till his eyebrows was singed off and his hands blistered, trying to save it. He's got a hollow-eyed wife and some hollow-looking kids. And he's the kind that really does turn the other cheek and give the coat off his back. I tell him it ain't practical. You just go around with both cheeks clawed, and getting pneumonia, in this altitude. But you can't pound sense into him."

The preacher arrived. One look at the desolate scene and the two shivering girls, and his mouth tightened. Feed my lambs, he had been enjoined, and these were certainly motherless lambs.

"Pack up some things and come along home with me," he had offered gallantly.

When his young wife Naomi saw him shepherding his woeful charges up the parsonage steps, she too had sighed. Feed my lambs, she murmured, with a look at her own three pale little girls and her ailing boy. But when the door opened, she gathered the two girls against her spare young bosom, and for a moment Roxana felt a little easing of her terror and her grief.

This morning Naomi Starbuck had fished the black veil out of a trunk and draped it around Roxana's hat.

"Funny thing about mourning," she said thoughtfully. "The world is mighty hard to please, Roxana. If you don't wear enough black rags and long looks, they criticize you for being callous, no matter how your heart is eaten away inside. But just let you mourn a mite too long, and they get impatient and restless. Morbid, that's what you are, and unwholesome, and they're put out with you for reminding them of your sorrows." She pinned the veil in place with awkward gentleness.

In spite of her own worries and her own sleepless nights, she could still appreciate the black veiling next to Roxana's white skin and drenched lashes.

"You two come back after the funeral and stay here until we figure out the next step," she said kindly.

But Roxana, standing at the graveside now, knew that they could not. With her new humbleness, she realized the added burden they were in the meager parsonage. She knew for herself the bone weariness that comes from day-and-night vigil by the sick.

"I will not leave you comfortless," the preacher's kind twangy voice quoted.

Comfortless. Roxana had thought that losing her father was the worst thing that could happen to her. But she found that losing her mother was worse, because she had not loved her mother enough. She had loved her father so much that she would carry his image with her always, giving him at least the memorial of a grieving heart. But her mother— Roxana winced. She hadn't thought her mother could die because she hadn't thought anything much at all about her mother.

If I'd loved her more— Oh, why can't you love the ones you ought to love? she reproached herself, as legions of other mourners have reproached themselves at a graveside.

"And there shall be no night there," finished the voice, sadness and hope intermingling. He closed the worn book.

Avis, who had an instinctive sense of the fitness of things, burst into thin hiccuping sobs and clung to Roxana. The preacher gently steered them away from the grave, his own mouth working. Gil Anker stayed behind to his lonely task. Roxana tried vainly, with swimming eyes, to see the rocky path before her, as she walked with the jerky held-back gait of one trying to keep from going downhill too fast.

Throughout the dinner at the preacher's house she remained firm about her intentions. They would both return to the shaft house for the present.

"We've got our dog."

Naomi Starbuck flashed her a glance of respect.

"Even so, it won't do for two young girls to stay there alone," Naomi mused. "Henry, you could ask one of the Bird girls—Mrs. Bird runs the bakery down below, Roxana— to come up and stay nights till we can work something out."

"That would be fine, just fine," agreed Roxana listlessly.

"I know you've hardly had time to make plans," began the

preacher. "But you'll go back home now to Iowa, won't you?"

"Oh, no!" Roxana's answer was an instant reflex. "There's nothing for us there."

"But you have relatives? Aunts, uncles, cousins?"

"Nobody."

Avis suggested in a small voice, "Roxy, what about Aunt Es—?"

The words were not even said before Roxana overlaid them with her own firmer, louder words.

"The only near relative we have is our Uncle John, who's prospecting in the Black Hills. We might write him General Delivery, Deadwood. But the last letter Pa sent there came back."

Her color had risen. That Avis! Bringing up Aunt Essie, their step-aunt, who would be only too happy to let her hired girl go if Roxana came back, and who would make Avis stop out of school at the eighth grade as she had her own children. They were never going back. This was their country, this Out West that she and her father had dreamed of and planned for. She forgot about the harshness and the chill winds and the barrenness.

"You expect to get a position, is that it? But what can you do, child?" asked the minister gently.

Roxana was at a loss. She dared not mention her dreams of the theater, for all ministers instinctively recoiled from the very word "theater." And she doubted that her knack for sewing or her way with bonnets could support them.

"Old lady—I mean, Mrs. Paxton needs a companion again," he offered.

"A companion?" She lifted her head hopefully. It had a genteel sound of wearing one's best dress and reading aloud from limp-leather gift books to an elderly employer with a face like a cameo.

He pointed up to the slopes where the high-toned people lived.

She followed his gesture, gazing at the tiered streets, each with its single row of narrow-gabled houses backed into the rocky hills as if to stare superciliously down at the rooftops below.

"Which one is it?" she asked, a little less buoyantly this time.

"That big one with the bay window and the cupola and the cut-out wooden trimmings along the porch. She's well-to-do; her late husband had mining interests here."

Naomi Starbuck could hold back no longer.

"Not that old harpy, Henry! She expects to get a combination cook, nurse, lady's maid, and listener, all for two dollars a week. And the listening would be the worst of all."

"It would only be temporary," he defended. "And we could find some place to put Avis for a while."

Roxana had already rejected the whole scheme; her quick mind was merely exploring various means of avoiding such a fate, when Avis unexpectedly came to her aid. Wrought up over the last weeks' happenings, she began to sob. In fact, she "carried on," in her mother's words.

"Roxy, you promised me! You said no one would separate us. You said you'd never let them 'put me somewhere.'"

Roxana patted her soothingly and said there, there. Naomi patted her and said there, there. The preacher blew his nose. And so it was settled that they must think of some other way to dispose of the Renner girls.

When the preacher and the two girls reached the shaft house, it was already late afternoon. Roxana opened the door, and Boots hurled himself upon them in welcome. Henry Starbuck grimly noted again the gaunt interior with its forge for a cook stove and its pallet on the hard plank floor.

He looked around miserably. He'd split a little kindling for them before he left, he said, rolling up the sleeves of his black preaching coat. There was pitifully little wood to split, only the few boards and pieces of stumps that the girls had found in foraging the hillsides. But his offer was as instinctive, in time of trouble, as a woman's putting on the kettle for tea.

At last he could think of nothing else to do. He left them reluctantly, almost self-accusingly, telling them he would stop by and see the Bird girl and that he'd be back tomorrow to find out how they had fared.

Roxana was still standing in the doorway wearing her black-veiled hat when Rob Evans appeared on the path. He came straight toward her, concern written all over his clear boyish features. In his hand was a wrapped oblong package. He held it out to her, thought better of it and drew it back, and finally let it dangle futilely.

Avis, who had a sweet tooth and could discern a candy box under any number of wrappings, solved his dilemma by relieving him of the package.

"I'm terribly sorry—" His Adam's apple worked painfully— "I didn't hear about your mother. I wanted you to know—"

Roxana had to guess what, for he had run completely out of words.

"Everyone is so kind," she whispered, including him and the box of candy and the town. But she was thinking drearily, My first present from a young gentleman—and it's on the day of my mother's funeral. She could hear the steady rustle of unfolding papers as Avis exposed the top layer of beehive-shaped mounds, whitish-brown from sitting in a hot showcase all summer.

Rob Evans looked around the shack and glowered fiercely. All that was chivalrous in him rose to protect these two women creatures suddenly abandoned in this heedless town.

"You know you can't stay here alone. It won't do."

"Mrs. Bird's daughter will sleep here nights till we decide," said Roxana.

"It's no place," he repeated. He must think of something; he *had* to think of something. And then he thought of it.

"My Aunt Edna—she'll know what to do," he said with relief. "She'll be up to see you first thing in the morning."

"That's very kind, I'm sure," said Roxana humbly. Her lip trembled. She had a sudden weak desire to lean against the strength and decency and kindness of this Rob Evans who was staring down at her with such speechless yearning.

He turned his hat around and around in his hands. He essayed further words but gave it up. With a blurted, "Oh, Roxana!" he turned on his heel and blundered down the slope.

Roxana stood there staring out into the sunset afterglow. The rustle of papers behind her brought her back.

"Avis, you'll be sick if you make a pig of yourself," she scolded in her mother's sharply absent-minded way.

"Pig yourself! Who was it always took all the cream for her oatmeal?" Avis flared back.

The two sisters quarreled vigorously and briefly, and both felt the better for it.

Chapter VI

IT WOULD PROBABLY have been better for Rob's innocent promises and Roxana's innocent hopes if his Aunt Edna had come to see the Renner girls that very night while Roxana's green eyes were still circled by smudges of fatigue and her skin was the transparent white of quartz. For after a night's sleep she woke to a brilliant Colorado September morning, and nothing could quite quench the light in her eye or the spice of color in her cheeks.

After Mrs. Bird's daughter Euphemia left—a large solid girl of nineteen, who promised to return again that night—Roxana fell to in a frenzy of preparations for her expected caller. She tidied up the shack and swept the gravel smooth in front of the door and ironed a dress for Avis and sewed a fresh ruching in the neck of her basque. She worked fast and well. Her mother always said that even a bow that Roxana tied had an air. Roxana wanted Rob's Aunt Edna to see that in spite of the shaft house, the Renner girls came from nice people; that they had had a nice mother. Her tears, close to the surface, started hotly.

She saw Aunt Edna before the latter saw her. From the gloom inside the shaft house she watched the woman daintily setting her feet down, all the while carefully holding a covered dish in her hands. She saw the approving glance Aunt Edna bent on Avis, who was sitting on a boulder working at her knitting spool.

Edna Evans was known as a "sweet" woman. Everyone back in Kaw Center spoke of how sweet she was. She had small agate eyes and frizzy grayish hair, cindery from the curling iron with which she made neat pursed curls around her forehead. She had a neat pursed mouth, well braced with tiny lines on either side to keep it that way.

She had been married for eighteen years, and her husband knew very little about her. He also assumed that she was sweet; wasn't she always making broths for the sick and flannel petticoats for the poor, and spending hours reading to old ladies? Outside demeanor speaks so much more loudly than does inside character.

He did not know that, left to himself, he would have been quite happy to live and die, a clerk in a small-town store. But his wife was constantly lacerated from having to give first place to the wives of the mill owner and the banker and the lawyer. If her husband were a store owner now— Yet it would take a lifetime of saving to buy a store. What they needed was a goodly sum all at once. The papers were full of tales of how immigrants—drug clerks, barbers, farmers—had struck it rich out west. So Nathaniel Evans thought he had conceived the idea of going to Colorado with his wife and nephew to make his fortune, in order that he might come back home and have "Evans and Evans" on his own store windows and spend his nights worrying over his ledgers.

One other unsatisfied longing gnawed at Edna Evans, and that was to have a little girl of her own to dress and mold to be a credit to her.

Something about this sedate little girl with her tan braids and her knitting spool appealed to her. So this was the younger sister Rob had spoken of. What a dear little thing. Why, the child looked enough like her to be her own.

"Hello, my dear," she said with brisk pleasantness. "I'm Rob's Aunt Edna and I've brought you a dish of floating island." She lifted the cover of the china tureen.

Avis smiled shyly. Better and better, thought Mrs. Evans. She liked a child who wasn't forward.

"Is your sister around?"

Then she saw Roxana in the doorway, and the agate eyes sharpened. Hmm—a rather stubborn chin. Not a bit tractable looking, not a bit. Such level greenish eyes under those black eyebrows. And what lashes! A foolish young man could be completely taken in by them.

Roxana was offering their guest their only chair, backless but with four sound legs, and murmuring thanks as she accepted the covered dish. The two women made company-talk while Mrs. Evans spooned out the custard. Afraid I didn't have quite as good luck as usual—the egg whites, you know—everything falls in this altitude (knowing full well that the floating island was perfect). And Roxana, gesturing deprecatingly toward their swept and scoured quarters, saying that Mrs. Evans must excuse the dreadful mess, but the wind blew so, up here. And all the while the two of them were circling and sniffing, with rippling hackles and inaudible growls, and deciding that they did not like each other.

"Rob has told me of your trouble, dear," said Mrs. Evans. "I'm so very sorry. I came to see if there's anything I can do." The conventional offer in time of trouble, to which Roxana made the conventional reply.

"There's not a thing, thank you, not a thing." Her eyes felt the quick scalding in them. She looked down hastily.

"Rob is quite right. You can't stay here," said the older woman, looking around her. Roxana grew very still.

Aunt Edna went on, "I happened to run into Reverend Starbuck yesterday, and when he mentioned your—ah—trouble, I told him about an opening I'd heard of. I wonder if he spoke of it?" She paused to watch Avis attack her custard. Roxana's brows drew together while she waited, tensely pushing her own white island back and forth in its yellow sea. "Such a cultured home you'd have with Mrs. Paxton. She belongs to one of Central's oldest families; I understand she's lived here fifteen years. And we would be glad to take Avis. She could have a nice little room of her own with moss rosebuds on the wallpaper."

Roxana stiffened incredulously. So this was how Aunt Edna would fix things. By taking Avis! And having her go to that horrible old lady Paxton. Well, Avis would show Mrs. Nathaniel Evans a thing or two. She looked hopefully at Avis, remembering how she had carried on at the preacher's over the idea of Roxana's going to this same Mrs. Paxton, leaving Avis to be "put somewhere." But Avis was intent on licking the last delicious drop from her spoon. The yellow custard with the snowy islands and the ruby dots of jelly was seducing.

"We're very grateful, but I promised Avis last night we would never be separated. Sisters belong together. I'll make a home for us somehow. We do belong together, don't we, Avis?"

Avis, maddeningly uncooperative, was still licking her spoon.

Mrs. Evans was disconcerted. She was not used to having her benefactions turned down.

"But you can't stay here. It's not fit."

"Oh, I'll find a position soon. We're much obliged to Mrs. Evans, aren't we, Avis? But we do think sisters should not be separated."

Still Avis said nothing.

"Hmm. Well, when you find out you can't manage, we'll still be glad to take Avis." Mrs. Evans smiled sweetly at Avis, who smiled back. "My husband's a great one for carving things. He makes doll furniture—little bedsteads and bureaus and dining-room tables."

She picked up her flowered dish and started for the door.

The day stretched out unexpectedly long after her departure. Roxana learned then that funerals, pagan orgies though they might be, have certain uses in busying the living. It is not until the last petal has been swept up from the floor and the last whiff of death and carnation has been aired from the house that the real emptiness sets in. The world has paid its respects; a little relieved, it goes about its business, leaving the mourners to a sudden hideous vacuum of inactivity.

She could not wash bedding, for the sun had gone under a cloud. Nor would it be seemly to start hunting a position so soon. There was nothing to do but wait, and think back to the past and ahead to the future, both of which seemed unutterably forlorn at the moment.

By late afternoon the cloud in the sky had become a leaden overcast with long layers of blue-black storm clouds in the west. The wind quickened; far-off thunder began to growl. Roxana went out to stand on the dump, the wind whipping her apron and bringing the first sting of rain. Fascinated, she watched the snow-capped distant peaks turn a sinister slate color, only to be blotted out by gray sheets of rain.

She watched the rain sweep down the slopes of the high peaks, then the nearer peaks, and finally the opposite side of the gulch. Only then did she realize that this was not a spectacle, but a menace. She threw her apron over her head and sprinted back to the shaft house. The storm burst as she slammed the door. She raced to fasten down everything loose. For she sensed that this was no mountain shower such as they had had before, that stopped as fitfully as it started, leaving only a dampish spatter on the floor, which soon dried. This would be a gully-washer. A flash flood. An avalanche-starter.

It was as if the elements had waited slyly until night, when the two girls were alone and helpless. For Roxana knew that no one could reach them in this storm. Lightning ripped up and down the canyon. Thunder crashed with terrifying closeness, sending Boots huddling against their legs in terror. The rain sought out every hole in the roof and thudded through with a hard cannonading on the floor. The air inside the building was full of a cutting mist. Gravelly water began to wash across the floor.

Avis clung close to Roxana on one side, and Boots crowded up against her on the other. What shall I do next? she asked herself in panic. I mustn't let on how scared I am.

She made Avis help her lift their bedding off the floor and pile it over the upended mine bucket. When the lantern blew out, Avis gave a shriek of pure terror and held on to Roxana frantically in the darkness.

"Don't leave me—the hole in the floor—don't leave me, Roxy!"

Roxana, who was afraid of the hole herself, could not find the matches and could only huddle on the pile of bedding with her arms around the cowering child and dog.

They would not soon forget that night. Time had never moved so draggingly. Roxana was afraid to hope that the faint grayness of the two small windows meant dawn. There were still snarling gusts of rain, and the heavens promised to loose another torrent at the slightest provocation, but the worst of the storm seemed over.

The two girls stretched their cramped legs and got to their feet looking like bedraggled little cats that have not had time to lick their fur dry.

They were trying to start a fire in the forge with scraps of wet kindling when Gil Anker appeared at the door. He stood there in silence, surveying them and the soggy interior. The steady drizzle made a gutter of his hat brim and sluiced down off his mackintosh.

"You two all alone here last night?" he wheezed angrily.

"Nobody could have got here in that storm," Roxana reminded him.

"I came to say good-by. I've been called back to Ohio by a death in the family. I'll be gone a week—or two—or three. But I can't go off and leave you in a place like this. I know my shop ain't much, but at least the roof is no leaky colander. I got two rooms in back, with a cook stove and plenty of wood. You could just pretend the coffins ain't out in front. Coffins can't hurt you—they're only boxes of wood and satin."

He looked from one girl to the other. At Avis, who was instantly dubious, like the sky outside, still weeping slightly and threatening at any minute to let loose a real cloudburst. At Roxana, who recoiled briefly from the idea and then as quickly embraced it.

It would be lovely, she told Avis in a rush, just to dry out—to sleep in a dry bed and get up and put on dry shoes in the morning. And cook on a real cook stove with a stovepipe instead of this open forge that let the smoke blow in your face. She half-carried Avis along on the swift current of her own enthusiasm.

Gil Anker helped them collect their sodden belongings. He closed the shaft house and boosted them up on to the seat of his wagon.

They were just setting off when the preacher sloshed into view. His first reaction to their plan was one of revulsion, too. Roxana's heart warmed to his concern for them. She felt less alone in the world. He was a good man, as Gil Anker had said. But not practical. His wife Naomi, a little less good and a little more beset by worldly considerations, would be easier to take your problems to.

When he said in a troubled, tentative way, "You don't think it might be better at Mrs. Paxton's after all? The Evanses say they're still willing to take Avis," Roxana stiffened. It was all she needed to congeal her wavering will.

No thank you, she told him. They would be perfectly comfortable in Gil Anker's nice dry rooms while he was gone. She would soon find a position. And sisters should not be separated. She repeated it until even the preacher looked abashed for having suggested anything else. With a troubled lifting of his battered hat, he finally left the girls in Gil Anker's care and retreated down the footpath.

When the wagon creaked around a turn, and their trunk slid the entire length of the wagon box, Roxana grew chattery with excitement. Her cheeks burned, as if to counter-balance Avis' listless pallor. She liked moving, she told Gil with feverish insistence. Moving anywhere.

"I guess I'm the true pioneer type, Gil. I never want to go back—only ahead. I'm like Pa—he said he'd drunk tea made from water from the Missouri and the Platte, and next he wanted to try the Arkansas. When he went to Leadville—" Her shrillness softened and then broke raggedly.

"Pioneers," Gil repeated. "Pioneers weren't only fur traders and prospectors, my girl. It took two kinds to pioneer a country: your father's kind to open it up, and your mother's kind to settle it down. It was your father that drove his team out west, but it was your mother that cooked biscuits in a Dutch oven and made a home out of an old shaft house."

He paused to hold his horses in on the slippery stretch of shelf road leading down to the town.

"Reckon maybe you two girls take after your two parents. You got your pa's itchy foot, Roxana; and Avis wants to put down roots, like her ma. Don't you, Avis?" He smiled at the solemn little girl, who looked pleased at her sudden importance. "Avis is the sort, I'll wager, that would build schools and raise money to pay the parson and start a reading circle. Yep, a country needs two kinds of pioneers. Though I notice each kind always looks down its nose at the other." He shook his reins in enjoyment of his own perspicacity.

Roxana frowned. She was not sure she liked this picture of Avis and her mother. She preferred to think that only she and her father were true pioneers at heart. Old stay-at-homes like Avis and her mother—imagine calling them pioneers!

"You spout like one of those lyceum speakers," she said petulantly.

"Hardly," he whispered with a reminding gesture toward his throat. "Not anybody that talks like a wheezy old forge bellows. Well, anyhow, none of my clients have ever objected!" He smiled at his grisly joke.

Roxana was instantly ashamed of herself.

They turned on to Spring Street. She remembered the night she had stopped in front of his shop to hide her tears and rage, feeling a certain hard satisfaction in eying the coffins within. Today she felt neither tears nor rage nor satisfaction. She had only a passionate desire to show the world, a world consisting mostly of Rob's Aunt Edna.

Gil drove around to the rear of the coffin shop and stopped. The back yard was a clutter of pine chips and saw horses and lumber piles. She saw the neighboring back yards, each with its own clutter and its flimsy privy on stilts. Across the creek she could see other back yards and other privies.

Gil opened the back door for them.

"Oh, look, Avis," Roxana cried. "A table to eat off of and a real bedstead with a nice hay mattress—and a Round Oak heater! How can we ever thank you, Gil!"

But Gil was already retreating toward his wagon.

"Sorry, but I got to keep moving if I'm going to catch my train. Have to leave my team at the livery on the way." He looked down anxiously at them from the wagon seat. "Help yourself to any grub you can find. Think you'll be all right?"

Roxana wanted to run after him, wanted to pluck at his sleeve crying, "What's to become of us, Gil, what's to become of us?" But she reminded herself that they had no claim on this kindly middle-aged man—no claim, in fact, on anyone in the world.

"Of course we'll be all right, Gil. Won't we, Avis?"

There was no answer from Avis. Roxana turned back to find Avis standing in the doorway that led to the front of the shop. The child was staring at the display of open coffins, each lined with its shirred silk, and each looking exactly like the one that held their mother.

[67]

Chapter VII

I F ONLY AVIS would reproach her! Instead of saying with that big-eyed look, "You take the last piece, Roxy. You're always so hungry." After all, at the Evanses' Avis would have had plenty to eat, instead of scrimping along here in Gil Anker's rooms, using up his supplies, and eking out with donations from Naomi Starbuck, who could ill afford to feed them. There was nothing more they could sell; she had sold her mother's cameo and her father's goldstone cuff links. They could not hold out much longer.

Rob had come with tentative eagerness to see her. But unfortunately he had renewed his aunt's offer in almost her very words. They would be only too glad to take Avis, and Roxana could stay with Mrs. Paxton, who lived in that fine house on Second High and belonged to one of Central's oldest families.

Roxana had glared at him. Everyone was against her, even Rob. To think that just because it was "respectable," he would be willing to see her go to *prison,* go into *slavery*— which was what working for old lady Paxton would mean. She could see his glance roving around the coffin shop as it had roved around the shaft house. Well, he could just disapprove. She wasn't going to old lady Paxton's, and she wasn't going to Aunt Essie's. She would find something yet.

But "positions" for unskilled but genteel young ladies

were scarce in Central City. She did not know how those other genteel young ladies in *Leslie's Illustrated,* wearing the long white aprons over their best dresses, had gone about learning to handle this thing called a typewriter or this even worse thing called a telephone exchange where they poked snaky tubes into little holes.

Her only knack, if you ruled out the cantata, was with her needle. But who was going to trust a sixteen-year-old to slash into expensive lengths of surah or *peau de soie?* Not that she had ever slashed into such lengths for herself; her only sewing had been confined to making over clothes and retrimming bonnets. (Ah, but she did have a way with bonnets!)

Maybe if she tried the new management at the Shoo Fly again, she might still get a job there. Probably every word that horrible Professor Jay had told her was a lie. A tide of confused anger swept over her at certain shameful memories. Her legs trembled under her seersucker petticoats. Skinny as a plucked pullet, was she? Well, Rob thought she was just right. He had said she was much too fine and delicate for Shoo Fly patrons to appreciate.

Yet her emotions about Rob were mixed, too. He made her feel wonderful and cherished and important one minute, and in the next he consigned her unfeelingly to old lady Paxton. How could he be so lacking in understanding?

Roxana reached for her bonnet on the nail behind Gil Anker's door. She might as well go down and ask for the mail even if there never was any. Avis was too tired to accompany her. Roxana tried not to think that it was lack of food that made the child so listless, with hollows like salt dishes at her collarbones. She tried not to picture all the good boiled dinners and fine rich puddings Avis would have had at the Evanses'.

When she reached the corner of Eureka Street she turned from habit up the steep walk. Tired and hungry as she was, she must still make that extra climb which took her to the Opera House each day.

Today she saw that bills were posted out in front. Her steps quickened.

The world is prone to lay much to chance: life is accidental, and things just happen, such as Roxana's trip to the Opera House today. But Roxana had begun and ended every journey downtown with a longing visit to the Opera House. A dozen times she had tried the doors and then walked around the side to the rear. There was no accident about her going to the Opera House today; she went as she always went—from compulsion, from desire, from need. But not by chance.

A stock company was in town! The DeForest Company. "Exciting Week's Repertoire," the bills said. She wondered what that was. They would put on a play every night. *The Lady of Lyons. Under the Gaslight. The Marble Heart.* Her own heart, which was not marble, almost burst from the combination of the climb and the knowledge that real live actors and actresses were in town this very minute.

As was her wont, she tried all the front doors of the building and then made her way around to the rear.

Today, for the first time, the stage door was open. She stopped outside it, staring up. In the doorway, which was at the side rather than the rear because the back of the theater was thrust deep into the rocky hillside, an old man was languidly sweeping. If he'd only let her look inside. Just one peep was all she asked.

He blocked the door against the supplication in her eyes. "No, they ain't no opening," he said testily. "Not for you or any other of the young ladies that's always pestering me. Only opening," he added slyly, "is for somebody to fill in for the wardrobe mistress that's took down with mountain fever. You'd have to mend tears and rips, press costumes, take out spots, make over—"

"But I can. I can do all of that. My mother will tell you—" She stopped abruptly, biting down hard on her quivering lower lip.

"You ain't pretending?"

"Oh, no. I can do it all. Let me show you."

"Mrs. DeForest!" he shouted over his shoulder. "Girl here says she's understudy for your wardrobe mistress."

A panting buxom woman with hair like oat-straw, holding a needle with a long thread attached, came to the doorway. She was sucking her finger, which she had obviously just pierced. She looked at Roxana with questioning despair.

"Can you really sew and press? I'm losing my wits trying to fix a torn hem and iron the wrinkles out of my dresses after their being jammed in a trunk for days. If you're any good, there's a week's work here till Mrs. Galliher gets better. We're opening tonight in *The Lady of Lyons,* and everything is at sixes and sevens."

Roxana took the steps in a leap.

"I can go right to work."

"Ten dollars a week if you're able to do it," said Mrs. De-Forest.

Roxana turned a look of incredulous gratitude upon her.

"Of course, that's a good deal for a young girl," hedged Mrs. DeForest, regretting that she had spoken so quickly. "I'll expect you to be here evenings, too, to help with the dressing." She waited for Roxana to object. Instead, Roxana looked as if boon had been added to boon.

"Can I stand out of the way and listen?"

"Well, when you aren't busy. Come along and I'll show you."

Roxana followed her inside. She found herself in a dim, cavernous shed that completely surrounded the stage. She was so occupied with craning to look upward into the cathedral gloom filled with painted stage sets hoisted up out of the way that she stumbled over a chair. She rubbed her shin absently. So this was what it was like backstage. She had not expected it to be so big.

"There's a couple of dressing rooms there on the sides and more down below," explained Mrs. DeForest. "You'll have to be everywhere at once while they're dressing and making up."

Roxana nodded. That was exactly what she wanted. She was inside a theater at last; she was a part of it even. She thrilled to its dark unwholesomeness.

From the lighted stage, painted screens extended out on either side. Wings, Mrs. DeForest called them. Roxana peered between them.

"Who's she?" She pointed to a rather pretty girl standing stiffly in the center of the stage, one arm extended.

"The one twirling the parasol? That's Miss Lovell, the ingénue."

Roxana looked again. So she was twirling a parasol, was she?

"Worst fumbler of lines you ever saw. And just walks through a part. But with that baby face, they forgive her anything."

"Is she rehearsing now?"

The woman flashed Roxana an indulgent glance.

"Rehearsing—and driving my husband crazy. Move over and you can see him in front of the footlights. He directs as well as plays leads. Tomorrow night Miss Lovell will play Laura in *Under the Gaslight,* and how we all dread it. She doesn't know half her lines yet. We always have to carry her. Slow study, she is."

Roxana listened with straining attention. That must mean the girl had a poor memory. She thought complacently of how quickly she had memorized poems for the Friday afternoon school programs.

"What about the play tonight?" she asked.

"Oh, that's *The Lady of Lyons,* and I play Pauline. I can do it in my sleep. Mrs. Harlowe is the mother." She pointed to a large woman at one side of the stage, overflowing a straight kitchen chair. She had her shoes off and was comfortably wriggling her stockinged feet. Roxana noted that her fat cheeks had run down toward her neck like melted wax and that her figure, in its shapeless dress, seemed to have melted down in the same way.

"Is *she* an actress?" Not that dumpy old woman who looked like a big fat bun in a wrinkled paper sack.

"The world will never see a better one. Wait till she does Mrs. Malaprop. Of course, she only plays character parts now—which is what we all come to."

The director was speaking with worn patience.

"We'll try that scene with Mr. Lynde again, Miss Lovell, and not so wooden, please." Miss Lovell tossed her head and forgot she was holding a parasol. "Remember, the young man is your betrothed," admonished the paunchy, but still handsome, man who was the husband of Mrs. De-Forest.

At his words, a languid young man doused his cheroot in a bucket of water evidently kept there for the purpose and crossed to Miss Lovell. He embraced her competently.

"That's Romney Lynde, the juvenile," volunteered Mrs. DeForest. "Sometimes he plays the parts that are too young for my husband." She sighed. "A leading man simply has to keep his hair and hold his stomach in."

Roxana noted that Mr. DeForest had been none too successful at doing either.

Miss Lovell, as Laura, in the circle of the young man's arm, was intoning, "We shall have cause to bless the morrow for it will bring the long-sought sunlight of our lives."

Roxana felt tingly. She had just heard her first lines spoken by a real actress on a real stage. She was jolted when Mr. DeForest gave a weary snort.

"Sounds like you're about to take a dose of calomel, Miss Lovell. Well, that will be all until tonight. Anyone who dries up and has to be prompted will be fined one dollar."

"One simoleon!" muttered an old man in a gritty, whiskey-ravaged voice. "Our dear little chicken-brain Miss Lovell will be owing the company if she doesn't watch out!" He looked across at Roxana, who was staring at him, taking in each detail of his bulbous nose and comic white tufts of whiskers.

"Monty," said Mrs. DeForest, "this is our new wardrobe woman—girl. I forgot to ask your name, dear, Mr. Montague plays character parts. He steals the scene if you don't watch out."

This seemed to amuse him. Roxana wondered why he did not mind. Stealing a scene . . .

"Wardrobe woman, eh? Don't let her fool you," he chuckled, his wise old eyes squinting at Roxana. "By the two-headed Janus, that girl's only using her needle to pry her way backstage. Stage-struck like all of 'em. And no harm in that, my dear," he reassured the alarmed Roxana. "But you do want to go on the stage, I'll be bound?"

She nodded timidly. "Ever since I sang in our church cantata. I've never been the same since."

"See what I mean?" he said gravely to Mrs. DeForest. "She probably dreams of playing Lady Teazle."

Mrs. DeForest grunted. "She's been hired for one week as wardrobe woman," she said dryly.

Roxana set to work downstairs in a dank little cubbyhole permeated by the sewer-like smell of the creek flowing beneath the building. She worked by lamplight. The Opera House was lighted by this wonderful new modern gas, but the system was capricious; it took all of one man's time to tinker with it.

She had never worked harder, as she whipped up hems, took in seams, let them out, mended torn laces, pressed wrinkled garments, and even managed to use a fluting iron. One by one the cast came to her with their costuming problems. She did not know their names as yet, but for each she had a wide lighted-up smile and an eagerness to please. She felt needed and important. The show could not go on without her.

It was almost dark before she remembered Avis, or that she herself had not eaten since breakfast. She sent a small

[74]

boy to Avis with a note telling her to stop at the store for some bread and cheese and come to the Opera House.

Roxana had two red spots of fatigue on her cheeks and a burning pain between her shoulder blades when Avis was escorted in by the old door man. While she wolfed down her bread and cheese, she explained to Avis about the wonderful new job.

"You can't stay home alone evenings, Avis," she mumbled, with her mouth full. "So you can come with me every night. They won't mind, I know. And just think, you'll get to see behind the scenes."

The prospect left Avis unmoved.

Roxana asked with an air of unconcern, "Did you tell Rob at the store where I was?"

No, Avis had not. Rob had been busy selling a lady boots for her little boy.

Roxana knew a small stab of disappointment. Avis might have hung around long enough to tell him.

Then she forgot Rob and Avis and the outside world. The evening was like nothing she had ever known. So this was what a play was like behind the scenes—all mad, but whispered activity. People running to and fro, or standing in the wings fixing each other's chignons and neck ruffles and bustles and swords, or studying their parts lashed to ropes behind the stage. And then between acts the swift pandemonium of pulling the canvas-covered frames up and down, or sliding them out at the sides, or shoving furniture around. Why, it was like the wrong side of a beautiful but sleazily made dress; lovely on the outside, but all raw edges and seams and basted linings on the inside. Yet thrilling.

Roxana thought that the matter of make-up was like the play itself. There was Mrs. DeForest, for instance, pantingly lacing herself into a terrible corset and piling her straw hair that was darker at the roots into a series of waterfalls and plastering layer on layer on her plump cheeks, to emerge at last, young and lovely and seductive. It was the miracle of the theater.

Roxana stood in the wings, her hands clasped together in an inverted V between her breasts. She could scarcely breathe as she listened to Mrs. DeForest, the lovely Pauline, whose voice could send little racing tremors through her.

"Sir! Leave this house. It is humble, but a husband's roof, however lowly, is, in the eyes of God and man, the temple of a wife's honor."

Roxana felt uplifted. That was what true love meant, a husband's love. Perhaps some day—

Later, when Pauline's worldly mother, the old actress Mrs. Harlowe, who had now become handsome and corseted and a veritable dowager queen, remarked pompously that a properly brought up young lady should think of only two things in choosing a husband: "First, is his birth honorable? And secondly, will his death be advantageous?" she hated the mercenary old dame, as did the audience, and found herself hissing, too.

Still later, when she had folded and put away the last costume and was ready to go home with Avis, who had fallen asleep on a pair of kitchen chairs, it was Mrs. Harlowe who stopped her.

"You two walk home by yourselves?"

"It's only a few blocks—just down along Spring Street."

"One or two things to remember, going home late from the theater. Move fast, eyes straight ahead, and keep to the outside of the walk. Never let a prowler crowd you close to a building or an alley. And never walk between a pair of drunks. After all, a girl who's been raped can't be exactly choosy about a husband." She gathered her ancient cape about her and marched off as calmly as if she had just been giving complexion advice.

Roxana was agape. She had never heard the word rape spoken above a whisper in her life. What a strange woman.

The two girls ran all the way back to the coffin shop, which in this short time had become home. With a feeling of reaching a haven, they locked the door and lighted the lamp and petted the excitable Boots. They started a little fire and put milk down for Boots, who drank it *callop-callop,* in a cozy way. They were safe, and Roxana had a position, and no white slavers had accosted them on the way home.

The next morning Roxana tried to infect Avis with some of her own excitement, but Avis had a constitutional immunity to excitement. She helped docilely about the two rooms, but when it came time for Roxana to leave, she grew quieter and quieter.

Roxana was fastening her bonnet.

"Now do like you did yesterday, Avis, and stop by Rob's store for something to eat. Tell the owner I'll be paid Saturday night and ask him to charge it please. And do let Rob know about my position, only don't tell him I said to." You had to warn Avis about things like that. And Roxana longed to have Rob know about her job, in a real theater, not the Shoo Fly. "Then bring my supper again and you can watch the show from backstage," she finished temptingly.

Avis looked untempted.

"All right, Roxy," she said in her lusterless voice.

Roxana looked back and saw Avis watching her forlornly from the doorway, her fingers pleating Boots' silky ears. She shook her head impatiently. Avis seemed determined not to like *anything.*

She was back in the maelstrom again. Tonight it was *Under the Gaslight.* Preparations were delightfully noisy. While she pressed and sewed she could hear the moving and pounding. This was one of the cast's favorites. A real train—well, a real stage train—would snort its way across the stage, spitting sparks and belching smoke. An innocent victim would be lashed to the tracks. The lovely Laura, locked inside the railroad station, would grab an ax and hack her way out just in time to save the victim before the train thundered past. Roxana kindled at the thought of it all.

Underneath her excitement was the triumphant realization that she had justified her stand with Rob and Rob's Aunt Edna. When Avis arrived with her supper, she questioned her sharply about Rob. Had Avis told him?

Yes, she had told him, but he hadn't said anything special. Avis was unsatisfactorily vague.

And then Roxana deposited her little sister in an obscure corner and forgot her.

It was a breathless evening, far better than the one before. Already she was swept up in the tempo of the theater. She sensed the quickened pulse of every actor before the curtain went up. She sensed the anxiety with which each peered through the peephole in the curtain to count the house. She was gratified to know that tonight the very last row in the balcony was filled. She heard the confused babble that came from the audience, the sound of chattering people waiting in gala expectancy for a play to begin.

Later, she could tell by the clapping and by the howls of glee and horror that the show was going like a prairie fire. She covered her ears against the explosions of the "real" train that went pounding across the brief tracks, with Laura coming to the rescue of the bound Snorkey just in time. Apparently all the coaching was bearing fruit; Miss Lovell did not "dry up" once.

It was almost time for the climax. Roxana was standing in the wings waiting, trancelike, when someone plucked her sleeve.

"She's crying—your little sister—she wants you," said a stagehand.

Roxana shook off the interruption. That Avis! Just when the play was at its height. But she turned resentfully and followed the man. She found Avis with her face huddled against a pile of coats. Two sheepish-looking stagehands were trying to placate her.

"We didn't know she scared so easy," one of them apologized to Roxana. "Maybe she was kind of asleep. We was running the locomotive out back, puffing away just fine. She jumped and rubbed her eyes, and we speeded up as if to run over her, and then swerved, of course. We wouldn't have hurt her. But she went down in a heap and started to cry."

Avis would! Roxana put her arm around Avis with impatient indulgence.

"It was only a joke, Avis. A stage locomotive couldn't hurt you. It was play-acting."

But the sobbing Avis was not easily comforted. Roxana had to assure and reassure her. The lovely play moved on to its finish, unseen by her. The closing lines were said. The curtain went down. It went up. It went down. Dimly Roxana could hear the unleashed roar of approval from the house. And she was missing it all!

Later, when she and a limp and still hiccuping Avis started out the stage door together, she saw Rob waiting in the shadows. He had come to take them home, he told her. He listened gravely as she recounted Avis' scare, comforting Avis with brotherly pats. Avis brightened. Masculine comforting carried more authority with Avis.

"This thing can't go on like this," he rebuked Roxana, who heard the new manly sureness in his tone and responded to it. Being scolded by Rob was oddly pleasant.

"Until your week in the theater is up," he went on, "Avis will spend the evenings up at Aunt Edna's." He never said Uncle Than's. "I'll call for you after the show and we'll walk around by Aunt Edna's and pick up Avis." He made it sound as if his only concern were for Avis.

That suited Roxana. Then she need not worry in the theater about her crybaby little sister. And she and Rob would have a lovely walk all by themselves up to Aunt Edna's after the show each night. She wanted to hear that note in Rob's voice again, authoritative and yet beseeching.

Roxana had never lived so fast or so completely as in the next few days. Stitching and basting and pressing, she was also storing up memories for a lifetime, she told herself. And daily the thought of Rob was growing like a once softly muted melody that had begun to swell and throb through her being. She must tell Rob this; she must see what Rob thought of that. Her craving for the stage was slaked, she told herself. Now she was ready to "settle down." She did not put into words what settling down meant, but it centered indefinably about Rob.

It was the next to the last night of her week as wardrobe woman for the DeForest Company. She was half-prepared for the significant new note in Rob's voice as they started away from the Opera House.

"I want to talk to you about something mighty important to me, Roxy."

She felt suddenly delightfully faint. All her untried woman's wisdom told her what was coming. And she was both eager and reluctant. He led her up the hillside to the steps of a church. The gulch spread out below, still brightly lighted. She kept her eyes studiously on the glinting panorama, but every nerve in her was tinglingly aware of Rob's shoulder touching hers, of his arm around her but not quite around her, of the masculine roughness in his voice.

"What . . . what do you want to talk about?"

"My Uncle Than has heard of a fresh strike. No one here knows a thing about it; gold flakes the size of watermelon seeds! I'm honor bound not to tell where it is. The folks pull out tomorrow, and I'll wind things up and follow in a few days. We're in on the ground floor, I tell you, Roxy. Know what that means?"

"What?" she asked, quite sure she knew.

"It means we can go back to Kaw Center and buy our own store." Roxana felt a sense of deflation. "It means we'll be able to put in a department of ladies' dresses—all made up, not just dress goods, and we can have those little cash boxes I saw in Chicago that whiz along on wires. It will be a regular emporium."

Roxana tried to share his enthusiasm because it seemed so important to him. "That will be lovely, I'm sure, Rob."

"And it means I can ask you to marry me!"

Now her waiting heart set up a wild thumping.

He turned with sudden young awkwardness and searched her face for courage, for words to go on. He gave up helplessly and tightened the arm about her, drawing her to him.

"Roxy, I love you so. Tell me you do—a little."

He kissed her. It was Roxana's first kiss, her first knowledge of the sweet, hot uprushing through her whole body that she took for love. Everything was rapturous. She and Rob would be married; they would make a home for Avis; he would strike it rich; they would all live happily ever after.

She reached out and touched his lapel with shy possessiveness. Then—as if she were the first to ask it in all time—she said, "When did you first begin to care?"

"When you watched me wind ribbons that day," he said positively.

That was the way with true love, she thought. It struck you like a lightning bolt.

They would be married at once, he told her with lordly simplicity. Next week. So she could go with him when he followed his aunt and uncle to the rich strike.

She did not recoil from the idea, but ran to meet it as she ran to meet all of life. Only last spring she had skipped rope and ridden farm nags bareback. And now, all of a sudden, she was grown-up. She was sixteen and quite old enough to be married, and have a husband, and keep house, and bear a baby. She was dizzy with the wonder of being a woman.

"Whatever you say, Rob," she said with her new-found woman's voice.

Quite as suddenly Rob was grown-up, too. His voice was husky with love. He trembled with the gusts that shook him. But his arms about her were tender, as he regarded her with the protectiveness of masculine twenty for feminine sixteen, and shielded her from what he was sure were the savage forces of his own passion. So little did he know about the armor of self-preservation possessed by even the most ardent of "nice" girls in 1879.

His words were muffled in her freshly washed hair.

"I didn't know anyone could be so sweet. Don't move—I love you so."

Roxana, with the profound subjectivity of her own state, could only feel. Every fiber in her was dizzily, swooningly aware of him.

"I . . . I love you too, Rob." And she was sure she did, in the old way, in the ancient way, through and through.

He turned her face up to his again, and his kisses were fire in the farthest depths of her. When she finally pulled away—what ancestor had told her it was best for the woman to pull away first?—she was shaking, and her knees would not have supported her. But it was a lovely weakness. She stared about her. The same splintery church steps under them, the same winking lights below, the same little mountain wind blowing. Only everything was different. She and Rob loved each other.

With her new and becoming maturity she reminded him of Avis.

For once, Avis' mood matched Roxana's. They found her happy and bright-eyed. Aunt Edna had washed Avis' tan hair with a lather made of yucca roots and put it up in curl papers, and now it shone with "real gold lights," Avis told them complacently. In addition, Uncle Than had carved her a napkin ring all her own, with a bluebird and her name on it. All the way back to the shop she caressed the napkin ring, her warm fingers giving it the patina of her devotion. When she had let Roxana admire it, she gave it back to Rob to return to his aunt for safekeeping.

As they undressed, she told Roxana, "When I stay with Aunt Edna I'm to have my own napkin and keep it in my own ring. Roxy, they have clean napkins every Sunday, and

Uncle Than put up a swing in the yard for me, and Aunt Edna makes fresh cookies on Fridays. And tonight we had Brown Betty for supper." Avis too was in love.

Roxana debated whether to tell her about herself and Rob. That in a week they would be married and Avis could stand up with them. She knew that Avis would be pleased, but she delayed the telling.

"Did they happen to say anything about their plans—that they might be leaving soon?" Roxana asked.

"First thing in the morning, and Rob is to go next week," said Avis, lowering her voice to a conspiratorial whisper. "But they don't want a soul to know about the rich strike. Gold flakes the size of watermelon seeds! I'm to visit them as soon as they get settled. Uncle Than is going to make me a handkerchief box with little pine cones glued to it. Aunt Edna says she'll write and tell me when I can come. She's going to teach me to make apple turnovers."

Roxana experienced a slight twinge of jealousy over Aunt Edna's obvious perfections. But the jealousy gave way to triumph. Aunt Edna would be off the scene by tomorrow. Not, of course, that anybody or anything could stop her and Rob from getting married. It was all arranged. But there was something about Aunt Edna's bright blackbird's eyes under the cindery curls, and the sweet little mouth so firmly pursed that made her glad Aunt Edna would be out of the way. Wanting to take Avis to live with them, but not Roxana. Well, Aunt Edna would just have to make up her mind to accept Roxana when she arrived next week as Rob's wife. Wife! Her heart flopped in her chest, and again it was like a great fish flopping.

Chapter VIII

WOODENLY ROXANA went through the motions of her work at the Opera House that last night. For Mrs. Galliher had come back, and Roxana was only her understudy now. Already the girl had moved on to her next role, that of betrothed young woman, and she was playing it with devout single-mindedness. Rob was the sun toward which all her sunflower thoughts now turned. She was eagerly ready for the next thing, which was love and marriage. To sixteen, love and marriage represented only the most abandoned rapture and the utmost freedom.

Because his family had already departed, Rob was taking care of Avis for the evening. He would probably tell Avis about their approaching marriage. She hoped so; she had been shy about doing it herself. Already Rob had a gentle big-brother attitude toward the little girl that boded well for their new life together when they would make a home for Avis. At the thought of that new life, little shivers raced down her spine. They would be married, and Aunt Edna could not stop them! She did not admit that outwitting Aunt Edna added fillip to the adventure.

And then an infected wisdom tooth changed her life. The tooth belonged to Miss Fanny Corwine, utility woman and walking lady, who mostly just walked on and off the stage. The tooth was not only painful but the gum had begun to swell. In the statue scene in *The Marble Heart,* where three

Greek statues in white wigs, robes, and tights must stand motionless against a black velvet backdrop, it simply would not do for one of them to look as if she held a butternut in her cheek. Miss Corwine moaned, her face pressed against a wrapped hot brick, while Mrs. DeForest paced back and forth, glaring about her in a distraught way. She focused her attention suddenly on Roxana and pounced.

"Here—why didn't I think of you before? You're just the same size. All you have to do is stand still."

She was snatching at Roxana's dress—right out in public she was undressing her and pushing her toward a dressing room at the same time. Roxana submitted in a daze. Several hands went to work on her at once. The white wig. The heavy powder. The long silken tights. The classic white draperies.

"We'll put you in the back where you can lean against the iron brace so you won't wiggle too much."

Like a jointed doll Roxana went through the next half-hour. She had no time to build up any stage fright. And when the three Greek statues, Lais, Aspasia, and Phrynne, were posed against the lush black velvet, she tasted the heady potion of applause. First, absolute breathless silence from the audience, then a relaxed *ah* of admiration, and finally a thundering battery of handclapping. She held herself so rigid that she had to be helped down from her pedestal when the curtain went down for the fourth time.

Her first stage appearance!

She wasn't even surprised when Mrs. DeForest said impatiently, "We'll take you along with us, Roxana, till Fanny's swelling goes down. She'll stay behind to have her tooth pulled. Three days ought to be enough. We leave on the stage right after the show tonight for Idaho Springs. Then we play Georgetown and Silver Plume. We'll pay your way back home and give you Fanny's salary besides."

Three days. Three days of being an actress. Her feeling of complete dedication to Rob went up like a wisp of chiffon in a candle flame. She must do this first. Oh, not that she loved Rob any the less, she assured herself. And after all, it was only till the middle of next week, and the company was in a terrible fix, and Mrs. DeForest had begged, and the show simply must go on. But the truth remained: she had to do it.

Rob and Avis were waiting outside the stage door for her. She could see their faces fall as her words tumbled out. Rob did not turn out to be so reasonable as she had counted on. He made a show of "putting his foot down." Roxana tried to push the foot aside.

"But I'll be back next Thursday, Rob," she pleaded.

"What are you planning to do with Avis while you're gone?"

She looked down at her little sister.

"Avis? Oh, Avis!" She had forgotten all about Avis, for whom she and Rob were going to make a home when they were married. "Why," improvising fast "Miss Fanny Corwine that's staying behind to have her tooth pulled—Avis can stay with her at the boardinghouse. She can feed Boots every day and go for the mail. I'll be back before you know it, and then you and I . . . you and I will be—"

"I won't be here when you get back."

"Why, Rob! Of course you'll be here."

"I won't be here."

"It's only for three days."

"I don't intend to hang around while my future—" He glanced at Avis—"while you go roaming off on a stage tour. An actress! Either you stay here, and we carry out our plans like we said, or I pull out for Aunt Edna's tomorrow."

She tried to argue, but his pride was stiff. And there was Avis listening with her solemn look. Her *orphaned* look, Roxana thought impatiently. If she could only talk to Rob alone—what she really meant was *be* with Rob alone—she could convince him. Already she had discovered that there were better arguments than words to use with a man.

But she had no time for anything, she thought distractedly.

She was forced to enlist Rob to help her, even while he disapproved of every move she made. He waited outside the boardinghouse while she went in to persuade the swollenjawed and extremely unenthusiastic Fanny Corwine to take in a young roommate for three days. He accompanied her and Avis back to the shop and then returned with them to the boardinghouse carrying Avis' needed items and her china doll. He waited frowningly while Roxana said good-by to Avis in the hallway, unlocking Avis' clinging arms from around her neck and drying Avis' sniffling tears.

Even when they were finally alone together, everything was wrong, Roxana thought. Avis' doleful presence stood between them. And the moving hands of the clock were between them, too. "Be on the steps of the Opera House, everybody, by midnight sharp," Mrs. DeForest had warned. And here it was past eleven-thirty already. Oh, dear!

As they reached the Opera House steps, with Rob carrying her gray-canvas telescope, he burst out with angry wistfulness. "I don't see how you could want to, Roxy, not if you really cared—"

Briefly she did not see how she could want to either; but she did, and there was nothing she could do about it.

Then voices sounded as the rest of the cast began to converge. Rob left her, tipping his hat politely. He would always remember to tip his hat to a lady. His back was very straight and his gait stiff-legged as he marched down Eureka Street.

But the moment Roxana settled back in the stagecoach her doubts dissolved. Everything would be all right, she convinced herself. Avis would be fine; and in no time Roxana would be back. As to Rob—he was just being bossy, the way men seemed to feel they had to be. After all, he really loved her; hadn't he told her so over and over? What if he did go ahead to Aunt Edna's? Maybe it would be just as well; then he could find a place for them to live. She had tried to make it clear that she would not live with Aunt Edna and Uncle

Than. Yes, maybe it was all for the best. She settled back in the jolting darkness, completely persuaded, so much more eloquent were her desires than her doubts.

The great iron wheels turned on the granite; the stage-coach lurched around narrow turns, as sharp as the loops of a whiplash. She was afraid to look over the edge in the moonlight, down into the bottomless black canyon below. The talk went on all around her. She was a part of the theater at last. She was carrying a champagne basket just like all the rest of them with her costumes—or rather, with Fanny Corwine's costumes—in it. She was an actress, on the stage!

For one who was only filling in until Miss Corwine's swelling went down, she was avidly interested and curious. Even though she had no part to learn in the next three days, since she was merely a walking lady, she learned everything else she could fasten her alert young mind on. About wings and flies and traps and borders and flats. She learned that "striking a set" meant dismantling it by pulling it out at the sides or hauling it up out of sight. She learned that her upstage hand or ear was farthest from the audience and her downstage one was toward the "foots."

She was fascinated by the sound effects: the shrieking winds produced by a crank turning a cylinder against a band of silk, the thunder pounded out against a thin sheet of iron, the box of dried peas shaken to make a gentle rain. She admired the stage properties, too: the pasteboard goblets, the stuffed canvas leg of mutton, and the complete sea scene with eight long blue-canvas waves. And her own private make-up box! She was a passionately interested pupil of Mrs. Harlowe and followed her raptly. The heavy foundation of grease first, the rosy tints of paint, the thickened eyelashes, the bluish shadows, the smothering layers of powder.

To Mrs. Harlowe's, "Careful, chick, too much make-up is aging," she returned only a pitying glance. As if she wanted to look *young*.

When old Monty, watching her seated before her mirror,

chuckled, " 'There was never yet a fair woman but she made mouths in a glass,' " she whirled on him in angry denial. Then she blushed foolishly. When would she learn that old actors' talk was likely to be inlaid with these strange shining bits from great plays they had acted in? Shakespeare mostly, she decided. She must get acquainted with this Shakespeare. What a lot she had to learn.

She found not a flaw in those magic three days. The hall over a store in Idaho Springs, with its rows of reflector lamps and its clattering chairs, was lovely. The whistling, stamping audience of miners was wonderful. The boarding house with its hay beds and cracked washbowls was cozy. Miss Delphine Delaney, with whom she shared a bed and expenses, was a lovely girl with only a slight tendency to take most of the bed and all the covers and to snore loudly on her back all night.

In Georgetown she was glad to be in an opera house again, the McClellan, and to stay at the elegant Barton House. Her hand shook so that she could scarcely sign the register. To think of staying in a real hotel, with a row of traveling men tilted back along the wall of the lobby, and a piano in the parlor.

They played in Silver Plume the last night. What a name that was. She said it over to herself, "Silver Plume—Silver Plume." The town was higher up the canyon, reached by a winding shelf road. They told her that the railroad was already planning to build a line up to Silver Plume from Georgetown. So steep was the grade that it would require a circular trestle on perilously high stilts that would make a complete loop over itself in order to accomplish the climb.

"It'll look just like a snake twisting around to bite its tail," remarked one of the cast as they jolted along up the road.

Oh, she *would* have something to tell her grandchildren!

Mrs. DeForest did not even give her a chance to demur when she announced that she had just had a telegram from

Fanny Corwine saying that although she had had her tooth pulled and was slowly improving, she would not be able to rejoin them before the end of the week. Of course Roxana must stay with them that long. Roxana needed little persuading. She was already under a spell.

It was a full week from the day she left Central City before she returned by train, carrying the battered gray telescope that had been her mother's. Returned, an actress! She was sure she looked entirely different—worldly perhaps, experienced, at the very least.

In the sudden affluence of a week's pay in her pocket, she contemplated taking a hack, but decided that was silly when it was such a little way to the boardinghouse where she had left Avis.

But at the boardinghouse the landlady looked at her queerly and said she didn't know where Avis was. Miss Fanny Corwine had eloped two days before with her dentist, and the little girl had naturally left at the same time.

"But she's only eleven! She was supposed to stay with Miss Corwine. Don't you even know where she went?"

The woman shrugged defensively.

"She said she was going back home—to some shop. She said you were due that same day, that you had promised. Something about how sisters shouldn't be separated."

Roxana paled a little. It was disquieting to hear Avis' words from the lips of this sullen woman. And it was true; she had promised to be back. What had Avis done with herself, alone in the coffin shop? She hurried away, her telescope bumping her legs.

She let out a sigh of relief when she saw that the back door of the coffin shop was open. So Avis was inside, safe and sound. She whistled to Boots. He would be jumping all over her in a minute.

But no Boots hurled himself out the back door.

"Yoohoo!" she called through the open doorway into the kitchen. "Why, Gil Anker, so you're back. Where's Avis?"

she asked of the man who came out from the display room in front.

Gil looked as if he had not slept.

"I only got in yesterday; found the front door of the shop swinging wide. Nothing stolen—nobody steals coffins. The bed in the back room hadn't been slept in, though there was a dish of water on the floor for the dog—but there was no girl and no dog."

Now she was beginning to be really frightened. She told him about her week's tour, about Avis' staying with Fanny Corwine.

"Oh, Gil, I thought she'd be all right. How could I know Fanny Corwine would elope with her dentist? Why didn't Avis go to Reveren' Starbuck's?" But she knew why—hadn't they both agreed they must not be beholden?

"I went to him first. He almost threw a fit blaming himself, but he didn't know a thing. I inquired for young Rob Evans, but he left town a week ago." He paused as if fiting his thoughts together, as if debating whether to go on.

"You know something more, Gil." She was biting down hard on her lip to control its trembling.

"The saloonkeeper across the way—" He hesitated.

"What did he say?"

"He said old Limpy Pete was seen staggering out of the coffin shop at dawn the other morning. The sheriff took him in charge, but he can't remember much. Just says over and over that he never harmed her."

"Her!" The syllable was agonized.

"He admits he was pretty well under the influence. He must have been reeling along, trying to find his way home, and turning the knob of every door he came to. The coffin shop was unlocked, so he wandered in. Can't recall a thing till he heard a scream that made his hair stand on end. He sat right up in bed—such a nice, satiny, soft bed, with sides, he said—and there was a little girl standing in the middle of the room yelling her head off. She turns and runs out the door. He swears he never harmed her. But all the same—"

Roxana gave a little moan.

"All the same, they're keeping him locked up in jail till he remembers more—or until they, er, locate your sister. There's mutterings of . . . a neck-stretching. They're out searching for Avis now."

Roxana collapsed on a kitchen chair and burst into body-racking sobs.

"It's my fault. I'm selfish, just the way my mother said. I only think of myself. If I'd thought of what was best for Avis, she'd be safe and sound this very minute. Oh, Gil, she's my little sister. We've got to find her!"

But they did not find her. Posses looked in abandoned mine shafts. They probed the stream bed of the north fork of Clear Creek for miles downstream. Every itinerant band of prospectors was questioned. The sheriff hectored the weak-minded old fellow in the jail until he was ready to confess to almost anything in order to be left in peace, but he still maintained he had never been within ten feet of the little girl.

Roxana stayed at the boardinghouse, scarcely eating or sleeping. She met each returning search party with hollow-eyed questioning. But the answer was always the same—a weary shake of the head.

But they *had* to find her, she told herself sickly. Nobody could just disappear. Somebody would have seen a little girl and a black-and-white dog trudging along the highway together. Maybe kind strangers had picked them up and taken them to a good safe home somewhere, too far from Central for them to know about the anguished foot-by-foot search for a lost little girl, along the bed of Clear Creek, and up and down the rocky defiles of the foothills.

There was something comforting about the thought that Boots was with Avis as a safeguard. And then a numbing fright fastened on her again. For Boots had been with her father on his trip to Leadville last summer, and the loyal little dog had been no safeguard. She shut her eyes tight against the picture Gil had brought back of the lonely rock-covered mound that was her father's grave.

The sheriff made fruitless trips to other mining towns. On one of them he ran into young Rob Evans down in Golden buying supplies. Rob acted surprised and sorry to hear about Avis, the sheriff said. But he was in such a hurry to get back to his diggings he didn't offer to help with the search, and he didn't ask anything about her, Roxana.

Roxana winced. Of course, Rob wouldn't ask, after the way she had treated him. She sighed. If only she had loved him more than she loved the stage, then all this would never have happened. But you couldn't make yourself love or not love, just because it was the best thing to do, she realized, with hard-earned wisdom.

"Did he mention where his diggings are?" she asked listlessly.

"No, ma'am. You know how a fellow is, on scent of a rich strike. It's easier to chop a fresh pine knot than to get him to tell where his new find is located."

Roxana's money gave out, and even though she had a telegram from Mrs. DeForest asking her to rejoin the troupe, she applied instead for the job at old lady Paxton's. It was her only way to do penance. After all, if she had gone there in the first place, Avis would not have disappeared. She went to live in the tiny back room off the kitchen (there was no use opening up the whole upstairs just for a hired girl). As she carried ashes and trays and coal buckets and slop-jars, she felt it was far less than she deserved. Because of her own wickedness and willfulness, she had lost everything, even hope.

She had to face it at last that they might never find Avis. Tossing on her lumpy bed in the back room, she was tortured by her thoughts. Suppose Avis had wandered off the road and got lost. You could get lost so easily in these hills, where one rocky gulch looked just like any other rocky gulch. Suppose she had staggered on and on, weak with hunger, spent with crying, chilled with the night cold, until at last she fell exhausted, with Boots scurrying around in helpless dog devotion, licking her nerveless hands. Wild beasts might have torn her body. Roxana saw her, staring sightless at the sky.

Or worst of all, perhaps no kind, worthy people had picked her up and taken her to their home. Perhaps cruel or crazed or evil persons had offered the tired child a ride. Perhaps some horrible man was holding her captive now in a filthy cabin, or a moldy dugout, or a black and dripping mine shaft. She could see her little sister, terror-stricken, cowering, fainting.

Roxana slid out of bed to her knees on the bare floor. It was the first real prayer of her life. All those years and years of long-winded prayers at church that she had never listened to; all those rapid, sheepish blessings her father had mumbled at every meal because her mother insisted on it; and now she was praying for the first time. Like most of the world she learned to pray only in the extremity of her despair. All of Roxana's brave, selfish, dutiful, heedless soul was in that incoherent prayer.

After a while she climbed wearily back into bed, to lie staring at the black void of the ceiling. Like all the world, too, she made her stumbling attempts at barter with God.

"I'll make it up to her, God. We'll never be separated again. I'll make a home for her somehow, if You . . . if Thou . . . wilt . . . wilst only help me find her."

But the days slid by, and the weeks slid by, and Avis seemed to have vanished from the earth.

Chapter IX

DAY BY DAY Roxana grew thinner and more like a plucked pullet than ever. She could not shake off her self-reproaches. They went to bed with her at night and got up with her in the morning.

As she handed old Mrs. Paxton her bottle of Sozodont mouthwash, she thought, If she'll just let me go downtown so I can see Naomi Starbuck for a minute (Naomi will let me cry on her shoulder), maybe I can go on a little longer.

But Mrs. Paxton said foamily, "You have plenty to do right here in this house. Young girls shouldn't walk the streets. I give you time off for church on Sundays." She spat resoundingly into the washbowl.

Roxana's stomach turned. But her revulsion was tinctured with self-flagellation, too. This was only what she deserved for neglecting Avis, so that the child ran away after that terrible shock. Ran away and met—who knew what fate?

Dully she watched Mrs. Paxton slosh her false teeth around sensuously in a cup before she ducked her head to insert them. To Roxana, her employer was a separate species put here solely to harass her, Roxana. It never occurred to her that Keturah Paxton had not always been old, with a protruding lower lip that reminded Roxana of a bad-tempered old horse, and with knotted swollen joints and a tendency to bladder weakness. Nor could she sense that Mrs.

Paxton's fault-finding was only futile jealousy of Roxana's imprudent, impudent youth. To Roxana she was the way she was, timeless and changeless, and wholly inimical to everything that Roxana wanted. All this talk about respecting the old. The old were a selfish lot!

Roxana dumped the contents of the washbowl into the slop-jar and rinsed out the bowl. Besides being selfish, Mrs. Paxton had a tiresome droning tongue, never buttered with a joke or a bit of flattery, that went on and on about her past glories. How many times had Roxana had to hear that the Paxtons were among the first gentlefolk in Central. This was no sunbonnet civilization, Mrs. Paxton would have Roxana understand. The late Mr. Paxton had been a mine superintendent who, along with the other managers and owners and professional people, made up a regular Upper Ten, as distinguished from the laboring classes.

Roxana had stared at her uncomprehendingly. Classes. She had not known that people belonged to classes until Mrs. Paxton probed about her father.

"Ah, a farmer, you say? And then a teamster." Her falling inflection dismissed him and all his kind.

Roxana was maliciously pleased over the way the Upper Ten were deserting Central (leaving the Lower Ninety to make shift as best they could). The Hills had already moved to Denver taking their smelting works with them. Mr. Bush had left the Teller House to manage the Clarendon in Leadville. The Halls had gone, and now the Eben Smiths. Mrs. Paxton ticked them off accusingly.

Sometimes Roxana wondered about the departed Mr. Paxton. Strange how the richer a man grew, the harder he had to work and the less his wife did. She remembered her own carefree father and her tireless mother. She guessed it was only in the despised laboring classes that the women had to be worth their victuals.

Mrs. Paxton ferreted out Roxana's weakness for going downtown, and hired a boy to do the errands. On Sundays she would look down and see exactly when church let out, allowing Roxana barely time to climb the slopes afterwards. Naomi and Roxana did manage a whispered word before or after church and a quick hand clasp, but Mrs. Paxton circumvented anything more than that. She could not spare Roxana to sing in the choir, because that would take her away Friday evenings for choir practice; Sunday school also was out of the question because who would put the roast in?

Balked, the girl would stand on the promontory of rock in front of the house and stare down at the rooftops, like stair steps below her. If she could just talk to somebody. To Gil, to ask about Avis. To Naomi, to bury her head on the other's thin shoulder and cry.

As her glance traveled over the town below, she always averted her gaze quickly from the Opera House. All her grief and remorse stemmed from the spot. She would never go near it again. Why, oh why had she gone off with the DeForest Company?

Her apprehensions over Avis had pushed the thought of Rob Evans into the background. When she did remember him, she told herself that she missed him sadly. In reality, what she missed was companionship with her own kind; her youth cried out for other youth. She was a scant seventeen and serving a prison sentence.

The first snow came early that year. It fell for days from a sky as gray as a canned oyster. It shut the two women in even tighter, the one seventy and the other seventeen. The house was battened down like a ship in a gale; but even then, the cold rolled in under the doors and numbed the feet; the wind pushed the smoke back down the chimney and puffed it out around the stove lids.

Mrs. Paxton used their enforced proximity to deliver one encyclical after another. Young girls mustn't lace (as if Roxana needed to, with her old corsets falling off her hip bones); they mustn't read novels (try and find one in this arid house);

they shouldn't be forward. (With whom? The pimply boy who did the errands?)

Roxana was relieved when Mrs. Paxton's attention was finally distracted. It took an Indian massacre to do it. The old woman read aloud with fascinated horror the accounts of the Meeker Massacre in the western part of the state. To think they had shot down the Indian agent, that nice Mr. Meeker, in cold blood. And abducted his wife and daughter. What was the government doing about it? She knew what *she* would do—wipe out every redskin in the state. Offer a bounty for Indian scalps—fresh—with both ears attached. Women and children, too. To kill lice, you had to get the nits. She rocked back and forth making bloody plans, until Roxana shut her ears. What a lot of hatred bottled up in one old woman—hatred of Indians and young people and the laboring classes and everybody who moved away from Central.

Roxana used any excuse to get outdoors: going to the privy, or hanging up clothes below the frowning cliff that formed the back wall of the house. The winds would tear at her shawl and numb her hands as she pinned up stiffening garments. But at least she was out of the sound of that grainy voice.

Roxana's mother could have put her finger on the worst hardship at Mrs. Paxton's. "It's sameness Roxy can't stand. Give her a spurt to do, and she'll work like a thrashing crew. Ask her to water the geraniums every day at the same time, and she pines and fidgets."

Then one winter morning Mrs. Paxton was forced to send Roxana downtown. The errand boy was in school, and Mrs. Paxton had developed a hoarseness that she felt would yield only to a box of Slippery Elm Lozenges.

"Wrap up well, Roxana. I don't want you coming down with something and sniffling all around the place."

Roxana could scarcely believe her good fortune. She hurried, so Mrs. Paxton could not change her mind. She took the money for the lozenges and put it in her reticule along with what was left of her wages. (Mrs. Paxton had docked her a dollar this week for the red-glass spoon holder that slipped out of her hands in the dishpan.) She wore her high buckled overshoes and her mother's dolman and her mittens, and tied a knitted fascinator around her head.

As she raced down the sixteen icy front steps she dared not look back. If she calls, I'll pretend I don't hear, she vowed.

But Mrs. Paxton did not call. She merely watched from the lace-curtained front window and felt sorry for herself. Crazy headstrong girl, breaking her neck to hurry down those glassy steps. She had done her best to make a lady out of her, telling her how the *bon ton* did things, and instructing her in manners and refinement. And look at her now bouncing around like water on a hot stove. Likely break a leg and then expect her, Mrs. Paxton, to pay the doctor bill. The young were selfish. Never a thought for an old woman whose husband had been dead these six years, and her boy, forty-two. It wouldn't be long until she followed them. And that little whiffet went skittering off without so much as a backward look. The young were selfish.

Roxana was so dazed by her freedom that she scarcely knew what to do with it. She would ask for the mail first. She had grown to hate the post office. How many times had she vainly hoped for a letter from her father last summer, and from Avis this fall. Surely there would be one today in Avis' round fifth-grade writing. But there was nothing. She went out to the street again, her throat constricted. Oh, Avis child, where are you?

She walked along, her head bent against the wind. She was not going near the Opera House, she told herself fiercely. And then she was climbing the hill toward it. A man was energetically slapping posters on the billboards out in front before the paste had time to freeze. She looked at the still-wet posters:

"Coming—*Uncle Tom's Cabin*. Mammoth Double Performance. Two of Everything. Two Uncle Toms, Two Evas, Two Topsys, Two Simon Legrees. The Spectacle of the Century."

She tried to conceive of such lavishness and let out a gasp of pure wonder. At the sound, the man looked around. He laid his paste brush on the edge of the bucket and gave her a broad grin of recognition.

"So it's the little cantata singer. Blast my ears if it isn't!"

"Professor Jay!" But she did not smile back. All the indignities he had perpetrated in the past rushed over her. Her hands inside her mittens balled into knots. Her wind-stung cheeks grew redder. "You lied to me. You pretended you were the manager. You made me show—" But she could not go on.

"So I did, so I did. Old Professor Jay—honest as the day is short." He was laughing at her.

"I didn't have any dangling raveling; I found out when I got back home. And I never tried to steal your old nugget. You . . . you—" As always, when she was very angry, she ruined her best dramatic effects.

"Of course not," he agreed blandly. "But I kept you from signing up in that dive, didn't I? From being a cancan dancer. I never saw anyone so set on going to hell."

"You had no business to—that raveling, I mean. You were simply terrible. Making me show you—I'll never forgive—"

"Sure, I know. Hate at first sight."

"All you had to do was *tell* me—"

"Tell you! Tell an Arkansas mule. Nobody could have told you anything right then, you were so far gone with footlight fever. Well, I'm glad to see you mooning around a decent theater today instead of a variety house."

"I've been on the stage since I saw you," she announced with haughty satisfaction. "The legitimate stage."

"You don't say?" He gave a low whistle. "Who? Where?"

"Touring—with the DeForest Company." She gave a gesture that included San Francisco, Seattle, and the Sandwich Islands.

"What's your stage name?"

She hesitated. She could not bear to confess that she had not been with the company long enough to have acquired a stage name.

"As a matter of fact, what's your own name?" he amended. "I never thought to find out that night at the Shoo Fly."

"I use my real name on the stage," she said with relief. "Roxana Renner. Mr. DeForest says it's better than all the Delphines and Fannys and Violettes."

"Roxana Renner," he repeated slowly. "Would anybody call you Roxy?"

"My family always called me Roxy."

"Roxy. Roxy Renner." He pursed his lips in thought. "That's the name. Somebody along the line was asking me if I knew a Roxy Renner."

"Who was? Who was asking?"

"A kid. A little girl hanging around the hall in some town I've been doing advance work in lately. Kept asking me if I knew a Roxy Renner that was on the stage. I never thought of its being you."

The strength drained out of her. She had to lean against the stone wall for support. Avis! Avis was alive and reasonably well, or she could not be hanging around a hall asking questions. She was as good as found already. The knowledge made a great roaring in Roxana's ears. After all these weeks— God *had* heard.

"What town was it?" she pleaded. "Oh, please try to remember, Professor Jay. You see, she's my little sister, and I've lost her. I ran away—I mean she ran away."

He gave her a surprised look, but before he could ask any questions, she went on desperately, "Think where it was. I've got to find her."

"Let's see, where have I been lately? Ward? No. Eldora, maybe? It might have been Gold Hill or Caribou. That's the place—Caribou. I'd just finished arranging for the hotel rooms and the hall and was slapping bills on out in front and painting in the dates when this big-eyed, hungry-looking kid came up and began to pester me. Did I know her sister Roxy?" Roxana flinched at the picture, forgetting that Avis always looked big-eyed and hungry. "She seemed sure that anybody in the show business must know everybody else in the show business."

Roxana stammered out questions. "Who was she staying with? How did she get there? How long ago was it?"

"Not over two weeks ago. But that's everything I can tell you."

Roxana was chattering with cold and excitement as Jay stooped to pick up his frozen paste brush and bucket.

"Do you know how far it is to Caribou? I've got to get there right away. The stagecoach has already gone. I believe I'll ask Gil Anker if he knows of anybody going that way."

"Hold on. Hold on. Won't your little sister keep until tomorrow?"

"No. I've got to get there today. Now. It's all my fault she ran away." Shiveringly she sketched in the story of her own willful departure with the DeForests, of Avis' dreadful fright, and of her own despair since.

"Well, look—I'm heading back to Boulder with the team and democrat wagon I hired there. Been arranging bookings all up through this country. Central today was my last stop. I can drop you off at Caribou; it's not much out of my way. You wait some place that's warm while I see the Opera House manager and pick up the team at the livery stable, and we'll be off."

"I'll wait at Gil Anker's shop. But please hurry."

She spun around, her overshoes squinching on the snow. The two of them set off down the icy slope of Eureka Street, the frozen paste bucket rattling and Roxana's skirts fanning out against the high snow bank along the edge of the sidewalk.

At the corner she left him, stopping to point out Gil's shop. As she looked up at him, her face was suddenly luminous— eager and solemn and washed of self.

"I don't know how to thank you, Professor Jay. It's as if I'd been given another chance." Her voice quavered. "When I find my little sister this time, I'll never let her out of my sight again. I'll forget all about the theater. I'll devote my life—"

He looked at her with his lopsided grin and lifted a hand as if to stem any further abnegations.

"Now, now, girl. Leopards' spots don't rinse out that easy. But we'll go find your little sister, since that's what you want."

She ran all the way to Gil Anker's shop. She found him shoveling snow from in front of his door. He invited her into his warm kitchen.

"Sit down till you get caught up with your heart-pounding. You look pretty as a fresh-painted Schuttler wagon this morning, Roxy. You must have good news."

She told him, the words racing each other in the telling.

"Looks like this advance fellow has got on track of Avis at last. You bring her back on the stage tomorrow, and we'll find a place for you both to stay. You can't very well take her up to old lady P's."

"No, oh, no," said Roxana quickly. "I don't want to go back there again—ever." She could not explain that now that she knew Avis was alive and well, she felt that her penance at Mrs. Paxton's was over.

He seemed to understand. "Are you all straight with her?"

She looked contrite. "Her Slippery Elm Lozenges! That's what she sent me downtown for. Will you buy them and take them up to her, Gil?"

He nodded.

"And while you're there, would you mind picking up my trunk in your wagon and leaving it at the Starbucks'? Oh, would you, Gil?"

"Sure, sure. You stuck it out longer there than anybody else ever did. I've known the sanctimonious old scold for years. One of those 'good' women that twine around a man till they smother him to death. Like bindweed. Reckon her husband was glad of an excuse to shuffle off. She never gave a thought to being a help to him. Had always been waited on; had always had a cushion under her back side—I mean bustle—when she sat down."

Roxana giggled.

"She's going to have to empty her own pot today."

While they talked, Gil was wrapping newspapers around the hot bricks he kept in his oven for such emergencies. He was stowing a half-loaf of bread and some chunks of cheese in a sack.

They heard the team drive up outside. Roxana ran to open the door. Jay had a warm cap with the ear-flaps down. He was holding in a winter-shaggy team, mettlesome with the cold. In the wagon box, under a piece of wrinkled gray canvas, were the humps and peaks of his rolls of posters and his paste buckets and long-handled brushes.

Gil went out with her while she introduced them. Jay had spread a blanket over the seat and down under their feet, where Gil now stowed the hot bricks. There was a thick buffalo robe to go over them. Gil stood back a moment, and the two men exchanged a long contemplative glance. Satisfied, Gil turned to help Roxana up on to the hub and thence into the wagon. But Roxana leaped lightly up. She looked down at Gil fondly.

"You're always helping me, Gil. I'll never forget it. Now don't stand out in the cold."

But he did stand there long enough to say thoughtfully, "Just don't get discouraged, no matter what. Life has a way of working out. Time drags for you young folks, with brakes on. But when you're my age, it's a runaway team." He glanced down ruefully at the palm of his hand. "The days slip through your fingers so fast you get rope burn."

He lifted the hand in a salute just as the horses lunged ahead, kicking up white clods, the wheels squealing on the hard-packed snow.

At first Roxana scarcely felt the cold. There was something tingling about racing down the long gulch road with the horses' breaths pluming backward, frosting their manes and rough coats. She glanced at Jay. His jaunty chestnut sideburns were frosted, too, and his eyes shone as he held the horses in on the rapid, coasting descent.

But when the road began to climb, the horses slowed to a walk. Roxana drew in iced needles now with every breath. They would need all these heavy robes and hot bricks before they reached Caribou. Her face felt numb; she had to cup her mittened hands around her cold nose. She spoke to Jay from between her mittens.

"What on earth would she be doing in Caribou?" she asked in a worried, muffled voice. "Why didn't she write? She writes a nice round hand, Avis does."

"Where would she send it? From what you said, she doesn't know you ever came back to Central at all. She probably thinks you're still gallivanting around with your precious DeForest Company."

She winced. That was true.

"Probably instead," he went on, "she's asked everyone who came near the hall about her sister Roxy."

"This Caribou—is it much of a place?"

"On top the heap right now. Claims a thousand population. But a bad fire cleared out some, and diphtheria cleared out more. Young ones died like fish in a tailings pond, I hear."

She moaned. "What if—?"

"No, that epidemic was over some time ago, and I saw your sister only a couple of weeks back."

She relaxed. The road climbed and dipped and climbed again. On the steep slopes the stiff dark pines were like black-paper cutouts made with a child's blunt scissors. The cold made her draw into herself. Her chin was tucked deep into her collar; her knitted fascinator was pulled low over her forehead leaving only the tip of her nose showing; her hands were thrust into her opposite sleeves to make a muff.

Uneasily she eyed the pewter sky and the blinding white clouds of snow churned up from the drifts by the wind.

As they crossed a creek, Jay pointed with his whip to the cushiony white humps of abandoned mining machinery rusting beneath the snow and to the remains of warped Long Toms and broken sluices beside the streams.

"Terrible waste. All that human backache gone for nothing." He stopped to slap a numbed hand against his knee. Then he leaned across her impersonally to pull the robe higher about her. "Mining's the poorest pay on earth—taken as a whole. Worse even than gambling. It's just the occasional lucky devil who happens to break the bank or hit pay dirt that keeps the rest of us betting on the red and sinking the shaft just one more foot. I ought to know—I've tried it all."

"You have?" she said in surprise. "I never thought of you as anywhere but around a theater."

"There's a lot you don't know about me," he said darkly, glancing down at her upturned face. "A half-baked little thing like you."

"I'm not so young," she protested. "After all, when a girl has had stage experience—"

"Stage experience!" He let out a guffaw. "Your cantata maybe?"

"You forget I was with the DeForest Company," she reproved him.

"Sure, one whole week as walking lady, you said. And you're proud as a kitten with its first mouse. Experienced!" He looked at her scathingly. It was as if her very youngness enraged him.

"What do you know about life?" he went on with the same angry intensity. "About a man—alone, homeless—about his hunger and his loneliness? What do you know, a child like you? Nothing!"

She shrank back, puzzled by his vehemence.

After a while she asked, "you still go under the name of Professor Jay?" Even yet, she could not say the name without a slight wincing.

"Yes; when I have an act, that is. I'm what you might call 'between engagements' now. But 'Jay' is easy to paint on signs, and it happens to be my first initial anyhow. Jay for Jared. Last name Withrow."

"Jared. That's a funny name. Different though."

"My mother found it in the Old Testament. But think what her eye might have lit on. Abimelech. Issachar."

She laughed. "Or Melchizedek. You must have gone to Sunday school, too."

"Not for long. I ran away from home."

"You did!" It was hard to think of this cynical, self-sufficient person as a runaway little boy. "Whatever made you do that?"

He did not answer at once.

"My father deserted my mother," he said presently. He seemed intent on the left ear of the near horse. "There wasn't much home left after that."

Roxana went *tsk* in a sympathetic way. She darted another side glance at his set profile, stung blue with the cold, at the slashing line of jaw and the thin flaring nostrils. If he would only go on; for some reason she wanted him to go on.

"Queer thing about fathers," he ruminated, peering ahead through the swirling whiteness. "Nature seems to take care of motherhood by making it an instinct. But fatherhood—I guess it has to be cultivated. Maybe that's one of the tests of any civilization—how much responsibility the fathers feel for the brats they've sired." He turned to her with an embarrassed little grimace, slapping his numbed right hand on his knee to get the feeling back into it. "I've always thought it was the test, too—of a decent man."

Where was the wry, caustic, insulting Professor Jay? Impulsively she reached out for his cold-numbed hand and drew it under the buffalo robe and began to chafe it. Her gesture seemed to be answer enough. He went on simply.

"When my mother brought home a stepfather, I joined the circus. I've always been crazy to. I guess I had a longing in my feet."

"I know." She lighted up with quick understanding. "I've always had a longing in my feet, too. Here, give me your other hand."

Obediently he changed his lines and let her knead his chilled left hand under the robe. She felt a sense of satisfaction in being able to do something for him.

"I was a roustabout at first. Then an old grifter taught me some sleight of hand, and I developed my own magic act. That's what I was doing when you wandered into the Shoo Fly that night, all set for a 'stage career.' " He turned to smile mockingly at her. The mocking look quickly gave way to concern.

"You're about frozen yourself, aren't you, young one?"

"I'm all r-right."

Almost roughly he pulled her over against him, his arm holding the robe high about her. She felt a little less chilled, snugged up tight against him. She liked the hard, comforting, impersonal grip with which he held her, even if it did give her a crick in the neck, and the fusty buffalo robe tickled her nose.

The horses' pace grew slower and slower. They were feeling their way through a whirling ground blizzard now. Not a trace of the road remained. The stinging snow pellets smarted against her face, blew into her squinted eyes, slithered down inside her collar. Jay was driving with the lines loose, letting the horses choose their own footing. All around them was this queer white darkness; yes, that was it, a *white* darkness.

The animals came to a halt beside an overhang of rock

that broke some of the wind's fierceness. Jay sat still for a moment. Then he tied the lines and clambered down.

"Horses know best. We'll wait here out of the wind. I'll go up ahead and see what it's like."

She was alone on the wagon seat. All she could see were the looming horses' rumps and the dark bulk of the cliff rising up. What if Jay got lost? People did get lost in blizzards; sometimes they froze to death. She was in a sudden panic.

"Jay!" she screamed, but the sound stopped at her teeth. She tumbled out of the wagon and floundered along in the snow beside the horses. She was thankful for her old high-buckled overshoes. More snow seemed to be scudding up from the ground than coming down from the sky. "Jay!" she cried again.

"Here," he called reassuringly. And there he was, looming up not far beyond the horses' heads. She ran to him, almost sobbing in relief.

"Oh, Jay, I was so afraid for you."

"We're on the road, as near as I can make out. We'll stay here until she clears a little. We'll be warmer in the back of the wagon." His voice was calming.

He took the blanket off the seat and spread it on the straw in back, pushing aside buckets and paste brushes. Then he boosted her up, spread the buffalo robe over her, and climbed in beside her. With the canvas cover, he made a tent of sorts over their heads, fastening it to the seat and weighting it down behind them.

Then, as matter of factly as if she were a chilled child, he gathered her close in his arms, trying to stop the uncontrollable shivers that shook her.

"We'll need each other's warmth," he said gently. He turned her face up to inspect it; he even rubbed the tip of her nose to be sure it was not frozen. He tucked one of her mittened hands under his armpit to warm it.

"I guess you're all right so far," he said with anxious relief. "That's the worst thing about cold—it sneaks up on you."

[109]

With his arms, with his hands, with the whole lean length of his body, he tried to warm her.

Presently her shivering subsided. A slow return of sensation began to course through her. Her face prickled; her feet stung. And suddenly she was terribly aware that she was in Jay's arms, and she was glad. She lifted her lashes and looked straight up into his brown eyes with the tiny embers far back in them. And she could not look away; their strange unmoving brightness held her. All she could see was his face bent over hers, so near, so near. She could feel him begin to tremble, too.

For an instant time came to a standstill. Their very breathing seemed to stop. Then she stirred in his arms and instinctively lifted her face to his, lips parted, eager young body fitting against him.

The embers in his eyes became a fire. But he made no move. He only frowned, and the lines bracketing his mouth deepened to a furrow.

"What are you—sixteen?" he demanded in a hoarse whisper.

"Seventeen," she corrected proudly. "Last month."

"Seventeen!" He let out a groan and pushed her away. "You and your experience! Come on, young one, it's time to eat. Where's that bread and cheese your friend was good enough to pack for us?"

It was as if he had built a wall between them. He unwrapped the frozen bread and cheese and managed to break off chunks for them. It hurt their teeth, but it was food, and they were both suddenly starved. They ate the last crumb and even shook out the sack.

Still with that wall between them, he said, "As soon as we locate your sister, I'll head back to Nederland to spend the night. Got to make it all the way to Boulder tomorrow to meet the manager of our show."

"Do you like doing advance work?" she asked almost formally, dusting the crumbs off her mittens.

"Sure. I like anything connected with the theater, just the way you do. Footlight fever, we've both got."

"I didn't know you wanted to be an actor."

"I don't. That's the one thing I don't want to be. I couldn't play the back half of a horse." He looked at her with a certain appeal. "You'll think I'm crazy, but I want to direct. Some day I'm going to have my own theatrical company." He dared her to laugh.

"I don't think you're crazy. I want to play Lady Teazle." It was her turn to look defiant.

"You could. I'll bet I've watched *The School for Scandal* a dozen times. You'll make a fine Lady Teazle some day. She's a lot like you—a fresh country girl, full of hell and hot water, and green as June grass."

She flashed him an annoyed look. There he went again, harping on her youngness. Then she subsided forlornly.

"I'll never get the chance now. I've given up the stage completely to make a home for my little sister."

"Don't you ever think it!" he chuckled. "You'll play Lady Teazle yet." He lifted one corner of the canvas. "Look, the wind has died down some. We'd better try to make it the rest of the way." He gave an unconscious sigh.

Part of her was crying out, Oh, don't let's go yet. Let's stay here a little longer.

"We've got a lot to do," he was saying briskly, "if we locate your sister before dark."

Avis! She felt the old twinge of guilt. *She* ought to be the one to be in a hurry now.

He gave her a last long look, as if he, too, were saying good-by to something.

"I'd like to be around, Roxy, when you're really grown-up. You're a cool-looking little thing on the outside, but there's plenty of fire underneath. Some day, when you're grown-up, somebody will come along and blow on the sparks. You're full of surprises and contrariness, as every woman should be. Take your lips, for instance. Prim one minute and in the next—"

[111]

He looked intently at her mouth, seemed to think better of it, and wrenched his eyes away.

"Come along!" he said unsteadily and helped her back up to the seat.

Roxana began to tidy her hair and tighten the knot of the fascinator under her chin. Jay clucked to the horses, and they set off; but he did not look at her again. As they left the shelter of the cliff, she felt suddenly bereft. They were leaving something behind, she knew—a small circumscribed moment of loveliness, snatched from time. She even looked back over her shoulder. But there was nothing to mark the place; only a bleak whiteness.

The horses plowed on through the drifts until at last Caribou came into sight, a dark stippling of buildings scattered over the white. Elbows of pipe let out smoke spirals from every roof, and heavy timbers propped up back walls against the ceaseless push of the winds. The charred wounds of the recent fire showed blackly: a lone chimney shaft poking up out of the snow, a staggering section of wall still left standing. Fires were an old story to mountain towns like Caribou.

They drove up the main street and stopped before the hall, where wind-tattered posters fluttered out in front.

"I declare, Jay! The DeForest Company played here, and they left only yesterday," exclaimed the girl, her voice going from hope to disappointment. Not that she had the slightest interest in any theatrical company, but she would like to know who was filling Fanny Corwine's place, and how Miss Lovell's romance with Romney Lynde was coming on, and whether Mrs. Harlowe had found her knitting needles, and if old Monty had managed to stay away from the bottle.

They climbed the stairs to the hall and found a man sweeping out last night's trash. Did he know anything about a young one, a little girl with tan braids, who hung around the hall?

The man stopped and leaned his chin on the handle of his broom.

"A little gingersnap of a girl about so high, with a black-and-white dog? Sure. Her name's Avis, and the dog's name is Boots."

Roxana had to steady herself. It was like pushing hard against a closed door and then having it open suddenly, letting her go sprawling.

"Where is she? She's my little sister."

He took them to a dusty window at one end of the hall and pointed to a dark blot of a cabin partway up the slope.

"She lives in that house, but I ain't seen her for several days. Never did know the child's last name."

"Renner," said Roxana in a strangled voice.

The man returned to his sweeping. Roxana and Jay hurried down the stairs. But even before they started up the unbroken expanse of snow, they knew the house was empty. It looked empty—cold and dead and deserted. Jay stamped out a path, with Roxana following.

There was no answer to their rap. Gingerly they opened the door. Inside, they peered about the marrow-piercing gloom. Frozen remains of food lay in the dishes on the table; a skillet with a layer of white grease sat on the stove; clothes were strewn carelessly about.

What could have happened? Had the occupants received news of a sudden death in the family? Had plague struck? Were they taking a stricken person to a lower altitude?

Roxana pounced on something on the floor.

"Look Jay, it's a girl's knitted cap. It must be Avis'. They went off and left it." She held the woolen cap to her cheek. It made Avis real.

Footsteps crunched in the snow outside. Jay opened the door to a woman bundled in shawls.

"I hope we aren't trespassing, ma'am," he said. "We were just trying to find the folks that live here."

"Lived here," said the red-faced woman, pushing back her shawls to stare at them curiously.

"But where have they gone?" demanded Roxana.

[113]

The woman shrugged. "Nobody knows. I thought, when I saw you breaking trail up here, if you was bill collectors, you'd have a hard time collecting. They took out in the night last week."

"With a little girl, say eleven or twelve?"

The woman nodded. "Evans, the family's name was."

Evans! Roxana looked at Jay.

"I might have known, Jay. They must have told Avis where they were going when they left Central, and she followed them. But they kept talking about gold, and this is a silver town. Maybe that was to throw folks off." She turned back to ask the woman diffidently, "Was there a young man about twenty with them?"

The woman was positive that there was no young man; only this couple named Evans and the little girl.

"But surely," protested Roxana, "they wouldn't just light out and leave all their stuff behind?"

The neighbor woman smiled a cynical smile.

"You ain't been around mining camps much, have you? Folks get wind of a new strike and pull out in the night so nobody will find out where they're going. Some darn' near forget to take the baby along."

"But they'd leave some way for mail to be forwarded? They'd have to tell the postmaster, wouldn't they?" Roxana implored.

"Sometimes they're afraid to tell, for fear of starting a rush before they get their new claims located," Jay explained, looking sorry for her. "The Rockies are full of houses just like this. And pretty soon the pack rats take over, and the roof starts to leak. Then the neighbors 'borrow' a few things like windowpanes and doors. And after a while the whole thing slumps down, and all that's left is a pile of rubbish with an iron bedstead sticking up and some broken crockery lying around. Whole towns are like that."

"But it won't be that way in Caribou," declared the

woman. "This is a live camp. The ore gets better and better the farther down you go. This camp is permanent."

Jay looked polite but skeptical.

The woman remembered something else.

"Was you looking for the Evanses or for the little girl?"

"The little girl. She's my sister Avis."

"Might your name be Roxana?"

"Roxana Renner."

"Then I got a letter for you. The girl gave it to me to mail just before the Evanses pulled out. But we were snowed in, and the mail only goes three times a week. I'll go back and get it."

"Let me—" began Roxana, but already the neighbor was retracing her way in her own footsteps to the cabin whose gable jutted out of a snowbank. Roxana followed.

Her numbed fingers could scarcely grasp the wrinkled envelope bearing Avis' round penciled scrawl. She made a jagged tear getting the lined tablet sheet out.

She was laughing and crying as she approached the open door where Jay waited.

"She needs me and wants me, she says. And she's written me several letters before this. She's even scolding me a little like she always does. Listen to this:

". . . but you never answered any of my letters that Aunt Edna mailed for me. Aunt Edna says likely you have forgotten me you're having such a good time traveling with those show people. But you haven't, have you, Roxy? I miss you lots. You said that sisters should not be 'sepperated.'" Roxana stopped to spell it out for Jay. "You know you did, Roxy. And now you never even answer my letters. Please write, Roxy. Your loving sister, Avis."

Roxana laughed again and abstractedly brushed off the tears that froze on her lashes.

"I'd like to meet that Aunt Edna!" Jay growled. "Sounds to me like she's been holding out the letters the kid wrote you. Trying to wean her away from you. Well, she didn't succeed."

"Now I've *got* to find her," vowed Roxana solemnly.

"Yes," he agreed. "You've got to. We'll try the post office first."

They tried the post office, and the general store, and the feed store, and finally the livery stable. No one had the faintest idea of the whereabouts of the Evans family. People were always drifting in and out of a boom camp. A rumor of a new strike, and off they went—to Lick Skillet Gulch, to the Black Hills, to Tombstone, Arizona.

"But we can't just lose her, now that we've found her," protested Roxana to Jay, her lip quivering childishly. She was so chilled; she was so tired; one more dash to her hopes, and she would sit down on a snowbank and bawl.

He did not try to buoy her up. He said gravely, "This is a wild new upset world out west, Roxy. None of the usual rules hold. People are around, and then they just drop out of sight. Men have come out here from the East and were never heard from again. Over in Leadville they bury an unidentified victim of pneumonia or a shooting every so often. Folks just melt away, out here."

"But not Avis! Why, she's lonesome for me. She said so. She said sisters should not be 'sepperated.' I can't lose her now, Jay."

"You haven't lost her. You're lucky the Evanses didn't change their name. Lots do. And remember, Avis is well and still loves her sister Roxy." He smiled his consolation.

"But what do we do next? I pinned all my hopes on this."

Even Jay was at a momentary loss.

"One thing we know is, they've moved on to another boom camp. We'll keep our ears open about all the new strikes. There'll be two of us hunting her from now on, remember. That means you've got to keep in touch with me, Roxy."

She nodded forlornly.

To divert her, he suggested they stop in at the Sherman

[116]

House to get warm. As they neared the frame hotel, he told her how, some winters, the snow was so deep the hotel guests crawled in and out the second-story windows on the packed drifts. It was called "taking the elevator."

She gave him a wan smile.

And then in the lobby of the unpainted frame hotel she let out a squeal of pleasure. The DeForest Company was sitting gloomily around in golden-oak rockers, knitting, reading week-old newspapers, playing solitaire, or tamping tobacco into pipes.

"Bless me, as sure as I'm a tie-walking old barnstormer!" shouted old Monty. "It's the little understudy for the wardrobe mistress!"

"Roxana Renner!" Mrs. DeForest beamed at her, straw hair awry, handsome face flushed. "What are you doing here? We've been held up for two days because of Mr. DeForest's frost-bitten foot, but we're pulling out tomorrow for the Black Hills. They say it's warmer there. Anything to get out of this awful timber-line country!"

Roxana looked around at the depleted company.

"Where is everybody?"

"Delphine Delaney went and got married—just like that little empty-head to take up with the first boiled shirt that ever paid her any attention. We never replaced Fanny Corwine, and Mrs. Galliher couldn't stand the altitude. We all look after our own costumes now. What are you doing here yourself?"

"N-nothing—now." Roxana was rigid with excitement. She swallowed rapidly, looking over her shoulder beseechingly at Jay in the background. She put out her hand and drew it back as if from a hot stove. "Then you don't have a walking lady or a utility woman?" she asked.

"We could use you, if you want to come along," said Mrs. DeForest amiably. "They say Deadwood is having a big boom now. Gold flakes the size of watermelon seeds."

Roxana was electrified. She turned back to Jay.

[117]

"Those are the very words the Evanses used about the place they were going to. 'Gold flakes the size of watermelon seeds.' "

Jay merely studied her, smiling a little.

"It would be a way for me to hunt for Avis," she defended. "Even if I shouldn't find her in Deadwood, the company would move on to all the other boom towns. It's the only way I'll ever have to hunt for her, isn't it, Jay?" She was openly pleading now.

He nodded slowly. "You're right. The DeForest Company can subsidize your search. But I've been in the Black Hills, Roxy. They're rough. Just three years away from wilderness, from bear tracks and Indian tepees. Hardly any roads. Poor excuses for hotels. Drafty halls over stores for theaters. You'd have to have a lot of the real pioneer in you."

"But I have, Jay. I'm like my father. I want to be among the first ones into a place." She had a prancing eager look, a quivering at the corners of her mouth, a straining to be off.

And then he said a little flatly, "Well, I guess that takes care of you. I better be moving on. Good-by . . . Lady Teazle." He was heading toward the door.

She forgot all about the DeForest Company. Jay was walking out of her life. She ran after him; she clung to his arm.

"When will I see you again? You were so good to bring me over to look for Avis."

"Just don't worry about your little sister. There'll be two of us asking for her in every town now."

He stopped and took her serious, flushed face between his hands. "Two of us, I said. Don't forget." He stooped and kissed her swiftly on the lips and strode out the door.

She ran after him, flung the door wide and called out across the snow, "You can't go like this, Jay. Come back."

But he did not look around. He hunched his shoulders higher against the cold and plodded on toward the livery stable.

She turned back slowly to the warmth and brightness

within. Jay had promised to write; he had said they would keep in touch with each other. "Two of us," he had said.

She saw the DeForest Company clustered around the wood stove at the end of the room, smiling expectantly as they waited for her to join them. After all, the little Renner was a welcome diversion in this God-forsaken iceberg of a place.

Roxana smiled back. Her steps quickened; her breathing quickened. "Why, I'm a trouper." She said the spine-tingling words under her breath. "I'm a trouper at last!"

Chapter X

ROXANA WAS BARELY seated on the train to Cheyenne before she began to study parts. She scarcely noted the charms of the lurching railway coach—the swaying brass lamps, the arching wooden fretwork overhead like the trimmings along the eaves of Central City houses, and the acrid smell of varnish brought out by the heat of the stove. She had half a dozen parts to learn at once. Later she would play several roles a night. Mrs. DeForest prided herself on portraying five different characters in *The Royal Slave*.

Walking around the coldly windy little Wyoming town of Cheyenne, called "Hell on Wheels" because of its riproaring railroad-building days, Roxana was mumbling, "As God is my witness, I meant no harm to my dear aunt who so tenderly reared me," and, "I may be only a humble serving maid, but I am not insensible of the dangers in what you suggest."

All the way across Wyoming on the Concord stagecoach to the Black Hills in Dakota, she was muttering and turning pages of scripts. "Sides" she learned to call them. She was so absorbed that she almost missed the first sight of the Hills, crouching on the plains like a low-lying bison, its back shaggy with black pines. Why, they're almost but not quite mountains, she thought. Maybe these would not have frightened Avis.

But as the stagecoach entered the Hills through a canyon that was like a deep claw gouge, and she saw the fanged rocks rising up, she knew that Avis would not have been happy here either. Nearing Deadwood, they came upon all the signs of mining activity that her mother and Avis had hated. The hillsides scarred and ulcerated by mine workings, the noisy mills, the slopes almost shorn of trees—she could hear the rhythmic *thuck-thump* of an ax still at work.

Just outside Deadwood the stagecoach came to a stop. The driver climbed down and brushed the clods from his shaggy six-horse team and shined their harness buckles. A stagecoach always entered a boom town with a flourish. The entire company sat up and began to smarten their appearance, with the complete unself-consciousness of theatrical people.

Mrs. DeForest put on a hat with arching blue plumes that hid one eye. Mr. DeForest, on the seat beside the driver, stuck a flashing stickpin into his cravat. (Roxana smiled patronizingly at her own ignorance back in Central when she had thought that Professor Jay's diamond horseshoe was "real.") Monty donned a flowing Joseph Jefferson tie. Miss Lovell unabashedly combed her long fair hair and coiled it up and then touched her lips with pink salve. Romney Lynde put on a biscuit-colored waistcoat which was much too good to waste on a long stagecoach trip. Only Mrs. Harlowe seemed to mind the sprucing up; she let out a grudging groan and bent down over her stockinged feet.

"I suppose I've got to put on my shoes, but that's all I am going to do for Deadwood."

Roxana watched all these preparations with interest. It was Mrs. DeForest who noted the girl's knitted fascinator and pulled a bonnet from the costume trunk and clapped it on Roxana's head. Roxana sat there, bonnet over one eye.

"Straighten your hat, dearie," admonished Mrs. Harlowe beside her. "And tuck up those mousetails of hair and bite your lips to make them pink. I don't have to look pretty, but you do."

Roxana obeyed. The driver climbed back up to his high seat and picked up the reins, which slipped expertly back and forth between his gloved fingers. With a crack like a shot, he snapped the whip over the backs of his horses, which promptly broke into a gallop. The driver was a soft-hearted man. Although he boasted he could cut a candlewick at fifteen paces with his whip without snuffing the flame, he never actually touched his horses with it; but they were gentlemen enough to respond to the sound.

With the rest of the troupe Roxana smiled from side to side as they pounded over the narrow gulch road along which Deadwood straggled for several miles. Jay might be right: it was rough, it was untamed, it was probably going to be uncomfortable. But it was "their" town—this Dead-wood—their first town in the Black Hills, and she had a proprietary feeling about it. She belonged completely to the DeForest Company now.

Then she remembered the really important fact about Deadwood: it was a boom camp, with gold flakes the size of watermelon seeds. Maybe the Evanses were here.

She saw the familiar main street of a mining town, worming its way along the bottom of the gulch, with the other streets cut in shelves above it. Log cabins and wooden shacks clung to the cliffs; dugouts burrowed into the hillsides.

She saw trudging women in shawls and calico carrying bundles of washing. She saw mincing women wearing muffs and fur tippets out airing their pug dogs. She saw miners with muddy jeans tucked inside their boots and candles stuck in their caps; and professional men who wore their jeans outside their boots; and dandies in broadcloth and patent leather. She saw silk hats for sale, as well as dynamite and scouring bricks. In front of a meat market was the sign: "Fresh Bear Meat, Antelope Steaks, Buffalo Hams."

Stumps which no one had had time to uproot still reared up in the middle of the street. The saloon doors never stopped swinging. Along the edges of the road were the usual mining-camp effluvia—tin cans and whiskey bottles. It was another lusty, greedy, roistering town full of whiskered young men who were said to throw gold watches and nuggets right on to the stage. Roxana drew in a long quivering breath.

She longed to tell Jay about her feeling of being a pioneer. Old Monty had put it into words for her. "We frontier stage folks do a job of civilizing the wilderness, too. We bring the first graces of life. For a little while—for a few hours—we take men's minds off the dirt, the weevily flour, the frozen socks that never dry, and the aches of rheumatism and homesickness. We help them to bear it."

Jay would understand; he understood so many things.

Afterwards, she remembered the Black Hills as a hurried excitement of learning parts, learning stage business, and learning about life. They opened at the Gem Theater in Deadwood; then they made a swing around through the hills. She played a scepter bearer in *The Royal Slave,* in Spearfish. In Lead City she was Miss Posie in *My Partner.* In Sturgis she took the part of Janet the innkeeper's daughter in *The Lady of Lyons.* She was a society girl in *Under the Gaslight,* in Rapid City. And in Custer she played a maid in *The Rivals* as well as a maid in *The School for Scandal.*

The company paused for a brief respite at the stage station on Fall River to "take the baths" in the hot springs there.

"Somebody's going to make a lot of money building a spa here some day," Mrs. Harlowe prophesied.

Roxana was too timid to ask what a spa was.

She grew used to theaters that were only halls over stores, where the curtain rolled up and down on a pole and fell with a padded thump. Where the dressing rooms were two screened-off corners behind the stage, one for men and one for women. She learned to put on her make-up, smoothing pomatum on her cheeks with the palms of her hands, while she peered over the shoulders of the older women at the scrap of cracked mirror. Everyone was helpful at first. She had as yet assumed no personality; she had made no enemies, stepped on no toes, aroused no jealousies. She was merely a green young thing with a wide luminous smile and eyes that lighted up at the smallest attention.

She was flattered when Miss Lovell suggested that they room together to save expenses. Even when she found that Miss Lovell left long fair hairs everywhere and never picked up a garment or wiped out the soap dish, still she was flattered. Hadn't Miss Lovell been on the stage five years and didn't Mrs. DeForest say she was the darling of the mining camps even if she couldn't act for sour apples?

They returned to Deadwood again, to the Gem Theater and the Grand Hotel. Deadwood—with its inexhaustible gold and its inexhaustible lust for living.

It took Roxana two months to save ten dollars toward the home she was going to make for Avis as soon as she found her. She sewed the money inside her corset, and every night she felt of the flat little wad of bills to make sure it was safe. How money did go, even when you were getting fifteen dollars a week. First, she had to buy her own costumes; she could not go on forever wearing cast offs from Mrs. DeForest and Miss Lovell. Then, a girl in the theatrical profession had to look—well, not like Mrs. Paxton's hired girl. She had to have new bonnet ribbons to match her eyes, and she could not go on carrying that moldy old gray telescope. Worst of all, she had to eat, and Roxana was always hungry.

Mrs. DeForest would watch her munch her third piece of corn bread dripping with syrup and sigh enviously, "You just wait. Keep on like that, and you won't be the willowy type much longer."

Roxana would merely look sheepish and reach for the syrup. She had all those months at Mrs. Paxton's to make up for.

In each new town she went to the post office to ask for

letters. When she finally received a brief, unsatisfactory little scrawl from Jay saying that he was still on the lookout for Avis and not to be discouraged, she was uplifted for days.

Mr. DeForest tried out Roxana's singing and dancing for the olio, those variety acts put on by the company during intermissions. He even taught her to do an Irish jig and sing "Hangtown Gals." Then he changed his mind and ended by having her sing doleful ballads like "Sweet Annie of the Vale" and "See That My Grave Is Kept Green."

"You just aren't the hoyden type, Roxana," he explained. "Better stick to refined heartaches and leave the foot-waggling to Lotta." He told the interested Roxana about Lotta Crabtree's famous curtain call. How the little variety actress had been recalled time after time by a hysterical audience until finally she opened the curtains a crack and merely waggled her foot through. Men went wild, and women screamed over such daring.

He snorted. "Daring! A woman that thinks nothing of exposing her brisket clear down to her belt buckle will faint at the thought of showing the calf of her leg. It's beyond me."

Roxana could not explain it either; but she did remember with painful clearness that dreadful moment when Professor Jay had made her show her—*legs*. Her chest rose and fell at the horrid memory. Plucked pullet . . . white meat . . . dark meat. She just wished he could see her now; why, she was going to have to let out her seams if she kept on.

Her eyes softened at another memory. Jay had also said he would like to be around when she was grown-up. She was sure that she was completely grown-up now; she would tell him so the very next time they met. And whenever she saw an advance man pasting bills out in front of a hall, her heart would give that great leap inside her chest, and she would rush up, all out of breath, to see if it was Jay.

She soaked in theater lore these days. She liked to stand in the wings just before the curtain went up, hearing the audience, that was like a restless animal out beyond the curtain. She liked to watch the cast doing all the last-minute things—fluffing their hair, crossing themselves, working their lips to loosen them, lifting and lowering their feet to ready them for a running start, or straightening twisted stockings.

"Your stockings look as if you'd done them up on curl papers last night, dearie," reproved Mrs. Harlowe when Roxana had been careless. "You've got to remember it's your feet and ankles that are on a level with the audience's eyes."

She tried to walk well. "Walk tall and spurn the earth," old Monty advised her. "You already carry your head nice and high."

She tried to learn how to speak, listening intently to both Mrs. Harlowe and Mrs. DeForest. Mrs. Harlowe, she noted, bit off her words like spiced morsels; her voice was clipped and precise and pleasantly gritty. But Mrs. DeForest's had the richness of caramel sauce. It sent little shudders through her. Both were actresses. Each had a leashed quality quite different from Miss Lovell's tinny declaiming. You mustn't be wooden, she learned; but neither must you rant.

Mrs. Harlowe was making tea for them backstage one day over the old brass spirit lamp she carried with her everywhere. It had been a long rehearsal. The company slumped wearily on hard kitchen chairs and drank the scalding stuff.

Mr. DeForest had been exacting. He had made his wife Julia go over and over a single speech until her voice grew thin with fatigue. He had called Romney Lynde's love-making too damned practiced. He had all but shaken Miss Lovell trying to get her to "show a little life." On the other hand, he had held up a hand to Roxana, like an orchestra leader muting the brasses, when she "let herself go."

"Restraint is what does it," he said over his teacup to Roxana. When Miss Lovell looked smug, he turned on her with, "But of course you've got to *have* emotions in order to restrain them."

"I've been thinking for some time," meditated Mrs. Harlowe, "that the day of the start-and-stare-and-clench-and-holler actress is about done. You've got to learn to think your part first, these days."

Monty shook his head.

"But not too restrained. You must remember that actors give expression to the things folks feel but daren't say. In the everyday world—particularly out west here—men take pride in hiding their feelings. The only time they really find expression for what's seething inside them is when they're drunk—" He grinned uneasily here— "or when they go to the theater. There, actors say it for them—these rough wordless fellows who long ago put their dreams and flights of fancy in their pockets. The actor has to express all those pocketed dreams, express the wonder of life, you might say." He looked defiantly over his glasses at them all.

"Fiddlesticks!" said Mrs. Harlowe. "You've got to think your part first, then live it on the stage—but never with more than half of you. The other half should stand back looking on, criticizing, feeling out the audience."

Monty refused to retreat.

"You can't fool an audience beyond a certain point. Take you, Roxana. You're playing mostly maid parts now. In time you'll be playing ladies. To act a lady, you've got to be one. You must cultivate the graces of the mind. No more reading Augusta Evans and Mrs. Southworth. I'll give you some books to read when you're not studying parts."

The talk drifted elsewhere, but he did not forget the books, which proved to be a worn complete Shakespeare and two thin volumes of essays, one by Montaigne and one by Carlyle. Roxana welcomed the Shakespeare; trouper that she was, she could recognize great plays when she read them. And she was sometimes surprised and pleasantly shocked by things the Frenchman said, things nice people seldom admitted. But she bogged down badly on the Carlyle. Her life at the moment had small use for contemplative philosophy.

But I will cultivate the graces of mind, she vowed savagely, even while Mrs. Harlowe laughed at her for poring over all that fine print.

"All you need do is act the way audiences think a lady acts," she maintained, adding slyly, "It's much like trying to interest a gentleman. (Don't think I couldn't, in my day!) You play the role of what he thinks a lady is. Chances are, he wouldn't care to have you be too much of a lady. Now take religion—"

Monty, who happened to be listening, shook his head in a distressed way.

"No, don't take it, Roxana. You leave religion out of this. It's not a piece of stage business."

Mrs. Harlowe was firm.

"Yes, take religion. And incidentally, so much luck enters into the theater that most folks in the profession are either superstitious or religious—or both. But what I was talking about was the gentlemen. Men like religion in their women if it doesn't interfere too much with their own pleasures. There's something mighty fetching about a pretty girl kneeling on a prie-dieu, head bent over a prayer book, long lashes dusting her cheeks, and the smell of incense floating around. One of the prettiest roles a woman can play. A man can't help thinking about wedding rings and settling trust funds on her—"

"Monica!" burst out the scandalized old man, his tufts of whiskers trembling. "That's no way to talk. Don't forget, she's but 'an unlesson'd girl, unschool'd, unpractised . . .' "

Roxana controlled a smile. Even when he was most disturbed, Monty was still the actor, unable to resist appropriating the fine old lines he had once mouthed.

"But my folks didn't go to a church that had kneeling and incense," she protested to the two of them. "Our preachers preached hellfire, and everybody saved up money in mite boxes, and we sang 'Work, for the Night Is Coming.' "

"Pouf!" said Mrs. Harlowe. "What romance or drama is there in that? But there's nothing to prevent you from—"

"Monica!" snorted the old man again. "This is a human soul you're tampering with." He turned to the girl. "Pay no attention to her; she's a wicked old woman with bleached hair and a blackened reputation. You go right on in the faith of your fathers. You can't escape it anyhow. As you grow older, it'll keep cropping up, and in the end you're likely to die by that faith."

"Hmm!" was Mrs. Harlowe's only comment.

"From what I've seen of you, Roxana," he went on, disregarding the old actress' curling lip, "you're a born protester—a nonconformist in more ways than one. You're a balky, conscience-hounded soul that has to work things out for herself. So you better hold on tight to your Bible-brimstone faith. By the way, you ought to be reading the Bible. No grander literature." He brought out a worn black book that looked almost as scuffed as the one Henry Starbuck had read from at her mother's grave.

Mrs. Harlowe voiced Roxana's thoughts.

"Fine words, coming from an old tosspot."

Roxana pocketed the tattered Bible with the tiny print. Funny, no one had ever before said that the Bible was grand literature. She carried it thoughtfully up to her room.

Roxana was learning other things these days. That a theatrical company is a nest of passion and jealousy and sly dealings, even a decent family troupe like the DeForests. She learned that Francine Lovell was hopelessly in love with Romney Lynde, who treated her with the same casual indifference he gave the ash on the end of his cigar, which he flicked off carelessly when it got in his way. Roxana sensed at once that it would be best for her always to be on the opposite side of the room or the stage from him when Francine was around. *Him,* she thought with mild scorn; imagine being jealous about him. I wouldn't have him on a Christmas tree; why, he's got just barely sense enough to lead a cotillion.

She learned that Mr. DeForest was darkly suspicious of his

wife, with her look of smiling ripeness. That was all Roxana could think of: how ripe Mrs. DeForest looked—her lips, her figure, her smile—all ripe for trouble. Only old Monty and Mrs. Harlowe seemed not to be involved in emotional entrapments. Doubtless that was why they wrangled so much about what was best for her, Roxana.

"That Monty!" Mrs. Harlowe would explode. "Don't listen to his maunderings. He's just an old bottle-man that's lost all too many bouts with delirium tremens. The reason he falls so easy is because he heads straight for the slippery places."

"Her!" he would retort with equal vigor. "A fair enough actress, I'll grant you, in her day. But a bad influence. Morals so loose they've fallen apart. The old rip!"

I can't tell whether they hate each other or are fond of each other, Roxana puzzled. She felt uncertain and upset about so many things these days. There was her search for her sister, which seemed to have come to a complete stop. There was her friendship with Jay, which seemed to have come to a complete stop, too. But of course, it hadn't, she told herself firmly. It was just that Jay hated to write letters; lots of men were like that. The minute she saw him again, everything would be all right. They would pick up where they had left off. But it was unsettling to have to wait and wonder, with only hope to feed on.

It was unsettling, too, to find that her feeling toward the theater had changed. After weeks and months of hard work, the stage had lost its early glamor; yet something else had taken its place. She found the stage more absorbing than ever.

The weeks slipped by, crowded with the constant change that finally became a sameness. Spring brought Chinook winds and sudden thaws. The spokes of the stagecoach wheels picked up thick gumbo mud and became clumsy, slowly revolving black discs. The troupe was always late getting from one Dakota town to another; there were times when everybody but Mrs. Harlowe had to get out and push. Icicles wept from the eaves. Audiences smelled of wet wool and dirty overshoes.

Roxana was quite ready for it when the company headed back to Colorado. They opened in Georgetown for a long run and stayed once more at the Barton House.

Mr. DeForest let her try her new role of Peach Blossom in *Under the Gaslight*. She remembered to be restrained, to think the part, but at the same time to let herself go enough to express some of the held-in feelings of the audience.

Monty congratulated her.

"You'll play Lady Teazle yet. You've got the makings of an actress, Roxy."

Jay's very words! She wondered wistfully where he was now.

"She's got the makings, but she'll never make it," predicted Mrs. Harlowe. "Roxy is a divided person, and the stage demands all of you. She's always looking back over her shoulder. One half of her wants to act, but the other half is stewing about making a home for her little sister. There's only one thing for her to do."

"What's that?" inquired Roxana with reviving interest, having already discovered that no subject can compare with oneself as a topic of conversation.

"Marry well. Then you can make a home for your sister. You can always express your stage yearnings in amateur theatricals, which would probably enchant your husband besides."

"Foo! I don't see any rich young men hanging around in the wings offering me their names and fortunes," protested Roxana, obviously titillated by the idea.

"You just wait." Mrs. Harlowe nodded wisely. "I've got an idea. This Georgetown is a regular hatchery for future millionaires. You wouldn't be the first to use the stage as a steppingstone. Look at those notorious British Blondes that came over here and took the country—and a lot of rich eastern bloods—by storm. You've got more than any of them; you've got true stage allure. In the early morning you're just a willow withe of a girl, all eyes and long legs. But at night, behind the footlights, you've got that something I'm talking about. You light up. No reason you shouldn't use your assets to take care of your old age."

"Don't pay the slightest attention to her, the old panderer!" shouted Monty. "Such talk. She'll be held to account. Laying up treasures in hell, that's what she's doing."

"A girl has to use her wits, if she doesn't want to have to live by them," said Mrs. Harlowe, unperturbed. "Now take the pretty baggage that snared the Silver King."

"What about her?" asked Roxana.

"A little nobody from Central. They say she hadn't a penny when she went to Leadville and planted herself in Horace Tabor's path, and now there's talk over there that he may divorce his stiff-boned wife and marry the chit."

"She's from Central?"

"Baby Doe, they call her. A silly name. But there's nothing silly about nine million dollars."

Roxana gave a little gasp at having been so close to drama once. So pretty Mrs. Doe had finally escaped that "mean smug little hole" and crowned her efforts with a millionaire. She felt no envy, merely the detached amazement with which one contemplates mountain climbers and aerial acrobats.

"They say she has jewels to match each frock," said Mrs. Harlowe, smacking her lips. "Nothing but the very best for her."

"The best! What's the best?" demanded the old actor passionately. "I'll tell you what it is; it's your young poor days, when you're sharing the same pillow and the same crust of bread with your true love—putting the baby to sleep in a bureau drawer, and having your youth and work and hope and love together—" He stopped, stricken suddenly silent.

"Listen to him! He isn't the only one can warm himself

with memories. I'll tell you that the best days of a woman's life are when she's adored by some man she can twine around her littlest finger. When she's wearing diamond earbobs and ordering canvasback and terrapin from a white-satin menu card. Make no mistake, those are a woman's best days."

Roxana smiled and let them run on. She wasn't likely at the moment to share either a crust of bread and a pillow with a poor young love, or to flash diamond earbobs at a rich husband. All the romantic opportunities of the theater had been greatly overrated. She would probably go on and on—an old maid—until at last she was ready for character parts.

Chapter XI

ROXANA WANDERED ALONG a Georgetown street on a still September afternoon. Already yellow splashed the mountain sides where the aspens were turning. She passed a clump of them, with thin gold coins quivering on every branch. She had been with the company almost a year, and what had she to show for it?

She quickened her steps. It would not do to mope along like this. Not an actress. The town was always curious about theater folks. You had to hold your head high and twitch your skirts and look remote and interesting. Like a visiting princess, Mrs. Harlowe said. A slightly venal princess, Monty always amended.

She came to the railroad station. A train stood on the tracks, with the door to its baggage car open. The baggage man was listlessly dumping trunks out on to the platform, scarred and well-labeled theatrical trunks and boxes.

She stopped to watch. Trains were interesting enough in themselves, but another theatrical troupe was even better. She tried to read the names painted on the boxes. This was the end of the narrow-gauge line. No doubt the company was on its way to Silver Plume. The stagecoach would pick up baggage and actors here and take them on the short, steep drive to the town above.

While she watched, a crate slipped from the baggage man's

hold and landed on its corner. A man who had been sorting trunks on the platform made a leap for it. A slat on the crate had come loose. From behind the slat streaked a loping white rabbit.

With her farm-bred instinct to head off any escaping animal, Roxana leaped. Skirts held wide, she danced back and forth, frustrating the frightened, darting rabbit. The creature was confused just long enough for her to make a lunge for its transparent pinky-white ears. She caught it up and held out the convulsively kicking animal to the man who had been making futile grabs at it.

"Jay!" She gave a gasp of delight, while he pushed the jerking, jackknifing body back into the crate. "Here, Jay, use this rock." She handed him a flat stone to pound the slat back into place.

Jay stood up when he had finished, dusted off his hands, and gave her his crooked grin.

"Well, Roxy! I didn't expect to run into you here."

She looked at him breathlessly, her whole face glowing, her heart in her smile.

"I'd about given up hopes of ever seeing you again, Jay. You never said— It's been so long since you wrote."

Her lips were parted. Her whole being was waiting for him, turning to him expectantly. She was saying, Here I am, Jay. Here we both are. You said there would be two of us —two of us together. Oh, life, start being wonderful!

But Jay was not looking at her soft lips or her radiant eyes. He was chuckling and glancing toward his caged rabbit.

"Of course, it shouldn't be any great surprise to have you be the one to capture him. You always did have a way with animals. First a horse, back in Central; now a rabbit, here in Georgetown." His raillery had a determined sound to it.

She stared at him, baffled. Things weren't the way she had expected them to be when she and Jay met. This was a different Jay from the one who had held her in his arms on that cold ride to Caribou, who had kissed her good-by, who had said that together they would find Avis. Who had written—honesty compelled her to add, who had written only once. There seemed to be so many Jays.

"Anyhow, I thank you for your efforts in my behalf," he said with a bow. "Aristotle thanks you."

"Aristotle?"

"My disappearing white rabbit. Magic act. I put a hat over him, and he vanishes. Of course, if he really did vanish, my act would fall to pieces."

He was busy opening a sack and strewing barley through the slats for the rabbit. Roxana bent down and plucked a handful of clover that grew beside the planking and pushed it in toward the quivering nose.

"They like clover," she offered uncertainly. "So you've got a magic act now."

Unconsciously they dropped down side by side on a trunk to watch the rabbit. The early fall sun was warm on their shoulders, a benign sun, a doubt-dispelling sun.

"I've had several jobs since I left the Tom Show. This one looks as if it might last. The company is waiting here now for the stage to Silver Plume. After that, we do the other Clear Creek towns, and then Leadville. We've got a pretty decent show; wish you could catch it sometime. The Tennessee Minstrels and a family of contortionists; and I've got an assistant in my act now—a Mlle. Fifi."

She was impressed. "Is she French?"

He laughed. "Paris, Illinois, maybe. I found her stranded in a girl show in St. Joe and gave her a job."

He said it with a benevolent air. Then he turned back to her again.

"What about you, young one? Any nearer Lady Teazle?"

"No. I'll never get the chance, and I know every line. I wake up nights thinking about stage business."

"All the fat parts go to the older ones in the cast, is that it?"

She nodded. "Just imagine Mrs. DeForest, in those tight stays, trying to squat on the floor behind a screen. Or Miss Lovell putting on a tantrum, when she's got about as much spirit as a pan of warm milk."

"It's a shame to let some big stuffed cushion or little lump of dough ruin the part when you're just made for it. But mark my word, you'll play Lady Teazle yet. Once you set that dainty little iron chin—"

She glared at him and then relaxed. It was wonderful to be with Jay, even when he teased her. She moved imperceptibly closer to him on the trunk. She smiled up at him invitingly. Any minute now they would recapture that moment in the storm on the way to Caribou. Her hand was close to his on the trunk between them. He had only to close his own hand over it—

The door to the depot waiting room banged open behind them.

"Jay!" called a petulant voice.

Roxana looked around to glimpse a young woman gesturing from the open doorway, her saucy little face an angry red beneath her fringed bangs, her fashionable braid-edged flounces twitching.

"Jay! Come here this minute and carry out my baggage. The stagecoach is due." Her voice was shrill with displeasure.

Jay shrugged and ignored the speaker. From the corner of her eye Roxana could see the girl stand there, furiously tapping her foot, and then go back inside the depot. Roxana's eyes questioned Jay.

"Mlle. Fifi," he said dryly. "Women and melons, so they say, are hard to know about in advance."

"So she's your assistant." She could not go on. Surely he would say now, "That's right. Like I told you, just a girl stranded in St. Joe that I gave a job to. She passes me my silk hat and wand in the magic acts. That's all."

But he did not say it.

"Let's see, we were talking about you and Lady Teazle, weren't we?" he inquired, trying to regain a lost lightness.

"Yes, I guess so. But Mrs. Harlowe, our character actress, says I'll never amount to much on the stage."

"She does! Why?"

"Because I live a divided life. One part of me wants terribly to be on the stage—"

"To put it mildly!"

"And the other part wants to find Avis and make a home for her."

"You'll find her. I'd have written, Roxy, if I'd had any news. I did ask in several towns." His voice was heavy.

Roxana had the feeling that half of his mind was back there in the waiting room with Mlle. Fifi of the mottled red face and the shrill, possessive voice. I'll bet she's common as pig tracks, she thought uncharitably, using her mother's expression. Her own color heightened. Her own foot began to tap. When she spoke, it was with elaborate innocence.

"Mrs. Harlowe says there's only one thing for me to do, under the circumstances."

"What's that?"

"Marry for money. That way I can make a home for Avis when I find her."

She was gratified to see that she had his entire attention now.

"Your character woman said that? Why, the old bawd!"

"But Monty disagrees. He thinks you should marry someone of your own kind—and share everything together, if it's only a crust of bread." Something in the red-brown eyes boring into hers stopped her from mentioning the shared pillow.

"Well, that's more like it." A thought struck him suddenly. "You haven't got your rich old man picked out, have you?"

"Certainly not. And I wouldn't dream of marrying just

for money. I'd have to *care*, too. But Mrs. Harlowe says money never detracted from a man."

His jaw had a rocky jut to it; his thin nostrils flared.

"It was bad enough when you were so stage-crazy you were willing to learn the cancan or work the boxes to get ahead. But to make eyes at some old codger with fat pockets would be worse."

"He wouldn't have to be so old, would he?" Deliberately she gave him a long-lashed, dewy look.

Why, he looked angry enough to break out of a box-stall, she thought. There was something exhilarating about making Jay angry.

"I saved you once from your mule-headedness, Miss Roxana Renner. I can do it again."

His enraged glance traveled reminiscently up and down the undulating back curve of her from her chignon to her bustle—wire, not newspaper now—that bulged so jauntily on the trunk upon which they sat. One corner of his mouth dented in ominously. His brown fingers twitched. He was outrageous! He was all but threatening to spank her again. She leaped to her feet, but she did not run away. Jay stood up, too.

A noise from the depot made her turn in that direction.

"You'd better go. Your assistant wants you. That's what she is—your assistant?" Poison was in her tone.

"Sure, she's my assistant." He was standing looking at Roxana, legs apart, eyes furious and derisive. He seemed unnecessarily vehement and sarcastic. "One thing about her, though. *She* wouldn't sell herself to some rich old rake, pretending she was doing it to 'make a home for her little sister.' If she did it, she would know exactly what she was after. Fifi would at least be an honest tart!"

For a moment she was speechless. Before she could think up an answer to this horrible person who said such insulting, searing, stick-in-the-craw things, the stagecoach rattled up with a clatter. The troupe boiled out of the waiting room.

Roxana found herself pushed aside in the flurry of last-minute sorting of baggage and strapping of smaller pieces on to the boot.

She retreated to the shelter of a towering pile of crates. She could not bring herself to leave. She huddled there, half-hidden, while the company settled themselves on the seats both outside and inside the coach; while Jay helped the now-mollified and preening Fifi up the step where they crowded together on the back seat; while the driver cracked his whip and sent the coach careening off up the street.

She was still standing there when it turned the corner out of sight.

Chapter XII

ROXANA SCARCELY NEEDED make-up that night, her color was so high. She had not been able to eat a bite of supper; a hard ball of resentment filled her stomach instead. She was jumpy as a cat as she slapped pomatum on her smooth cheeks for the role of Janet the innkeeper's daughter in *The Lady of Lyons*.

She looked blankly at Mrs. Harlowe, who came to the dressing room door and whispered for her to take a look through the curtain peephole. There was someone out front she wanted Roxana to see.

Without enthusiasm Roxana applied her eye to the hole.

"See the row of gentlemen in dress suits? And the one in the middle with the mustache?"

Roxana saw the row of gentlemen, chaffing each other and smiling with knowing anticipation toward the curtain. Her eye fastened on the solidly built man in the middle, with the gravely pleasant face and the thinning hair.

"Yes, I see him. What about him?"

"He's the one I've been saving you for. The one I want you to meet."

"That old man?"

Mrs. Harlowe looked annoyed. "He's not old. Barely ripe, my child. Middle forties, at the most. What did you want, some young sprout without two farthings to rub together?"

That was exactly what Roxana did want, although she would not have admitted it.

"What's his name?"

"Grover Hull. Well-known mining man—that is, he deals in mining stocks. Came out here from Cincinnati and pyramided his holdings. They call him the Silver Prince—Tabor's the Silver King, of course. I'm going to fix it so you meet him. He's widowed, decent, and free—or he would be free, if forward females would leave him alone."

In spite of herself Roxana felt a faint pleasurable quickening. At least he did not look bold and mean and vindictive and insulting—the kind who would talk gentle one minute and then throw a Mlle. Fifi in your face the next. And as Mrs. Harlowe so often remarked, wealth was not exactly a drawback to a man.

"You can let yourself go a little tonight," suggested that old woman with a witch's gleam.

Roxana needed no such advice. She was already keyed up. She threw herself into the part; she gave it all her pent-up emotion. Right straight into the smiling, admiring eyes of Mr. Grover Hull she played that night. She was electric with feeling. The audience sensed it; the cast sensed it. She was not overacting; she was simply a blaze that threatened to become a conflagration at any moment.

"Nice work," said Mr. DeForest when she came off. "You can do Pearl in *Under the Gaslight,* and I'll put Miss Lovell in as Peach Blossom."

There were many curtain calls that night, some of them for Miss Roxana Renner. The opulent row of white-shirt-fronted gentlemen was insistent. And then came the climax: her first bouquet of hothouse flowers. Clear from Denver they had come. Even as she accepted them and sank in the curtsy she had been practicing in secret for months, her glance took in the card which said in the firm black letters of a man who knows his own mind, "With the admiration of Grover Hull."

When she came back with the rest of the cast for the last curtain call, the roses still in her arms, she had the presence of mind to wrench off a handful of blooms and toss them with reasonable accuracy at the row of applauding gentlemen. She saw Grover Hull capture one, bow and touch the flower to his lips and tuck it into his buttonhole. She smiled brilliantly across the footlights.

She took extra pains with her dressing that night. Usually she was so tired after the show that she hardly laced up her corsets properly or saw that her petticoat tapes were safely tucked inside her placket. But tonight she borrowed Miss Lovell's curling iron, and she dusted her face with rice powder.

It came as somewhat of an anticlimax when Mrs. Harlowe stuck her head in the dressing room door and said, "How about a nice cove-oyster stew tonight? Monty says he's hungry. Bring your flowers along, and we'll put them in a water pitcher at the Barton House." She paused and added as if it were an afterthought, "I understand there's a gentlemen's party going on tonight next door at the Hotel de Paris. You know, the French proprietor who hates women and caters only to men guests and imports his wines clear from France? A gourmet he is, and the men talk about his dinners for weeks afterwards."

Roxana felt oddly letdown; and she felt even more so in the morning when she found that the financier's special car was gone from the siding and that Mr. Grover Hull and entourage were far down the canyon already.

So the roses and the smiles and the flower in his buttonhole had not meant a thing. She tried to cover her discomfiture. Mrs. Harlowe seemed surprisingly unmoved; in fact, she continued to act pleased and mysterious. When another sheaf of roses was delivered to Roxana that night, with a similar card attached, Mrs. Harlowe indicated that it was no more than she had expected.

"Just don't be in a hurry," she said cryptically.

Not be in a hurry! Roxana was in a fever of impatience to meet this Grover Hull. Vengeful blood boiled up in her veins. If there were only some way to let Jay know that she had already met—well, almost met—her rich, eligible older man.

The delay and the second bouquet whetted her interest. As the troupe moved on, out of the canyon to the towns along the front range, and they played Colorado Springs and then Pueblo, she thought a great deal about Mr. Grover Hull and as little as possible about Professor Jay.

She was so wrapped in her own thoughts that she scarcely heard the talk going on about her on the train: Mr. DeForest quoting silver statistics; old Monty announcing that President Hayes had said we were on the doorstep of better times. She sat almost unmoved during the trip up through the Royal Gorge where only a frail steel spider web kept the sinuous line of cars from hurtling into the torrent below.

But, passionate egotist that she was, even her self-absorption was pierced as they neared Leadville. The name brought her up with a jerk. Leadville, her father's goal. She gazed down into the rushing Arkansas. Her father had said he had drunk tea made from the Missouri and the Platte, and next he wanted to try tea made from the Arkansas. She peered up at the cold, beautiful, angry-looking ranges on either side of the valley and thought that somewhere in one of those desolate gorges lay her father's body under a cairn of rocks.

Dear Pa, she thought, holding her mouth in a tight trembling line. Just when she thought she had got so she could bear a thing, something happened to start the pain up afresh.

When she reached Leadville and walked along the teeming, jostling streets, she could see her father everywhere. This was his kind of country, as it was her kind of country. It was Central City and Georgetown multiplied many times. To think that only a handful of people had lived here two years ago, and that now thousands—some said twenty; others, thirty—swarmed its hastily laid out streets.

Looking at its raw ferocity, she remembered her mother's refusal to go to Leadville. From her mother's point of view, she had been right. This was much worse than Central. Two miles above sea level, with timber line grimly close on the surrounding ranges, the cold hand of winter was already clamping down.

Smelters spewed their poisonous fumes over the town. On every side, fresh mine dumps cascaded down. Fine brick buildings elbowed makeshift saloons and stores. Strings of pack animals stepped daintily along the ruts. There were houses with cupolas and turrets; there was a splendid new opera house. Flapping tents crowded against new log cabins. On State Street the doors never stopped swinging, nor the painted women beckoning, nor the wheels of fortune spinning.

She picked her way decorously among the crowds of men and knew the old wild exhilaration. She was short of breath. Maybe it was the altitude. She felt that there was something portentous and agitating about this Leadville. It was a place where things—all sorts of things—could happen.

When she saw Mrs. Harlowe back at their boardinghouse, the latter greeted her in high spirits.

"We're going to a party tonight, you and I."

"Are we?" said Roxana.

"With Mr. Grover Hull."

So that accounted for Mrs. Harlowe's mysterious admonitions not to be in a hurry; she had expected to meet Mr. Hull again in Leadville.

"It's a supper party after the theater, at the Saddle Rock Café," explained Mrs. Harlowe. "He'll have a carriage waiting for us at the stage door to take us the whole half-block to the restaurant. Now look your prettiest. Not too worldly wise, but not too young and green either. They never want to be cradle-robbers, but they certainly do like to think they're first."

"Procurer!" muttered old Monty, overhearing. His white tufts of eyebrows met in a line; his white tufts of whiskers quivered.

Roxana was too engrossed to take in all the implications of Mrs. Harlowe's advice or Monty's anxiety. She gave the old man a pat on the arm and hurried off to her and Miss Lovell's dressing room in the handsome new opera house built by Horace Tabor, the Silver King. She was so occupied thinking about Mr. Grover Hull, the Silver Prince, that she gave only a passing glance to the special seat reserved for Mrs. Doe, which Mrs. Harlowe pointed out to her.

"There's a covered passageway on the third floor connecting the opera house with the Clarendon Hotel where this Baby Doe has rooms," said the old woman with relish. "See what I mean, dearie, about interesting a gentleman of means?"

She failed to mention any of the other fruits Baby Doe had reaped, along with her Silver King: her anomalous position at the moment—neither wife, maid, nor fiancée—until such time as the present Mrs. Tabor should reluctantly let her husband go. The scandalized lifted eyebrows of the world. The cold, cold shoulders that would be turned toward Baby Doe if she should ever try to assume a place in society as the second Mrs. Tabor.

Assured that Mr. Grover Hull was not present in the theater that night, Roxana walked through her part.

"Now, now!" chided Mrs. Harlowe, who, with all her scheming, was still an actress. "The only time you're supposed to play a marble statue is in the tableau. Better come to life."

Roxana came to life.

After the play she put on her new iridescent blackish-green dress (exactly the shine and color of a mallard's neck in the sun). It had the latest tied-back look that made her waist seem outrageously small.

"You really could span it with your two hands tonight," Mrs. Harlowe noted with voluptuous approval.

Roxana stood tilting forward like a goddess on a promontory in the wind. The front folds of her skirt were swept back, to cascade with billowing abandon in the rear. It made her walk with a slight Grecian bend. Wearing her tight kid gloves and her new mantle and her hair in a smoky waterfall of curls, she pleased even the critical Mrs. Harlowe.

"Don't chatter. And only one glass of champagne—make it last. Smile and listen and let your looks do the rest."

Mr. Grover Hull was waiting at the stage door with Leadville's best rented carriage. Mrs. Harlowe presented him to "our pretty ingénue, Miss Roxana Renner—I believe you two know each other by sight," and he bowed low over Roxana's hand. The two ladies climbed in, disposing of their pleats and billows, while Mr. Hull sat opposite them. The driver set off over the brief distance to the restaurant, with Mrs. Harlowe capably handling the small talk.

Presently they were being ushered into the dining room. Roxana moved slowly, her lovely back fullness twitching with her mannered gait.

When the three of them were seated, she said demurely, "The roses were lovely. You have beautiful taste, Mr. Hull."

He looked almost unduly pleased, she thought.

"Buds would have been more suitable than full-blown roses, of course. But coming all the way from Denver, one does the best one can. I presume that actresses—lovely actresses—get a great many?"

She swallowed rapidly and looked at Mrs. Harlowe. What if he knew that those were her first hothouse flowers? She smoothed her kid gloves in her lap.

"It's the giver that makes them different—and special, I always think," she said hesitantly.

Mrs. Harlowe looked approving. Roxana flushed. She had

[147]

not actually said that she had had dozens and dozens of hot-house bouquets. Of course, she had had nuggets thrown on the stage, and once a gentleman's gold watch fob, and even a shower of gold coins in the Black Hills—all merely the customary evidences of the miners' approval. But never hot-house flowers before.

The bowing waiter handed her a large and glossy menu card, which happened to signalize the arrival of some visiting dignitary to Leadville. Roxana picked hers up with a feeling of awe. White satin! She recalled Mrs. Harlowe's spirited arguments with old Monty about which were the best days of a woman's life. And Mrs. Harlowe's "I'll tell you what they are—they're when she's adored by some man she can twine around her littlest finger . . . and when she's wearing diamond earbobs and ordering from a white-satin menu card. Make no mistake about it—those are a woman's best days."

She looked around her with startled greenish eyes. So these were a woman's best days. She wished she didn't keep remembering some frozen bread and cheese that hurt her teeth, eaten under a canvas shelter in a howling storm on the way to Caribou.

Chapter XIII

ROXANA HAD A protracted siege of temperament that winter. One minute she was enjoying her role of admired woman, coveted and sought after by a man of wealth; the next minute she was distrait and wondering why Jay's troupe did not get here. He had said they were coming to Leadville, and here the whole winter was slipping by without a sign of him. She had the feeling that if she could just see him again, he would make everything right. She had long ago accepted the fact that he was a poor letter writer. But if she could just hear him say, "Shucks, Roxy, you women are always imaging things. Every magician has an assistant. It's part of our act."

As frequently as he could get them in winter-locked Leadville, Mr. Grover Hull had flowers delivered across the footlights to Miss Roxana Renner. She accepted them with demure but distant politeness. But when more lasting gifts were waiting for her in her dressing room—French kid gloves, a carved ivory fan, a lace handkerchief as delicate as a frost pattern—she returned them to him politely.

Mrs. Harlowe told her not to be a fool. What difference did it make, flowers that cost a fortune because they had to be shipped all that way on ice, or a bauble or two? Hadn't Roxana accepted plenty of trinkets tossed on the stage? But Roxana was perversely firm; she sent back everything but the flowers.

When she received insistent, but not particularly ardent, invitations from Mr. Hull to after-theater supper parties, she accepted them only occasionally. More often she sent careful little notes saying that she was sorry but she was otherwise engaged, or that she had a headache—that omnibus excuse in the eighties whenever a lady was disinclined, though not necessarily indisposed.

The cast, housed in a boardinghouse on Fourth Street, grumbled over Roxana's touchy ways and snappish outbursts.

"Who does she think she is—Lady Macbeth?" growled Romney Lynde. "Notice how, when she reaches for a chop, she stabs it to death?"

"It'll wear off," old Monty chuckled. "A girl has such a short while to be capricious, to blow hot and cold, and such a long time to be sensible."

Mrs. Harlowe was vexed. Exasperating girl! All her carefully laid groundwork wasted. The winter was almost gone. She did not know how much longer they could keep her old acquaintance Grover Hull dancing attendance. After all, he was a man of affairs. True, he was out of his wits over Roxana now. But how long would he stay that way, with the contrary little snippet treating him like some common miner that threw nuggets on the stage? In fact, not treating him so well, for she had kept the nuggets.

Mrs. Harlowe need not have worried. Grover Hull was obviously bewitched by this icy young thing who so primly sent back his presents and nightly ravished him from behind the footlights. Mrs. Harlowe could not have done better, had she been coaching Roxana in her present role.

The ordeal of a Leadville winter neared its end, with high mounds of snow still banking the sidewalks, and cold winds still swooping down off Mt. Massive, nipping noses and making chilblains burn.

Roxana had never worked so hard. The troupe was making the most of their long run in Leadville. They were playing that tear-soaked perennial, *Camille,* with Mrs. De-

Forest probably the healthiest-looking case of phthisis ever to cough her life away on a canopied bed with lace coverlets. At the same time, they were rehearsing for *The Taming of the Shrew*. Gradually Roxana was edging Miss Lovell out of her supporting roles and inching her back into the status of utility woman; Roxana was to play Bianca to Mrs. De-Forest's Katherine in *The Taming*.

Grover Hull was frequently away on business trips, but he always returned, drawn back by a force stronger than his good judgment.

He was no fool; hence he knew that he was being one now. They could talk all they wanted to about young love. But when love waited to hit you—a man along in his forties—it was a cataclysm. He had a fatalistic feeling that it might even be a catastrophe. He knew as well as anyone that he ought to be interested in a suitable woman his own age. He knew it was folly to choose ambrosia in place of bread, a brocaded waistcoat in place of a warm coat. And he ordered more roses.

Not for the world would Roxana have admitted that she was enjoying herself. She continued her airy, trying ways. "Uncertain, coy, and hard to please," quoted Monty. "Damned hard to live with," said Mrs. Harlowe.

Then, one day, because she had still heard nothing from Jay and was beginning to suspect that she never would hear from him again, she relented toward Mr. Grover Hull. It was spring at last, with a warm wind taking off the snow in the hollows. No, she would not accept an aquamarine necklace, nor dine at the Tontine Restaurant, nor wear a pearl brooch that had belonged to his mother (so he said). But she would go on a picnic to fashionable Turquoise Lake the following Sunday, provided Mrs. Harlowe would go along.

Mrs. Harlowe was only too willing.

Picnic, to Roxana, meant a checked tablecloth on the ground and hard-boiled eggs and her mother's marble cake. (It meant even frozen bread and cheese in a snowstorm.) Picnic, to Grover Hull, meant fringed damask napkins and cold roast capon and marrons glacés.

They set off along Chestnut Street down California Gulch for the long drive. There was none of the Sunday calm here that she was used to. Even the creek, which elsewhere would have run clear on Sunday, was roily and opaque with tailings.

Mrs. Harlowe probably enjoyed the picnic more than did anyone else. In the first place, she liked being driven in state by a coachman (well, by a man from the livery stable). She liked the elegant hamper packed by the chef at the Clarendon; she was the only one who did justice to it. She liked the soft rugs spread beside the glittering jewel of lake, and the cushions and champagne and all the unnecessary graces provided by money. It took her back to the time— She was drowsy with memories and good food and quite ready to have Mr. Hull take Roxana off for a stroll.

They followed along the shore of the lake. Roxana played at skipping stones, making them dart in and out of the ripples. At length they paused where the bright twigs of red-barked willows made a show of color. Mr. Hull spread his handkerchief on a rock before he let her sit down. She was impressed; the handkerchief was of far finer material than her old mulberry alpaca.

He sprawled opposite her on a bank of grass, leaning on one elbow. She wondered if he really ought to do that. The ground was still coldly damp. Older people—

"Pleasant, isn't it?" he said, looking up at the blue dome. "There's something about spring; each year it makes you feel—" He did not finish. "Doesn't it make you want to play hookey, too? Or are you so wedded to the theater that you never think of anything but rehearsing and learning new parts?" He looked at her quizzically, but with a certain seriousness, too.

"I don't think of very much else," she admitted. "All my life I wanted to go on the stage. There's something about it—"

"I know," he said with sympathy. Then his eyes crinkled in self-derision. "Judging by my attendance this winter, I'd say I found considerable fascination in the theater myself."

She looked at him in swift surprise, and they both broke into easy laughter. He's nice, she thought. You can laugh with him; you can even laugh at him.

"But I do think of something else besides the stage," she amended. "My little sister."

"Sister?" he asked.

"We're orphans." Queer how she could not say the word even yet without that quick pang. "We got separated while I was off on my first tour. She ran away to be with some friends. And now—oh, I know it sounds strange—but I can't find her. I ask at every town. Avis Renner her name is. She'd be thirteen now. A quiet little thing with big hollow eyes." Roxana's chin quivered.

"It's easy enough to lose folks out in this new country. No postal service to speak of. People and towns are here today and gone tomorrow."

"That's just it. And Mr. Evans didn't want anyone to know where he was going. He's a prospector. I'll never rest till I've found Avis. You see, it was all my fault." She told him about the past year. He listened with understanding soberness.

She found him friendly and easy and not at all exigent. Dusk came on, and a little wind sprang up. When he pulled her to her feet—he was barely an inch taller than she—and she staggered on a hummock and fell lightly against him, he did not take advantage of it. She saw his jaw set; she felt the hand holding hers grow tense. But he maintained his rigid decorum.

Then the sun was gone behind the sheer wall of mountains that formed the backbone of the continent, and it was suddenly winter again. They were reminded that they were two miles above the sea and that the weather here was harsh and implacable.

[153]

They hurried back to Mrs. Harlowe and the waiting carriage. Mr. Hull was solicitous. He tucked robes and propped cushions. At the boardinghouse he waited until Mrs. Harlowe had lumbered majestically inside and the driver had driven off with the carriage. Then he escorted Roxana up to the door and took her hand with an air of quiet ceremony.

"I hope you enjoyed the day, Roxana."

"Oh, yes, very much," she breathed.

"You didn't find it too tiring?"

Tiring? She who her mother always said was strong as a yearling mule?

"Oh, no," she breathed again.

"I liked it, too. I like doing things for you. If you'd only let me do more. I hope you enjoyed being with . . . me." It was strange how he seemed to feel his way, this man who was so sure of himself with others.

"I did. I like being with you very much, Mr. Hull." She could not say less. His very humbleness embarrassed her. With all his wealth and all his years, he ought not to be the humble one now.

"I know I'm a lot older than you," he said, sharing her thought. "I'd not ask much, Roxana—only that you'd let me try to make you happy."

"But you do make me happy. Indeed you do," she assured him. And his pleasure was all out of proportion to the worth of her statement. It was such a meatless bone to offer such a beseeching dog.

Suddenly he lifted her cold gloved hand to his lips. She fought off an overwhelming impulse to pull the hand away. It made her uneasy. Having one's hand kissed was not nearly so—well, it was entirely different from what she had expected.

A door opened and shut somewhere inside the boardinghouse. She must go right in! she said with relief. Mrs. De-Forest wouldn't like her to be out late, even if it was their

Sunday off. She had to be fresh for tomorrow's rehearsal—Bianca, you know, in *The Taming*. She rattled on.

When she was inside the dark vestibule, she glanced back through the etched-glass doors and saw him standing bareheaded on the sidewalk, hat against breast, watching the door that had just closed after her. He looked as if something rare and valuable had just disappeared through that door. She was uncomfortable again. She did not feel either rare or valuable; she felt merely uneasy.

Roxana walked out of the Boot and Shoe Emporium wearing her new shoes. She knew she had been a spendthrift. Five dollars for a pair of shoes! Her mother would have been scandalized. But she felt unsettled and reckless and keyed up these days, as if she were waiting in the wings for a cue. The lovely, silly, costly shoes in the window exactly fitted her mood. With their embroidered cloth tops and their teetery spool heels and their bobbing tassels on the front, they could scarcely have been less suited to Leadville's cold and slushy spring weather.

"I'll wear them," she announced, even before she had found out whether they pinched her feet no worse than did most new shoes.

Outside the store the wind snatched at her bonnet and billowed up under her skirts so that she had to clamp her hands about them to hold them down.

A man was halted in the lee of the building, bent over by a fit of coughing. She eyed him commiseratingly. This cruel spring weather that anywhere else would have been called winter. There was so much pneumonia. He ought to be home and in bed.

He straightened up, and she saw his face.

"Jay!" She stopped beside him, appalled.

His smile, his "Why, Roxy—" were broken off by a fresh fit of coughing.

"What are you doing out in this wind? Jay, you never take

any care of yourself!" All her defenses had crumbled at sight of him, ill and miserable.

"It's nothing. Just a cold I caught coming up on the train yesterday. We don't open till Monday at the Grand Union. I'll be all right then. We took longer getting to Leadville than I'd expected. I didn't think you'd still be here."

"We've had a long run. Oh, Jay, why didn't you write? You said—" Her voice shook.

"I wasn't sure you'd want to hear from me."

"All winter I've looked for a letter. But I never heard from you, and I never heard from Avis. You said we'd hunt for her together. Both of us." She was near tears.

"I know I did. But I'm not much good at writing. I'm not . . . much . . . good—" He looked apologetic and ill and chastened.

"You ought to be in bed. Where are you staying?"

He nodded toward the side street.

"Boardinghouse," he gasped between coughs. "Stoop out in front."

She dug down into her reticule and came up with a hoarhound cough drop. He took it obediently. She winced at the unfamiliar meekness. He must feel bad indeed—the once-arrogant, cocky, top-of-the-world Professor Jay.

"Oh, Jay, I can't bear to see you so wretched. Come on, you're going straight back to your room and to bed, do you hear me?" The sharply tender voice might have been her mother's.

"All right, Roxy. But I don't deserve it—your bothering about me, I mean."

"I'm going to tell your landlady to make a mustard plaster and put it on your chest," she said. She took hold of his arm and began to propel him toward the two-story frame structure.

"Oh, no, don't come in with me. I'll tell her about the plaster," he said uneasily, trying to shake off her hold. "It's only a cold."

"Cold! You aren't two steps from pneumonia." They were in front of the boardinghouse now. She hated to let him go in alone, dependent upon the grudging care of some overworked landlady. "Take a hot drink and just pile the covers on; will you promise, Jay?" He looked so weak and feverish and hunched over. She longed to follow him in, to do for him, to stand guard over him. Perhaps because he had always been so self-sufficient, his very helplessness now was the more heart-wrenching. Both the woman in her and the mother in her yearned over him with passionate protectiveness.

"Good-by, Roxy," he said a little nervously. He looked at the entreaty in her face. "I'll see you again. When I get over this, I'll see you. You're different from what I expected. Different from everybody else in the world, I guess. You've certainly been doing a lot of growing up, haven't you, young one?" He tried to grin, but it was only a grimace.

She said, "Oh, yes, Jay; I'm grown-up now," but he was already going up the steps. She watched him fumble for the door knob and stagger into the house.

She walked slowly back to Harrison Avenue, where the stores were. Maybe Mrs. Harlowe would know what was good for a chest cold. Or old Monty. A pharmacy on the corner with its beautiful glass urns of colored water caught her eye. Surely they would know.

The gentleman back of the counter, standing before a ceiling-high honeycomb of pigeonholes, each containing its mysteriously labeled square bottle, was helpful. There was nothing better than a capsicum plaster on the chest, he said. Might redden the skin, but it drew the congestion right out. You applied it thus.

I don't care what anybody thinks, she decided with a lift of the head as she marched back to his boardinghouse with the plaster. He's a sick man. I'll explain to the landlady that we're old friends—theatrical friends. Stage people always look out for each other.

[157]

She twisted the handle of the bell, which twanged just inside. She waited a moment and then went in. After the high brilliance out of doors, she could make out nothing at first in the gloom. Even in a town so new that the pine siding had not had time to darken nor the floors to warp, the place had a boardinghouse smell. She wondered where the landlady was.

Now she could see that a hallway bisected the first floor and that a steep stairway rose directly in front of her. A door in the hall above opened with a flimsy clatter. A sharp voice called out something indistinguishable. The flimsy door banged shut. Hard little heels pounded along the upper hall, reached the top of the stairs, and descended the uncarpeted flight toward Roxana. The heels landed on the steps with mallet-like blows.

Roxana could see that it was a woman, dressed to go out. One of the boarders, no doubt. The woman stopped in front of Roxana, who blocked her way.

"I wonder if you could tell me," began Roxana in her most ladylike voice. "That is, I'm looking for—"

The other waited with a certain truculence. Roxana blinked, trying to accustom her eyes to the darkness of the hall. She could make out the hair the color of new rope that did not go with her snapping black eyes, the too-girlish hat that did not go with her woman's face.

"Who did you want?" asked the boarder ungraciously.

"A Professor Jay, who stays here. I met him on the street, and he had a terrible cough. I thought I'd bring over a plaster for his chest. If you can just tell me which room he's in—"

The woman stiffened. Roxana could feel the impact of her hostility like a blow. But there was something more than hostility there.

"I'm taking care of Professor Jay," the other said shortly. "If he needs any plasters on his chest, I'll put them on."

"Oh," said Roxana. "I didn't know. I thought—" And

then she gave a start as she recognized her. Mlle. Fifi, of course! She was thrown completely off balance. Why hadn't she been prepared for this? Naturally, this Fifi would be staying in the same boardinghouse with him. A company always stayed together; they got better rates that way.

"And why shouldn't I be looking after him, I'd like to know?" demanded Fifi. The something else in her voice might have been fear.

"I guess you're his assistant. I—I ran into him in Georgetown last fall, and he said he had an assistant."

Fifi did not reply for a moment. Instead, her eyes raked Roxana from head to foot, from the bird on her bonnet to the foolish tassels on her new boots.

Roxana was beginning to see more plainly now, and she did not like what she saw. A furious young woman with violence in her eyes, and a face that, under its powder, looked puffy and raddled from rage or weeping.

"So you're the one!" Fifi's voice was explosive. "The one that was lallygagging with him at the depot till you almost made him late for the stagecoach to Silver Plume!" To the shrinking Roxana, her fury seemed unwarranted. "Well, after this you can just keep your prissy little nose out of his affairs, do you hear? We'd get along fine in this company if it wasn't for all you stage-struck ninnies lining the circuit. And if it's anything to you, I was just going out to get something for his cough myself."

Roxana broke in weakly, "Here, take this plaster. The man at the pharmacy said it would draw out the congestion. Jay looked like he had a fever, too. If you'd wrap him up well and give him a hot drink—" Every word she said only inflamed Fifi further.

"Fever! Plaster! Congestion! Who are *you* to tell *me?* Didn't he toss and turn all last night so I hardly got a wink? One minute hot as fire, and the next, shaking with chills and dragging the covers off me. Well, I don't need advice from any of you actor-crazy little chippies!" She grabbed the

[159]

outstretched package and hurled it to the floor so hard that Roxana backed away. Fifi followed her, her angry little face close to Roxana's. She was furious; she was common; and she was wildly agitated about something besides Professor Jay's cough.

"Trying to edge me out of my job, that's what you are"— Fifi was livid—"on the stage—and under the blankets, too!"

A speechless Roxana whitened and fumbled behind her for the door knob.

A heavy tread lumbered toward them. The landlady came into view, a stooped untidy woman, worn with trying to make a living off these precarious and unreliable theatrical folks.

Roxana turned the knob and managed to get out just as she heard Fifi say sweetly, "I think he's a little better, thanks. I was just going out to get a plaster for his chest. And I'll thank you if you could make him a little hot broth for his supper. I thought if I wrapped him up good—the congestion, you know." Her voice was concerned and wifely.

Roxana stumbled down the steps, the treacle-sweet tones following her. Even though she broke into a run, she could not seem to get rid of them. They followed her and followed her.

Now you know why Jay was no good at writing; why Jay was—no good. Now you know exactly what it is his assistant does for him. I hope you're satisfied. I hope you've had a plenty.

Mrs. Harlowe watched Roxana anxiously during the next few days. Something had happened to the girl. It was not like her to go around with that queer tight look. Surely, Grover Hull had not jilted her? But that was impossible, for he was still obviously fatuous about her. Yet the girl was as nervous and fidgety as a bee-stung filly.

Monty was concerned, too. She had had a blow of some sort. Only a wounded heart could make a girl look so reckless and beautiful and unstrung. Who could have hurt her? Certainly not that slow-moving rich chap with the rather decent face.

Mrs. DeForest thought with satisfaction, The little Renner seems to have waked up at last. We can let Miss Lovell go any time now, and take on just a utility woman. The girl's ready for real dramatic roles. She'll put some fire into Bianca.

Her husband mused, She'd make a wonderful Lady Teazle if I could talk Julia out of the part.

Romney Lynde's eyes widened, and he ran his tongue over his lips as Roxana swept past him with a fluid gesture. She certainly looked different lately; maybe he'd been overlooking something.

Francine Lovell, seeing his look, hated Roxana afresh.

And then, three days later, in the midst of final rehearsals for *The Taming*, Gil Anker's letter came. The writing was labored; it must have taken him a long time to write.

Now don't get your hopes up Roxy I haven't much to tell, but I know you been hunting and hunting your sister. [Her conscience lashed out at her; she had forgotten all about Avis lately.] Rev Starbuck was transferred over to St. Elmo where he travels a circuit from Alpine to Romley to Hancock. His wife was just back here to tend to their little boy's grave. [Roxana's heart was squeezed with pity. Oh, poor Naomi!] She mentioned she was on track of a Mrs. Evans that has a half-grown girl. Now I know there are lots of Evanses in this state, it being a good Welsh name, but this girl was called something like Alys or Mavis or Avis. They been having sickness and trouble, she heard. You better get over to St. Elmo. Good luck, Gil.

Sickness and trouble! Roxana stood unheeding in the Leadville post office while the crowd jostled her this way and that.

Lacerated and raw as she still was from her encounter with

Fifi; hurt and frustrated by her meeting with Jay; unsettled by the attentions of Grover Hull, she was quiveringly vulnerable at the moment to the sense of her own guilt. Self-reproaches swooped down upon her like angry birds.

A fine sister she was! Eating roast capon and buying a fancy new surtout to wear with her gray marceline and silly embroidered cloth-topped shoes to wear with the surtout, when she ought to have been saving her money. Mooning over a man who didn't deserve it, when she ought to have been hunting for her sister.

When could she get the first train out? Where was this St. Elmo? Oh, if she hadn't tossed away all that money on foolish kickshaws when she might have been saving it to make a home for Avis. And Avis undergoing sickness and trouble. She was shocked and shamed and frantic.

With her customary recklessness she threw away the rewards of two years' devoted work. She must find Avis at once. She barely remembered to tell Mrs. DeForest her intentions.

No, it simply could not wait, she told that horrified woman in the hallway of the boardinghouse. She was on track of her sister at last. At St. Elmo, the letter said. No, she couldn't stay over even for one more day until they got a replacement for her. She might lose her sister again. She had to go now, on the next train. Yes, of course she realized what she was giving up—her chance to play Bianca tomorrow night in *The Taming,* her first serious dramatic role. Sure, she was sorry the company would have to shift back to *Camille* if she went off like this. And she knew perfectly what it meant in the code of the theater to pull out, leaving the company in the lurch.

Mrs. DeForest tried every argument. She stamped her foot and breathed so hard she threatened to burst her corset lacings.

"All right, you bull-headed little wretch! Running out on us just for a whim, with the notices already in the papers, the bills posted in front of the opera house, and the new scenery all painted. Lucky thing Delphine is back in Denver and wanting work. I'll wire her this minute. But don't ever come puling back to me begging for a job again. It'll be a cold day, Miss—" She marched out of the boardinghouse. She had not played tragedy roles for nothing.

Roxana scarcely heard her. Avis, at last! She shook with an ague.

Monty regarded her with sorrowful admiration. Crazy, rash, conscience-ridden Roxana. He was proud of the girl. She was the stuff heroes and great ladies are made of. But it did seem kind of a pity, after she'd worked so hard.

"Little fool. Not a lick of common sense!" snorted Mrs. Harlowe.

"That's right," he agreed. "Not a lick, God bless her. But what's so wonderful about common sense? A little comes in handy, like table salt. But it's only the people without common sense who make the great crusaders and great martyrs. Common sense saves you your own skin and loses you your cause."

"Shut up, Frank Montague!" Mrs. Harlowe shouted. "All your pious mouthings may have helped the girl ruin her life. Just when she and Grover Hull were on the verge of an understanding. What will he think when he comes back and finds she's gone kiting off? Wealthy men don't take kindly to having their hopes dashed again and again. A little is all very well—"

Roxana was oblivious to them all. She flung her clothes into her new telescope and departed on the morning train. If only she had saved more money, she mourned. Twenty-two dollars would not go very far.

Chapter XIV

CARRYING HER TELESCOPE, Roxana picked her way along the edge of the muddy road. The early summer sun beamed down on her shoulders. That was mountain weather for you: snow yesterday, mud today, dust tomorrow. But she was grateful for the sun—a drying sun. Naomi must be grateful for it, too, she thought with a chuckle as she recognized the Starbuck cabin by its long line of washing dripping wetly in the back yard. It was past noon; Naomi was always the last to get her washing out.

She waved to the three tow-headed little girls playing in front of the cabin and went around to the back yard. When Naomi saw her, she dropped her clothes basket and ran to enfold Roxana in her arms. They two would always be friends; they had known trouble together.

"Henry!" she shrieked over her shoulder. "Guess who's here!"

The beaming, raw-boned young minister came out of the cabin, holding his sheets of sermon in one hand. With the other, he picked up Roxana's telescope and carried it into the house.

"Let's go right out to that place, Henry. We mustn't wait," urged Naomi, when they had listened to Roxana's brief explanations. "We were planning to go ourselves first chance, but it's several miles up the gulch." She meant it involved hiring a livery rig, which one did not do lightly. "We understand she's a widow, this Mrs. Evans, and that he was killed in a mine cave-in. She's running a boardinghouse at the Royal Flush mine. Henry, do hurry and get a horse and buggy." As always, she had to prod her husband a little.

While they waited for Henry to return, Roxana and Naomi wept softly together over Naomi's lost little boy. But there was a look of hope and sweet planning on Naomi's face as she ran her hand shyly down over her swelling body. She could not say more; after all Roxana was not a married woman. But as she waddled over to ask a neighbor to watch out for the little girls while they were gone, Roxana looked after her and prayed earnestly, "Oh, let it be a little boy, God; please let it be a boy!"

All the way out to the mine the three of them talked. As they neared the buildings that clung like tough lichens to the rocky slopes, Roxana leaned forward, peering out. Avis! How would it seem for them to be together again after all this time? Was Avis starting to be a young lady now, with curves of her own?

They stopped on the road below the frame boardinghouse with the narrow porch across the front. Roxana raced ahead up the steep flight of steps; Naomi had to follow more slowly. Roxana rapped insistently. It took forever for heavy footsteps to sound along the uncarpeted hall within. The door was opened at last by a middle-aged woman with a knob of gray hair like a frowzy cruller on top of her head.

"Is Avis Renner—?" panted Roxana. "I mean, will you please tell Mrs. Evans that Roxana Renner is here? Oh, where's Avis?"

Henry and Naomi Starbuck had reached the porch by now. Henry explained more coherently.

"We understand that a Mrs. Evans runs the boardinghouse here at the Royal Flush mine."

"She used to run it. But I took over everything last week,

including her debts. The girl was getting over a fever, so they pulled out for a lower altitude."

Roxana clutched at the spindly porch pillar.

"But where did they go? The girl is my sister. I'm terribly anxious to find her."

The woman wrinkled her forehead. "Mrs. Evans didn't write it down. I guess they didn't expect any mail."

"But she must have mentioned the name of the town."

"Seems like it was Plainfield, or Plainview, or maybe Broadview."

The three on the porch stared at the woman in shocked incredulity. Roxana was crying now, not covering her tears. They couldn't have come this close, only to lose her again! The woman was regretful; she stood there helplessly wrapping and unwrapping her hands in her soiled apron, trying to dredge up some recollection.

At last they left her, the minister patting Roxana's arm, and Naomi saying stoutly, "We'll try the former postmaster. He still lives in St. Elmo. Probably Mrs. Evans left a forwarding address with him."

But the one-time postmaster, who had given up his job for the more lucrative one of carpenter in this growing town, only shook his head. He kind of remembered a Mrs. Evans, and he thought he could place the girl—a big-eyed pretty little thing that used to come in and ask for mail and then fall back disappointed-like when there wasn't any. But they didn't leave any forwarding address.

He picked up his saw again. He was being paid by the job, and after all, the past was past, with little merit or meaning in this busy new world.

Dejectedly the trio returned to the parsonage.

"You must plan to make your home with us until we get track of Avis, Roxana," offered the preacher gallantly.

Roxana's eyes softened. That was like him—never count the cost, offer first, and trust that the Lord will provide, afterwards. Please, God, give them a boy!

[166]

The little girls were put to bed. The three sat long at the uncleared supper table talking, stirring their coffee with slow figure-eight motions. But their ponderings led nowhere. Quite simply, Henry Starbuck decided to talk it over with the Lord. Down on their knees they all went, Naomi grunting a little. Elbows on their chair seats, the three of them knelt while Henry Starbuck prayed. Damp-eyed and uplifted, Roxana got to her feet. This is what I've been needing, she thought with mild surprise. Why do I always lose it between times? She went to bed comforted, to sleep dreamlessly on a crackling hay mattress in the loft with the little girls.

It was midmorning of the next day, and Roxana was letting down hems—Naomi had no skill with her needle—when a livery buggy stopped out in front. Sudden color dyed Roxana's cheeks. There was no mistaking that groomed and brushed and well-shined person deliberately wrapping the lines about the whip and descending from the buggy. She hurried to open the door.

"Why, Mr. Hull, this is certainly a surprise. How did you ever—?" she stammered. She introduced Grover Hull to Naomi, who came in from the kitchen just then, brushing flour off her cheek and rolling down her sleeves.

He knew how to put Naomi at ease. He spoke of the welcome warm weather and how important it was for the little girls to be out in it all they could before winter closed in again. He regretted that he could not accept her invitation to stay to dinner, but he was in town only briefly on business and he must catch the afternoon train back. He would, however, like to take Miss Roxana for a little ride first, if Mrs. Starbuck had no objections.

Naomi was too startled to know whether she had any or not. She looked inquiringly at Roxana, but Roxana already had her bonnet on.

Grover Hull headed the horse out of town, past the last

straggling cabin. He stopped in a little open meadow to let the horse graze. It was suddenly very quiet here in this high mountain valley, with only the occasional soft thump of the horse's hoof as it stamped and jerked portions of its flesh to redistribute the flies.

She liked Grover Hull's directness. Without any meandering, he told her that the minute he got back to Leadville and learned from Mrs. Harlowe that Roxana had thrown up her job to come over here to find her little sister, he had decided to come, too, and see if he could be of any help.

"I told you once how I felt. All I ask is to be able to do things for you. Have you found her yet?"

It was a relief to talk to him. She held back nothing. When she had finished, she spread out her hands helplessly.

"So here I am, without a job, and with only the smallest clue as to the name of the town where they've gone—and just twenty-two dollars left to my name." She flushed at that last. She had let it slip. A lady never mentioned her financial straits to a gentleman.

"Do you want to find your sister worse than you want to have a stage career?" He waited, very still, for her answer.

Her face grew suddenly pinched. Put baldly like that, did she?

"I—oh, dear, I only know I've got to find Avis first. She's my little sister, and I was to blame for her running away. She's been sick with a fever, and Mrs. Evans is a widow now —and sisters ought to be together."

"If that's how you feel, we'll find her. I'll start things moving at once. I'll write Washington; I have friends there. We'll check on every town in the country with those names." He was very businesslike.

She almost wept with relief. Her tautness slackened. He was so competent, so resourceful. She felt a profound gratitude welling up inside her. No one would have been more surprised than Grover Hull to know that at the moment

Roxana was regarding him through tear-matted eyelashes as the direct and obvious answer to Henry Starbuck's prayer of the night before.

"How can I ever thank you? I didn't suppose anybody in the world cared except maybe Gil Anker and the Starbucks."

"Well, I care for you, Roxana." He turned and gathered her two hands in his large firm ones and searched her face. "At first I thought it was just infatuation. Older men make such fools of themselves. You're so young. But things don't seem to change any for me. Would you be willing to marry me right away?"

She was quite calm for a moment after he had said the words. In a way, she had known they were coming from the moment she opened the door to him at the Starbucks'. And then she was not calm at all. She was startled and frightened and in a not unpleasant turmoil.

Marry him! Marry this kindly older man with the steady eyes and the steady hands and the steady heart. Who had decency and soundness and dependability written all over him. Who would take on all her problems so she need never be worried or troubled again. Who would be gentle and admiring and even—well, *grateful* for whatever she gave him. Who would never harrow her with savage words or throw a cheap little slut in her face.

"I'll be very good to you," Grover Hull said simply, and took her in his arms.

She said no words, neither yes nor no. She just rested there in his arms, trying to think. Everything was a vast confusion. Why, this was the climax of her whole life; everyone said it was. It was what a girl lived for—and she could not seem to take it in at all. She could only smell the livery-stable smell of the laprobe and hear the wind in the pines and feel the comforting, undemanding strength of the arms about her.

"You're so kind. I'll never forget it. I'll try—I'll try to make you a good wife, Mr. Hull."

[169]

Wisely he knew when to shift moods. He smiled at her, tightened his arms briefly, and let her go. He picked up the lines and drove straight back to the Starbucks. With an air of deep respect toward Henry Starbuck, who must have been fifteen years his junior, he asked the Starbucks' approval of his marriage to Roxana.

"There's nothing sudden about my feeling for her," he assured them gravely. "Ever since I saw her last fall, I've felt this way. I know what you're thinking—our ages and all. I've gone over it a hundred times myself. But sometimes there are other considerations: And now that she has left her position and has just got track of her sister again and wants to make a home for her—" He stopped delicately.

The Starbucks saw the point. There were indeed other considerations.

Roxana looked shyly pleased and proud and almost tender. Doubtfully they looked at each other. This was not what they had wanted for Roxana; this was not what they had had themselves. But what was there to say? He was so obviously a man of honor and kindliness and good intent. If only—

All the while that Roxana was dressing for her wedding, with Naomi flushed and helpless and handing her the wrong things, and the three girls peering in through the open door, Roxana was talking feverishly to herself.

She was a very fortunate girl, she assured herself. Hadn't Mrs. Harlowe told her so, over and over? Mr. Hull was a man to be proud of—the Silver Prince. He could have had his pick of any number of rich widows, Mrs. Harlowe said, and instead, he had chosen her, a penniless actress with a sister to find and a home to make for that sister. He would build a lovely house with stone turrets and a porte-cochère and a room in it for Avis. He would set the machinery in motion at once to find Avis, and at last Roxana would be able to make a home for her sister.

She'd give up all thought of the stage and its raffish hangers-on, and *their* hangers-on—she flinched at certain memories—and she would settle down to a lovely, ordered, sensible existence. She only hoped that some day, somewhere, when she was the wife of the Silver Prince and Jay was a tie-walking barnstormer, they would run into each other.

In fifteen minutes she would be Grover Hull's wife.

Roxana was married in her gray marceline. Once, as Henry Starbuck was saying ". . . for richer or for poorer," a horrid picture flashed through her mind of Professor Jay glaring at her on the platform of the depot at Georgetown, legs apart, eyes blazing. She hated him for intruding again. "Sell yourself to a rich old rake" (but Grover was nothing of the kind; he was fine and good and honorable) "on the pretense of making a home for your little sister . . . at least Fifi would be an honest tart!"

Then they were saying good-by to the Starbucks: Naomi questioning, tearful, tender; the minister hopeful, a little blind, looking only for the best in people. They were on the train heading back to Leadville where Grover had wired ahead for rooms.

After all the flurry of the wedding, with the exhilaration inherent to all weddings, it seemed suddenly strange to be sitting beside this man in the varnished railroad car, with the train lurching and complaining its way around the curves.

She could not think of anything to say. She had the eerie feeling of being caught in a gentle downhill landslide. There was nothing menacing about it, nothing dangerous, except that it was carrying her along just a little faster than she could run uphill against it.

The best suite at the Clarendon was waiting for them. Grover Hull was an important person. They had a pleasant corner sitting room and a bedroom dominated by an immense black-walnut bed with a headboard eight feet high, carved with lilies and grapes and various uncatalogued flora.

No matter where she was in the room, Roxana could not shut out the sight of that puffy white island of bed. Standing before the marble-topped bureau clasping on the necklace of aquamarines that Grover had just given her, all she could see was that great white expanse over her shoulder in the glass. Determinedly she focused her attention on the greenish aquamarines. They did just match her eyes, as Grover had told her. She snapped the clasp of the bracelet and held her arm up to admire the delicate sea-water jewels.

Strange, to think it was proper to accept jewelry from him now. Those few words spoken in the Starbucks' parlor made everything proper between her and Grover Hull. Everything! Irresistibly her eyes were drawn back to the white bed. She had a sudden hollow feeling in the pit of her.

She went out to the sitting room to rejoin her husband, who was pacing back and forth along the flowered Brussels carpet. At sight of her, his whole face lighted up incredulously. He started toward her; then he halted and contented himself with ceremoniously crooking his arm for her.

"You look as beautiful, Mrs. Hull, as every bride hopes to look on her wedding day, and seldom does."

At the supper table in the restaurant—her wedding supper table—Roxana found to her relief that there were plenty of things to talk about. For seated at a table across the room from her was pretty Baby Doe of Central City, with her round blue eyes and her Lily Langtry bangs. Curiously Roxana inspected the man with her. Why, he was older than Grover even, and not half so handsome. Both his hair and his mustache straggled. He was bending across the table searching his companion's face, while she returned his gaze with equal fervor.

Roxana stared openly. She must be in love with the man! she thought with faint resentment. Baby Doe laughed aloud just then, and the pompous dining room was the gayer for it.

Roxana was envious of the happiness in the laughter; it seemed to her she was always envying Baby Doe.

"That's Mrs. Doe, Grover," she whispered. "They call her Baby Doe. She used to ride horseback in Central. I knew her over there."

Grover turned slightly to follow her glance.

"Oh, her. Hmm, well, you may have known her once, my dear, but you don't any longer." He smiled at Roxana.

"You mean because—? But Mrs. Harlowe says he'll undoubtedly marry her when he's free."

He shrugged.

"That remains to be seen. In the meantime—"

She nodded docilely. She felt evened-up in the balance of life. She was smugly aware of the "Mrs." in front of her name, and that this was her husband opposite her. And then the hollow frightened feeling rushed back. For "Mrs." in front of your name meant more than a smug safeness. It meant that you were really and truly married; and marriage wasn't all wearing aquamarine necklaces and sitting opposite a man at a wedding-supper table. There was always that room, and in it a vast puffy white island—waiting.

She began to talk, as if she were running away from something. Her color was much too high to be the result of the one small glass of champagne Grover allowed her. She talked about the theater company, and the towns they had played in, and about Central City, and her parents, and her sister Avis. She talked about Georgetown, and Mrs. Harlowe and the night the latter called to Roxana to come look through the peephole in the curtain at Mr. Grover Hull.

"Mrs. Harlowe said you were handsome and well-fixed and could have your choice of any number of rich widows, but that she had been saving me for you."

She began to slow down. What, exactly, had she been saying? Lackaday, how that bubbly little drink did unlatch the tongue! Grover Hull was listening, a little smile twitching his mustache.

She came to a dead stop at last. No matter how fast she ran, she could not run quite fast enough.

It was almost daybreak when her husband's even breathing told her he was asleep. She had never been more wide awake. Cautiously, so as not to disturb him, she reached out and lifted one corner of the heavy window drapery to look out. The sun was just tipping the high peaks with color. She lay there watching the shell-pink light sink slowly, slowly down the craggy sides to the valley below. She drew a long breath. She had felt so closed in here in this room with the heavy draperies and the heavy bedding and the heavy breathing beside her.

Chapter XV

N ow that bustles were getting larger—her dressmaker mincingly referred to them as "tournures"—Roxana found a bed almost more comfortable to sit on than a chair. She perched carefully on the edge of their bed in the new Windsor Hotel in Denver, so as not to muss her green-and-blue plaid visiting dress, and listlessly turned the pages of a thumbed copy of *Theater News.*

With one ear she listened for her husband's footsteps in the elegantly carpeted corridor outside. The minute she heard his key in the lock she would chuck the paper under the bed. She had learned soon after their marriage six months before that stage talk made him uneasy, that he did not like to take her to the theater, and that on those rare occasions when he did, it was better not to comment either technically or wistfully upon the acting.

"Thank God, that makeshift life is over for you, my dear," Grover would say. "A hand-to-mouth existence with a bunch of helter-skelter barnstormers."

She could not very well explain that the hand-to-mouth existence had been stimulating, and the helter-skelter barnstormers friendly and gay. Her present life had a vaguely unsalted flavor. As old Monty used to say, "We show people aren't cut out for a safe, sane, orderly way of living, or we'd never have become actors in the first place. We've got to have the forced draft of the stage, the self-made fevers. We'd wither and die in a neat regular life."

She was not exactly withering or dying. She was probably as happy as most, she told herself staunchly. Nowadays she could look at the towering black-walnut bed with neither fears nor anticipations. Instead, she thought in a superior way, novels and silly whispering girls and sly older women had greatly exaggerated the importance of—well, the secret side of marriage. What a "to-do" they made over it!

Love was really a very minor part of life, she decided. She recalled Mrs. Harlowe's acrid comment; and it was Mrs. Harlowe who quoted Shakespeare this time: "Men have died—and worms have eaten them, but not for love." As always, Monty contradicted her. But Mrs. Harlowe and Shakespeare were right. She felt very grown-up, knowing all about life and love. For she had found out for herself how much of the talk about it was only airy embroidery.

Sometimes she had the feeling that she was living in a suspended state. She did not know exactly what she was waiting for. To find Avis?

It was not Grover's fault that they had not found Avis. He had done everything in his power. She eyed the center table with its pile of letters. He had used all his Washington connections. He had written to every Plainfield and Plainview and Broadview in the whole United States. Roxana had been for setting off in person to each town, but Grover had persuaded her not to. What if, while she was gone, the real clue should pop up?

So she had stayed here at the Windsor and collected this stack of letters. "Sorry to report we have no record of such a person or persons" . . . "You might try Broadplains in the eastern part of the state" . . . "About two years ago a family by that name resided in this city, a man and wife and several children, but their present whereabouts is unknown."

She had even written to the Evanses' home town, Kaw Center. The postmaster there had answered promptly. "A

Nathaniel Evans and wife used to live here, but they left for the West several years ago. Last address was Central City, Colorado. You might try there." She had come around full circle.

At times she suspected that Grover was good and sick of the whole business and was secretly relieved that the search had come to nothing. But he was an honorable man who had given his word. He had all but neglected his business to hunt for Avis.

Being married for six months to a successful business man had taught her many things about wealth. Chiefly, that it was no granite rock on which to build your life, at least not Grover Hull's kind of wealth. It was as erratic and delicate as a young turkey poult and had to be tended quite as carefully. He was always making trips to various parts of the state to keep an eye on certain mining properties. His fortune seemed a touchy, temperamental thing of shares and short-term loans and London Syndicates and Eastern Capital.

When he was in the city he spent most of his time at the Mining Exchange, a narrow little store on the ground floor of the Windsor. Sometimes as she walked past on the sidewalk, she would glance in. But it was only a surreptitious side-glance, for the place was as exclusively masculine as a barber shop. All she could make out were crowds of men milling around in the cigar smoke, hats on the backs of their heads, arms waving in gesticulation. There was a blackboard up in front, with a man standing on a chair before it making notations. It was an awesome place, where money changed hands fast, and fortunes were made or lost on things called "weaknesses" and "rallies."

It was when Chrysolite stock went to six eighty-five, she remembered, that Grover had come hurrying up to their room to grab her by the elbows and lift her clear off the floor. "It means a fur jacket for you, my girl," he had crowed; and he rushed straight out to buy her the lovely copper-brown mink jacket. And then again, when Bull

Domingo "slid" to a quarter (she wondered how anything so cheap could cause so much havoc), he had gone around for days looking sleepless and haggard. When she begged him to let her return the mink jacket to the store, he only smiled ruefully and shook his head.

She stood up now and straightened the shirred plastron over her bosom before the diamond-dust mirror that reared to the ceiling. Gliding back and forth, she admired her intricate draperies. If Jay could only see her now! Rich, adored, sheltered—while he, no doubt, was still junketing around with that—that— She wrenched her thoughts away and returned to a determined contemplation—a complacent contemplation—of her new frock.

She was wearing a half-hoop or "tilter," with tapes underneath to hold the front fullness back. She smoothed the crosswise folds over her stomach, which were archly referred to in the fashion pictures as "an effect *à la lavandiere.*" She would laugh and say to Grover, "Isn't that funny? I'll bet the designer never pinned her skirts back to do a washing in her life." Grover would smile as he always did over her conceits and would satisfactorily admire the visiting dress.

Not of course that she had many places to visit. She had had exactly four callers. Well-dressed ladies they were, wives of Grover's business acquaintances and twice her age, who lived in fashionable houses on Champa or away out in the new section on Lincoln and Sherman. They acted a little standoffish at first; after all, they had come only because their husbands had insisted. They had never even seen the first Mrs. Hull, and had scarcely been introduced to Mr. Hull.

But presently they were telling her where to buy her boots and about the nicest little hairdresser who would come right to her room to wash her hair, and they were calling her "My Dear Child." Later, when she had correctly returned their calls in a rented barouche, things had come to a sort of standstill. Until she and Grover had a home of their own (that home she was planning to make for Avis), she could scarcely hope to stick more than the pointed toe of her little French boot inside the door called Society.

For a brief time after their arrival at the Windsor, she had thought of resuming an old acquaintanceship. Pretty Mrs. Doe had a suite here also. Roxana had contemplated calling on her. Not that she approved of her. My, no. For even if Mr. Tabor did succeed in divorcing his wife and marrying her, they would still be divorced people, and a divorce was almost as bad as living in sin. To the end of her days, Baby Doe would be "that woman" to respectable people. But Roxana wanted to see Baby Doe again because there was something she needed to know; she thought she could find it out from the expression in Baby Doe's eyes. She wanted to know if she herself was missing something.

But Grover had been stern. She was not even to recognize Mrs. Doe if she met her in the halls. "No man that will throw over a faithful wife who's slaved at his side all these years for a little chit—"

Fortunately Baby Doe moved to another hotel. "To stop gossip," Grover said with a brusque laugh, adding, "about a year too late!"

As if to make up for her not having a house, Grover never tired of shopping for surprises for her: clothes and jewels and hats. That only left less for Roxana to do. She could always retrim the hats, of course, which she did; they were far prettier afterwards, she admitted. But when that was done, what else could she find to do? They even made the bed for you here and dusted daily. Grover had told her that the hotel had 140 employees in all—140 people, just so she would not have anything to do.

She could always rearrange the various objects she had interspersed among the hotel furniture, her sandalwood fan, her Japanese screen, and her mottled glass. She could polish the silver card tray again (with the four cards on it) and touch up the bright spindly faucets in the bathroom.

Would she ever get used to the glories of that bathroom?

Up one step, and there you were, all private and luxurious, with the gray-marble washbowl, and the tub sitting up high and white on its four legs, and the water closet with its swinging chain and magic swish and roar. How her cleanly mother, who had never seen a bathroom in her life, would have loved it.

But they even came in and scoured the bathroom every day. So when she had twitched a picture here and straightened an antimacassar there and moved the card tray a quarter of an inch, what then? Of course she could read. She had read all of Shakespeare through twice and got as far as the Psalms in the Bible (the stories were better nearer the front). But she did love the Psalms. She read them over and over. They must have been written especially for her—so full of longing, so full of regrets, so seeking.

And she devoured the theatrical sheet when she was sure Grover was nowhere around. For she realized with a certain sympathy that he was jealous of the stage in the same way that he was jealous of her youngness. He would shy away from mention of either like a horse from a wind-tossed newspaper. She tried to humor him. After all, he had been good to her. Never hurrying her, gently leading her into marriage, patiently putting up with her hesitations and whims and tears. She had heard dreadful stories of other brides, until she knew how lucky she had been. Oh, she did so want to be a good wife to Grover. He had satisfied her every wish, that is, except to find Avis—and he couldn't help that—and her longing for the theater. She had stopped hoping to see a real stage play again. Music, he seemed to feel was safe for her to hear, but plays were dangerous.

So when he had brought home tickets for the opera, on the opening night of the fabulous new Grand Opera House built by Mr. Tabor, he dropped them in her lap as benevolently as if they were a pair of bracelets.

She had picked them up incredulously. "Not the opera!" she shrieked. "Oh, Grover, you're taking me to the opera!"

It was *Maritana*, sung by the Emma Abbott English Opera Company. Miss Abbott, who proved to have a husband, had stayed right here at the Windsor. Tiptoeing with enraptured curiosity along the halls, Roxana had stopped outside Parlor C to hear the famous voice run up and down scales.

She thought back to that evening, dressing for her first opera, and how she could scarcely comb her hair or pull the new ice-blue *peau de cynge* over her head. When she had settled the rich silk about her hips, she turned to Grover to have him lace the dress up the back. That proved almost disastrous, for he had to keep stopping to kiss her bare perfumed shoulders, until he was quite beside himself, and she began to fear they would never reach the opera at all. But she reminded him of their expensive tickets and the hack already ordered, and at last he let her go.

As they started out of their room together, he made her stop just to look at her, flowers cascading down the side of her hair, great hillocks of ice-blue billowing out from her waist, and long tight gloves with rich bracelets clanking. She might have been a picture he had painted himself, he was so pleased.

While they settled themselves in their opera chairs and unfolded their ornate programs, Roxana had looked about her eagerly. At the glitter of silk, and the glow of red velvet, and the gleam of cherry wood that was as rich and dark as Grover's glass of port. The finest opera house in the country, the papers boasted.

The painted stage curtain captured her attention. How romantic it was, with its ruined pillars and trailing vines and the poignant little verse below.

She read it over softly in Mrs. DeForest's throaty accents.

> So fleet the works of men;
> Back to earth again.
> Ancient and holy things
> Fade like a dream.

[181]

"Fade like a dream." Strange words to find on the curtain of this rich and massive theater that had been built to last a century.

The lights began to dim. She was quiveringly sensing that moment when the theater slowly darkens, when the chatter of voices quiets down with a few warning hushes, when *the curtain is about to go up.*

Miss Abbott herself was a legend come to life. Graciously she came out alone from the wings and announced that she would sing the mad scene from *Lucia* as an opening gift to the audience. What a beauty; what a lady, thought Roxana reverently. She preferred not to think of how one of the newspapers had snickered over the diva's excessive refinement, accusing her of removing the last taint of love from *La Traviata* and of singing "Nearer My God to Thee" in the third act of Faust.

Miss Abbott retired amidst applause. Roxana could hear sounds of scene-shifting. Perhaps now the opera would begin. But no, the millionaire benefactor came out next. With embarrassed pomp Mr. Tabor accepted a Token of Esteem, a giant watch fob composed of solid-gold mine ladders, ore buckets, and replicas of his first store and even of the opera house itself.

"It'll hit him on the knees when he walks," derided Grover in a whisper.

At last, the opera! Grover might think that music was safe, but he had forgotten that opera was acting, too. When it was over, he had to nudge her and pull her mantle up around her shoulders and even assist her to her feet before he could bring her back to the present.

As they made their way out in the sluggish current of people, she was glad she need not talk. She was still living in that other world of canvas and tinsel and paint and make-believe that was so much realer than this one.

They stepped outside to find that it was sprinkling and the street clogged with vehicles.

"Let's walk, Grover. You'll never get a hack in this bed-lam. It's only a little way."

He made a few attempts to call the number of his cab-man and gave it up. They walked back to the hotel through the September drizzle that was as cool and damp as a dog's nose. Roxana was grateful, after all that heat and exhaustion inside. She was staring rapturously straight ahead.

Grover eyed her quizzically, the star-lit look, the mist that made chip diamonds in her hair. Once or twice he tried to talk to her, but she was far away and lost. It was weeks before he dropped another pair of tickets in her lap, and they were for a concert that was about as exciting as a church anthem.

"How would you like a house like that?" he had asked one day as they rolled along in a shiny hired carriage. He pointed with his whip to one of the handsome new houses lining the street. It was a gold-and-blue Colorado day. The arching cottonwoods that had sifted white fluff down all summer were now shedding their brittle yellow leaves into the irri-gation ditches that ran along the sides of the street.

"It would be lovely, Grover. Avis could play croquet in the side yard."

"We'll start drawing plans as soon as this deal over in the Valley of the Blue goes through."

The Valley of the Blue had come to have a legendary meaning for her, a sound of an other-land, an up-in-the-sky sort of place. Actually it referred only to a mine that he hoped to develop, somewhere above the Blue River, across the range. But he said it the way some men say, "When my ship comes in."

"We'll build a nice brick house on Lincoln," he would say, "and you can have days to receive. Living in a hotel puts a woman at a disadvantage. But right now I find the Windsor useful; with the bartender a good friend of mine, nothing

[183]

escapes me, see?" She did not see, but she had nodded brightly.

Ho hum, she thought wearily now, as she tucked her *Theater News* out of sight and went over to look out the window. What a long day. She glanced down at prosperous Larimer Street below, where street lamps were bursting into bloom on tall black stalks.

A key grated, and her husband walked in, his eyes widening in admiration of the new dress.

"It's a visiting dress," she vouchsafed wistfully.

"Let's take it visiting then, or at least for a little walk before supper. I realize you're indoors too much, my dear."

She was like a puppy offered an airing. She had not realized how cooped up she felt. She whirled toward the tall wardrobe and reached for her tilted pancake hat and her new mink jacket. The jacket was deftly fitted in at the waist, making her look like a graceful decanter; small and curved above, bell-shaped and flaring below. Its copper-brown turned her eyes the blue of turquoises.

He smiled at her dainty flurry. This moon-lit creature. A white-violet of a girl on the outside, but with steel underneath. It was a constant surprise to him to find so much gallantry and courage and generosity behind that flower-like exterior.

His feeling of a miracle had grown rather than diminished with the months. At first he was ashamed of the passion of tenderness he felt for her, the yearning to shower her with treasures, the longing to protect her forever. People laughed about older men and young girls; they couldn't possibly understand how much of one's feeling was unselfish and how little of it was carnal. Finally he had dared let himself be happy, since Roxana had convinced him that she was happy, too. But he still had nightmares from which he awoke in the black self-searching hours. What if she were not quite so happy as she seemed? What if—?

He drew her hand into the crook of his arm. Youth was unable to appreciate itself. It took an older man. Roxana had a funny little-girl way of deprecating her charms. If anything ever happened to her—!

She almost skipped as they went down in the cautious boxy elevator and out through the marble-floored lobby. Under the massive porte-cochère Grover debated which way to go. He turned toward the station. There were so many shops that way, and Roxana liked to look in the windows.

On the corner beyond was a pitchman with his layout before him. Grover quickened his pace, pulling her along with him. He always enjoyed a pitchman's spiel. He wondered what this chap was selling.

Early dark had already descended. The chill brought a tingle to Roxana's cheeks. She noted the street vendor ahead, the gasoline flare hissing beside him. Before him was an opened suitcase on a tripod, with a velvet lambrequin about it trimmed with tarnished gilt. She smiled to herself. Grover could never resist somebody selling something. He seldom bought. He merely had a professional interest in the other man's business methods.

The fellow was just finishing a banjo selection—"Long Tail Blue." The twangy plangent sound on the chill night air drew a crowd. Roxana could hear the first drifting inflections of his voice. He was going into his patter. The voice did not drone; it had a crackling electric sound that made you want to hear more.

They reached the outskirts of the crowd. She craned to see over the heads. She could hear the hissing sputter of the gasoline torch and the incisive voice going on and on.

". . . and now, my friends, I have brought you a little piece of magic straight from the Orient. In the olden days alchemists toiled their lives away in dark cellars trying to find out how to change baser metals into gold. I shall show you the even more difficult trick of transmuting one material into another. The Great Alzigone could do it. But few others in

[185]

this country have ever accomplished it. Step closer, please."

Instinctively Roxana stepped closer. Magic! She was child enough to respond.

"Here in my fingers you will note a fine crimson silk handkerchief. A gift to me from Zuleika, favorite of the Shah of Persia. It was spun from cocoons grown in the royal courts of Tokyo and woven especially for an Emperor's pleasure." He waved the handkerchief in the air, a scarlet flag for all to see.

She stood on tiptoe. The hissing flare of the gasoline torch lighted up one side of the speaker's tomahawk-lean face. Her fingers dug convulsively into Grover's arm. Why had she not recognized that irritating, provoking, yet oddly tantalizing voice? Professor Jay!

Instinctively she jerked back. But Grover did not notice. She must get out of here, she thought. All these months she had been hoping to meet Jay, hoping to find him seedy and run-down and shabby, so she could flaunt her good fortune in his face. And now that she had her wish—for there was nothing so seedy and run-down and shabby as a corner pitchman—she felt no triumph whatever. She did not want to flaunt her good fortune, or Grover's devotion, or her fine clothes. She did not want to meet his eyes at all. She simply wanted to get away before something happened.

Against her will, she was caught by Professor Jay's words.

"My sleeves are rolled up—everything is right out in the open. Here, mister, touch the handkerchief for yourself. Smooth and soft as your sweetheart's cheek, isn't it? Notice carefully—no pulls, no draws. Now watch"—as if they weren't —scarcely breathing—"I hold absolutely nothing in my hands but this silken handkerchief." He held the crimson square delicately by the corners with the thumb and forefinger of each hand. He was facing away from Roxana now; his face looked darkly chiseled there, in profile.

"You are now about to witness an example of purest magic —the miracle of transmutation. I hereby call upon all the powers of the black arts—" His voice had dropped to mysterious depths. The crowd was hushed.

"Hocus pocus—ginger locus—presto changibus."

She ought to laugh. But there was something oddly compelling about his tone and those crazy words and the way he waved the silk square up and down, up and down, cupping his two hands around it while he worked it into a wad between his palms.

"Hocus pocus—ginger locus—magic change take place!"

Now his voice was urgent, calling upon some esoteric force. He seemed to be exerting all his strength and will as the handkerchief grew smaller and smaller until it finally disappeared between his tight-pressed palms.

"I shall now invoke *both* magic and muscular strength." He ground his hands together; sweat glinted on his forehead; he grunted with the effort. Then he extended his tightly pressed hands toward the audience.

"We shall see whether I have been successful. Remember that every eye has been fastened on me every second. I have used no stage properties; I have touched nothing. I shall now unclasp my hands containing the wadded-up silk handkerchief, and we shall see whether or not the magic has worked."

Silence, craning silence.

Slowly, as if the hands did not belong to him at all, the lean brown fingers uncurled before them.

"What have we here, ladies and gentlemen? Our silk handkerchief completely transformed into a shining red billiard ball!"

He picked up the ball with the fingers of his right hand. There was a gasp. The handkerchief was gone. The light shone on the red ball. He tapped it on the wooden suitcase top, where it resounded sharply. Before any heckler in the audience could say, "Let's have a look at that ball," he went smoothly into his next routine.

"I hope you enjoyed the demonstration of magic, ladies

and gentlemen. And now, for your edification, I shall perform another little feat. This one is neither trick nor magic. It requires none of the black arts. It merely demonstrates to you a remarkable piece of craftsmanship. I have here, as you see, a pair of scissors, made from finest Damascus steel at the famed cutlery works of Sheffield, England. They will cut anything short of a railroad tie and will halve a human hair. Best of all, they will cut metal. Think of that! Precision scissors that will cut metal. Watch me while I take an ordinary paper of household pins." He unwrapped a paper of new pins. "I shall now proceed to cut the heads off of an entire row of pins at one cutting."

With a crunching of metal he snipped off a row of pin heads; they fell on the table top with the sound of rain. He snipped off another row, and again came the light metallic clatter.

"Think you could buy such scissors at any emporium in your fine city? You can not. And if you sent to England for them, you would pay anywhere from five to fifteen dollars for them. Plus duty! I alone have the distribution of these extraordinary scissors in America." He waved the glittering blades in the light.

"So, ladies and gentlemen, to introduce these marvelous scissors, I am going to let them go for the astounding price of one dollar and fifty cents. I'm not joking. One-fifty is what I said. Your wife can throw away her old scissors or give them to the junk man."

He looked around benignly.

"If you're in bad at home, now's your chance, gentlemen, to get in right again with the little lady. Been holding some losing poker hands lately? Been imbibing too freely? Fallen from the wife's good graces and want to climb back up again? Then take home a pair of these amazing scissors for her sewing basket, and all will be sunny as a baby's smile."

He seemed to debate some further largesse. Then he

[188]

shrugged ruefully as if his benevolence had got the better of him.

"I'm even going to offer a bonus to the first fifty purchasers. A combination offer of several handsome presents. A package of golden-eyed needles—solid gold eyes they are—made in Redditch, England. And a spool of best-grade white thread and one of black. With the scissors. And I'm going to offer this ree-markable combination, not for one-fifty, but for a single lone dollar. One measly silver cartwheel. You can see I'm no business man. I'm a missionary at heart, a crusader, a lover of my fellow man. *Man,* I said; I leave the ladies for you gentlemen to win over with my astounding combination offer. It goes to the first fifty who plank down their dollars."

What had got into Grover? He was dragging Roxana forward, all the while that Roxana was pulling back. He was slapping a five-dollar bill down on the opened suitcase with a lordly gesture that disdained the change.

She tried to hold her head down and melt into the shadows behind Grover. But his grip on her arm was tight and possessive. As if sensing an alien presence, Professor Jay turned his hawk face toward her and sought her out in the shadows. His fiery carnelian eyes flashed in recognition. She felt the flash go through her, disturbing, a turbulence in her very depths.

His pitchman's spiel faltered. He almost lost the rapid pace of his words. He glanced down at the bill before he picked it up gingerly. He seemed to debate whether to toss it back in Grover's face. Then one corner of his mouth furrowed in grimly.

"Thank you, sir. See the five dollars the gentleman has thrust upon me?" He held up the bill for all to see. "Five dollars because he feels he can not accept so prodigal an offer for only one dollar. I'm sure his little lady will live to bless his generosity. Step up, the rest of you. My offer still holds

—the gift offer of a lifetime. Only a dollar, to the first fifty
—or forty-nine it is now—who step this way."

The crowd stepped that way. Grover had started the rush.
He smiled genially at Roxana as he presented her with the
special gift of a lifetime.

"That fellow's a jim-dandy. I couldn't help it. Never
heard a better patter."

Professor Jay's voice went on, like a sparking electric wire.

"The offer is open to you ladies, too. Only one silver dollar, ladies. With these scissors and needles and thread, you
can be dressed to the nines. If you're still single—a lovely un-
plucked peach—you can easily deck yourself out to capture a
rich nabob. It has been done, ladies." His voice dropped to
a conspiratorial undertone. "Why, I know a pretty little
doxy not far from where I'm standing that set out deliberately to trap a rich mogul. If she could do it, you can. All
you have to do is set your cap—first using these beautiful
gold-eyed needles to sew the cap—and in no time at all—"

His eyes, malevolent, ruthless, roamed the crowd, coming
to rest on Roxana's shocked face. His voice had a vicious
lash to it. Roxana was terrified. What was this insane man
saying? Was Grover taking it in? She must get away from
here. She tugged at her husband's sleeve, but he was still
blandly enjoying the evening's chance diversion.

"You know the old saying, ladies, every rich man owes his
fortune to his first wife—and his second wife to his fortune.
Yessiree, I've seen it happen. You'd like a rich husband
yourself? Well, gather closer and I'll tell you how to tree
your game. Less than a dozen feet from where I stand . . ."

The blood was roaring in her ears. She knew the dreadful
things this mad-brained creature was capable of. She must
get Grover away before this fellow wrecked all that she had
worked so hard to achieve in her marriage. The hard-earned
peace, the friendly trust. For Grover, in spite of his corrod-
ing jealousies, was a happy man. But he would not be much

longer, if this cruel mountebank went on. And she must keep Grover happy; it was the least she owed him.

"Grover, I'm chilly. This silk dress and short jacket—the cold goes right through me."

It was like Grover to put aside his pleasures instantly for her frailties. He forgot all about the pitchman as he reached out and turned the collar of her mink jacket up about her neck until it made a soft fur frame for her distraught face. For a minute he held her like that, eyes on a level with hers, devouring her, loving her. She was a prisoner in his uxorious grasp. She could well imagine the pretty domestic picture they made. She flushed and drew back. To think that all these months she had longed to prove to Jay how greatly her husband cared for her. Yet now that she had, all she asked was to get away from that bitter, knowledgeable scrutiny. Would Jay always have the upper hand?

Then, thank God, Grover released her and took her arm preparatory to leaving. But the voice of the pitchman only grew louder. It sought them out and followed them through the crowd.

"Nothing a lady can't do if she sets her mind on it, I say, folks. You've all heard the old saw that you can't get a silk purse out of a sow's ear? But I assure you ladies that a smart young woman can easily get a fur jacket out of an old goat."

The crowd laughed. Roxana was shaking. She must have caught a chill, Grover said contritely. He ought to have taken her back sooner, but that fellow certainly did have a patter, didn't he? Wonder how he did that billiard ball trick; he'd watched it carefully, but he couldn't figure it out. Shrewd, some of these street-hawkers, in a foxy sort of way. It was odd that with all their surface cleverness, they spent their lives in a cheap game like this and finally had to be buried by the county.

She made no reply. She tried not to look back. She would not look back. But she did.

The scissors must have gone in a hurry; already the crowd

was dispersing. Somewhere in it, she was sure, Fifi was waiting. She would join him any minute. Roxana saw the Professor close his suitcase with a practiced sweep and turn to dismantle his gasoline flare. She kept looking back over her shoulder, but it was Grover who was in a hurry now. Solicitously he pulled her along toward the hotel. If she could only find out for sure.

Later that evening, while Roxana and her husband were undressing, Grover turned around from the bureau where he was going through his nightly ritual of brushing his thinning hair. His suspenders dangled; his starched white shirt cuffs, with their heavy links unfastened, were turned back from his strong hairy wrists. He glanced at her curiously because of her long silence. Then he let out a roar of delighted laughter.

"Bless you, you weren't taken in by all that stuff, were you? Didn't you know he either had a pair of good scissors that he palmed, or else he used a special kind of soft-headed pins?"

Roxana was savagely sawing away with the new scissors at a paper of pins, without so much as denting them.

"So you really believed him? A cheap grifter like that? Oh, my dear child!" He laughed again, fondly and indulgently.

Her cheeks blazing, Roxana hurled scissors and pins into the wastebasket. She ought to have known. Of course he was only a cheap grifter. She would know better than to believe him again—ever.

Roxana lay in the big bed beside Grover, as wide awake as a teething baby. She must not flounce or turn. Grover needed his sleep. As if burned on her retina, she carried to bed with her the picture of Jay, insouciantly shutting up shop for the night, smiling into the crowd—no doubt at Fifi —and never once bothering to glance after her, Roxana.

She could picture the two of them setting off to a room

somewhere together. She knew it all—stained wallpaper, cracked washbowl, sagging bedsprings.

Lying beside Grover in the luxury of her own soft white bed, she stared burningly into the dark that was only half-dark because of the reflected glow up from Larimer Street. It gleamed on the pale marble fireplace columns, glinted on the brass chandelier, and glanced off the cut-glass bottles on her bureau.

Jay and that . . . that creature, brazenly climbing the creaking stairs of some cheap boardinghouse, brazenly entering their awful room, brazenly locking the door and turning to each other. That terrible man—rude, demanding—pulling the girl Fifi toward him in the dark. . . . She would not let herself think about them. And she could not stop thinking about them.

She lay there rigid in her bed, her hands doubled into hard knots, her legs stretched out straight and taut, her teeth clenched until they ached. And then she began to tremble uncontrollably. She had to cram her knuckles against her mouth and bite down hard. It was either that—or shriek aloud, or laugh wildly. Or weep.

Chapter XVI

THE NEXT YEAR the Grover Hulls moved from the Windsor to the American House. Roxana insisted on it, after Grover took to sitting up nights working on columns of figures.

"It's only temporary," he assured her. "It's only temporary," she assured him. Besides, the American House was really very nice.

"By next year we'll have a house of our own," he said, adding, "and then we can make a home for Avis."

Grover's fortune, the queasy temperamental fortune of the mining speculator, was ailing these days. He tried to explain what was wrong with it to Roxana. It was queer, she thought, how she had always been a quick study, yet she could not understand how you lost money—or made it.

The mining industry, he said, was having a shaking down. The first easy gold in the placer bars and rich pockets had been exhausted twenty years before. After that, it required expensive processes to extract the stubborn deep-buried gold.

"Is that what they mean by 'refractory gold'?" she asked brightly, and he smiled at her as at a precocious child.

Then along came silver, and now even the silver boom was subsiding, since the shafts had gone so deep and the seep water had come in. Big capital decided the issues today. Luck played a smaller and smaller part. There were no more bonanzas.

"Like when the fellow looked down into his gold pan and yelled, 'I've got all of California in my pan!' so they called it California Gulch?" she asked.

He nodded. "And like the other young fellow who panned some dust and hollered, 'Eureka, I have found it!' and so named Eureka Gulch and Eureka Street."

But moving to the American House did not help enough, for Grover continued to sit up nights worrying over columns of figures. Roxana wondered what else she could do. As season melted into season, she had to sit by and watch him lose weight, and with it a certain padded affluent look. He looked a little seedy instead, even though he was twice as careful to brush his fine hat and have his shoes shined daily. All the external glossing and brushing was not enough. He was down-at-the-heel in spirit.

He told her in their second year at the American House how he had been caught short. He had made commitments, he said, because he had reason to believe a certain eastern syndicate would back him. Then it had changed its mind. He handed her the letter. She had seen it in his hands many times as he read and reread it, smoothing the creases in the letter paper and deepening the creases in his forehead.

There it was, terse and dignified, as if it were not wiping out a man's fortune and with it his faith and his hope. It was signed, The Vanguard Mining Properties, Incorporated. She would gladly have fought the whole Vanguard Mining Properties, Incorporated, with her bare hands, if it would have helped Grover any.

She suggested that they rent a little house where she could take boarders. If she had offered to sell herself on the slave block, Grover could not have been more shocked. Roughen her pretty hands with dishwater? Bend her slim back over oven and tub?

So when, that third winter, she found a refined boarding-house on Twenty-Third, he let himself be persuaded into moving again.

[195]

"Only till I develop that property on the Blue," he assured her stoutly, as they moved into a second-floor room at Mrs. Pfaab's, with its select clientele.

Mrs. Pfaab was insistent about the selectness and refinement of her establishment. There is no one so snobbish as an ex-ladies' maid and hairdresser. Her manner toward her guests was subtly graded by the price of the rooms they occupied. Yet she had learned to be careful, too. Men's fortunes took such quick turns for better or worse out in this country. Take this nice Mr. Hull and his young wife—only a short time ago his name was in all the papers as a big mining operator. Probably tomorrow his luck would change, and he'd be in the money again. Mrs. Pfaab was guardedly cordial to the Grover Hulls, in their second-floor room that looked out on the alley.

Roxana watched Grover with concern these days. Adversity did such different things to people, she noted. Some grew quiet; others ran over with words. Grover, who had always been a man of deliberate speech because someone was always hanging respectfully on his words, now grew slower and more tentative than ever. He chose each word as if he were selecting it with tongs. He would look at her appealingly as if to say, "You haven't lost faith in me, have you? Because my money is gone? It wasn't just my money, was it, Roxana?"

And Roxana would throw her arms about him with an ardor she had never shown in his prosperous days.

Prosperity was a queer thing, too, she decided. It lent one a false importance. A man who had been born rich and stayed rich never had to know either doubts or humility. He could go to his ornate mausoleum thinking he was made of superior bone and flesh simply because he had inherited wealth or had made it by a chance coup. He probably never put the feeling into words, even to himself; he merely acted upon it. He felt set apart, of greater consequence. Strip him of his wealth, and something happened to his inner assurance.

Grover's inner assurance was gone. He was no longer certain that anything he had to say was worth hearing. When you lost your money, she thought sadly, people no longer listened to you as if you were Moses returned from Mt. Sinai. You actually had to have the graven tablets of the Ten Commandments under your arm if you hoped to convince anyone that you had been there.

For herself, she did not mind being poorer, except for not having a home for Avis. She found the select boardinghouse cozy. The ladies had little to do but ply their needles and their tongues. As soon as they discovered Roxana's skill with her needle, they flatteringly brought her a dowdy hat or a puckery basque to ask advice about. It always ended with Roxana's happily making over the offending article closer to its owner's heart's desire.

The first time anyone offered her money for her work, she flushed and refused. The second time she took it. She needed a new chemise and she hated to ask Grover for money when he always explained so miserably that he didn't happen to have that much cash on him at the moment.

She sometimes thought with self-reproach that he would have been happier married to another sort of woman, one nearer his own age—plump and comfortable and a little scuffed by life. But nothing could change the Roxana who must make an extra detour every time she went downtown, in order to circle the Tabor Grand Opera House. Nothing could keep her from preening a little when she went past a reflecting shop window, or from walking like the piquant Lady Teazle, or wearing her bonnet like the lovely Laura Courtland, or holding her head like the fair Pauline.

The day that she had been married four years was a little frightening. Perhaps because she had just had a letter from Naomi Starbuck, whose husband now had a circuit out of Crested Butte, to Gothic and Irwin and Ruby. The letter told Roxana that Gil Anker had succumbed to pneumonia.

Roxana wept a little. Life would be poorer without Gil.

He had been a link with the past—with her father and her mother and Avis. Gil was someone you could hold on to.

The day was frightening because she realized that Avis was now eighteen and would soon be beyond needing a sister to make a home for her. Perhaps, too, Roxana realized that life itself was flowing swiftly past—with her in this scummed little backwash, where no current freshened the waters and no storms lashed them. She was twenty-three years old, a settled matron, and she had nothing to show for it. If she could only have had children! She had taken bottles and bottles of elixirs. She had talked to the midwife. She had eaten lots of dandelion greens and cove oysters. And nothing happened.

Grover did not seem to mind.

"It would be better to wait till we have a home of our own, dear. You're all the baby I want now," he would mutter against her hair. And he meant it.

Then the plague struck. Ever so many people in the city had it. Typhoid fever, they called it. It must have been some miasma in the air; for they ate good home-cooked food at Mrs. Pfaab's and drank sparkling piped-in water and milk delivered daily by a nice old man who poured it foaming out of a crooked-spouted can into a crock.

First Roxana had the fever, and then Grover had it. The doctors were too busy to give much attention to any single case. People were dying here and there. Roxana recovered first, after an eternity of weakness and misery. But she looked forty, and her hair fell out, and she was as wasted as a winter-gaunted heifer.

Grover on the other hand did not seem to recover.

"Keep him in bed on liquids, gruels and such, and sponge him off often," the tired doctor suggested.

Grover snorted weakly when he had gone.

"A man never would get on his feet if he paid any attention to these calomel peddlers. I've got to get up if I'm ever going to gain my strength back." He crawled determinedly out of bed, and fell in a dead faint in the middle of the carpet. It took both Mrs. Pfaab and Roxana to lift him back into bed.

After that, Grover just lay there, staring at the water stain on the ceiling. It was about this time that he got word that a certain vein in a certain mine had faulted, so the bottom had dropped out of that stock, too. His eyes would follow Roxana with a beaten look. She sensed that he was mourning her lost beauty, worrying about her future, and wincing over all the humiliating things she must do for him.

She did not really mind. She remembered how she had cared for her mother and she was deft and gentle with him. Doubtless she even fancied herself in her new role of nurse. Her starched white apron made her look as crisp and fragile as a stalk of white hyacinth. She "walked tall" these days; there is nothing like a halo for making one hold the head high.

When Grover seemed better she tried to revive his hopes with talk of his property in the Valley of the Blue. There was always that mine to develop. He brightened at once.

"You'd like it over there, Roxana. Not much of a hotel, and the trip is hard. But the air, and the view— If anything happens to me, don't forget the Canaan Mine, above the Blue." Even as he talked, his color was rising; he was lifting himself up on his elbow. "There's still a fortune to be dug out of those hills. Why, with one more round of dynamite, we'll likely break through. It will be four feet across and run a hundred ounces to the ton." His eyes shone.

She regarded him tenderly, remembering her father. The next venture would set them on their feet. Tomorrow. Next year.

But the weeks went by, and still Grover could not throw off his weariness. She had to call the doctor again. He came and listened, with his ear flat against Grover's chest. Afterwards, in the downstairs hall, he said that Mr. Hull had a tired heart. This typhoid—

She went back to the room for money to pay the doctor. Grover's eyes flinched.

"Ask him if he can wait a little, will you, Roxana? Tell him about my mine, the Canaan. Tell him—"

Roxana told the doctor nothing. She pried up the velvet lining of her jewel box and dragged out the twenty-two dollars that she had put by before she was married to make a home for Avis. She had all but forgotten it. When she did remember it, she had thought only of using it to buy skates for Avis, or a croquet set. She paid the doctor, who was wearily waiting in the hall below.

The jewel box gave her an idea. She began turning her trinkets into money. Amazing, how these flashing gems that had cost Grover so much should suddenly have become flawed and second-rate and inconsiderable when viewed through the little glass of the jeweler. "Hard as a pawnbroker's eyes" took on new meaning.

It was all an old story that gained nothing with the retelling. Her mother's cameo, her father's goldstone cuff links— she was back in the shaft house and the coffin shop.

Instinctively, next day, when she went downtown for Grover's tonic, she walked past the Tabor Grand Opera House. For a moment she had a hope. Then she saw her reflection in the polished glass windows—a haggard crone whose short hair was just beginning to come in like beaver fur and who was skinny as a mop handle. Who would look at her now?

But a thought slowed her; she still had her needle. Once she had pried her way into the opera house at Central City with it. Maybe Grover would not mind if she found something drab and everyday, like sewing, to do in the theater. He had to have his medicines, and their board bill was mounting.

She walked up and down looking at the bills and trying to

muster the courage to go around to the stage door. With a sigh she noted that *The School for Scandal* was opening tomorrow night. All-Star New York Cast. The lovely Ina Farley as Lady Teazle. Ah, once long ago a young and halfway pretty girl named Roxana Renner had dreamed of playing Lady Teazle.

She read the names of the rest of the cast and wondered who they were, these unknown persons playing Sir Peter and Sir Oliver and Joseph and Charles and Lady Sneerwell. Then her hand went up to her throat.

Mrs. Candour—Monica Harlowe.

Rowley—Frank Montague.

Her old friends—Mrs. Harlowe and Monty! She ran around the corner of the building and along the narrow passageway to the stage door. Oh, to see her friends from the DeForest days. Her dear friends. They had really cared.

She smiled at the hostile old man guarding the door. She wondered gaily where they grew this special brand of churlish old men who guarded stage doors. When she had finally convinced him that she knew two in the cast, she slid past into the strange yet oddly familiar region backstage. This was finer than any she had ever seen. Rows of dressing rooms here, instead of one long single barracks for the lesser female members, where everybody scrambled for places at the make-up shelf and turned the room into a jumble of flounces and flying powder.

A dressing room door opened, and old Monty came out. She gave a squeal and threw herself at him.

"It's Roxana, Monty. You haven't forgotten me?"

He patted her on the back and then disengaged her to hold her off for a good look. She loved his lined old face with the white tufts, and the wrinkles around his mouth like the dry courses of old smiles.

"You looked peaked," he said. "Eyes as big as kettle drums. Don't tell me marriage has disagreed with you that much."

She smiled in spite of herself.

"It isn't marriage. It's typhoid. My hair is just coming back in. I lost twenty pounds."

"And you always were—"

"Skinny as a plucked pullet," she finished imperturbably. "But I'm going to drink lots of milk and fatten up. I didn't come to see about acting though; I know I look like one of the three witches. But you remember how I got into the theater in the first place? I came to see if they needed a wardrobe woman. My husband has been even sicker than I. And, well—he's waiting for some properties to start producing, and in the meantime—" She did not need to continue, to anyone on the stage.

"Wardrobe mistress, eh? Come in and say hello first to Mrs. Harlowe. She's a little bunged up."

"What's wrong?" Roxana was concerned.

"Nothing serious." He rapped on Mrs. Harlowe's door. The old actress was sitting with her foot in a pan of steaming water. At sight of Roxana she held out her arms.

"What on earth have you been doing to yourself, child?" Roxana told her.

"And what have you been doing to your foot?"

"Oh, this." Mrs. Harlowe lifted a fat reddened foot from the hot water. "I sprained my ankle and am soaking it in epsom salts."

"Sprained her ankle—my foot! She ran a tack into her toe running around in her stocking feet and she won't admit it."

"Sprained my ankle. Whose ankle is it?" asked Mrs. Harlowe. She looked at Roxana consideringly. "We open tomorrow night in *The School for Scandal*. I was to play Mrs. Candour. Remember the play?"

Remember it!

"I knew every part once," said Roxana tensely. "Of course, it's been a long time."

"It would come back. You were always a quick study.

You're thirty years too young for the part, but you don't look it at the moment. Monty, go get the director."

Monty came back presently, accompanied by a distracted man with the day-before-the-opening conviction of utter failure. He looked gloomily from Roxana to Mrs. Harlowe to Monty.

"You say she can act? She don't look it," he said with the frankness of the theater. "But maybe it's because she just got over the fever. I certainly wouldn't cast her as Mrs. Candour from choice. But with Mrs. Harlowe crippled up and no understudy and the programs all printed—"

He stopped and frowned. Then he thrust a paper-covered bunch of sheets into Roxana's nerveless grasp.

"Here, girl, take these sides and look them over. The part is a thin one, thank God. You remember Mrs. Candour, an old rip full of scandalous stories and always waving her fan? We'll fix you up with costumes and make-up. You'll have to be a scrawny old rip instead of a stout one. Do your best and don't dry up. Rehearsal in ten minutes." He walked away.

Hugging her script to her bosom, Roxana flashed a smile at her two old friends that was, as Monty said, so wide only her ears stopped it. She followed him out into the wings to watch until it was time for her to go on.

When the director called out, "All right, folks, places," a shudder of pure ecstasy went through her.

She sniffed the familiar theater smell, the dust, and the great dank emptiness out front, with the faintly eerie moving currents of air. She was amazed by the mechanics of the modern theater, with its intricate lights and its webs of ropes and pulleys in the flies. She stared at all the people scurrying about: stage hands, property men, dressers, extras.

She thought of the theater as she knew it with a little family company like the DeForests, where often they shifted their own scenery and rolled the curtain up and down; where they had to be careful in crossing behind the backdrop or it would ripple like muscles; and where they thought nothing of making a cliff scene do for a city street or a drawing-room interior for a county jail.

She studied her brief part with passionate concentration. The pattern of the play was coming back to her. When she stepped out on to the stage to read her lines, she remembered to take a deep breath to quell her nervousness. Her voice quavered a little at first; then it strengthened; and finally it was the grainy rasping voice of an old beldam. She was living in the days of curtsies and snuff boxes and claret punch; of marble-pure young ladies and conniving old ones; of half-tipsy young blades and rakehelly old ones.

She heard Sir Peter say sadly to Rowley, who was Monty, "When an old bachelor marries a young wife, he deserves— no, the crime carries its own punishment along with it." Briefly she caught a wicked gleam in Monty's eyes as he looked past Sir Peter and straight at her, in the wings. She bit her lip and looked away. She had forgotten that line, "the crime carries its own punishment with it." Oh, dear, she hoped not. Poor Grover. She must be extra kind.

It was a little difficult to be kind when she found Grover resentful and fidgeting as she hurried in late from rehearsal. She bustled around him fluffing up pillows and talking fast.

"It's only until Mrs. Harlowe can walk again. A few days at most, Grover." She paused and then said the words, "We *are* getting a little low on funds, you know."

He was silent after that.

She drew the shade and smoothed the quilt and stopped at the foot of his bed a moment before she went back to the evening dress rehearsal. How could she know that for the first time in five years she wore a mettlesome, prancing look, the look of someone tasting freedom, eager to be off? That she had color in her cheeks and a sparkle in her eye?

"My one wish," she parroted out of the long-gone past, "my one wish, dear, is to try to make you comfortable."

Winged feet took her out the door. Grover turned his face to the wall.

The bride and groom in the third row of the dress circle riffled their theater programs and looked about them. They must not forget to tell the folks back home about the ruby-colored plush and the chandeliers dripping lights and the curtain painted by a fine artist. Everyone said that the Tabor Grand Opera House was the finest west of the Mississippi.

They spoke of it in respectful accents and looked at each other shyly and then quickly away. They tried to act as if their shoulders were not touching, sending currents of burning awareness through them.

Presently the lights began to dim, and the orchestra broke into the portentous music that announced that the play was about to begin. Slowly the curtain rose. For a moment they almost forgot each other.

It was during the intermission that they turned to each other with baffled expressions, "It's the strangest thing." "Did you have the feeling, too?"

Simultaneously their eyes sought their programs.

"Mrs. Candour," they read aloud, "Monica Harlowe."

"It's out of the question," she said positively. "Even without her make-up, that woman is forty-five if she's a day."

"But the way she walked and held her head—"

"She was always thin, but she wasn't scrawny like this. Besides, she isn't on the stage any more. Don't you remember, they told us in Central City they heard she had married some years ago? Nobody knew who. If only Gil were alive! There is a kind of resemblance," she admitted.

"Maybe she went back on the stage," he persisted. "People do. And acting was certainly in her blood." There was a hint of bitterness in his tone.

"I used to think—when I was little—I used to wonder if perhaps you and she—?"

"My darling!" He was shocked at such blasphemy. "I was only waiting for you to grow up."

She sighed in delight, and they settled back together, arm against arm, and gave themselves over to the rapture of touch that was only a foretaste.

Before the last act, with a faint sadness that was filled with longing, but longing dulled by time and disappointment, she said plaintively, "I'll never understand how she could go off and leave me like that. And then never answer my letters. For eight long years I've tried to find her."

He was silent. When they were gathering up their wraps he said with a certain casual eagerness, "What say, we go around in back to the stage door and see what she looks like when she comes out? Just to make sure?"

"No. It wouldn't be any use. Just one more disappointment." She was drearily firm. "I guess I ought to know my own sister!"

Chapter XVII

ROXANA RAN to rehearsals. She whistled tuneless little airs under her breath. Oh, not inside a dressing room; that was bad luck. And not in Grover's presence; that was tactless. But she was enamored of living again.

She would not allow herself to hope that Mrs. Harlowe's indisposition would be prolonged, even though she knew she would be dismissed as soon as the old character actress could get her shoe on again. But until that time came, she might as well be happy. Mrs. Harlowe appeared to be in no hurry to return to her role of Mrs. Candour. In fact, she seemed to enjoy sitting on a kitchen chair in the wings, her bandaged foot on a box, while she coached Roxana on her acting and about the ways of the world.

"You're pretty careful, Roxana, going home late at night?" she asked one evening during the intermission. Her sharp eyes missed little, under her fluff of white hair that was like a gone-to-seed dandelion.

"I've never forgotten what you told me once. Keep on the outside of the walk and go like a galloping horse."

"Of course, Larimer is pretty safe, being one of the good streets. Keep off Holladay though. You've got to remember something, now that you're a married woman, and that is that virginity is a girl's best protection. Most men respect it (if they're sure of it). But look out, when you're widowed or married. You're fair game then, that's never out of season. They figure no one should begrudge a slice from a cut loaf. Of course, if the time ever comes that you *want* to step off the straight and narrow on to the broader, gayer path, that's different. In that case, let me suggest—"

"Don't you suggest!" muttered Monty, who had come up behind her. "You've done enough damage to that girl's life already. I'd think you'd be ashamed."

Mrs. Harlowe remained unruffled.

Roxana spoke in quick defense. "Everything's all right with me. I've had a good life and a good husband. He just happens to be having a run of bad luck at the moment. But he has some properties over in the Valley of the Blue; when they come back—"

"That's the way to talk," approved Monty. "Never let on. Be like a duck that glides along calm on top, but paddles like sixty underneath."

"I have to be calm on top," Roxana admitted with a rueful smile. "Because my husband is the kind—"

"I remember Grover Hull's kind very well," said Mrs. Harlowe dryly. "He doesn't want to think the women he married can even swim, let alone paddle like sixty."

Roxana shot her a look of surprise. How much that old actress knew.

"He'd much prefer it if his wife just floated gracefully, waiting until he could rescue her," Roxana sighed.

"A smart woman encourages such delusions—all husbandly delusions, in fact," said Mrs. Harlowe. "A wife must make a man think he's taking care of her, no matter what. I say it's kinder even to let him wear horns than to strip him of his man-pride."

"Horns?" asked Roxana.

Monty looked ready to explode.

"Pay no attention to the old harpy, Roxana. 'Horns,' says she. 'The broader, gayer path'! She just means pulling the wool over an unsuspecting husband's eyes. Have you ever

[208]

noticed, once they've strayed themselves, bad old women try to read the same straying into every other woman's conduct? Makes them feel that if they've got company, then they can't be so wicked themselves. Harpy, I say!"

"Tush," said Mrs. Harlowe with the calmness acquired over many years, off and on, of sparring with him. "Pay no attention to that brass-mouthed, copper-lined old sot, Roxana. He's only so saintly-talking because his stomach's gone back on him. He wasn't always like this. Back in the days— Ah, Roxana, the man was a handsome devil. What a Captain Absolute he was in *The Rivals!*"

She beamed at him. He beamed back.

"You made a pretty seductive Lydia yourself, ma'am," he said with a bow. She bridled.

Roxana regarded them with tenderness. Through the fleshy folds on Mrs. Harlowe's fat cheeks and dumpy figure she could see briefly the young Monica Harlowe, sharp-tongued, racy, arch, with a heart that was perhaps a mite too easily conquered. As Monty often said, "Scratch a grandmother, and you'll find a coquette." For a moment she had seen the young, flirtatious girl who played Lydia, instead of the dumpy old actress who played Mrs. Malaprop. And for a moment, too, she had seen the Frank Montague who did not need to wear "symmetries" to pad out his scrawny legs, and whose voice made girls at matinees shiver, and who could wield a cutlass or a fencing foil with the best of them.

She sighed over them both. But it was an impersonal regret that age had to creep up on people—other people, of course. For growing old had nothing to do with her, now that her hair had come in again, and her curves had returned, along with her love of living.

With every happy busy week with the stock company, she grew younger. When Mrs. Harlowe was able to return, Roxana was not let out. The director had found that she was sensitive and quick to learn. The next time they played *The*

School for Scandal, she was given her old part of Maria, an appealing role.

Monty rubbed his hands together.

"What did I tell you? You'll be doing Lady Teazle yet. You've got everything for the part, Roxana. Best of all, you've got real stage music. You light up at night."

She thought to herself, Oh, I could—I could play Lady Teazle. She walked home that night with her pointed button shoes scarcely touching the red-sandstone sidewalks.

But she had to mute her happiness and dim her shine when she was in Grover's presence because he was so eaten by his own frustration and despair. To think that his wife must work in the theater to support them; must leave early for rehearsals and stay late at night, running all the way home through the darkened streets by herself. And all because he had a tired heart. A woman should be sheltered; her place was in the home or the back seat of a carriage. The most embittering thing of all was the thing he could not bring himself to face: the fact that his wife could seem so electrically happy leading her unsheltered life.

"As soon as I can make that trip over to the mine— I think I'm on track of some fresh capital, Roxana."

Roxana nodded sympathetically, and her ears heard not a word he said. But her heart heard. She was genuinely sorry for him, and she reached out in the only way she knew to comfort him. In the dark, in the softness of the night, where once again she could be tender and submissive; and he could be masterful and conquering. For a little while he would be assuaged, and the old quiet confidence would return—until he saw her skipping away from him with such lightheartedness the next morning.

The All-New York Company moved on, taking Mrs. Harlowe and Monty along. Roxana was tearful at the parting, but Monty patted her on the shoulder philosophically.

"Never say good-by except in death. That's one thing you learn in the theater. Folks are always turning up again.

Look how you ran into us here. It's like putting a message in a bottle and throwing it out to sea—like as not it washes ashore at your feet some day."

Roxana gulped and nodded her head.

Following their departure, she continued to be lucky after a fashion. For although she had had to refuse the offer to travel with the troupe, there was nearly always a part for a walking lady or utility woman in the companies that followed. It was a little ironical that it had been Grover's illness which had freed her to go back to the theater, but it was also his illness which prevented her from getting anywhere in the theater. For so long as she could not go on tour, she was doomed to minor roles.

Then, one day when she pulled her stays in a little too tight in her dressing room at the opera house, the world up-ended crazily. A great queasy gorge rose within her. She had to hang on tight to the edge of her dressing table. She knew without being told. In the early days she had watched so longingly for just these symptoms. And now—to have it happen now!

She stood there, one hand holding on to the make-up shelf, the other with knuckles pressed against her mouth in the old gesture of angry despair. She bit down hard on her knuckles trying to right herself. Not after all those bottles and bottles she had taken, when nothing happened. Not when once she had wanted it so, and longed and prayed for it so. It couldn't be now; it mustn't be now, with Grover sick and the pay from the theater all they had for the board bill. The minute her figure went, her job went, too.

She stared into the mirror with haunted eyes.

I can't, I simply can't have a baby now, she told the mirror. (How many women have sighed the words, or groaned them, or sobbed them.)

Clumsily she went on with her dressing and make-up. It did not seem possible, after all these years. Why, she was twenty-four. She had only meant to be kind, to make Grover

[211]

feel proud and triumphant again. And how cruelly nature had repaid her!

I must get hold of myself, she thought. She was breathing hard in a spent way. Her hand could scarcely brush the powder over her cheeks.

But Roxana was an actress. She sailed through her part that night, and the next, and the next, and through the weeks that followed. She even managed to keep Grover from knowing, so that he was no more wretched than he had been.

The day she could not get into her gown to play Dorothy Blossom in *Black-Eyed Susan* she had to give up her job. Heavy-footed, heavy-bodied, she plodded back to the boardinghouse.

Grover seemed unaware that she was not hurrying off at the usual time right after supper. She sat with downcast eyes in their room mending her skirt braid, every jab of her needle a venomous thrust.

When it was long past time, he looked up and said mildly, "You aren't traipsing off to the theater tonight, Roxana?" The very way he said "traipsing" was belittling.

"I've lost my job."

"You have? How did that happen?"

"Because I'm going to have a baby, that's why. And I wish I were dead!"

He looked as if she had struck him, and she had. She was sorry the instant the words were out. She need not have said that last. But she had to take out her fury and disappointment on someone. If only it had not been Grover. He was gray-looking and quiet now.

Later in the evening, returning from an errand, she was just in time to make a leap and knock Grover's arm aside. The bullet lodged harmlessly in the plaster. Grover cried after she wrenched the gun away from him, the middle-aged tears of a man crying because his life has crumbled about him and he sees no way of rebuilding it.

The next afternoon when Roxana was walking along the

street toward the pharmacy for medicines for Grover, she saw a sign in the window of a shabby little millinery shop.

"Experienced Milliner Wanted."

She halted and stared at the sign and then at the row of slightly dusty bonnets on stands in the window. Well, she was experienced, goodness knows.

She took a deep breath, the standard remedy for stage fright, and braced herself to walk on in a new and difficult part. She opened the door; a warning bell tinkled weakly.

A troubled woman, chewing the corner of her lip, parted the lank brown portieres at the rear and came in. She looked Roxana over. Probably estimating just how many months along I am, thought Roxana, cringing.

"I saw your sign. I've had all sorts of wardrobe experience with theatrical companies," Roxana offered. "Dresses, hats, retrimming, pressing, work with buckram. I can cover buckles and steam velvet and make flowers." She stopped. It sounded pretty impressive, she thought.

"Can you keep books?"

Roxana was jolted.

"Not very well. But my husband can. He's sort of run down now, but he knows all about things like that."

"Got any references?"

References, thought Roxana, her mind darting about. The bank? Hardly, when they kept getting those little notices about overdrafts. Their pastor? But they had gone only to the big downtown church and sat in a back corner and hurried out afterwards; because that was the only way she could get Grover to go with her.

"Let me see," she said aloud. "Would our landlady—? We've been at Mrs. Pfaab's quite a while."

"Gertrude Pfaab? I'm well acquainted with her. That will be all right then." The woman relaxed visibly. "My trouble is, I don't know how long I'll have to be away. My mother back in Illinois has had a stroke and can't be moved. There's nobody but me to take care of her. I don't want to lose my business here. I need someone honest and experienced to leave in charge while I'm gone."

Roxana followed her into the back workroom with its long table heaped with scraps of velvet, wiry pieces of buckram, airy feathers, and curly-petaled flowers. Her darting glance took in the rest of it—the untidy bed over to one side and the small rusted cookstove.

"If you leave the curtains open in cold weather, the heat goes into the front room," said the woman.

Along with the smell of cooking, thought Roxana. But she was making rapid plans.

"You can have half you take in," continued the shopowner. "The rest will go for materials and rent and a little to pay me. Will that be satisfactory?"

"Perfectly," said Roxana, who was not one to haggle. Besides, the hats in the window were really most unappetizing. She was sure she could put bonnets out there that would lure more customers in. It didn't look like much of a bed. She wondered if the stove would draw. But at least, if they lived right here, there would be no board bill mounting higher and higher.

"I think I'd better move my husband into this back room where I can look after him and the shop at the same time," she said tentatively.

The other took it as a favor.

"Then I'm sure you won't mind feeding my cat. I didn't know what to do about Blackie."

Roxana did not mind Blackie, who arched a shoulder confidingly against her skirts. And so it was agreed.

Even after Roxana, in one of her wild spurts of industry, had scrubbed the back room and blacked the stove and put a flower on the table and a clean spread on the bed, it was not much to bring Grover to. Standing back to survey it, she quickly banished the thought that it would not be much to bring Avis to either.

Grover paled as the hack driver and Roxana helped him

through the shop and into the back room. Not this, his anguished glance said; oh, God, not this!

Roxana fluttered around, pointing out the virtues of the
place. He would be right where he could call to her, and she
would cook the nicest things on the little stove; and while
she sat at the table working on bonnets, they could talk. Oh,
she did have a way with bonnets! She was not pretending this
time. She was so glad to have this roof over their heads that
she was chattery with relief.

In the days that followed, Grover watched her from the
bed, his eyes narrowed and puzzled. Either she had a child's
gift for happiness, with no thought of yesterday or of tomorrow, or else she really did like to make bonnets. She seemed
almost as happy as when she was trotting back and forth to
that accursed opera house. And vastly happier than when
they were staying at the Clarendon or the Windsor or the
American House.

He shook his head. Women were strange, at least this one
was. If only he could get on his feet; if he could just get up
to look at that mine above the Blue. He wondered if the ad-
joining claims had been taken. He wondered if someone had
jumped his own claim and was working his Canaan Mine.
He wondered . . .

"If I can just get up to the Valley of the Blue—to Montezuma—to my mine," he would say, shutting his eyes to her
swelling bulk, and his ears to her lumbering tread. He could
not bear to watch her when she tried to hoist herself out of a
chair and fell back and tried again. Because it was all his
fault. He ought to be dead. Well, he had tried to be, and she
had stopped him. She would be better off if he were out of
the way, he told himself, averting his eyes from her shapeless
body. Yet she seemed to be illumined by a peace from within.
I don't understand her, he thought; I never understood her.
I only love her, and I'm no good to her.

The fall merged imperceptibly into winter. The daisies
on the hats in the windows gave way to feathers and bits of

fur. Business had improved slightly, but not so much as Roxana had hoped. The shop was in a poor part of town. Women who wore shawls and saved their one hat for Sundays did not go in for style. And to the longing-eyed servant girl who tried on a hat and then handed it back reluctantly, eyes moist with yearning, Roxana could only say, "Take it, my dear, and pay me when you can." Adding under her breath, "And let's hope it brings your young man around in a hurry."

At the end of each month there was little left after she had paid for Grover's medicines and bought coal and groceries. Sometimes Roxana thought with forlorn humor that she was like the lost wayfarer stumbling on and on through the wilderness, only to find that he has staggered back at last into the very clearing from which he started. Her life had gone from rooms back of a coffin shop to rooms back of a millinery shop.

She said to herself a little hysterically, But I would rather trim hats than coffins.

With the callousness of the desperate, she was glad when the owner of the shop wrote that her old mother just lay in a stupor, and the doctor couldn't say how long it might last.

A dime at a time, Roxana was putting aside a sum for the future, which meant the baby. She must be ready with the little sacques and slips and tiny blankets and the pile of diapers.

Mrs. Serafini, whose husband ran the boot-repair shop next door in the row of stores, was a midwife. She told Roxana what preparations to make during their back-yard conferences on the way to privy or ash pile.

"Don't worry, Mis' Hull, you look fine. By the way you carry him, it looks like a boy. I take care of you. I bring many a fine boy into the world. I've had twelve children of my own—five of them living." She seemed proud of such a record.

Roxana would not ask what had gone wrong with the other seven. When you were That Way, you must not think of all the baby graves in all the mining camp cemeteries, or the graves of the young mothers there, too. You must think only of eating for two and getting lots of sleep and keeping Grover's spirits up.

She was coming home in the early dusk of winter carrying a basket of groceries. The street lights had not come on yet. Naturally she had to go out after dark for her groceries because it wasn't decent to be seen on the streets in daylight in her condition. Luckier women who were in the family way went for short walks with their husbands after dark, thus managing to get their airings without offending respectable people.

She walked gingerly, steadying herself with one outstretched hand against the walls of the buildings. She guessed she must be pretty close to her time now. She wished she had not come out tonight. For since she had left home, the melted snow had frozen into terrifying sheets of ice. It wasn't easy, when you were so big and lumbering, to carry a heavy basket of groceries in one hand and balance yourself against the store fronts with the other.

The stars were large and cold and brilliant tonight. They made this little city on the plains at the foot of the mountains seem small and flimsy. She thought of all the people who had gained strength and comfort from gazing up at these stars. They gave her no comfort. They just glittered, remote and uncaring. Her own troubles were so near and looming.

Suddenly she choked on a sob. She wished she could see the Starbucks again. She needed Henry Starbuck's praying that brought God close—right into the room with you. She needed Naomi's arms around her to give her the sense that other women had gone through this, too, and had come out safely. Stars only made her lonely: for Gil whose rasping whisper she would never hear again; for Avis, who used to follow her around with that looking-up-to-her gaze, all the while pretending that she wasn't.

[217]

She stopped to rest. The basket was heavy. She looked down at the contents: the knuckle of veal in brown wrapping paper, some turnips, six potatoes, a head of cabbage. Her father used to remark that if you were finicky, you could be sure you weren't hungry. These days she was not finicky; she never got enough to eat. It was only Grover who assured her that the food was very nice and then left it all on his plate.

She slipped a little and caught herself up with fright. These terrible walks—like skating rinks. Her old buckle-galoshes were worn so slick on the bottoms they were worse than nothing. Now was no time to fall.

She shuffled cautiously past a lighted shop window. Someone came up behind her, steadied her by the arm, and gently took her basket away from her.

"Let me," said a voice.

She faced around dreadingly.

"Jay!" Waves of humiliation washed over her. It had been five years, and he had not changed by a hair. The same jaunty manner, the same Indian-lean face, the same cynical drooping eyelid. While she had come to this! She would have cowered, if so unwieldy a shape could have cowered.

He appeared to notice nothing.

"It's been a long time, hasn't it? I wondered what had become of you. I thought I recognized that haughty lift of the head, even under your shawl. The same lift as when you told me you were going on the variety stage and neither God nor Professor Jay could stop you. I always said, The face of a Botticelli, but the spirit of a Texas Ranger." He was laughing at her, but at least there was no pity in his laughter.

"Please give me back my basket. I'm quite able to carry it."

He did not relinquish it.

"I'm going your way."

She had to admit it was easier to walk without that heavy basket, and with his hand steadying her arm. She tried not

[218]

to move her feet in a sliding shuffle, so different from the dancing pace of the younger, lighter Roxana. Everything in her was rebelling at accepting his help.

As they passed another lighted shop she cast a little side glance at him. She saw all the signs of prosperity written large: an even shinier stone in his cravat; a handsome tight-curled astrakhan collar on his coat, that gave off rich black gleams; the twinkle of new patent-leather boots. He glowed with good fortune. She could not bear it any longer. She tried again to jerk her arm away, but he continued to hold on.

She felt herself tremble. She wanted to cry, she hated him so much. Look at how he upset her; it was always like this. Why did he have to come back into her life just now?

"You must have a profitable pitch!" she said spitefully.

"No pitch. That was temporary, because I got cleaned out soon after I saw you in Leadville. The manager of our company skipped with all the proceeds, and the sheriff attached everything we had, including Aristotle. It ended my act. I had to go into a pitchman's routine till I could get some cash. Right now I'm assembling a little medicine show that will tour the farm regions next summer. That too is only a step. I told you once I want to have a real stock company some day —no medicine." He stopped, and she could feel the smile in his voice as he went on, "I even have plans for putting on *The School for Scandal* when I find the right Lady Teazle— somebody full of hell and hot water!"

She pretended not to hear. There was something else she had to find out.

"I'm glad you gave up that pitch. Those cheap awful scissors that would hardly cut paper, let alone pins. And the needles that broke. What did you do with all that trash you were selling?"

"Tossed it in the gutter that same night—the night your husband threw down the five-dollar bill on my table."

"What became of your assist—I mean, your accomplice, Mlle. Fifi?" She had to ask it.

"Oh, her. I tossed her there, too. The same day I ran into you in Leadville." He was openly mocking her now. "Wasn't that what you wanted to hear me say?"

She darted a furious, baffled glance at him. What a maddening man. Did he mean he had got rid of Mlle. Fifi? Tossed her into the gutter, he said.

"Well, the gutter was certainly the right place for her," she said nastily. "And I think you were dreadful, what you said in your spiel—I mean, hinted at. You had no right. You were very impertinent. It was a wonder my husband didn't catch on." She was getting slightly tangled. She had better drop the whole subject.

"I trust he didn't. Too bad to have him learn the truth from a corner pitchman."

"It was not the truth!"

"By the way, I've been meaning to ask, since I caught up with you tonight, where is your husband? You shouldn't be out alone. Judging by the way he looked at you five years ago, I'd have said he wouldn't let you out of his sight."

"Oh, he wouldn't. But he's had a siege of typhoid. It left him with a tired heart. He's trying to get his strength back so he can look after his business. Luckily, he's still director in a lot of companies. I'm trying to hold him back, but he's set on making a trip over to the Valley of the Blue to look after some mining properties he's got there. You know how these business men are!" She laughed airily.

He said nothing; his eyes slid from her shawled figure down to the basket of groceries in his hand.

"Don't you think I'd better call a hack to get you the rest of the way home?"

Her cheeks went hot in the cold air. She had not figured on his taking her all the way home.

"Oh, la, I'm not going directly home. I'm taking a basket of groceries to a poor family in the next block. Such a nice little woman, who makes my hats. She has a sick husband, and I'm afraid they're terribly hard up. I thought I'd take a few goodies to her as I go to try on my new bonnet." There. She felt better; so much better that she almost lost her balance.

His grip tightened on her, righting her.

"Here's her shop now," she said. They had stopped in front of the darkened millinery shop. She could see the splinter of light coming through the brown portieres from the back room. She held out her hand for the basket. The moon shone down menacingly on the great hummocks of recent snow mounded up along the outer edge of the walk.

Almost reluctantly he gave up the basket. He wanted to say something. Instead, he reached under the skirts of the elegant astrakhan-collared coat for his pocket and drew out a coin that gave off a yellow gleam.

"You better take this tenner to your worthy couple in the back room. It can't be any joke for a man to be old and sick and to have lost all his money. Bad enough when you're young and single. But far worse, to be down on your luck and tied to a young wife that only married you for what she could get out of you, and now is stuck with a bad bargain she doesn't know how to break. Give this to the nice little woman and the sick husband—poor man—with my compliments."

He tucked the gold piece under the tight string that held the brown paper around the bulging soup bone. For a moment she stared at him in horror and rage. Why, he was throwing her very words back in her teeth, even imitating her patronizing tone. She hadn't fooled him for a minute. He was a devil.

"You—you—" She was completely incoherent.

He merely tipped his hat politely, smiled the lopsided smile that matched his drooping eyelid, and turned on his heel. Debonairly, jauntily, a man without a care in the world, he marched off.

"Here, take it! I won't have anything to do with it." She wrenched the yellow coin from under the string and threw it after him with a clumsy left-handed swing. She missed his retreating back. The coin bounced from the walk into the snow bank. He must have heard it, but he did not look around.

Shakily she let herself into the shop. She had to stop inside the door to pant.

"That you, Roxana?" called Grover.

It was several seconds before she could answer. "Yes, it's me."

"Are you all right? What's happened?" Faint alarm tinged his voice.

"I'm all right, Grover. It's just that I dropped something outside and must go back for it."

She set her basket on the chair and opened the door again. No one was in sight. She looked apprehensively at the expanse of sloping ice between her and that mound of snow by the curb with the small black hole in it where a coin had disappeared. There was nothing to hold to. She began to shuffle across the ice.

Halfway across, her feet slipped out from under her, and she went down jarringly. She sat there for a moment, dazed. But she was not hurt. She knew, however, that she could never hoist herself upright again in the middle of that glassy expanse. And she would not give up. She lurched over on all fours like a bear and crawled the rest of the way, the ice cutting her bare palms and bruising her knees through her petticoats. Toward that pillowy white bank and the dark spot that was like a bullet hole in it.

She reached the spot and plunged her hand down into the snow. Ten dollars. Ten dollars would feed and warm them for days. Her fingers closed on—nothing.

"Oh!" It was a moan. Her bare hand was already numb from the wet snow. It *had* to be there. She pawed the snow; she combed it with her fingers. She plunged her arm in clear to the elbow. At last her fingers closed on a small cold disc. Ten dollars! She extracted the coin and rubbed the snow off on her skirts.

With the gold piece clutched tightly in one wet chilled hand, she began her slow lumbering crawl back to the shop door. Now to get up over the doorsill. Now to haul herself to her feet, pulling on the knob with all her weight. Inside, she shut the door carefully and picked up her basket again.

If she could only get her breath; she was panting so. If she could only make her voice sound steady and cheerful. She drew herself up to her full height and forced herself to smile in the darkness, so the smile would be there in her voice when she spoke.

"Guess what, dear?" she called out brightly. "I found the nicest knuckle of veal at the butcher's to make soup out of. We'll simmer it on the back of the stove with all these good vegetables. You've no idea how nourishing it will be, Grover. In no time you'll be feeling better."

Roxana was an actress.

Chapter XVIII

I N THE MIDDLE of the night Roxana woke with the queerest backache. Could it have been from crawling around on the ice? Maybe she had strained her back when she fell.

She lay there trying to find a comfortable position in the sagging bed. There, that was a little better. The ache seemed to have gone away. She slept again.

The next time she woke, the ache prodded her awake. It was a pulling pain this time, sharper than before. The pain was followed by a little surcease. And then the pain again. And the respite once more.

So this was what it was like! She had thought she had several weeks yet. She lay there with little waves of fright running coldly down her legs. Her mind scurried around trying to remember what she was to do first. The longer she could wait, the better it would be for Grover. The room was so cold. Maybe she could hold out until morning. Night cold seemed so much worse than daylight cold.

Hands clenched at her sides, she began to count between pains. One—two—three—four—five—six—seven. It would be better if she could be up and doing something. This lying here counting was unbearable.

At last she heaved herself out of bed and lighted a lamp. Grover still slept. He never dropped off until nearly morning, and then he fell into this drugged slumber.

She must start the fire. She stuffed paper and kindling into the cold black maw of the firebox that refused to hold a fire through the night. She laid chunks of wood on top. She made each move jerkily, stopping to hold on to a table, or the back of a chair, or the foot of the bed. The pains were more commanding now.

She was relieved to see she had a full scuttle of coal in the house and a full teakettle of water on the back of the stove. She hoped she had the right things ready. She wondered how long it took. She had heard awful tales of women in labor for days. Oh, she hoped not, for Grover's sake. Waiting helplessly out in the other room, he would go mad if she suffered too much. Poor Grover.

At last the fire began to take hold. She held her cold hands over the stove lids with the darting firelight around their edges. The chill in the room began to retreat into the corners. She laid out the clean white cloths and the blankets and the doll-sized garments.

"Oh—oh—oh." It was a clenched, guttural groan. She caught the edge of the table and held on so tight that her hands were corded with tendons. The pains were closer now. Sharper, too. Maybe she ought to wake Grover.

She could hardly bear the look in Grover's eyes when he blinked and realized what she was saying. The concern for her, the loathing for himself.

"You can't go through this without a doctor," he said doggedly, dragging on his clothes. "I'm going out to find a doctor." She saw him reel as he got to his feet.

She laughed huskily.

"You mean you'd go out and round up some old calomel peddler just to bring a baby into the world? Well, I should hope not. I told you long ago that Mrs. Serafini would take care of me. She knows all about it. She's a midwife and she's had twelve of her own." She did not say what had happened to seven of them.

When she had finally established him in a chair out in

the shop, she pounded on the wall that separated her from the Serafinis'. Two raps and then a third. That was to be the signal. She waited and pounded again. More urgently this time, and this time there was an answering rap. Good Mrs. Serafini, dear Mrs. Serafini.

That voluble, kind-hearted woman, carrying her little black bag, puffed through the back door a few minutes later, her white apron tied on askew, her splayed bedroom slippers flapping.

Things went along so slowly. The lamp guttered and went out. The fire had to be replenished again and again. Mrs. Serafini made coffee for them all and saw to it that they drank it. The hours dragged on, the whole day dragged on.

When it finally grew very bad, Roxana bit down on her knuckles in the old gesture of pain. She mustn't make any more fuss than she could help. She remembered Grover out there in the shop going through his private hell. And then she forgot even Grover and was lost in her own private hell that ground on and on.

At last she dimly heard Mrs. Serafini saying proudly to someone, "A fine boy, Mis' Hull. Perfect." Why, she was talking to her, Roxana. "Perfect, Mr. Hull." Now she was talking to Grover.

There was a sharp spank. Satisfied and relaxed, Roxana lay there waiting for that next sound. But all she heard was another sharp spat of hand on newborn flesh.

Then she heard Mrs. Serafini rustling rapidly around and talking to herself and pouring water and panting a little. And nothing else. She waited for it, that little sound that had to come soon. She was too tired to rouse up, but every fiber of her was waiting.

She could hear Grover's low voice and Mrs. Serafini's broken, anxious one.

"I do everything. I spank, I blow, I try warm bath."

Roxana tried to raise herself on her elbow.

"Is it a little boy? You say it's a little boy?"

"Yes, it is a little boy. A perfect little boy, Mis' Hull. But he never breathe. Not once he breathe." Mrs. Serafini was crying now.

Roxana sank back. All those dear little baby clothes. She could not swallow. She could not even wipe away the helpless tears that ran down her cheeks and into her nightgown ruffle. But why, why? She had felt life—such a lively baby before he was born. Why?

A thousand times she would ask the question before she could put it away forever.

After a while Mrs. Serafini left them. But Grover was beside her now; a haggard Grover, but a calm and resolved one. He knelt beside her bed, holding her hand and comforting her. It was a strangely fortified Grover who lined the little box and took it away, who cared for her and brought her food. He had forgotten himself. Instead they were parents, grieving together. And she leaned on him.

Chapter XIX

G ROVER'S NEW ENERGY was in marked contrast to Roxana's lassitude. She was drearily slow getting her strength back. If there had been any reason to be strong; if she had been needed by a young life; if the terrible, wonderful urgency of motherhood had been upon her so that she had to get up and around, she might have recovered faster.

So many if's. If she had not taken that slippery walk, if she had not run into the infuriating Professor Jay, if she had not fallen down and then crawled after that despised, that needed, that life-giving ten dollars.

She kept asking Mrs. Serafini, who came in to bring hot soups and the comfort of her sorrowing glances, "Do you suppose it was because I fell? Do you suppose it was because I got so cold? Do you suppose—?"

Mrs. Serafini did not know the answers.

"One woman fall down a whole flight of stairs and have a healthy babe. Another, she take the best care, and her husband carry her around like in a market basket—and the baby dies." She sighed and gave a shrug that said, "Five living— seven dead."

Roxana would think that maybe tomorrow she could raise the front shade and take down the sign that said, "Closed Until Further Notice." Maybe tomorrow she could start work on the early-spring bonnets.

Then the old anguished sense of loss would flood through her again, a great rush of sorrow that was like the hot rush of milk to her breasts.

Grover would sometimes sense her empty desolation and come over and hold her quietly. All those hours of shared suffering had done something to Grover. He dressed every day now and set off cheerfully to the Mining Exchange. But he was still thin. Roxana's heart twisted as she saw how the cords at the back of his neck stood out. His hair was lank, and he no longer tried to comb it over the sparse spot on top of his head. His shoulder blades showed through his coat. Roxana's first stitches were to take in his clothes.

But his color was certainly good; or was it? From being sallow, he now had a perpetual flush on his cheekbones. He breathed fast; he talked fast, too, instead of in the slow tentative way he had of late. She was relieved to see some of his old confident spirit back.

"I'll get on my feet again," he kept saying. "Many a man has gone through a business slump like mine and then pulled out of it. I'm due for a change of luck. I've got a feeling it's in that property in the Valley of the Blue."

He was buoyed up when the supposedly worthless stock of a mine near Leadville paid a sizable dividend.

"You see? That whole region is having a revival."

He was a different man now, with a little money bulging the wallet in his hip pocket. When the owner of the millinery shop returned, they moved back to Mrs. Pfaab's.

"Even this is only temporary, Roxana," he assured her. "When I develop my mine, we'll have a room at the Windsor again. And then we'll build a home of our own."

In the meantime she found the gossip at Mrs. Pfaab's enlivening. The ladies chittered like squirrels, she thought with a smile. She began to ask questions, to try her hair a new way, to look at fashion magazines, to retrim a hat. On cold, brilliant days she went for walks. Her strength was coming back.

[229]

She was sewing a strip of fur on her dolman one evening when Grover returned in haste from an unwonted visit to the Windsor bar.

"Things are happening, Roxana. There's a revival over on the Blue. Silver stocks are booming. I've got to get over there to see what's happening. I've said all along we'll recoup everything with that property of mine."

She listened indulgently. It was good to see him exhilarated, even if he did look flushed, and his breathing was too fast.

"Here, chick, pack my valise for me," he commanded with new vigor. "I'm going to catch the morning train. It's quite a trip: first to Dillon on the train, and then several hours by stagecoach to Montezuma. But I want to be there on the ground floor. There's a likely claim right next to mine I plan to get hold of."

"Oh, Grover, you aren't able to go!"

He was already lifting his portmanteau down from the top of the golden-oak wardrobe and reaching for clean shirts and underwear and nightshirt. She was compelled to help him, in spite of her misgivings. Then she hauled down her own valise and began to throw things into it.

"I'm going if you're going," she announced. "All of our married life you've talked about the wonderful Valley of the Blue. Now's my chance to see it."

He smiled doubtfully at her.

"I don't know whether you ought to. It is wonderful though. It's the Promised Land. When my time comes, I'd like to be buried on a hillside looking out at Mt. Lenawee, high above the Valley of the Blue. I—I think I'd sleep better there." He stopped apologetically as if death were something indecent to mention.

Neither slept much that night for thinking about the morrow. They ate a hurried breakfast and took the shoe-box lunch Mrs. Pfaab had packed and climbed into the hack. The driver caught the feeling of festive urgency and laid his whip smartly on the back of his heavy-footed horse, who lumbered off toward the station.

Their mild hysteria lasted until they were seated in the railroad car. Trains always delighted Roxana. As the engine snaked its way out of the yards and toward the mountains, she thought of all those railroad builders of the past ten years who had pushed tracks into the most remote canyons, until they made a pattern on the map like veins in a leaf, so that now the stagecoach had become almost a rarity. Railroad builders were pioneers, too, she decided magnanimously.

She could scarcely sit still. She was going somewhere! She realized with surprise that she was well again, her weakness forgotten.

She smiled at Grover, and he smiled back and leaned across her to see that the window beside her was shut tight against the cinders and the cold. It was like their first days when Grover was all quiet happiness, watchful of her comfort—a little jealous, it was true, but endlessly protecting and thoughtful.

Her febrile gaiety lasted throughout the trip up over Kenosha Pass, down through Como, over Boreas Pass, and down at last into the Valley of the Blue. Then Grover became the animated one.

"You see?" he said over and over. "The mountains, the air, the rushing Blue. It's a better country, Roxana. That's why I named the mine the Canaan. The Promised Land."

But presently he sagged back. Only his will was keeping him going, she realized.

"Grover, let's stop off at Breckenridge for the night. I've got old friends there—the Starbucks, you remember them. You ought to rest up before you finish the trip."

He looked at her with grim appeal.

"We mustn't stop. We've got to go on. You never can tell—"

"Tell what?" she asked with a little stab of apprehension.

"Oh, I don't know," he evaded. "Someone might jump my

claim, or get there first and pick up the one next to it that I've got my eye on. If I'm ever to make my stake back—for your sake, dear—this is my chance."

When the train let them off at Dillon, she followed him anxiously along the cindery bank.

"Grover, please, this is far enough for one day. Let's stop here. The stagecoach trip to Montezuma will be a hard one."

But his thin shoulders hunched higher, and he continued toward the stagecoach which was waiting to take passengers to Keystone and Montezuma. It was a hard-used vehicle with a driver who was small and red-wattled and big-voiced.

"Right this way to the Montezuma stage. Right this way."

As they neared the stagecoach, drawn by four winter-shaggy horses, Grover looked beyond her and tightened his hand on her arm.

"What did I tell you! They're all trying to get in on the ground floor. We're not a second too soon. There's the fellow that was standing right at my elbow in the bar last night when we got news of the boom up this way. I thought he gave me a queer look when I said I was coming. He certainly didn't lose much time getting here himself."

She followed his glance, and her muscles jerked uncontrollably. Professor Jay! She came to a dead stop; her legs would not carry her any farther. Not that grinning, gloating, insulting creature! He was here for no good purpose.

I won't get into the same carriage with him, she vowed. No telling what he might do. He'll be sure to say something dreadful that will upset Grover—or me. She began to shake. If he hurt Grover now— Whatever could have brought him up here? He couldn't have come merely to torture her. Perhaps he really had become infected by the news last night and had decided to get in on a good thing, too.

She glared haughtily past him as their paths converged at the stagecoach. He gave no sign of recognition. He merely stood back to let her and Grover climb in first.

The stagecoach accommodated six passengers inside. She

had Grover sit in the back seat in the far corner, facing forward. She sat beside him in the middle. Professor Jay took the seat opposite Grover, his back to the driver. She was relieved that he was not directly facing her. You had to sit so close to people in a stagecoach. If, when they lurched around a bend, his knees had touched hers—! The very thought made her green eyes flash and her breath come fast.

She kept her head studiously turned away from Professor Jay, so that only the tip of her left ear lobe was toward him.

The other passengers were slower to arrive. First came a large-boned woman who took the space next to Jay and across from Roxana. Curiously Roxana looked from her to the small trunk which the driver was lashing to the boot. It was a theatrical trunk, with the name "Mrs. Sophie Blackwood" painted on it. But surely this gaunt straight-lipped woman was not of the theater. Then Roxana saw the words on the other side of the trunk, "For God and Temperance."

She glanced at the woman uneasily. Mrs. Sophie Blackwood had such steely, penetrating eyes that took in all your weaknesses. Would she know, just from looking at Roxana, that she had drunk a glass or two of champagne under Grover's watchful eye? Would she know that Grover picked up some of his best tips—or that he used to—at the Windsor bar? She could see Jay watching the woman, too, and thinking inscrutable thoughts about lady temperance lecturers who brought their message to lonely mining towns.

The fifth passenger, next to Mrs. Blackwood, was a fit subject for her efforts. He was a watery-eyed man, with mustaches that drooped downward like curving steer horns, who just made it into the stagecoach, where he slumped down in an alcoholic haze. Roxana looked at his hard hands and seamed face, rough as a piece of conglomerate, and was sure he was a miner returning from a celebration in Denver with empty pockets after emptying all too many bottles.

The last to climb aboard was a plump little man. At first you thought he was a jolly prankster, doing a variety act por-

[233]

traying the complaining traveler. And then you realized he was in earnest. That his high nervous monologue was the natural outburst of a shrill, selfish little man, worried about the roads, the rickety vehicle, his digestion, his asthma, and catching a chill.

He fastened all the curtains tight to keep out the drafts. He understood there had been a terrible epidemic of mountain sickness up this valley and he hoped none of them were coming down with anything. No one volunteered any information. He opened a little bottle and shook out two pills, everyone watching him with fascination as he tilted his head back like a drinking chicken and swallowed them noisily, one after the other.

Quietly Roxana unfolded the rug she had brought and tucked it about her husband's shoulders. Grover was slumped back in his corner of the carriage, his eyes closed. She watched him with concern.

The softly plump little man with the hard blue eyes said waspishly, "The gentleman isn't coming down with anything, is he?"

"No, he isn't," she said shortly. "He had typhoid last year, and it left him run down."

The little man looked unsatisfied, but she said no more. Outside, the driver was strapping the last of the luggage to the out-jutting boot and fastening canvas over it.

Professor Jay broke the unfriendly silence by remarking equably, "I hear there's quite a mining revival up this way at Montezuma and at Saints John, just beyond. There's a name for a wide-open mining town—Saints John."

Mrs. Blackwood's mouth thinned.

"Judging by all the other mining towns I've seen, it's just one more sacrilege. Like giving gambling halls and drinking saloons such names as St. Anne's Rest and The Church and The Chapel." She turned a poisonous glance upon the miner beside her (who was only average-sized and well-slumped, while she was overly tall and very erect). "Liquor—the devil's

[234]

handmaid!" But her companion was too far gone to care. He smiled fuzzily and waved a hand like a flipper before he lapsed into slumber.

The stage turned to follow along up a tributary of the Blue. By an effort of will Roxana kept from looking at, even from thinking about, the silent man opposite Grover. She must think only of Grover now. She held her arm around him to keep the rug in place, and the feel of him against her was of an utter weariness that gave slackly with each lurch. He was so thin, this once-solid bulk of a man who had exuded health and vigor. They ought to turn back. She had no business taking a man with a tired heart to an altitude of over ten thousand feet. Yet she had no choice. He was set on going. Somehow, they had to reach Montezuma, high above the Blue; Montezuma that looked out upon his beloved Lenawee Mountain, and his Canaan Mine. The Promised Land.

The lurching, the terrible lurching. The little man complained with every jolt. Grover had lapsed into a limpness that required all her strength to hold him upright. Had he fainted? Was he unconscious? Then he stirred slightly. She was like a mother, all shielding, hovering anxiety.

The stagecoach jolted to a stop. The driver climbed down to open the door.

"We're late, folks. We'll never make Montezuma in time for supper, so we'll stop here in Keystone for half an hour. You can get a quick meal or tea and coffee." He winked at the lady lecturer. "Plenty of time for a little nip at the Miners' Choice, ma'am. This mountain air chills the innards."

"Better chilled than rotted!" she snapped.

The driver laughed.

They had drawn up in front of the boardinghouse. Roxana made no move to get out.

"We'll stay here. My husband is tired," she said.

"You sure it ain't mountain sickness or anything?" inquired the pill-swallower. "Maybe you ought to get off here where there's a good place to stay." His concern was obviously not for the sick man.

"We're going to Montezuma," said Roxana.

Professor Jay said nothing. He merely stood up in his far corner, thus forcing the rest of them to get out ahead of him. They scattered toward the boardinghouse. Roxana was left alone in the coach with her husband. She had one goal now: to reach the end of their journey—the hotel—and rest for Grover.

As the swift mountain dusk descended, it was suddenly cold inside the stagecoach. She saw the yellow lights of kerosene lamps go on in the houses and the handful of business buildings. How quiet it was. She drew the rug closer around Grover; she tried to warm him with her arms and her body.

He stirred slightly. He was trying to speak.

"I'm afraid I'll not make it after all, Roxana."

"Of course you will, Grover. I'm going to see that you do."

"Are you?" he asked wonderingly. "I believe you will. You're a good girl. I only insisted on coming because . . . I wanted to leave you well-fixed . . . taken care of, Roxana."

A shudder, a jerky little shudder, went through him. She waited for him to speak again. The minutes stretched out.

"Grover?" she whispered shakily.

Only his silence answered her.

"Grover!" she repeated insistently and a little sharply. Panic went through her, a sharp unreasoning animal fear.

Still he said nothing. Her arms tightened convulsively about him. His head had fallen back now; he was a sacklike weight in her arms. She reached up urgently and touched his cool leathery cheek.

"Grover, can you hear me?" Even as she sobbed out, "Oh, Grover!" she knew. He would never hear her again. Yet she must try to reach him somehow. "You've been so good to me, Grover. I ought to have—I could have done better."

Her voice sank to nothingness. Grover was dead. Death

was here in her arms. For a moment she sat quite still, stupefied by the fact. And then she felt only grief; her whole being was hollowed out by grief. Everything was finished for Grover. Poor Grover, whose last words had been for her. Trivial, touching last words about wanting to leave her well-fixed. When he was dying, when he ought to have been thinking about his own soul's welfare and about meeting his God. But maybe it was all right. Maybe those who died unselfishly, thinking of others, were already prepared to meet their God.

She pulled the robe up higher about him. All she wanted was to be allowed to sit here and shield what was left of him. But in a minute the rest would be trooping back, that terrible little man among them. He would know instantly. He would insist that they take Grover—she winced—Grover's *body,* off here at Keystone. He would never ride in the same coach with a dead man.

But Grover wanted to reach the end of the trail—Montezuma and a hillside overlooking Mt. Lenawee, high above the Valley of the Blue. What could she do?

Here they came! The light from the open door of the boardinghouse slanted across the road behind the passengers straggling back to the coach. The miner, sobered by black coffee, was lighting his pipe. The complainer was holding his handkerchief over his nose so as not to breathe the cold night air. Mrs. Sophie Blackwood stalked along taking deep gusty breaths of that same air and gazing out at the purpling mountains. The driver was wiping the dripping tips of his mustache. Rapidly overtaking them was Professor Jay, carrying two steaming tin cups in his hands. He swerved past the rest and reached the coach first.

He climbed in and bent over Roxana in the half-darkness. He said quickly, "How is he?"

She looked back up at him. No words came. She shook her head desolately.

A stillness in him answered her.

[237]

She whispered, "He wanted to reach Montezuma . . . and his mine. I promised him—" A sob racked her.

The others were crowding into the coach now, tilting it downward with their weight. The suspicious little man leaned forward to peer at the trio already there—the sick man and his wife and the passenger facing them holding the tin cups in his hands.

"There's a doc at the boardinghouse. Maybe he better take a look at your husband?"

No one answerd him. He bent farther forward, his nostrils twitching as he scented trouble. He began to clamber out of the coach.

"He's the company doc. He's in there eating his supper. He'd know if it was mountain sickness. I'll go get him."

"Sit down!" said Jay in a voice like a whip-crack. "All this man needs is a hot drink." He bent over Grover.

"I've brought a cup of coffee and one of tea, sir," he said solicitously. "Which will you have?"

Roxana's blood chilled. What had got into this madman? He knew that Grover was dead.

Professor Jay bent even closer to Grover now as if to catch his reply.

"Tea," came the whispered answer from the blanket.

"Tea you shall have," said Jay cheerfully. "And coffee for madame."

"No cream or sugar," added the weak whisper from the blanket.

"That's the way I brought it. Plain. Now if you'll just hold your head a little higher so you can swallow—"

Jay held the cup to Grover's lips. Roxana had a panicky desire to scream. So in addition to all his other trickeries, Professor Jay was a ventriloquist!

With sober care Jay held the cup to the dead man's lips; then drew it away as if to let him swallow, and held it back again. His every movement was anxious and careful, a kindly fellow passenger helping out a woman with a sick husband.

At length he straightened up and called to the driver.

"We're about ready to start. He drank a little tea." He turned to Roxana. "You better drink your coffee, madame. It gets mighty cold up here at ten thousand feet, in the spring of the year."

She managed to swallow a gulp and returned the tin cup to him. He shook the contents of the two cups out on the ground and tossed them in the direction of the boarding-house, where they clattered on the rocks.

"All aboard," he called to the driver. The vehicle lurched into motion.

The passengers settled back in the dusky interior. The complainer sulked suspiciously in his corner next to Roxana. The miner began to come to life. The lady lecturer with the augur-like eyes glanced her way now and then. Roxana thought, She's the one we've got to fool. Professor Jay was quiet, yet alert too, leaning forward as if on guard, his knees forming a protection for the wrapped figure across from him.

Once he said to Roxana, "Want me to change places with you? Your arm must be tired."

She shook her head. The arm had long since lost all feeling.

The darkness thickened. It was cold and black and silent inside the coach. Would they never get there? On and on they went, around narrow curves, along shelf roads, and beside the rushing waters tumbling down toward the Blue.

She was numb in mind and body and heart, when at last the lights of the little mountain town of Montezuma pricked the darkness.

"It's about time," the lady lecturer said wearily.

"I could do with a drink," muttered the miner.

The complainer peered out at the settlement.

"I suppose the beds are terrible," he groaned.

Jay and Roxana and Roxana's husband were silent.

The miner climbed down first and headed for the bar. The suspicious little man took his time getting out. He kept looking back at them, and when he reached the hotel porch, he stopped to watch with morbid interest.

Roxana was at the end of her strength. She had no idea what to do next. Even Professor Jay seemed to have used up all his ingenuity.

The brusque voice of the temperance lecturer took command.

"I think I see a doctor's office in that small building near the hotel. We'd better get your husband to him first. No use trying those hotel stairs. You've had a difficult trip, madame. The gentleman and I, one on each side, can help your husband into the doctor's office."

Help him—help a dead man? Roxana tried to say something, but the words stuck in her throat. She could only sit there, her arms, her whole body, numb and strengthless. There was no stopping the woman; she was a great gaunt iron-willed machine as she pushed Roxana aside and slid an arm under Grover's shoulder.

Professor Jay took his place on the other side. Between them they managed to get the limp toppling figure out of the coach. Roxana walked behind them, carrying the rug. Slowly they covered the few feet of road, made the steep step up to the walk, entered the tiny one-room office of the doctor, who was seated at his desk in a yellow circle of lamplight.

Mrs. Blackwood said to him with brisk gentleness, "Doctor, you're probably the coroner, too? This gentleman . . . came to his end . . . on the journey up here. The lady is his wife. The other gentleman and I were passengers on the coach. The lady hasn't had an easy time of it. When you've taken care of her husband, I suggest you give her something to make her sleep. Perhaps the gentleman will accompany her over to the hotel?"

Jay nodded gravely.

The rock-jawed woman gave a jerky little farewell salute, and backed out the door. Roxana could only stare after her.

[240]

She looked at Professor Jay, waiting there in sober deference. You never could tell about people.

She explained brokenly to the doctor, "We had to keep on. Grover, my husband, said he'd sleep better up here. On a hillside . . . looking out at Mt. Lenawee . . . high above the Valley of the Blue."

Chapter XX

S UMMER PASSED SLOWLY in Breckenridge for Roxana. The Starbucks had insisted that she make her home with them until she decided what she wanted to do. As if she would ever want to do anything again. Her arms were empty; her heart was empty; she was a dry husk of a woman.

She helped with the housework and went to church and took long walks. It was a beautiful country, Grover's Valley of the Blue, she admitted; so prodigally supplied with mountains that the range to the west was called merely Ten Mile Range and the mountain brooding over the town was known as Peak Eight. But mountains were like stars. When she was happy they stirred her; when she was sad they were only coldly pure and far away.

The Starbucks were kind; they surrounded her with kindness. They were tactful; they knew when to leave her alone. She drew slow healing from the life that went on around her in the crowded log cabin, where she shared a room with the oldest of the girls, who was now a shy, gangly fourteen.

It was a life of normal bickering and making up, but it was lived in confidence and serenity. The Starbucks were so sure —perhaps not always sure about the here, but completely sure about the hereafter. The Bible was neither a duty nor great literature to them. It was a solace, a guide, and a promise. When Henry read aloud at morning prayers, "My times are in thy hand," or, "I will trust and not be afraid," you sensed a Presence there beside him.

I only pray when I want something desperately, mused Roxana guiltily. Oh, God, let some of this faith rub off on me.

Winter came on. Roxana helped Naomi bank dirt up about the cabin, chink the cracks between the logs, and paste another layer of paper on the inside walls. A thick coat of wallpaper was as good as anything to keep the wind out. But there was no keeping this wind out.

Roxana said nothing to the Starbucks about Professor Jay and his conduct that last night of Grover's life. Of course, if he should follow her here to Breckenridge—wasn't he always bobbing up in her life?—she would explain to them how helpful he had been.

When she had asked Jay that night in Montezuma why he had made the trip, he explained simply, "I overheard him say he was coming, and I was afraid for him." And then when she went to thank him the next morning, he was gone.

There were times now when she knew a driving need to talk to Jay about it. Yet she shrank from seeing him. He did such dreadful things to her, stirring up her thoughts, churning up her feelings. She both wished he would appear and she hoped he would not.

She could not bear one of his grinning, hateful remarks right now. In spite of herself, a comment of his came back to her. The day they were sitting companionably on the trunk feeding Aristotle, a woman, ostentatiously swathed in black, had passed by. Jay had given her one narrow side glance and muttered, "I've noticed that a widow's grief is often like a pain in the elbow—sharp, but soon over."

Just thinking about his cynical tongue made her wrathful. But she was ready for him and anything he might say.

And then he did not come. Her rehearsed speeches grew stale. The weeks and months slipped by, and nothing, absolutely nothing, happened.

Her money was almost gone. Henry Starbuck had come to Montezuma promptly in response to the telegram Jay had sent. Henry had taken care of all the arrangements about Grover and had even found a man who was willing to buy the machinery at the Canaan Mine for two hundred and seventy-five dollars. It was enough to pay her way at the Starbucks' throughout the winter.

Christmas came and went. Roxana plunged into family sewing. She made over clothes for the girls from the dregs in the mission barrel. She relined Henry's ancient overcoat, keeping a record of his measurements. When she got back to her trunk in Denver, which Mrs. Pfaab was holding for her, she would see what she could do about making over some of Grover's clothes for Henry.

She flinched at the thought that mere *things,* made of wool and leather and linen, could so long outlast the flesh that had worn them.

She even managed to make a suit for Henry Junior out of his father's oldest. Such careful cutting to find enough good places. Roxana delighted in the small trousers and bobtailed coat. To make things for a little boy! When Naomi found her crying, she cried too, thinking of that other little boy sleeping on a barren hillside above Central City. For a moment they were two women weeping for their lost sons.

"You don't ever get over it—losing a child?" inquired Roxana thickly.

Naomi shook her head. "You don't ever."

They had gay moments, too. Roxana made costumes for the three girls for the Living Pictures at the church bazaar, where they represented "Miss Rosy-Cheeked Apple," "Miss Plum Pudding," and "Miss Bounteous Harvest."

As Roxana knelt and pinned folds around the skinny, owl-eyed little girl of nine, her eyes met Naomi's, and their stomachs shook with deep subterranean giggles. Miss Bounteous Harvest, indeed! They dared not look at each other again, for the child was scanning each adult face for the first

[244]

sign of ridicule, her nose quivering like a doubtful chipmunk's.

And then it was spring. There was something about spring, Roxana thought, that made you both happier and sadder. And more restless. She must find work; she must take up her search for Avis again; it was time for her to move on. Without words, Naomi understood. Sadly she helped Roxana pack. She would miss her; when you have had a friend you can laugh with and weep with . . .

Roxana took a small attic room at Mrs. Pfaab's. Denver was growing fast. It was a large city now—seventy-five thousand people. To think that it had been only a cluster of huts on a creek bank twenty-five years before. And now it had telephones, and horse cars, and there was talk of cable cars soon and of building a capitol up on the bluffs. She took long walks to view its wonders.

One afternoon she saw a crowd gathered around a man on a street corner, and her heart set up a frantic drumming against her ribs. She moved quickly up to the outskirts of the crowd. Then her tumult subsided. She could see the pitchman now and hear his nasal drone. He was shabby and old and glibly unconvincing as he intoned the merits of pills containing tiger-marrow and the fat from he-turtles, guaranteed to revive gentlemen's failing powers and cure their secret diseases.

She let out a slow exhalation and moved on. For a moment there she had thought—she had hoped even—

All this delay was not improving her finances. The opera house was deserted for the time being, with no companies coming or going. No one seemed to need an experienced milliner. She studied the newspapers for listings of openings. Mrs. Pfaab was no worse than any other boardinghouse keeper, which meant she was no better, and Roxana knew she must not fall behind with her board money. If she was to find Avis, she must have a job first and a little money ahead.

She almost missed the small notice hidden away among the fine print at the back of the newspaper.

Young lady wanted, with carnival or stage experience—willing to travel—able to sing or dance. Apply Great Divide Traveling Tent Show, end of carline.

Willing to travel! She tried to quell her sudden inner tumult. Of course, it could not be Professor Jay's traveling show; he had said his was a medicine show. But if by any chance it should prove to be his, she would pretend to be overcome with surprise. She would be a little remote, even haughty. It was always best to take that stand with him.

She would wear her best black dress, dyed of course, with the twenty-six crystal buttons down the front. Naomi had said with an admiring chuckle, "My, that bodice fits like skin, doesn't it? Better than skin—skin has wrinkles!" It had a beautiful projecting back with little postilion tails lying out on the bustle. Her bonnet was of the same material —it was lucky she had had some scraps left over—and it tied under her chin with a tulle bow. Black really made everything about her more so: her skin whiter, her eyes greener, her hair blacker.

She mentally hurried the poky old horse car toward the end of the line. When it reached the loop, where it turned around, she saw the tent off to one side in a vacant lot. It was not so large as she had expected. Its sides were covered by a vast sign: "The Great Divide Traveling Tent Show."

Holding her furled black umbrella (there was something impeccable about a furled black umbrella; you could not imagine a fast woman carrying one), she approached across the carpet of young dandelions. She could see a man and woman practicing a dance routine in the soft sand. A man with bulging knots of muscles was ponderously raising and lowering weights. Clothes dried on the guy ropes. A half-eaten sandwich rested on a stump. The small community on the vacant lot had already assumed a comfortable family look —untidy, lived in, workaday—like the caboose of a cross-country freight.

They neither paid any attention to her nor slackened their practicing. She wandered on into the tent, with its rows of backless benches, its heavy center pole, and its rough board platform at one end. A man with his back to her was working with a screwdriver over the row of kerosene footlights.

She started to say, "I wonder if you can tell me—" when the man turned around.

He let the screwdriver plunk into the sand.

"Roxy! So it's you!" as if he had been looking for her hourly.

Professor Jay! She forgot all about her remoteness with the tinge of hauteur. Forgot to act surprised, forgot everything in her bewildering rush of feeling. They were close together now, facing each other, breathing hard, smiling yet tense. He caught hold of her arms above the elbow and half shook her in a glad welcoming.

"You look fine, Roxy, you look just fine," he said over and over, gazing deep into her face. "I've wondered about you. I started a couple of times to come and see you. And then I didn't. I guess you know why. You being the kind you are, I figured I ought to wait." His eyes went on drinking her up.

She laughed back up at him.

"Was that why you never came? I wondered. Well, me being the kind I am, that's why I *did* come today." She was blushing at her own boldness.

He still had her by the arms; he still smiled at her. But something else was in the smile. His eyes had caught fire. The umbrella dropped unnoticed to the ground. He was drawing her slowly nearer. She felt hot and cold and shaky and wonderful. She couldn't pull away; she couldn't even look away.

And then someone outside stumbled over a guy rope and

howled out, "Well, blast my cats!" and the whole tent shivered under the impact.

She jerked back from him self-consciously. Suddenly she remembered that it was bright noonday in a tent with people all around. She began to tuck up her hair and speak with trembling laughter.

"The minute I read the notice, I wondered if maybe it could be you. After all, I *can* sing a little, and I *do* have theatrical experience, and oh, Jay—I'm certainly willing to travel!"

Chapter XXI

CAREFULLY ROXANA applied her daytime make-up for the noon ballyhoo. The heavy cream, the cloud of face powder, the delicate pink on cheek and lip, more powder, and last, the arched dark brows. There was a definite convention about make-up: fast women flaunted scarlet mouths and bright red discs on their cheeks; theatrical women wore paint too, but more discreetly applied. Jay said that the "rubes" liked the tent-show ladies to look like pink-and-white apple blossoms, in contrast to their own clabber-colored women.

Roxana hummed in her cubicle in the railroad car that bore on the outside the gaudy sign, "The Great Divide Traveling Tent Show." She tried to closet her happiness. But each day held such aching loveliness for her; each day was lived at such high intensity. She had to keep reminding herself to be careful. If you were too happy, the fates lay in wait to trip you. She had a faint sense of guilt besides. Grover had been dead only a little over a year. Wasn't it a little disloyal to Grover to be so happy?

This gypsying summer with the tent show had been her closest approach to a carefree existence since that covered-wagon trek so long ago when she and her father had munched their bacon and corn bread, standing over a roadside fire that brought smoke-tears to their eyes and laughter to their lips.

Roxana admitted to a momentary sinking feeling the first time she had seen the tent-show car. Jay had taken her down to the railroad yards to look at it, battered and patched, but boastful with red and yellow paint. She had winced at the flamboyant sign along the side, "The Great Divide Traveling Tent Show," and underneath, the words: "Dr. Langworthy's Famous Mineral-Vegetable Elixir; the Renowned Ever-Lather Indian Root Soap; the Alaskan Polar Bear Hair Oil."

Jay promptly dispelled her squeamishness. With his hand under her elbow (how a woman needed a man's hand under her elbow!) he had proudly forced her to admire the ancient rolling stock that housed his show.

"First step up the ladder," he had gloated, albeit with a slightly sheepish air. "It may not look like much to you—a medicine show is probably a far piece from art—but it's a starter. The medicines we concoct don't hurt anybody; most of these farmers need a good dose of salts anyhow. At least, we don't carry an oversized tapeworm in a bottle to scare them to death. And our programs are several notches above the usual 'physic show.' With a seasoned actress like you along, we can even put on a decent one-act play."

He had snugged her arm tight against him, as if he were never going to let her get away again, and all the lovely swooping pit-of-her-stomach feelings rushed over her. Right there in the cluttered railroad yard, with engines chuffing and whoofing on all sides, and men shouting and signaling. She had flushed and tried to pull away, but he only laughed at her, gently, triumphantly, with a look that said, "Now none of your airs, Roxy, you know this is where you belong."

He took her inside the ancient combination car, which had a partition across the middle, with the front half for baggage and the rear half for passengers.

"See," he explained cheerfully. "We carry the tent and the gasoline flares and the footlight lamps up here in the baggage section. There's room for what stage properties we've got—front curtain, sides, backdrop—as well as for my magic paraphernalia and the stuff to make the 'medicine' with. We rent lumber in each town for the benches and stage."

He led her into the passenger half of the car, which was divided into small sleeping cubicles, with a meager space at one end of the car for cooking and eating.

Looking at it—decrepit, crowded, but blithe with new paint—she had been caught up in his enthusiasm. She was eager to start. She had not long to wait, for Jay had used up his savings and borrowed to the limit, and they had to get on to the road. The Great Divide Traveling Tent Show set out the next day.

The company of six settled into a comfortable routine: Jay, "Dr. Langworthy" since he had become the owner of a medicine show; Winnie and Chet Lazier, dancers and acrobats; a lumpish weight-lifter billed as Sutro the Strong Man; Roxana, now Mlle. Roxane; and Ferd the canvasman who slept in the front section on a bundle of tent. A show-crazy farm boy, Ferd had obviously run away from home; and Roxana suspected that Jay had a soft spot in his heart for him because, not so many years ago, Jay himself had run away from home to follow the big tent.

Winnie Lazier did most of the cooking because she liked to cook, and the rest helped her. Roxana, who hated the ever-recurring monotony of cooking (you spend hours at it, and then they gobble it down in ten minutes), but who loved to sew (when you're done, you've got something to show), worked on their costumes. Everybody did what came to hand. It was a haphazard, scarcely respectable, slightly sleazy, but infinitely merry way to live.

Jay had not hurried her. They had the rest of their lives, his confident look said.

Oh, surely it could not be wrong to be so happy, she thought, leaning forward to look at herself in the small square of watery mirror. As she darkened the feathery arches of her brows, it came to her that it had been a long time since

[251]

she had thought about the look in that other girl's eyes, in the pretty blue eyes of Baby Doe Tabor. She knew now that she need wonder no more. She had a look in her own eyes these days; she had her own private claims to bliss. Her mouth curled up at the corners; her whole face was softly luminous.

The weeks had been a slow revelation of this other Jay. A kinder Jay (because he was happy too?) who passed over young Ferd's costly mistake when he gave some rube the wrong change, who only grinned when Winnie let the meat scorch, who shrugged philosophically when Sutro broke one of the footlight lamps: "Those big muscle-men never have enough sense to spit downwind," and who let a dozen little boys in free in every town because he, too, had once gazed yearningly at the outside of a big tent.

Jay could be granite-hard, too. She had seen him ruthlessly grind his heel down on the foot of a foul-mouthed drunk, sending the man hobbling off home with perhaps a broken bone. She had seen him knock the front teeth out of a thief caught trying to make off with their gate receipts. "It's best to be your own law and order," he said grimly. "Mix with the local authorities, and you only get into worse trouble."

The gentler Jay had gone to church with her once or twice. She wore her dyed black dress and no make-up and carried her respectable black umbrella. Jay had looked like a deacon in his soberest clothes, had never smirked once, and had even known most of the words to "Praise God from Whom All Blessings Flow," which he sang with sonorous enjoyment. But still the townsfolk watched them both as if they were two-headed calves.

They had had a hundred stolen moments together, so brief, so enchanting, so disturbing. Sometimes it was only a look, electric with awareness. Sometimes it was the touch of his hand when they were practicing the magic acts. Once, with the audience rustling and chattering out front, he had looked at her in the canvas lean-to dressing room and murmured,

"You are just the right height, Roxy; your shoulder would fit under a man's." Only the fact that there were always people around kept her from, as she termed it, "making a fool of herself."

For she was learning things about herself these days. Mrs. Harlowe might have warned her of another truth, when she was telling her that a girl's best protection against a man was her very virginity and that once she was a widow, no rules held. She might have told Roxana that a girl's virginity was also her own best protection against *herself*. But no one ever hinted that a woman had feelings, Roxana thought with a flush. Why, every time Jay touched her accidentally, that rushing weakness came over her. She had not been prepared for it. No one had told her she would have to fight herself. It both shamed and kindled her.

She twitched aside the calico window curtains of the car to look out at the little town. Endless prairie, with too much cloudless sky above and too much plate-flat land below. Land should be broken up and hemmed in by mountains and trees. It should not stretch away and away, bisected by a pair of shining rails that met at the horizon.

She wondered where they were. Nebraska? Kansas? Somewhere in the dry-farm country of course. Jay said that any ordinary one-gallus farmer was a better sucker for medicine-show slum than was a miner in a mountain town.

"Slum" she had learned meant any liquid medicine. "Grease" was salve. "Buckshot" was pills. They sold them all.

She could hear Winnie Lazier in her cubicle next to Roxana's muttering, "Whew, it's hot today. This'll make our paint run, sure." Winnie, she knew, was bending toward her square of mirror and putting on her pale-pink layers and arched dark brows.

Roxana liked the hearty, slightly battered ex-circus performer who had sought the comparatively safe routine of the tent show after a bad fall from a high trapeze. Winnie Lazier could crack a joke or bang a skillet or dance a breakdown with equal gusto. Roxana sensed the inarticulate bond of affection between her and her toothpick-chewing mate.

For Ferd, the young canvasman, Roxana felt only sisterly concern. She dosed his throat when he had tonsillitis and saw to it that he ate his stewed prunes and pieplant sauce. Toward Sutro the Strong man she felt nothing whatever. He was, to her, a mere mountain of writhing muscles. She had seldom heard him voice a statement of any kind. He made his wants known at the table chiefly by grunting. He was useful in putting up the tent, however, and he *was* strong. The weights he lifted were almost as heavy as the figures on them said. She sometimes wondered what went on behind those small eyes, like horehound drops in color and size. Once she had seen him in his cubicle staring dully at a tiny cup and saucer in his hand. What was he thinking, what was he doing with that small cup and saucer? She gave up trying to figure it out. Jay had dismissed him with the remark that all weight-lifters were too stupid even to know their AB-abs.

They had spent the evening before, making up a fresh batch of slum to be used in the new town they were opening in today. While Jay measured in the ingredients, they all took turns stirring the mixture with a heavy wooden paddle in a washtub. A generous amount of epsom salts, some cascara bark, aloes, sassafras, and aniseed, with just enough alcohol to add "authority." Jay said the suckers liked the flavor of aniseed, and the aloes were bitter enough to make them think the medicine was good for them, while the cascara and the salts did the work.

"Sure, it's just a pitch," he said defensively to Roxana, who was watching the proceedings with an air of doubt. "As soon as I can, I aim to quit selling this bilge and have my own stock company. We'll kill off Dr. Langworthy and paint 'The Withrow Repertory Company' on the car, and carry our own properties to the farthest backwoods mining camps on the Kerosene Circuit. We'll put on *The Rivals* and *She Stoops*

to Conquer, and even take a whack at Shakespeare." He
cocked an eyebrow at her. "As I said, if I have the right
Lady Teazle, we'll do *The School for Scandal.* We'll give
those miners the best. They deserve it, poor devils, hacking
away all day at a wall of rock in the black underground. I
always figure that good theater is like—well, like opening a
window on a fairer land." He stopped, embarrassed at being
caught spouting idealism.

He gave the slum a swish with the paddle and began talking about prospects in the new town, and hoping with a
cynical droop of his eyelid that the weather would be good
so the suckers, the rubes, would flock to town in great numbers to buy the slum.

Roxana only smiled to herself. Let him talk now. He had
given himself away. He, too, saw good theater as a reaching
out, a stretching upward. He wanted to take it to the far
frontier. Her heart yearned toward him. Oh, Jay, you're a
pioneer, too.

Winnie Lazier had evidently finished making up her face.
She called out now through the thin partition to Roxana to
come along. As Roxana caught up with her, Winnie flashed
her a gold-toothed smile, and the two women went out to the
cinder bank beside the depot, where the company was assembling for the noon ballyhoo.

Jay had been lucky today. He had found a shabby open
barouche for the two ladies to ride in and a man from the
livery stable to drive. Roxana and Winnie draped their
plumes coquettishly over their cheeks, saw to it that their
frivolous little parasols would open, worked on their tight
kid gloves, and picked up their froth of skirts and climbed
into the carriage.

Noon. Time for the bally. Roxana felt her usual pleasant
tensing of the nerves. The little boys who always hung
around the medicine-show car had already started off up the
street carrying fluttering banners; they would each earn a
quarter and a free ticket to the show tonight. The band,

"windjammers" in the trade, were limbering up their instruments. Only four men in the band, in shabby red uniforms heavy with tarnished gilt, even to epaulets; but to Roxana they looked gallant in their finery.

Jay led off with a competent cornet; he was truly a musician, she thought. He could play a cornet, drag rhythm out of any old rented piano, and lead the band with verve and grace. Ferd played the alto horn; Chet Lazier played the clarinet; Sutro pounded the bass drum.

The sun was a blinding dazzle on the brass instruments. The dust lay thick as flour on the streets.

"Let's go," said Jay.

The four men swung into place, forming a square behind the barouche. Even the sedate old livery-stable horse picked up its feet like an anxious dowager. Winnie muttered out of the side of her mouth to Roxana that the old plug had such a pious look, she bet it asked a blessing over its oats each morning.

In spite of her familiarity with it all, at the strains of the "Tenth Regiment March," Roxana's pulse jumped visibly in her throat. There was something about band music—well, about Jay's band music—that made her feel high-mettled and tingly.

Tootle—tootle—tum—tee—dah. Her foot in its pointed French shoe beat time under her lace flounce; her parasol jerked to the rhythm. She smiled her fixed bright smile from right to left as the procession moved slowly up the main street. Past the block or two of false-fronted stores moved the creaking barouche and the high-stepping band. The brassy music seemed to fill all the spaces between the frame buildings and to cascade out across the prairie.

People swarmed out on to the walks. A parade. A band. Will you look at those two in the buggy. Fast, I'll bet. That's sure a looker on this side. See how she holds her head? How'd you like to—? Sure, I'll bet so, too. The other ain't so bad either. They say these theayter people . . .

It was all good business.

Up the street they went, to circle around and return. The faces of the band were red with exertion and shiny with sweat. The two ladies looked as cool as dishes of pink ice cream at a strawberry festival, although they surreptitiously patted at little beads on their upper lips.

In the central square they all came to a halt, with the carriage off to one side now, giving precedence to the band. On and on it played, until the sidewalks were banked with curious folk. Drop everything—dishtowel, cash boxes, dinner trays, receipts. Hurry out to hear the music. It isn't every day you can have music right outside your door.

The music stopped. Jay doffed his band-leader's cap, tucked it under one arm and stepped into the middle of the street.

"Friends: ladies and gentlemen—" His voice sounded pleasant and folksy. But looking at him, Roxana knew he was not one of them. He stood out from them like an eagle in a chicken yard. "We hope you enjoyed our little concert. To tell the truth, we almost didn't get here today." He paused for a broad wink. People moved closer, their faces crinkling with anticipatory enjoyment; a joke was coming. "Fact is, our train was held up for a while on a siding so our cowcatcher could drop a calf."

The audience exploded. They clapped each other on the shoulders. That was good. Cowcatcher dropped a—

The bandleader went on gravely enough.

"This little music you have heard is but a sample of to-night's entertainment at the tent up the street. There, you shall have a veritable feast, my friends. Songs by the beautiful Mlle. Roxane. Dancing and acrobatic feats by the famous Laziers. Deeds of incredible strength by Sutro the Strong Man. And magic acts, straight from the Orient. We close with a play—*The Beautiful Spy,* with a New York cast. And all this prodigal wealth will be yours for just ten cents or one dime."

[257]

Little ripples ran through the crowd.

Benignly Jay added, as if he had been saving the best for the last, "Above all, my friends, I want you to bring your aches and pains with you. Why? So we can cure them. Troubled with gas? Heartburn after eating? That logy feeling? Lacking in vigor, you men? Too tired to beat a carpet, you women? Then come tonight at eight o'clock to the tent, and we'll cure your troubles, or give you your money back. Thank you now, one and all."

He bowed to a little chorus of ah's and a crackle of hand-clapping. The band burst into a march; the barouche moved on its way; the noon ballyhoo was over. A good bally, Roxana decided, running her practiced eye over the crowd.

It was a good day. For one second her eyes met Jay's over the top of his golden cornet, and their glances locked and held. She looked away quickly. Oh, it was a very good day!

Chapter XXII

ALL DURING the hot afternoon Jay and Roxana worked in the tent on the new one-act play, *The Beautiful Spy*. She had a chance to wear two costumes, one an army uniform, the other Civil War hoopskirts, both of which became her. Jay proved to be a surprisingly exacting director as well as a sensitive one.

When they had finished, they stopped to rest, sitting on the edge of the platform, dangling their legs over and mopping their hot faces.

"You've got it, Roxy—the true actress-quality. I can't tell what it is."

She laughed. "Mrs. Harlowe says it's when you light up at night. You can be as ordinary as mashed potatoes in the daytime, but behind the footlights—"

"That's it. You and I could go far, Roxy. 'Jared Withrow presents Roxana Renner—' "

She stared past him down the long years, the shining years, ahead.

"Today I paid off my last note." He was suddenly shy. "From here on, I climb. I want to have something to offer a woman. I'm not much now. Just a circus sprat that came up the hard way. You know: chicken today—feathers tomorrow."

"I think you've done wonders, Jay."

"If a woman were willing to go along with me, and take the lean with the fat—"

"I'm sure the right kind would. A really unselfish woman," said Roxana nobly.

He studied her for a moment; then he threw back his head and laughed raucously and joyfully.

"You had me fooled for a minute. You and your Botticelli face—almost made me forget the spirit of the Texas Ranger underneath. 'A really unselfish woman,' " he mimicked her pious accents. "Back in Central you'd have sold your immortal soul to get on the variety stage. You'd do it again today to play Lady Teazle. Only thing that sometimes balks you is that crazy conscience of yours," he conceded.

She glared at him. His mouth was laughing at her; his red-brown eyes were full of the lively knowledge of her. Then she wilted in laughter, too. It was wonderful not to keep up any pretenses, to know that he sensed her deepest weaknesses and longings and still liked her, and wanted to see her name in lights with his: "Jared Withrow presents—"

Three small-boy faces peering under the edge of the tent reminded them that curious townspeople hoped avidly for details of the loose lives of the tent show folks. Their laughter died to a chuckle. It was time to be getting back to the car on the siding. They gathered up script and cash box and reticule.

The tempo of the day always relaxed momentarily in the late afternoon when the shadows took long strides across the prairie and the faintest coolness descended. Supper was leisurely tonight. Roxana and Winnie went out to stand on the narrow back platform of the car while they spread out the dish towels on the handrail to dry.

"Nice, ain't it?" sighed Winnie, looking down the tracks. "Between the time the flies stop and the mosquitoes start in. Makes you feel good."

It did. Everything made Roxana feel good today. She

dressed for the night's show with little wordless anticipations running through her mind and body.

The two women were the last to leave the car. They gave each other a careful inspection as they started off up the main street toward the tent on the vacant lot. They were fully aware that every passage through the town of their alien ruffled selves was part of the glamor and mystery of visiting show people. So their gait was studied. They twitched their full skirts and held their heads like blossoms on frail stalks. No farm wife ever walked like that or held her head that way. It was all part of the bally, Roxana or Winnie would have said.

The blare of brassy music came to them from the band stationed in front of the tent. The flaring gasoline torches out in front of the tent made it a bright island in the gathering dusk. People were already clotting around the tent flaps. When the two women reached the tent, the band dispersed, and Winnie slipped inside to begin pounding the piano. Ferd took his place in the ticket booth. Chet Lazier stood at the entrance to take tickets. Sutro lighted the row of reflector-lamp footlights in front of the painted street scene on the lowered curtain. Jay was in the lean-to dressing room hastily changing from his band uniform into the habiliments of Dr. Langworthy.

Roxana peeked out at the audience through a crack in the curtain. The tent was rapidly filling. It would be a good house tonight. She watched until Jay—Dr. Langworthy now —brushed by her and out to stand on the narrow strip of platform in front of the curtain. She smiled because the audience was so obviously pleased with him—splendid in his braid-edged coat, his fawn waistcoat, and his narrow string tie. All he needed were more years and less hair to look like a Kentucky colonel.

He might pretend that he had no acting talent, but he was an actor, all the same. In his opening bally about the remedies he had come to dispense, his voice was rich and unctuous with concern for their well-being.

Now he was announcing a song by the lovely French actress, Mlle. Roxane. She knew exactly how he raised his eyebrows and put a finger to his lips to suggest all sorts of titillating things. She would sing a ballad for them, a slightly naughty ballad, his manner implied, called *Maître de Chant*.

Her face was still quivering with laughter as the curtain went up, disclosing her in her lace and ruffles, waiting to warble her innocuous little verses about the singing master and his dear little pupils. She pursed her lips and trilled her bad French in imitation of all the Gallic singers she had ever heard.

The crowd was electrified. A song in real French! That was going pretty far.

They were now in a mood to be impressed by Sutro's weight-lifting. Sutro looked appallingly muscled, wearing his fake leopard-skin trunks, while he lifted and grunted and strained.

Would some young man in the audience care to come up and lift the weight? queried the doctor. A free gift of Alaskan Polar Bear Oil to any who would. How about the gentleman in the third row? The scarlet but willing young farm hand was pushed forward by his neighbors. Gratifyingly he could raise the weight only a scant two inches. The crowd was respectful; it was the real thing then, that weight. The show was the real thing. The doctor and his medicines were the real thing, too.

And now for the magic. The curtain went down; it went up again. The doctor had become the magician, standing aloof behind the small table surrounded by the inevitable velvet lambrequin. In the rear stood Roxana, demure as his assistant.

"We bring you tonight, dear friends, not only the herbs of the far East, but also its mysteries. On a visit to a remote Tibetan monastery in search of simples for my medicines . . ."

On and on went the hypnotic chatter. Against her will Roxana recalled his pitchman's spiel one night on a corner in Denver. She must not remember things like that; she must keep her mind on her business.

He opened with the trick of turning the red silk handkerchief into a billiard ball. It was all mundane enough now, since she knew that the ball was hollow with a hole in one side of it, and that Jay held it hidden against his middle under the lower edge of his waistcoat until he was ready for it. All he had to do then was draw in his lean stomach and catch the ball with his left hand, while the audience was intent upon the waving silk handkerchief in his right. It was easy after that, as he was wadding the handkerchief between his two hands, to poke it with one finger into the hollow ball.

The audience was as baffled tonight as that street-corner crowd had been years ago. They gasped when Jay opened his hand to disclose the shining red ball. She knew that if a knowing rube should ask to see if the ball was hollow, Jay would have his reply ready.

"You're mistaken, mister, about what's hollow. It's your head, not the ball." Whereupon he would thump the ball resoundingly on the table, slip it into his pocket and go into his next number.

Tonight there were no hecklers. The crowd shrieked when Jay mixed a cake in a man's Sunday hat, breaking eggs messily into it and then stirring it over a lighted candle, while the owner squirmed in red-faced anguish; only to end with Jay's pulling a bunch of flowers from the hat and returning it unharmed to the owner. So simple a matter it was to use a metal liner in the hat.

They always loved the magic. They would have sat through a whole evening of it if Jay had been willing. They would be awed and puzzled by all of tonight's acts, and tomorrow's, and the next night's. The mind reading, for which she and Jay had memorized a code of questions and answers, the vase and ball tricks, the flying glass of water, and the Chinese rings that could almost fool Roxana herself. The Cabinet of Proteus, with its ingenious mirrors which could make a person inside disappear in a twinkling, left them shaking their heads. Nor did they ever figure out the aerial suspension trick, saved for the last night in each town, when Jay passed a metal hoop completely around Roxana's recumbent body while she lay, apparently floating in air. What they never noticed was that he did not pass the hoop quite all the way up over her head. Some nights the iron support, hidden by her draperies, made a terrible crick in her back.

The curtain went down for the first intermission. Jay—Dr. Langworthy again—stepped out on the apron of the stage at the front and began the true business of the evening, the selling of the medicine. The rest of the company gathered on the ground below him to act as ushers. Bottles of elixir were piled at his feet.

Jay had never been more persuasive than he was tonight, or more cajoling, or more convincing. Just one dollar that might well be the turning point in your lives—one dollar to wake up with the joy of living—one dollar so you can do your housework and dance till dawn—one dollar to enable you to milk twenty cows and break a bronc before breakfast.

They laughed, but they also dug down into their pockets. It needed only someone to start the buying. Jay took care of that. He gestured to Ferd and pointed to a nonexistent purchaser in the rear. "Take care of that gentleman holding up his dollar."

That was all that was needed. Bona fide dollars sprouted in upheld hands all over the tent. The doctor would point out this man or that woman to the ushers. "Over there, that lady . . . off to the left, the gentleman with the silver cartwheel."

Each time, one of the ushers picked up a bottle and ran breathlessly all the way back to the eager purchaser. But Jay was careful to see that no two ushers ever ran at the same time. It prolonged the process and added tension and drama to it.

Jay's—the doctor's—voice went on and on in what was, Roxana knew, the most skilled act of the evening. The soft padding of feet on the dirt went on and on, as Winnie or Ferd or Chet Lazier or Roxana or Sutro ran swiftly down the aisle holding aloft a bottle in the air, to return a moment later and toss a silver dollar with a clatter into the metal cash box.

Jay, the sensitive pitchman, could sense the exact moment when interest began to flag. With a customer's upheld hand holding a dollar in full view of the audience, Jay shook his head regretfully.

"I'm mighty sorry, sir, but I see our supply is getting low. We've got to keep some elixir for the folks who couldn't get here tonight. Afraid I can't let another bottle go. Some other time."

The audience was impressed. Getting low, was he? Must be mighty good stuff, that elixir.

It was time for the Laziers' number. The versatile Jay took Winnie's place at the piano, while Chet and Winnie went into the old, old routine of song and dance and joke and acrobatic feat. Roxana had heard every threadbare joke in some olio long before, but she enjoyed them tonight nevertheless. Chet Lazier grinning apologetically at Winnie, his stage wife, and saying, "Dear, let me explain how I happened to come home so late last night with a black eye;" and Winnie answering tartly, "Don't bother—let me explain that when you came home, you didn't have a black eye."

The audience collapsed with laughter.

The ponderous Sutro now lumbered on to the platform and pretended to make off with the willing Winnie, with Chet Lazier in full pursuit across the twelve-foot stage, shouting, "Leggo that woman! You're stealing my wife, you horse-thief, you!"

The guffaws were satisfactory.

The second intermission's selling act was as good as the

first. Roxana never tired of the soap spiel. Majestically Jay ordered Ferd to go out to the lot behind the tent and bring in a wagon wheel, any wagon wheel that was handy. While he was gone, Jay extolled the virtues of the Ever-Lather Indian Root Soap. His patter went on until Ferd returned, hands black with axle grease, a smear across his cheek, and rolled a wheel noisily across the plank stage.

The ladies gasped as Jay drew out his snowy handkerchief and proceeded to wipe off the black grease around the hub—hadn't they tried and tried to get the stuff out of their husband's jeans? They gasped again when Jay airily swished the handkerchief up and down in a bucket of cold water, rubbing it with his famous soap, and lifting it out a moment later for all to see—spotless.

My goodness, a soap that will do that! Here, John, I want three bars.

They couldn't know, thought Roxana wryly, that before the show Ferd had carefully prepared that wheel by cleaning out the real axle grease and filling it with soft black tar soap and then replacing it on the rented livery vehicle.

Before she knew it, it was time for her one-act play when, briefly, she was a star. This might be only a countrified audience in a medicine-show tent, but into her performance Roxana put all her pent-up love of the stage and its trappings. When the curtain went down on her last lines, with Roxana wrapped in the American flag and Jay pounding out "The Battle Hymn of the Republic," the audience was cheering. People turned to look at each other in dazzled delight. Hadn't they just seen a real stage play with a real New York cast and a real French actress for the leading lady?

The lovely sediment of her excitement remained while Roxana unwound herself from the flag—the beautiful letdown feeling of a good day's work behind her. The crowd departed. The kerosene footlights were blown out, one by one. Sutro faded away. The Laziers set off for "home" arm in arm. Ferd was locking up the stage properties in a chest, safe from prying small boys.

She and Jay were the last to leave. He tucked her arm under his, and they started off slowly down the silent main street, as vacant now as an empty picture frame. They reached the tracks, but an impalpable pull on her arm turned her in the opposite direction from the company car. They moved dreamily along toward the water tower, the only break in the level skyline of the treeless prairie.

It was very still. They spoke of surface things, the first things that came to their minds. The size of the night's take; Sutro's stumble as he made his entrance; the kid that bellered straight through the Laziers' dance number. Their talk was as light and aimless and drifting as cottonwood fluff. They talked with the tops of their minds, as if they dared not let themselves look deeper.

Then Roxana was doing all the talking. Her voice was a little high and breathless. Jay was oddly quiet. The air between them felt charged with electricity as before a storm. Roxana was afraid to stop talking. Their feet made soft crunching noises on the cinders. They reached the shadow of the water tower. It had a damp mossy smell underneath and the pleasant sound of dripping, in this arid land.

And then Roxana ran completely out of words—those light airy cottonwood-fluff words. It was suddenly alarmingly still around them, with only the *drip, drip, drip* of wasting water. She leaned back faintly against a heavy upright timber.

"Roxana," Jay said softly. He took her by the shoulders and turned her around so he could see her face in the star-shot darkness.

A treacherous tide of feeling swept through her, along with a curious heavy thudding in her veins. She was unable to move. She stood there dreamily, sensing the approach of something momentous and wonderful and frightening.

"Roxana!" he repeated, with a sharply indrawn breath. He was shaken beyond all concealment now.

[267]

"Yes, Jay," she whispered.

Like a flash of summer lightning, their longing seared away all their sparrings, their uncertainties, their postponings. It drew them together; it flung them together. He caught her tight against him. She felt his whole lean toughness straining against her, the hard muscles of his thighs, the iron ribs of his chest. His heavy watch chain made imprints on her breasts.

His arm was behind her head now. He bent her head back across his arm and kissed her. At first with quick haste that sent tremors along her nerves to her very finger tips. Then slowly, hotly, passionately, as a man kisses a woman he has long hungered for, has dreamed about, has starved for.

"I've waited a good many years for you, Roxy," he said in a roughened voice. She looked up into his fiery dark eyes. "How much longer are you going to keep me waiting?"

She moved even closer to him, so close she was a part of him, until the feeling of him was in her very bones.

"Not much longer, Jay. I need you, too."

Pleasure was like a pain in the depths of her.

Chapter XXIII

THE THROUGH TRAIN, which seldom halted at this little whistle stop, squealed and chuffed to a standstill. The noise roused Roxana. She wondered drowsily who could be getting off.

How nice, she thought, not to have to get up when something woke you. That was one of the best things about being theater folks. You did not have to get up in the morning; in fact you were supposed not to, for you had worked the night before. Perhaps that was back of some of her mother's disapproval of play-acting. It let you sleep late, and it was sinful to sleep late, turning over and burying your head in your pillow for another downy, delicious nap. The time to get up, according to her mother, was when you did not want to.

She rolled over and slept.

It was late when she finally awoke. She lay there staring unseeing at the roof of the car, her eyes wide with held-over dreams. In that half-waking, half-sleeping state, she abandoned herself to a resurgence of last night's feeling.

She shivered, remembering Jay's strength and her own weakness. It had been Jay who had thrust her from him almost roughly at the last.

"You're too lovely— It's time for you to go back to the car!"

Oh, Jay, I love you for being strong!

With a swift gesture, she raised her arms, in her ruffled long-sleeved nightgown, high above her head. Her silky dark braids slid downward over the round curve of her bosom. Now at last she dared make plans. She was standing right at the door of happiness—of marriage—and all she had to do was stretch out her hand and open the door. She and Jay would go up in the world together. What a lovely word, *together*. Her whole being knew a delicious disturbance, a profound agitation of the senses.

She smiled radiantly at the roof timbers. Some day, what a Lady Teazle she would make! With a childish gesture she hugged herself. That screen scene in *The School of Scandal*—with Jay to direct her. With Jay. Was ever a woman so foolishly, so idiotically, so gloriously happy?

She raised herself on her elbow to listen for sounds from the rest of the car. How quiet it was. Winnie and Chet Lazier must be up at the tent practicing. Where was everybody else? She could hear only the raspy sounds of insects outside, the faint clicking of a telegraph key from the depot, and somewhere a horse's feet clopping softly along a dusty road.

She got out of bed. Leisurely she unbuttoned her nightgown, let it fall to the floor and stepped out of the circle. She poured tepid water from the pitcher into her washbowl and swished her washcloth around in it. As she sponged herself from head to foot, she remembered without envy the elegant tub in her own private bathroom at the Windsor. But she knew no nostalgia. Today was all she asked for. With Jay. She thought that living today was unbearably lovely. She did not see how she could stand any more happiness.

It was getting on toward time for the noon bally. She would fry herself an egg. There was no use looking frowzy, so she put on her flowered dressing sacque. You never knew when Jay would come hurtling into the car.

As she walked down the short corridor that separated the various sleeping cubicles, she noticed Sutro peering silently out of his window toward the depot. What was he staring at? He seemed to have been packing. That was queer.

At the stove she found a few embers and added enough dry cobs to make a blaze. She broke an egg into the skillet, cut two slices of bread from the loaf in the food cupboard, and pushed the coffee pot forward.

Footsteps crunched on the cinders outside—Jay, striding hatless along on some business of his own. She bent to wave at him through the window, but he did not look toward her. It gave her a lonely feeling, watching him hurrying past, so intent upon affairs that did not include her.

Jay, she cried out to him in her mind, look at me, wave at me, smile at me, *love* me. I need you. I want you to think about me all the time—well, practically all the time. I guess I've always loved you. Even when you were so mean and I was so spiteful—I loved you.

Her glance came to rest on the trunk standing on the depot platform where it had been put off the train. There would have been nothing unusual about a trunk on the depot platform, except that this was a theatrical trunk, well pasted with dirty labels. An indistinguishable name was painted on one end. Hmm, that was odd.

She flopped the egg, sprinkled salt and pepper on it, and transferred it to a slice of bread. She ate absently.

Where could Jay be racing to? Why didn't he come into the car to see her—after last night? She wondered how they would greet each other. Would he say anything? Would she? Who would have thought that love was like this? A fever, a clamor, a wild commotion in the heart that made one weak and dizzy and blissful.

Her eyes followed Jay's straight lean back as he made his way toward the depot. In her mind she raced after him, she hung on his arm, she smiled rapturously up into his face. I'm crazy in love, she thought.

Still chewing, with her thoughts all on Jay, she noticed the woman perched on a baggage truck in the shade, with a child beside her. Jay went up to her and began to talk as if he were continuing a previous conversation. Who on earth?

She held her forgotten sandwich in her hand while she bent to peer out. Even from this distance the woman was stagy looking; she had stagy gestures. The child wore ruffled skirts and darted here and there like a water bug, with the woman reaching out automatically to haul her back. The child had evidently had her yellow hair put up on rags the night before because her ringlets were little coiled springs that bobbed up and down when she ran.

Jay was talking earnestly. How well she knew his every gesture. She saw him hold out his hands, palms up, in the age-old expression of defeat, of emptiness, of pleading even.

Roxana was goaded by curiosity.

The woman slid down from the baggage truck, reached for the little girl's hand, and walked slowly along beside Jay toward the company car, talking volubly. Something cold clamped around Roxana's insides. She knew her now. Mlle. Fifi!

She stood there staring, rigid with dislike and fear. What was the woman doing here now? After all these years! Hadn't Jay got rid of her long ago; in fact, the day he was so sick with the cold in Leadville? Doubtless Fifi had been leaving at the very moment Roxana bumped into her in the board-inghouse. Perhaps that was why she was so ugly; Roxana could still remember the vicious way Fifi had flared out at her.

As they came nearer, she saw Jay's face. It looked blankly stony. He stepped aside to let the woman precede him.

The child bounced up the steps of the car screeching, "Mama, Mama, lookit. There's a table and a cooking stove and a lady eating."

So she was! Roxana looked down in dismay at her forgotten sandwich and then at her frilly wrapper. She hated to be caught at such a disadvantage. If only she had on her best green walking dress; if only she weren't holding this eggy sandwich.

Jay introduced the two women brusquely.

Roxana waited, biting her lip, for Fifi to say, Yes, we've already met. I threw her plaster in her face in the boarding-house in Leadville and called her an actor-crazy chippy and told her just what I was—besides your assistant. But Fifi only stared at her coldly. She hasn't changed for the better, thought Roxana. The same vixen. How could a man be taken in by that crafty little face with its tarnished pretti-ness?

Jay was saying carefully, "Fifi used to be in my magic act some years ago. She heard about the medicine show and she thought—since she's kind of down on her luck and with a young one to support—" He was floundering now, avoiding Roxana's glance. "I—well, I thought maybe we could find a place for her in the show, until she gets on her feet."

His last words made Fifi scowl. Roxana was speechless. That trollop . . . in their tent show. What had possessed Jay to take her back? Why didn't he send her packing as he had done once before?

Jay continued, "I figured she could do her old act as as-sistant in the magic. You can keep on, Roxana, with the bal-lads and the play. I've asked Sutro if he'd mind moving into the baggage section with Ferd and give his quarters to Fifi and—and Crystal. That's her name, you said, Fifi?"

Fifi nodded.

"Come here, Crystal. Yes, her name's Crystal. Stand still, Crystal. Shake hands with the lady, Crystal." But Crystal would neither come here nor stand still nor shake hands. She had already investigated the contents of the food cupboard and was starting in on the flour bin.

"Would you care for something to eat?" asked Roxana in confusion. "It's almost time for the noon bally, and we don't eat dinner till afterwards. But I could get you something."

"Just a cracker for Crystal, if you have it," said Fifi. "I'll wait until we all get back from the bally."

So Fifi was planning to be in the bally, too. Jay would not meet Roxana's accusing eyes. The Laziers came across the open lots and entered the car. Apparently they had met Fifi and her offspring; they bowed briefly and went into their own quarters. Sutro had already vacated his cubicle for the newcomers. So that was why he was packing this morning.

Fifi appropriated his room as if it were hers by right, and the car was filled with the cricket-like questions of the little girl.

On legs that seemed turned to aspic, Roxana got herself back to her own compartment. Shakily she began to dress for the noon bally. She was sore of spirit and sick of heart—and jealous—and frightened. She had been right about happiness; hers was too good to last. For there was something menacing about the reappearance of this pert little trull from Jay's past, with her pert little Crystal, and an air of rightfully belonging here.

The three women, Roxana, Winnie, and Fifi, accompanied by the bedizened child (wearing paint on her face! fumed Roxana), climbed into the carriage.

Winnie managed to mutter to Roxana, "I couldn't be any happier with a boil on my neck."

Roxana nodded bleakly. But she was an actress. When the carriage started along the main street, she pivoted her head and smiled and lifted her eyebrows, as did Winnie and Fifi and the grimacing, posturing little edition of Fifi called Crystal.

The wretched day wore on. Winnie was a distrait cook, and the pork chops were shriveled. Crystal upset the sugar on the floor where it gritted under their feet; she broke the round butter-dish cover so that the flies settled in the swimming butter. Winnie made futile darting efforts to right things and move objects out of Crystal's reach.

[274]

"It's like trying to tromp on a grasshopper!" she said darkly.

Only the elephantine Sutro found Crystal's antics amusing. His barrel sides shook when she daubed mustard on Ferd's coat.

Jay was too busy to eat. He stuck his head in the car door and told Fifi to be at the tent to practice in half an hour. He had added some new tricks since she had last worked with him.

Again Roxana tried to catch his eye. She must talk to him; she had to. But he was off and across the vacant lots before she could get his attention.

After Fifi had left for the tent, Roxana humbled her pride enough to ask Winnie what she knew about this Mlle. Fifi and her little Crystal.

"All I can tell you is, she didn't give him any warning she was coming. Jay had been going around here this morning looking like he'd just struck gold in his back yard, and then the express train stops and lets off this—this package out of his past called Fifi. A collect package, I reckon you'd call her. His chin dropped clear down to his wishbone when he clapped eyes on her."

"But he got rid of her once. Why doesn't he do it again? Why does he take her back into the show?"

Winnie shrugged. "If I know this Fifi, she holds some kind of a mortgage on him."

"What do you mean—mortgage?" Roxana did not want to ask, but she had to.

"The little Crystal, would be my guess. Jay and this Fifi had a long argument on the depot platform, him trying to get her to take the next train out and her saying she wouldn't."

Roxana turned her tortured face away from Winnie and went to her own room. I don't believe it. I can't believe it. She's nothing to him; he said she was nothing. But she remembered them—crowding together into the back seat of the stagecoach in Georgetown—staying at the same boarding-house in Leadville. Shakily she sewed a patch on the elbow of Chet Lazier's band costume. Jay is just being kind to an old companion of the road, she told herself. As soon as she gets on her feet, he'll send her packing.

At supper time when Jay came in to eat, Crystal, obviously coached by her mother, went up to him and tried to sit on his knee. He set her firmly off, with a look at Fifi that was both still and dangerous.

"Must give you a funny feeling, seeing your own kid for the first time," Fifi said loudly with a toss of her head. "Of course, I've had a good while to get used to the idea, but it's new to you. And don't think I've had it easy either, Jay. Waiting on table and doing variety show acts. If you hadn't changed your name to Dr. Langworthy—! I hunted and hunted for you. And little Crystal, all that time without a father."

Jay leaped to his feet, pushing his plate back. His face had turned a grayish color.

"That's your story. How do I know—?"

"Oh, you know, all right," she said with venom. "And if you don't, I can refresh your memory with a signed statement from the boardinghouse lady where we stayed in Leadville. My lawyer says—"

He stamped out without hearing any more, leaving his untouched plate. The only persons who did justice to their food that night were Fifi and Crystal and Ferd and Sutro.

Fumblingly Roxana dressed for the evening performance. You could powder your face, but you could not cover up the sick misery in your eyes. You could put carmine on your lips, but you could not keep them from trembling. Even her hands shook with a palsy of desolation as she tried to tie her petticoat tapes.

What did you do when your whole life fell to pieces? How did you keep going? She felt ill; she would have to lie down;

[276]

she simply could not drag herself out for the evening show. But she kept right on dressing.

You could fight for a man who was poor or in trouble or down on his luck, but not for one whose common-law wife and illegitimate child had just popped up again.

She recalled those hesitant, sober words of Jay's on the road to Caribou long ago, when he had told her how his own father had deserted them. He had said he guessed the measure of civilization, of a man's decency, was how responsible a father felt for his children. Motherhood was an instinct. Fatherhood had to be cultivated.

Ha! she thought, jabbing tortoise-shell pins into her hair. Fine words.

Her mother had been right; how often her mother had been right. There was an earth-root morality about this thing that you couldn't shut your eyes to. A decent man "gave his child a name." He "made an honest woman" of the child's mother. He had no choice.

How woefully mixed up her own standards had become. But right was right, and wrong was wrong, just as her mother had said. The morals of the theater *were* loose. They winked at wrong things, and gave them evasive names, and looked the other way. Back there in Georgetown, and later in Leadville, she had known quite well what a Fifi traveling with a Jay as his "assistant" meant, but she had shut her eyes to it. It was only when a concrete proof, like Crystal, appeared that she grew offended and outraged. Yet the underlying facts were the same.

I'm tainted by this whole life, she told herself. I'm not fit to make a home for Avis, if I should find her. What would the Starbucks, tolerant as they are, think of all this? I've come a long way—and all of it downhill.

The evening show went badly. The band numbers lacked spirit. Jay had no zest in his pitch; he "walked through his part." Roxana sang her own ballads with conscientious care, but while she warbled wanly of moonbeams and honeysuckles and undying love, her green eyes were hollow and haunted.

When she came off, Winnie was pacing back and forth in the cramped lean-to dressing room.

"I'm nervous as a gambler's wife," she told Roxana. "Something's got to give. The show can't go on like this."

Roxana watched the magic act from the dressing room. She could not wrench her eyes away from Jay and Fifi when they were together. Fifi, wearing a page's velvet doublet with black mesh tights, simpered and made eyes at the audience and then turned to smirk upward at Jay. Roxana's nails gouged her palms. She saw Jay fumble and almost expose a trick. Once, he dropped a property and had to talk fast to cover his mistake. A little more of that, and even the stupidest rube would catch on.

Jay studiously kept away from the dressing room and Roxana. The medicine was not moving well tonight either. Perhaps the weather had something to do with it. The drought was becoming a worrying thing. You smelled dust; dry whorls of dust like midget cyclones danced along the roads; the ground in the tent was churned by feet until a haze filled the air. The prairie wind sucked the canvas walls in and out and snapped the guy ropes up and down like whips.

"Sure makes you jumpy," commented Winnie.

Roxana nodded absently.

"Give me a hailstorm or a gully-washer, to one of these dust storms. You can't get yourself clean. It makes a phlegm in your throat and corn meal in your ears. I never did like wind. All this company needs now is a tent blow-down," Winnie said ominously.

Roxana scarcely heard her. As if anything could happen that would be worse than what had already happened. She picked her way around Crystal, asleep on a pile of coats in the dressing room, and lifted the tent flap to step outside, as was the custom, while the Laziers changed for their act.

There was a quick rustle off to her left. She saw two figures spring apart, and she retreated hastily. Her cheeks burned. Fifi and Sutro! Fifi *was* a little slut. Hadn't been here twenty-four hours, and already she was lolloping around in dark corners with the muscular but stupid weight-lifter. Roxana would be willing to wager she knew how Fifi had made her way in the world since she and Jay had parted.

At length the show dragged to a close. The last member of the audience had come back for the dropped handkerchief or the forgotten palmleaf fan. The dust had begun to settle. Ferd and Jay were totting up the night's receipts at the little table on the stage. It was then that Fifi went into action.

She flounced angrily over to the two men, who were counting stacks of silver coins.

"Make it in two stacks, Jay. One for you, one for Fifi. I've talked to my lawyer. Half the proceeds are mine from now on. You've got all these years' back keep of this child to pay for. Unless you cut me in on half of what you take in, I'll get an attachment on all you've got—everything. If I file suit, you can't move a thing. This here is a courthouse town. I've got a good lawyer."

Jay stood up and looked at her. The muscle in his jaw was a small jumping cord.

"You can't do that to me, Fifi. You'll break me. It isn't even smart business for you. I've got salaries to pay and license money and a little pay-off to the town marshal, besides grub for the company. You want to close me up completely?"

All her naked hatred of him was in Fifi's face, the hatred of a woman who has been cast aside and now has her chance to get even.

"I don't care what happens to you. I intend to get mine, whether it breaks you or not. I hope to God it does. You didn't think much about what would happen to me when you chucked me out, without a thought for my feelings or—or the kid that might be on the way."

She gave a sob that sounded as false as a horsehair wig to Roxana. Crystal, who was awake now, came romping out of

[279]

the dressing room. She upset one of the kerosene footlights, which Ferd hastily righted. She kicked the piano. She knocked three bottles of the elixir to the ground. Then she reached into the open cash box and grabbed up a fistful of silver dollars. Jay caught her wrist and shook it until the money clattered loose from her small paw.

"I see she takes after her mother. Will you try to cage your brat?" he snarled at Fifi. "All right, here's half tonight's take, and I hope it chokes you." He counted out the money into two piles with virulent care. "One for you, one for me, and one for you—"

Fifi turned with an injured air toward the rest of the company. Her glance stopped at Roxana. There was a sleek look, almost of triumph, about her.

"Don't you think a woman who has a man's baby has a right to some protection from him? Don't you think so?" she prodded Roxana.

"I think a man has to take care of his own child," said Roxana in cold rage, rage at Fifi, rage at Jay. "I believe it's considered by some to be the test of a decent man."

She turned and walked out of the tent and across the weedy lots toward the company car. But the rage was soon gone, and only the defeat was left. The taste of it was bitter as brass on her lips.

Chapter XXIV

WHEN SHE REACHED the car, Roxana dragged herself to bed like a gun-shot animal. And like a wounded animal she thrashed around in her pain. For hours after the others had come in and settled down for the night she lay awake.

She longed to hurt, to maim, to kill. She pictured Fifi shoved under the wheels of an approaching train, pushed off the trestle into a dry wash, mangled under the hoofs of a runaway team. She called the other woman all the short sharp ugly words she knew. She covered her face with her hands and silently groaned. She had no tolerance, no sense of justice, no mercy left.

She hated the child, too. Precocious, undersized little rat, who never got to bed before midnight and drank coffee three times a day. Roxana was without pity. She could remember only that she had thought, this very morning, lying here dreaming in her fool's heaven, that some day she would bear Jay's child.

Jay's child! Well, someone else had beaten her to it, and here was the child to prove it. She hated the grimacing little monkey, with all the poisonous hatred of a woman denied her own right to motherhood.

The humiliation! She burned inwardly with a wasting fire. Last night, in Jay's arms . . . they were going up in the world together. And now this!

Just let Jay try to make excuses for himself. Just let him come honeying around in the morning with explanations. She had her knife-edged replies all ready.

But morning came, and Jay did not come around at all, which made it worse. At dawn the men had struck the tent, loaded it into the baggage section of the car, and attached the car to a local that hauled it a few miles up the line to their next stop. Appropriately the town was called Dry Creek.

She waited, smoldering, all through the busy morning, all through the noon bally, and then through the long afternoon while the tent was going up and the benches were being knocked together. She supposed Jay was relieved that there was so much to do, so he could put off facing her.

Fifi was swollen and insufferable with power. She treated Winnie like a hired cook when the latter objected because Crystal emptied the salt box in the stew. She treated Roxana like a cheap cancan dancer she was about to fire when Roxana angrily dragged her best hat away from Crystal, with the plume broken. Fifi and Crystal appropriated the choice seats in the carriage for the bally, while Winnie and Roxana rode backwards. She talked about "my show" and "my railroad car."

Jay did not appear to notice. He merely went about the business of getting his show ready, eyes straight ahead, jaw clamped tight.

Even through her blinding resentment, as the days dragged by, Roxana could not help seeing the gravity of the situation for Jay. After Fifi had extracted her half of the proceeds there was nowhere near enough left to pay the bare running expenses of the show. The attendance was meager; people had other things to think about than a medicine show. The country was drought-baked. The crops had shriveled on the stalk. The sun glimmered palely through veils of dust. Dust was in everything—in their food, in their beds, in their hair, in their lungs. The wind, the snarling prairie wind, blew day and night.

Jay tried all the traditional methods for pumping life into a dying medicine show. He got up a testimonial night, with several glib loafers hired to extol the curative powers of the elixir. The audience remained apathetic, except for the few who hooted at their neighbors' testimony.

Jay started the usually effective popular-lady contest, with the prize, a gaudy silver tea set, displayed in a pharmacy window. One hundred ballots went with each bottle of medicine bought. But the men of the region were far more concerned about their fields blowing into the next county, than about buying votes for the most popular lady. So few ballots came in that Jay begrudged the cost of the tea set, even though it was the cheapest silverplate, bought wholesale from a carnival-supply house. At the drawing, to everyone's surprise except the company's, the winning number went to the mayor's buck-toothed daughter.

It was their last night in Dry Creek.

"Listen to her blow," groaned Winnie through the thin partition to Roxana while she dabbed cream on her cheeks with angry slaps. The wind pushed steadily and shudderingly against the side of the railroad car. "I hate to go up to the tent when it's like this. The sound of those canvas walls blowing in and out—*slip-slap, slip-slap*—seems like I couldn't stand another night of it. That and some other things," she concluded gloomily.

Roxana found her comb almost too heavy to pull through her long hair tonight. Her clothes hung loosely on her. There was no need for her to use blue eye shadows. She thought with self-loathing, If I had a grain of pride, I'd walk out of the whole mess. The show must go on? Bah! Not this show.

She and Winnie started across lots toward the tent. Just ahead of them walked Fifi and Crystal. Jay was in the lead, alone. Fifi grabbed up Crystal's hand and hurried to overtake him. He turned a startled look upon them, but walked along, with Crystal skipping in the middle, and for a moment he and Fifi looked like any decently married couple with their child between them.

Roxana bit down savagely on her lip. She would not look at them, and she could look nowhere else. After all, a man's own child— She drew weak satisfaction from the fact that Jay broke away from Fifi and Crystal at the first corner and hurried up a side street.

The last night's performance in Dry Creek started off badly. Jay was delayed in town, and the band could not play without him. The wind blew harder every minute. Only a few teams were tied at the hitch racks.

Roxana had taken Ferd's place in the ticket booth so he could tighten tent pegs, when Jay came striding across lots, his hair standing up like wild black jackstraws. He headed straight toward her, ignoring the handful of ticket-purchasers before her booth.

"I've got to see you alone afterwards. Something's come up. Something I want you to know—"

Only the flutter of her lashes betrayed that she had heard him. "Two tickets? Children under six in free," she murmured mechanically to the couple holding out their dimes.

What was there left for Jay to say to her now? "I'm sorry for ruining your life, Roxy." "Better luck next time, old girl."

The band blared forth, but only a handful of people drifted up, attracted by the torches or by the occasional valiant blurts of music that sounded above the wind. Ferd hovered anxiously near those gasoline torches. Claws of wind pulled ragged streamers of flame from them. At last he extinguished them. This was no time for gasoline flares.

The only light left outside now was the continuous nervous display of lightning. Roxana shut up the booth, picked up the cash box, and joined the rest of the company in the lean-to dressing room. The air seemed both close and gusty in its cramped confines.

The company was as uneasy as caged circus animals that

smell smoke. Wisps and fragments of Jay's selling talk out front penetrated to them through the roar of the wind. From outside came the *whack, whack, whack* of Ferd's mallet pounding tent stakes in tighter.

The company muttered among themselves. Would the show go on? A tent blow-down was bad. People got killed sometimes. Jay ought to send the audience home.

Even Sutro, immense and powerful in his leopard-skin breechclout, fidgeted. The Laziers glanced at each other anxiously. Fifi's face looked years older. When Crystal began to whine, Fifi's thin patience ripped. She whirled and slapped her hand down so hard over the child's mouth that she left a red welt. Crystal's bellow stopped before it started.

There was a spatter of sound on the canvas above. Rain! It would settle the dust. Maybe the wind would die down now.

But the wind did not die down. It caught up the rain and skirled it along with howling inhuman wails.

During her opening ballad, Roxana might have been singing in pantomime. Her voice was lost in the fury of wind and beating rain and flapping canvas. Only a chord here and there of Jay's vigorous piano accompaniment, only a word now and then of "The Letter that Never Came" sifted through to the audience.

Jay whirled suddenly around on the piano stool to shout at her, "Keep back from those foots!"

She jumped back. Her froth of ruffles had brushed dangerously close to those kerosene wicks sending up vicious yellow tails of flame.

As she finished and smiled fixedly to right and left, she noted with alarm the strange behaviour of the heavy hexagonal center poles. They were beginning to heave up and down, like giants' feet, in a slow rhythmic dance. With them, the whole tent was ballooning—in and out, in and out. Her eardrums felt ready to burst.

Pale under her paint, she backed slowly toward the lean-to

dressing room. Jay stood up and faced the audience. He was the regal Dr. Langworthy now, wearing his masking smile and his unctuous selling manner.

"Ladies and gentlemen, your kind attention, please. This wind is a little too much for us. There may be a real storm heading this way. I want you to empty the tent now. Not the slightest danger—simple safety measure." His voice was genial and composed.

But the crowd had become suddenly aware of the macabre dance of the great center poles. A blow-down—what if the tent collapsed on top of them? A child wailed. A woman screamed. Panic broke loose.

But Jay was there to quell it. He was down in the midst of them, standing on a bench directing their orderly withdrawal. Reluctantly Roxana sensed his strength, felt the iron in him. This was his show; these were his people; he was responsible for their safety.

"Don't crowd. Plenty of time. Who belongs to this nice little girl?" He lifted a child across several benches to her distraught parents. He helped a woman up who had tripped. He found an old gentleman's cane.

But before the last straggler was even gone, Jay had leaped toward the center pole and was hanging to it with all his strength. He shouted to the company.

"Sutro, douse those foots. Chet Lazier, herd the company out through the dressing room; the wind's from that direction. Quick, everybody! Out!"

He was gasping now, trying to hold down the evil, gyrating pole. He was no longer the suave Dr. Langworthy shepherding out his audience. He was the foreman of a gang, and they were all in this together.

The pole was lifting him clear off the ground with every upward lunge. All of his strength availed nothing against the power of the winds that lifted the tent, and with the tent, the pole. Each upward lunge was accompanied by a straining of canvas, the ripping of torn guy ropes outside, and the pop-ping loose of wooden tent pegs.

As Sutro blew out the last footlight, Jay let go the pole and leaped across the intervening space, up on to the stage and down the steps into the lean-to dressing room.

"Out, all of you!" he shouted angrily. "Are you afraid of getting your feet wet? This is a twister. If the tent goes, with us inside, we're goners."

They were all in the lean-to now. One lamp remained in a bracket on a pole. Fifi lifted it down to blow it out, when the light gleamed on something in Jay's hand—the metal cash box he had scooped up as he ran. Her whole face sharpened as her vast cupidity conquered all her other emotions, even her sense of self-preservation. She halted balkily, lamp in hand.

"Douse that light and run!" Jay commanded.

"So that's your game? Hustling us out, so you can sneak off with the cash box in the dark. I want my half now."

"Are you crazy? Get out."

"Not till you hand over that cash box. Here, I'll carry it for you." She reached out with her free hand, but he held the box out of her reach. She leaped at him, raking his face with her nails.

Jay swore and fended her off.

"Goddam you, get out!"

"I'll show you." She hurled the lamp straight at him. He ducked. It grazed his shoulder and shattered against the wooden steps leading up to the stage. Kerosene splashed. Flames raced up the canvas backdrop.

"Holy Mary!" moaned someone.

Screams, shouts, curses—intermingled. Roxana was caught in the jam of buffeting bodies, all trying to get out at once. Outside, the wind shunted her against a fence post. She clung to it with both arms. Over her shoulder she saw the tent, eerily illuminated from within like a Japanese lantern at a lawn social.

[287]

A man's voice shouted, "Crystal? Where's Crystal?"

"Crystal!" squawked Fifi. "My baby!"

A child's muffled scream answered from within the burning lean-to. The thick shoulders of Sutro dived into the smoldering canvas; he was back a second later carrying the wailing child.

"Look out. The tent's going."

With a great final ripping, the tent broke loose from its last mooring, taking the burning lean-to with it. Like an ungainly monster—alive, flapping—it began an uncouth humping progress across the fields.

The last Roxana saw of it, the rain was pounding down on it as it turned and rolled its way toward the lightning-torn horizon. She looked back at the spot where it had stood, a bare open lot now, with a ticket booth knocked over on its side and some scattered lumber that had once been benches and stage.

The rest of the company clung to the fence in the whipping wind and rain. The constant eerie lightning flashes showed them up in sharp relief, turned their faces into staring white blobs and their eyes into black holes. Jay was swaying and looking about him in bewilderment. The storm had pasted a ragged swatch of hair across his forehead. He was seeing the suddenly stark lot, the end of everything he had worked and dreamed toward.

Just beyond him Fifi was crowded against Sutro, who still held the child. Jay turned his stunned gaze on them. When he recognized them, he tightened all over—face, muscles, fists.

"You did this to me!" he raged at Fifi. "You burned up my tent. You, with your greed. Get out of here. Take your brat and your muscle-bound man. You . . . you . . . get, I say. You lying Holladay Street whore!" He was incoherent.

"I'll kill you for that!" screeched Fifi.

She threw herself at him. He tried to shake her off, but she clung like a rabid animal. He shoved her away. She came at him clawing. He struck out with a lashing blow. She went sprawling to the ground.

Roxana froze. She had never seen a man hit a woman before. Jay had knocked a woman down before her eyes.

Then Sutro moved. He chucked the child to the ground and charged Jay. Like a pasture bull, Roxana thought, head low, hardly looking where he was going. But deadly, all the same. The lightning gleamed oilily on his bare shoulders. Sutro the Strong Man, of the bone-crushing grip.

But Jay had gone crazy. He sprang to meet Sutro.

"Thought you could flim-flam me too, eh? Bloodsucker!"

Jay was the quicker at the start. He was all over the ponderous Sutro. He shouted obscene names with pagan abandon. Sutro seemed unmoved by Jay's blows. It was as if he knew that one bearlike grip of his great arms could squeeze the life out of a man and leave him a crumpled shape on the ground. Yet Jay seemed momentarily possessed of the strength of the mad.

Roxana saw only a confused weaving of figures now. She heard Fifi yell, "Kill him. Kill the bastard!" She heard the flat slapping of fists on flesh, the sharper thudding of fists on bone. There was a lustful bacchanalian quality to it all.

It was the spat-out words that were the worst. The short ugly curses, the shorter uglier obscenities. Roxana was ashamed to hear it, ashamed to see it. Two men fighting because of this—this trollop who had once belonged to Jay and had now become the property of Sutro, who was "defending" her.

Fifi was down on one knee, an arm about the child to hold her back, while she leaned forward and watched gloatingly. Two men turned into beasts because of her. Even the child was spellbound.

A great sickness came over Roxana. She turned away from the sight—but she had to look once more. This time the treelike torso was toppling. Surely Jay could not be overcoming that bull, Sutro! But he was. And then she saw Fifi crawling along the ground toward a pointed white stake, gleaming in the dim light. She clutched it; a tent peg, a two-foot-long hardwood weapon with a lethal tapered point. In the hands of Sutro—

Without reasoning, Roxana threw herself upon Fifi. She must get that tent peg away before the other could use it. The two women fought for possession of it. They fought for the sake of fighting. She, Roxana of the Botticelli face, scratched like an alley cat, and bit and clawed.

Fifi gave way, whimpering. In shame Roxana backed off. Oh, no, she said to herself incredulously. I didn't—I couldn't have fought with another woman. Over a man.

The struggle between Jay and Sutro was all but finished. The barrel-chested figure was down. The lean rawhide one was crowing over him, mauling him, kicking him in the ribs and shouting, "Stand up, you big bunch of tallow. Stand up and fight!" But there was no fight left.

Roxana could feel the blood on her face. She wiped it away with the back of her hand. She must get out of here. She felt soiled and degraded. She hated herself with a nauseous hatred. As she looked down she saw that she was gripping the wooden tent peg. She threw it as far as she could hurl it.

Alley cats . . . common alley cats!

As if the storm had fulfilled its purpose of spreading destruction and fury, it now abated. The wind let up. The rain settled into steady slanting needles.

Roxana panted up the steps of the medicine-show car. She had only a few minutes before they would all be here. In a frenzy she tossed things in on top of her partly filled suitcase. She twisted her dripping strings of hair up under her hat, wiped the blood off her clawed face, and threw a cloak over her wetly plastered dress.

As she stumbled along the main street toward the livery stable, she thought, This is what life with Jay has done to me. I know now what he is underneath—a savage, a cruel man, a coarse man. I know now what I am underneath—an alley cat.

She was both sickened and appalled.

She turned into the open door of the livery stable, her telescope bumping against her knees.

"I've got to hire a rig," she stated faintly, "to take me to the next town so I can catch the train to Denver."

Chapter XXV

MRS. PFAAB LISTENED with diluted sympathy to Roxana's bowdlerized version of her summer with the "stock company." It was the tent blow-down, of course, that had sent her back to Mrs. Pfaab's.

Roxana could almost see the woman thinking, while she led her up to the attic room, Well, she always *looks* like a lady anyhow, and Mr. Hull was such a fine gentleman, and she did make over my brown merino very nicely, and business is terribly slack in midsummer, what with everyone away at resorts up Platte Canyon. But "show people"—!

Roxana moved back into the stuffy little attic roost that was as hot as a brick kiln in the daytime. Surely now she would find peace. But it was a queer thing about peace; running away from turmoil and disruption did not necessarily lead you to it. There was still your heart to live with, and Roxana's heart was an untamed pony these days. She took long lonely walks to quiet it—clear out past Grasshopper Hill to the park laid out on the prairie with spindly little trees planted in rows. She did not want to meet anybody she knew. She had to take stock of herself first, and she was finding the results disquieting.

It was a shocking thing to learn what you were really like inside—violent, unstable, sullied. It was a shocking thing to find you had given your heart to a man who was unworthy, too.

But surely if you faced the truth, then the truth would make you free. (Echoes from Henry Starbuck's sermons went through her troubled mind.) The truth would wash away all the lingering fascination such a man could hold for you. Every time she thought of that last night in Dry Creek, of the fight, of *her* fight, the same nausea smote her. She hated both Jay and herself.

The flatness of her purse began to nag her. As she tucked her few remaining dollars back under the bottom layer in her telescope, she came across a rectangular package which had lain there undisturbed during her weeks with the tent show. She unwrapped it curiously.

Of course. It was the small bolt of fine China silk she had bought at a wholesale house here before she started out with the tent show. She had been planning to make silk handkerchiefs for one of Jay's magic acts where he would pull a long fluttering string of them out of the back of a gentleman's watch. At least, that was how it would look. She had never got around to hemming the handkerchiefs; there had been so much else to do.

The bolt had not been touched. She remembered the dim warehouse where she had bought it. Even with professional discount, it had cost her several dollars. And she was wondering how she would pay Mrs. Pfaab. She would never again be hemming handkerchiefs for Professor Jay.

She put on her dyed black dress with the twenty-six crystal buttons; she wore the matching bonnet and carried her furled black umbrella. Surely they would refund the money at the wholesale house; no one could refuse such an obviously refined young woman.

As she walked along the hot city streets there was no spring to her step. She did not look at her reflection in the shop windows. She did not care whether she walked with a pleasing Grecian bend, or even whether her lined, heavy skirts trailed in the dust.

Her black garments had a hot, dyed smell. With a feeling

of relief she turned in at the wholesale house. The interior seemed cool in its high-ceilinged gloom. No clerks bothered her. She wandered along between great heaps of carpets on one side and counters piled high with bolts of material on the other. It was clean and impersonal, a dim world filled with the dry pleasant smell of new cloth. She found it healing.

She stopped at a counter holding a pyramid of ribbon-wound cylinders. I believe I'd like to sell ribbons, she thought. So sleek and shining. They make the world prettier; ribbons never harmed anybody.

Out of the corner of her eye she noted the quiet couple standing several paces down from her at the same counter. They were speculatively fingering a length of dress goods. Nice mannerly folks, she thought. Probably here in the city on a buying trip from some out-of-the-way general store. Their voices were low.

From the rear a clerk in a black alpaca coat, pencil over ear, paper cuffs around his wrists, came toward the waiting couple. His air was one of businesslike servility.

"Very sorry to have kept you waiting, Mr. Evans, but we know the grade of flannelette you stock. If you will just wait a little longer, we'll have this last shipment unpacked. Please make yourselves comfortable, Mr. Evans, Mrs. Evans."

Evans, she thought idly, turning to glance for the first time at the man a few feet down the counter from her. Her package fell from her nerveless fingers.

Evans. She stared openly at the pleasant profile of the youngish man, thirty or so, who was looking at dress goods and talking in low tones to the woman beyond him. A little heavier perhaps, thought Roxana excitedly, but with Rob's nice high-bridged nose. If he would only turn around so she could be sure.

As if sensing her scrutiny, he turned at that moment and looked her full in the face. His mouth fell open a little. His face went from red to white.

"Why, it's you. But it can't be. Yes, it is. It's Roxana."

He started forward, hands outstretched—and then stopped as suddenly as if he had run into an invisible wire fence. He turned and laughed in a high-pitched boyish way.

"It's Roxy, Avis. It's your sister Roxy!"

He moved aside, and there stood Avis, slack-faced and staring. The same little old Avis, who always looked big-eyed and hungry. Only this Avis was a very pretty young woman, in a gentle self-contained way.

"Why, Avis." "Why, Roxy!" The two sisters laughed together. "Why, Avis." "Why, Roxy!" They sobbed. And then they were in each other's arms.

Chapter XXVI

THEY COULD NOT talk enough. They talked in long stretches and in short snatches. Facing each other on the plush train seats on the way to the new little plains-country town northeast of Denver called Eden, they tried to build a bridge across the years.

Briefly and without blame, Avis recounted the events on the night of her dreadful scare, when she had run away to the Evanses at Caribou, taking Boots with her. She and the dog had walked until they were tired. Then a couple in a wagon had picked them up and given them a ride the rest of the way.

Briefly, but blaming herself abjectly, Roxana told how she had returned to find Avis gone, and had never given up searching for her during the long years since.

Rob, sitting beside Avis, listened to them with smiling sympathy.

"But you've found each other now, and everything is all right," he consoled them. "I've got my own general store at last, and Avis has a new house."

"Painted frame, Roxy," put in Avis with decorous pride. "Not those old dark logs, like in the mountains. My lilac bushes are up to the window sills. We've got a spare room, and I call it 'Roxy's room.' "

Roxana's throat ached with wanting to cry. The two sisters

blinked hard and reached out at the same moment to clasp each other's gloved hands. They held on tightly.

The wonder of it! After all those letters she and Grover had written. After all the clues they had followed. After the notices inserted in the papers, and the inquiries made at post offices. And then to bump into each other standing at the same counter in the wholesale house. Roxana could not get over it.

Avis looked up to say wistfully, "Why didn't you ever answer my letters, Roxy? I wrote and wrote."

Roxana told of her trip to Caribou with Jay.

"That was the only letter I ever got from you—the one you left with the neighbor woman. The rest just couldn't have been mailed."

They were silent. For Mrs. Evans was dead—Edna Evans of the birdlike eyes and the tight neat mouth and the need to possess completely those around her.

"When we went to Central on our honeymoon, we couldn't find a soul that knew what had become of you, could we, Rob? The Starbucks had been gone for years, and Gil was dead."

"Yet it was the Starbucks who finally did get track of you, even though we lost your trail right away," said Roxana. "In St. Elmo they heard of a Mrs. Evans, a widow who kept a boardinghouse up one of the gulches and had a girl about your age, Avis. But there didn't seem to be any Rob." She smiled shyly at her new brother-in-law.

"I had an offer to work in a store in Topeka. I figured I'd get to own a store quicker by working in one than by gouging up the hillsides with a pick. Our store here in Eden has the best assortment of dry goods in our part of the state," he said with honest complacency.

She regarded him respectfully, this solid citizen who spoke with such earned authority.

"And then we moved some more," went on Avis. "And Aunt Edna took sick, and things were pretty bad, and finally she died. Rob—Rob was so good. He came out to help me—"

"And since I couldn't do anything else with her, I married her," explained Rob with a laugh.

Avis looked at him fondly and slipped her gloved hand under his arm, and a little flush appeared on his cheekbones.

A break came in the sisters' talk. They stopped for a reckoning up. So this was Roxy. So this was Avis.

To Roxana it was all completely unreal. They were only playing at being grown-up—one of them married, the other one widowed—dressing up in their mother's long skirts and clumping around the neighborhood. One single teasing word from their elders, and their disguise would have been punctured. They would have dissolved into the Renner girls again. Roxy—coltish, dreaming; Avis—big-eyed, wistful. These two proper-looking women sitting opposite each other in the railroad car, with their wide band wedding rings and "Mrs." in front of their names, couldn't be Roxy and Avis. They couldn't be.

Roxana sensed that Rob and Avis approved of her, a widowed Roxana in straightened circumstances. They approved of the whole idea of a deceased and highly respected Grover. They approved of the black dress and the black bonnet and the black umbrella; it showed the proper feeling, they were thinking.

"There's a vacant store building in Eden, Roxy. Rent's low. I could help you start up a millinery business," Rob suggested.

"Do, Roxy. You always had a way with bonnets," Avis said. "And you say you've actually had experience running a millinery shop."

"You could also sell ribbons," added Rob with a twinkle. "You used to like ribbons, you know."

Was he remembering that they had met across a ribbon counter? Was that what his smile meant? Roxana flashed him a look. Then she beamed gratefully at the two of them.

"The millinery shop was only for a few months, before

my baby was born, when I couldn't act," she explained conscientiously. She had so many gaps to fill in; there was no use putting it off. "Mostly I've been on the stage. A couple of years before I married Grover. Then after he got sick and lost his money, I went back for a while to play supporting roles."

They looked at her uncertainly. They looked at each other. The idea of a millinery shop in her past had been so satisfactory. They could even swallow the fact that she had been on the stage before she was married. But to have gone back to it afterwards! Perhaps a sick husband made it all right.

Roxana decided that she would have to go slowly in telling them about the tent show.

"Will you ever forget, Rob, on our honeymoon when we went to the Tabor Grand Opera House in Denver? What was the name of that play?"

"*The School for Scandal*," said Rob instantly.

"There was an old woman playing the part of Mrs. Somebody. So hard-looking. Just for a minute, Roxy, we thought we saw a resemblance to you. But I told Rob you couldn't look like that—ever."

"It was me," confessed Roxana. "Of course I was made up to look older. But I didn't need much making up. I had just got over the typhoid. Grover was sick at home. We—we needed the money."

They were apologetic and pitying. They talked quickly about other things. Pleasant things like their new home—*her* new home.

Eden, they explained proudly, was different from most small irrigated towns along the front range. It was modeled after Greeley; it had been started by good sound people. (Roxana stifled a wry chuckle. Greeley was a notoriously bad show town because its founders were so upright.) Although Eden was only four years old, already it had two

[299]

churches and a school and a singing society and a circulating library.

"Rob is on the town council," boasted Avis. "I wouldn't be surprised if he was our next mayor."

"Pshaw, Avis. I don't know about that."

"Yes, you will be. You've worked harder than anybody else to make it a good town, to keep the lower element out. No saloons. No gambling. No tent shows. We don't want that sort of people. Oh, not *you*, Roxy. I didn't mean you. You're different."

Roxana smiled shakily. Yes, she was different. There was nothing left of the old stage-mad Roxana. She was going to feel right at home in a place like Eden.

Monty was wrong about the lure of the stage. It could vanish completely. He used to say, once you'd been exposed to the rays of the footlights, you were 'touched' from then on. Unfitted for a sane, sensible life. Let a woman marry and try to settle down, and ever after, one part of her was looking backward.

But forsaking the stage, for her, would be like sailing away to a fair new land, leaving behind on the dock all her old, soiled, travel-stained luggage. She would never want to return for it again; she would never want to see it again.

Eden. It was well named. Not that it was exactly a garden yet, thought Roxana, as the three of them walked up from the railroad station. The main street was immensely wide, designed for future heavy traffic of countless buggies and surreys and farm wagons. The fresh new stores were irregularly spaced, with weedy lots between. There was something proud and confident about the rows of cottonwood saplings no bigger than buggy whips set out along the sides of the streets, where some day towering trees would rustle starched leaves across the road. It took vision. Only people willing to stay and work could build an Eden.

Avis gestured toward the little white church with its stubby finger of spire pointing warningly upward.

"I sewed miles of carpet rags for our aisle carpets. Of course, it's only hit-and-miss pattern, but so clean and bright. Some day we'll have a good ingrain."

Some day. When you grew up with a place, you planned for years ahead.

They stopped before a white-painted store with a false front and a covering extending over the sidewalk. Two wooden benches ran along under the two front windows. Hitching posts sprouted in front.

"Why, Rob, it's your store! With your own name on the window. 'The Evans Mercantile Company.'" Roxana was impressed.

"When you get rested you must come in and look around, Roxy. I've got everything arranged in departments—we're a department store. Maybe next year I can put in those little cash boxes that whiz along on wires."

As they turned a corner on to a side street, both Rob and Avis darted expectant glances at her, waiting for her to remark on something momentous.

A very new, very neat frame house painted gray, wearing its white trimmings like freshly washed collar and cuffs, sat in the middle of a dirt yard that was bounded by a white picket fence. Three scraggy bushes grew in front of the narrow porch.

"Can that be—I believe it is—your pretty house," said Roxana obligingly.

They relaxed into smiles.

"Of course, when the ditch is extended this far, we can grow grass. Now we have to water our lilacs with pails. I always dump my washwater on them; aren't they doing well? We had two blooms this spring."

Roxana looked at Avis' shining face and thought of their mother and the yellow rose bushes. Tears pushed against her lids. She felt suddenly full of years and memories.

"I think it's lovely. And you have a little porch to sit and rock on, too."

"I don't find much time to rock," confessed Avis. "What with my housework and helping Rob at the store sometimes and teaching a Sunday school class and taking turns at the library and planning club programs. And there's so much to do in a new house."

"I think you're a wonder, Avis. Rob, too. Remember what Gil told us once? It takes two kinds to pioneer a region. The reckless adventurers like Pa"—like me, too, she thought—"who come in and then move on. The put-down-roots kind like our mother, who stay and make a home of it. That's you, Avis. And you, Rob. You make me feel so useless," she said humbly.

The inside of the house was exactly the way she had known it would be. The center table in the parlor holding the lamp with the round painted globe and the Rogers group, "The Peddler at the Fair." The artistic rack for newspapers, hanging by pink ribbons on the wall. The caster on the dining-room table and the row of plates on the sideboard.

Avis said modestly, "Oh, this isn't a patch on what we hope to have some day. We're just starting."

Roxana relaxed with a sigh in the spare room, "Roxy's room." It was so clean and good. The ruffled pillow shams lovingly embroidered. The ruffled starched splasher on the wall behind the washstand. Even the husher on the slop-jar lid had a knitted ruffle around it. The room smelled of clean dry matting and sun-dried sheets and the crumbled leaves of sage under the papers in the bureau drawers. When she had unpacked and hung her clothes on the hooks beneath the curtain in the corner, she took off her hot dyed black dress and flung herself down on the bed.

This is paradise, she sighed. Truly, the Garden of Eden.

She slept dreamlessly, waking in the late afternoon to lie looking out the window toward the thin wavy line of violet peaks to the west, with miles and miles of tan and green lands between. The sun would rise early and set late here, with no mountains hemming them in. They were out in the flat country where Avis could "see out."

It was a pleasant, predictable country, as bland as a dish of tapioca, with a future that stretched ahead as long as this good prairie soil could be watered by ditches from the far-off mountains.

Corn and potatoes and wheat and cattle and hogs. Children growing up. Thanksgiving turkeys and Christmas trees and birthday cakes. An addition built on the house. An Estey organ in the parlor. The trees reaching to the lintels of the doors, and then to the eaves, and finally towering overhead. Children reaching to the elbow, and then to the shoulder, and finally towering overhead, too. A silver wedding anniversary, and finally a golden, with the children and grandchildren coming back and saying indulgently, "Aren't they wonderful? Fifty years in this same house. Why, they planted those huge trees themselves—no bigger than buggy whips when they put them in, Grandpa says. Pioneers, real pioneers!"

She thought fleetingly of the mountain country, that wavy line of peaks she had once called her land. Where towns and fortunes and people came and went, and nothing was permanent. Where Presidents dined and lovely ladies flirted —and then, of a sudden, pine trees grew in rotting sluices and pack rats took over the houses.

She thought of her other world, the theater, where nothing was permanent either. Everything make-believe—curls, smiles, characters. Here today and gone tomorrow, even fame. Just when an actress was at the height of her fame, she was already starting down the short steep path to obscurity.

Rob and Avis had chosen the right way. Every hour in their house proved it. When Rob brought in a pail of water from the well on his way to supper that night and kissed the flushed face of his young wife, who was stirring something on the stove, Roxana was sure of it.

Rob had the look of a contented man. You knew he enjoyed his food, liked to sit evenings in the patent rocker under the hanging lamp in the dining room reading his paper, and never ran if he could walk. You knew his store help liked working for him because he was fair. His opinions on the town council would not be lightly given nor lightly received. He was a man of substance. Life with him would be good.

He was no lean splinter of a man with a smoldering fire back in his eyes and a droop to one lid and a tongue that was sharp as a yucca spear . . . with a savage temper and a streak of cruelty . . . a bit of a mountebank and a bit of Robin Hood.

Avis was lucky. Roxana wondered enviously if she knew just how lucky. To think that she, Roxana, might have had it all: this clean sweet peace, this security of the mind, this safety for the heart.

For supper, she put on an airy summer dimity, sprigged with violets. She had made it the summer before Grover died.

She found Rob watching her as she sat back in her chair and sighed with satisfaction when the excellent meal was over. Potatoes creamed with new peas, ham fried to a lace-edged brown, green-apple sauce. Avis was a good cook, like their mother.

"Such wonderful food, after a boardinghouse and those haphazard meals in the company car."

"Company car?"

"On the road."

"Did your stock company have its own car?"

Roxana hesitated. It had to come out some time.

"It wasn't exactly a stock company. It was a tent show. A traveling medicine show." She looked at them almost defiantly. "We had some music and a comedy routine and put on a one-act play . . . and sold medicines—an elixir, besides hair oil and soap."

"But you didn't finish the summer out," said Rob.

She wilted. "No, I left, as I told you. We had a tent blow-down—and other things. I left—"

Avis was still staring at her uncomprehendingly. A medicine show!

Roxana laughed recklessly.

"We might have found each other a bit sooner, Avis, if Rob hadn't been on the town council that kept out 'the lower element.' I've been through Eden several times this summer with our show, known to the trade as a 'physic show.' "

Avis got up from her place and came around to put her arms about Roxana's too-squared shoulders.

"That's all behind you now, dear. You need never think of it again. We'll none of us think of it again," she said magnanimously. "In fact, I believe—don't you, Rob?—it will be best if we don't *any* of us mention about the medicine show. We'll just say you played a few Shakespearean roles. You know how people are."

Roxana nodded meekly, all the stubborn starch gone out of her. She knew how people were.

It was Avis' turn to take care of the library that night, when the farmers came in to do their Saturday trading. Would Roxy like to come along? She could see what a worthwhile project their circulating library was.

Rob spoke up. "We'll walk you down to your library, Avis; then I want Roxana to see the store. And before it gets too dark, I'd better take her over to look at the shop she can rent. It isn't much, Roxy. Just a small front room and a smaller back one. A cobbler had it. There's never been a real milliner in Eden. I think you could do well here."

Roxana nodded obediently. She went into her room to smooth her hair.

Avis came to stand in the doorway to watch her. Roxana touched her white skin with rice powder and tidied her hair, with the feathery dark fringe across the brow and the mass of curls caught into a chignon in back. Avis' own tan hair was parted smoothly in the middle, and her compact braids were crossed on top. She wore a figured dove-gray dress, and she looked not unlike her own neat gray house, clean and fresh and well-ordered, and without an ounce of style.

"You—that light ruffled dress—everybody will be downtown on Saturday night. You being a widow and all—You're so wonderful, Roxy, I want people to think well of you. How about wearing your nice black?"

Roxana turned and looked at her sister. Then she shrugged amiably. Avis knew best what the people of Eden would think. That dyed black was pretty hot and stuffy for a summer night, but if Avis wanted it—

As the three of them set off down the street, Roxana reminded herself chidingly that she was an *insider* now, a rube, and that it was important to her what people thought.

They left Avis at the furniture store where one corner was given over to the circulating library. She and Rob went on to The Evans Mercantile Company.

She was suitably impressed by the two busy clerks and by everything arranged in departments instead of "with the gingersnaps all mixed up with the coal oil and the suspenders." Rob added slyly, "We advertise our suspenders as conscience suspenders—they're so elastic."

She looked at him and burst into surprised laughter. She was still laughing when he took the key from his desk and ushered her down the street to a tiny building standing by itself. It was a child's playhouse. It had a pitched roof and a door on the front with a small display window beside it.

"The light's good enough for you to get some idea, Roxy. Next time we come, I'll measure for a counter and shelves. I think there's a work table in back, and a stove."

She stopped in the front room to look at the distempered walls.

"Why, this will be fine, Rob. It's nicer than the shop I ran when Grover was sick. That front window—it would hold one or two bonnets—smart ones though. I always think a few are better than a whole windowful."

"That's what I try to tell my clerks." (There might have been twenty instead of two.) "You don't have to put a sample of every item you stock in the window. But you know how the old-fashioned clerks are—they want a store window to look like the fish-pond at a church bazaar."

They laughed together—two business people laughing over a business matter.

It was purely business, too, when they went back into the dusky rear room, with its stove and table and one backless chair. The very smallness of the place threw them together. She felt herself appallingly close to him, looking up at him and laughing nervously.

"Another back room! I seem to be forever moving in and out of back rooms. First Gil's. And then the millinery shop in Denver. And now this." She knew she was rattling on.

But he did not rattle on. He merely looked at her. When he spoke, his words came unevenly.

"You know the real reason I didn't stay out west, why I went back to Kansas? You know, don't you, Roxy?"

"Why, Rob?"

"You. Because you chose to go off with the DeForest Company. Deliberately chose it . . . to me."

How dark and close it was in here! She tried to back away from him and only bumped into the chair. She felt confused and giddy. Her laugh was strained.

"I expect you've often thanked your stars I did go off with the troupe. If I hadn't, you wouldn't have Avis today."

"That's true," he agreed gravely. "I wouldn't have Avis today."

His words, his tone, alarmed her. She looked around the shadowy little room. Anything to avoid meeting his burning glance.

"This workroom will be fine, simply fine, Rob. And now I

expect we ought to be getting back. We can't measure until the light is better."

"We'll go now. I know we mustn't stay here. But why did you do it, Roxy? Choose the stage instead of love? Because you did love me when you were sixteen. And no later love can ever be quite like first love. Can it, Roxy?"

Fright made her breathing ragged. This was the Rob who had once consoled her and loved her. And this was Avis' husband.

"I'm twenty-five now, and that was a long time ago, Rob. Why did any of us do the things we did? Because we couldn't help ourselves. The pull of the theater—it was bigger than I was—it tore at me. C-can't you understand?"

"Yes, I can understand."

She backed into the one chair again, and it went over with a crash. She had to get out of here! She turned and walked with swift unsteadiness out into the front room, lighted with the apricot afterglow of a prairie sunset.

He followed her.

"Nobody knows better than I," he repeated doggedly, "what it means to feel a secret inner pull that is stronger than you are."

His face looked older and sterner as he opened the door for her and let her precede him out into Eden, on a Saturday night.

Chapter XXVII

How many things you forgot about small towns, particularly tidy little plains-country towns founded by a picked band. She had lived in a different world so long, thought Roxana. First, with the vagabond stock company, then in the rootlessness of a hotel and a boardinghouse, and recently in the gay shoddy round of the tent show. None of it had fitted her for an Eden. She must try harder. Avis was always having to remind her gently. Even about such things as the way she walked.

"I—I guess it's your theater experience, Roxy. You're different from the ladies here. You carry your head so high and when you walk you sort of twitch your skirts. Oh, I know you don't mean to, but you do."

She *had* meant to, that was the worst of it. Always, as theater folks, you tried to walk with an air; you kept up the pretense of a sweetly icy remoteness, like the visiting princess. And with the tent show, every appearance on the streets was a bally. I must sort of trudge along, she thought, plumping my feet down as if my bunions hurt and my back was stooped from the washtub.

"You're so much prettier and with so much more style," went on Avis bravely. "You stand out. Like when you sing in church. It's all that ballad singing, I suppose. But people—well, I see them looking out the corners of their eyes. You let your voice out—"

"And why not?" defended Rob loyally. "She's the only one in this town that can sing."

But Roxana paid him no attention beyond a flashing half-smile. For Avis knew best; Avis listened to woman-talk. I must swallow the hymns. No more lifting my head and opening up all the stops for "How Firm a Foundation," she thought regretfully. There were so many things to remember.

"I'll try, dear," she told Avis. "I know what you mean. I knew a man once in show business—" She wished she had not started this; the very mention of Jay set her heart to pounding painfully. "I used to take him to church with me in towns like Eden, and he had the same effect on the congregation. I sometimes thought he was as out of place as . . . as an eagle in a chicken yard."

Avis looked gratified at Roxana's sensibility.

There was the problem of the Murdochs—Mrs. Murdoch, who was president of the Shakespeare and Milton Society, and the wife of Jethro Murdoch, who was, in turn, president of the Stock-Raisers' Bank, which held Rob's notes. Avis and Rob used a special tone in referring to the Murdochs. Roxana had a mounting curiosity to see this remarkable pair who were the guardians of Eden's faith and morals.

It was a slight shock, after a whole day of preparations: of sweeping the carpet, with shredded wet newspapers scattered over it; of shining the best silver; of putting on one's Sunday clothes—with the whole house smelling of furniture polish and roast chicken and spiced peaches—to have the Murdochs finally walk up the path.

So these were the Murdochs. This darting-eyed woman who moved her head with little pecking motions. This big squeak-booted man with the bellowing laugh.

"I smelled your roasting hens clear out to the gate!" he shouted, nudging Rob, who was standing beside Avis on the porch. "Nothing like putting tasty feed in the trough for the old codger that holds your notes, eh?"

Avis flushed, and Rob laughed uncertainly. Mr. Murdoch

was not a cruel man; he was simply not endowed with a thin skin himself.

Avis asked to be excused to return to the kitchen, leaving Roxana to accompany Mrs. Murdoch into the spare bedroom while she took off her hat. Roxana watched the other remove the brown magpie's nest from her head. The woman reminded her of Rob's Aunt Edna. The same careful sweetness, the same quick glance that took in everything—the mars, the patches, the let-down hems. Perhaps it was not so surprising that Avis had turned to her; perhaps Avis needed an Aunt Edna in her life.

She wondered how such a precise, buttoned-up woman could endure Jeth Murdoch and his bullying laugh and bullying tongue. I wouldn't touch him with a toasting fork, she thought scornfully. And then she realized that Jeth Murdoch had a crude attractiveness, the magnetism of power. He was the kind of man Aunt Edna had wanted her mild and ineffectual husband to be. Mr. Murdoch owned so much already that he almost succeeded in buying your respect, too.

Mrs. Murdoch was inspecting Roxana's black dress.

"Avis tells me you're handy with the needle. Did you make that dress yourself?"

"Yes. I dyed it first; it used to be sage green. I made the bonnet out of the black scraps." She reached up to the shelf above the curtained corner for her hat and exhibited it on her forefinger. "Rob and Avis are trying to get me to start up a millinery shop here. I had some experience in Denver."

Mrs. Murdoch looked at the bonnet with measured enthusiasm.

"Very citified. Of course, here in Eden—" Her glance touched the magpie's nest on the bed.

Roxana misread the glance.

"I know," she said with sympathy. "You can't expect to get becoming hats in a small town. I could do a lot with that hat of yours, Mrs. Murdoch, if you'd let me try." She picked up the magpie's nest from the bed.

"Oh, no, you mustn't trouble. Please, I'd rather—"

"But I'd love to, really."

With a swift snipping sound, Roxana's scissors sheared off several buckles, a sheaf of brown wheat, and a handful of desiccated flowers. She perched the denuded frame on Mrs. Murdoch's reared-back head, wrenched the folds higher on one side, tucked a flower in here and there, and pinned the whole confection into shape. She stood back to view it with the narrowed eye of the artist.

"You've no idea how fine you look. Wait while I tack it in place. I work like lightning, you know. Now if you were to wear some nice fresh tones instead of those deadening browns, it would bring out the color of your skin."

There was nothing the matter with the color of Mrs. Murdoch's skin at the moment, except that the red was in splotches. Roxana noted with surprise that the woman's hand shook as she gathered up her discarded hat trimmings and stuffed them into her reticule.

The gaiety at the supper table was labored, in spite of Mr. Murdoch's draft-horse humor. Mrs. Murdoch sat through the meal with an air of explosive stillness. They left early.

The three stood on the porch speeding their departing guests, who needed no speeding.

Rob asked in a troubled tone, "What on earth happened? You could have cut the chill in blocks and stored it in the ice-house."

"What happened to her *hat?* Roxy, you didn't—?"

Roxana nodded miserably.

"I did. She admired mine, or I thought she did. So I re-trimmed hers all in a wink and tried to make it look like something. I'm sorry, Avis. I wouldn't for the world—"

"Oh, Roxy, how could you!" Avis' despair welled up in her voice.

Rob swallowed once or twice. What if old Murdoch did hold his notes and entire future in those knobby-knuckled hands of his? He spoke out manfully.

"I noticed her hat when she left. I thought it looked real stylish, Roxy."

Roxana flashed him a glance, soft with gratitude. How like Rob. He had always tried to heal her hurts.

The next time the two sisters saw Mrs. Murdoch, the latter bowed politely to them from across the street and hurried on her way. The magpie's nest had assumed its original form, the buckles were firmly mortised back in position, the brown wheat nodded, the desiccated flowers burrowed in the dun-colored folds.

When she was out of sight, Avis drew in a quivering sniff that was close to a sob.

Roxana could only murmur again, "Avis, I'm sorry!" If it had been anybody but Avis' idol, her present-day Aunt Edna.

Something went out of the sisters' relationship that day—a certain fond indulgence; and something came into it—a new critical sharpness. Roxana knew that she could never make hats that would satisfy Eden. She probably could not make a hat that would satisfy Avis.

At the next meeting of the program committee of the Shakespeare and Milton Society, which was held in Avis' parlor, they discussed having a paper on the Influence of Shakespeare on Drama. (Influence on! thought Roxana; why, he *was* drama.)

She suggested diffidently, "Why don't you actually read aloud some of the great scenes from Shakespeare? There are some wonderful bits you could lift out. From *Romeo and Juliet*. From *The Merchant of Venice*. From *The Taming of the Shrew*. I once knew all of Bianca's lines—" She stopped before she had offered to give a whole scene from *The Taming*. She hoped she hadn't said anything new to upset Avis; after all, Avis had let it be known that her sister had once been on the stage briefly—in Shakespearean roles.

There was an uncomfortable silence before Mrs. Murdoch spoke in pained reproof.

"We don't put on plays here. We aren't actresses. We're

[313]

just a study club—for ladies." There was the faintest stress on the word *ladies*.

Now she's even, thought Roxana. Maybe she'll feel better.

Avis' critical sharpness took on an even keener edge over the near-catastrophe at the meeting of the women's society of the church to plan the annual baked-goods sale. Because all gatherings in a small town are eagerly attended, Roxana and Avis were there. Roxana sat through endless haggling over booths and decorations and who should bring what. It was decided to be daring this year and have an auctioneer auction off the cakes and pies. But what should they do if the bidding was too low?

Without thinking, Roxana spoke.

"What you need is a couple of shills planted in the audience to start the bidding and keep it climbing. You'd be surprised how that sparks a dull crowd. Always in the medicine show—" She caught Avis' anguished expression—why, Avis looked actually white around the mouth—and she retrieved her sentence smoothly. "Even in medicine shows, I understand, as well as at big cattle auctions, they have someone planted to start the bidding, or to raise the bids when interest flags. But maybe you won't need it after all; maybe you'd be better off just to let things take their course," she finished lamely and sat down. Whew! That was a close shave. She touched the sweat on her upper lip. She must be more on her guard. She had come perilously close to wrecking the careful edifice Avis and Rob had erected here in Eden.

Placatingly she suggested after supper that they leave the dishes until morning and the three of them go for a walk to see the sunset.

"After all, it's the only dramatic thing all day, out in this flat country," she urged.

"Sure, come on," agreed Rob, brightening.

"You two go if you want to," said Avis. "Some of us haven't time to wander around looking at sunsets. Some of

[314]

us haven't time even for 'drama' in our lives. We have to be satisfied with doing our work well and keeping our homes nice and . . . and doing our duty."

How like their mother, Roxana thought with vexation. But Rob Evans was no feckless Dan Renner. Avis had no right to take out her rancor on Rob, who was faithful and serious and getting on in the world. She doesn't appreciate him. He needs understanding and approval (such as I could give him). He's so good, so open-faced, so kind. She thought of a certain dark, raffish countenance with a smile that was half-grin, half-sneer.

First love is right, after all. It's impulse and instinct. I should have listened to my heart back there in Central, instead of trailing off with the troupe. If I had, Rob would be happy now—and I would be happy. But it's too late. Poor Rob.

She spoke briskly. "Avis has had a hard day, Rob. She does far too much. You take her for a walk then while I do the dishes. All I want is for somebody to see the sunset. Look, it's starting to fade already."

Avis would have objected, but Roxana hustled the two of them out of the house, flapping a dish towel good-naturedly after them. Then she turned to the dishes.

Such a neat kitchen, with its yellow-pine woodwork and its iron sink with a drain that let the water run out on the ground and saved so many steps; you only had to bring water *into* the house.

My, what an orderly saving little thing Avis was. A box of burned matches to be used over again; Avis always reminded Rob to light one of them from the stove embers, for his pipe. The withered turkey wing for a stove brush. The apron made from Rob's shirt tail—the tail of a shirt always wore out last, Avis explained. The pile of wrapping paper to be used again. Oh, no! she said to herself as she touched the pile. But it had been—every sheet of brown paper had been pressed by Avis' careful iron to make it look like new.

[315]

Roxana shook her head compassionately. Avis would be her mother all over again if she didn't look out. The same terrible urge to be dutiful and good and see that everyone else was the same. She hoped Avis hurried up and had six children, so it wouldn't all be concentrated on Rob and the study club.

She opened the food safe to put the bread away and saw the little square of folded paper under the edge of the bread box. Smiling, she drew it out. Avis was always writing reminding little notes to herself and tucking them into conspicuous places around the house; notes that said, "Remember to tell Mrs. Beck how pretty her cosmos looked in church Sunday," or, "Ask butcher to put in *all* the meat trimmings, for soup." Today's note read, "Tell milkman to leave double order for Roxy's oatmeal."

Roxana's laugh was mirthless as she put the note back. Well, it was true, wasn't it? How many times had Avis remarked smugly as a child, "At least *I* don't gobble up all the cream in the pitcher on my oatmeal."

Nettles, little nettles. But they smarted.

Roxana was sitting quietly on the front porch in the darkness when Rob and Avis returned by the back way. She heard the snick of a match and the squeak of a lamp chimney. She heard Rob settle himself under the dining-room lamp to read his paper. She heard Avis moving stealthily about the kitchen, accompanied by subdued rattles and clinkings.

This flimsy little house, where every sound carried to the farthest end of it! She listened curiously now, trying to decipher the meaning of Avis' movements. She heard cautious little jangles as Avis rearranged the silver in the drawer where Roxana had carelessly dumped it. Now she was pouring water from the teakettle into the dishpan and swishing towels around in the suds. Oh, dear, I forgot to wash the tea towels, Roxana thought in horror.

Nettles, only nettles. But they burrowed in and festered.

In the days that followed, Roxana found herself in a dilemma. She did not want to be alone with Avis for long periods because they had completely run out of things to talk about, and Avis had started in to improve Roxana. She did not want to be alone with Rob because of the intent way he looked at her. She dared not be alone with him, in fact; for when she was, the past rushed at her. She found herself both carried back and swept along. She tried not to answer his look; but she was always conscious of those deep-set eyes following her about.

My sister's husband! My little lost sister that I hunted for, these nine long years. Her mouth dented in with pain and remorse.

I'm a misfit everywhere. I thought everything would be all right as soon as I found Avis. I thought all I longed for was to settle down in a place like Eden. But Avis wants to make me over, and Eden suspects me.

She began to take long walks by herself. Late one afternoon she returned from a walk to Mallard Lake, a flat depression almost covered with a cracking mosaic of dried mud, but retaining a pond in the middle, which was dotted now with southbound wild ducks.

She thought suddenly, I'd like to tell Jay about Eden. I'd like to see his eyes squint into slits when I tell him about all these nice plump setting hens staring at me with suspicious little hens' eyes from the nests—me, the outlandish wild mallard that's just stopped off on my flight south.

Imagine me, Jay, boxed up with a lot of women exchanging receipts for salt-rising bread and debating whether it's better to use wood ashes on the kitchen knives or a scouring brick. Imagine me having to muzzle my tongue and cover up my past as if I'd been a . . . a Holladay Street whore.

But that thought brought her up with a bitter grimace. She would tell Jay nothing. Eden was exactly where she wanted to be. She was through with Jay and his cheap tent-show life forever.

[317]

She was so absorbed, as she neared Eden, lying puny and vulnerable on the large flatness of the prairie, that she did not realize the sky had clouded over. A spat of raindrops in the dust made her look up in surprise. But it smelled good. Did anything ever smell so good as a late summer shower, when the roads were ankle-deep in dust and every roadside weed was furred and gray? She turned up her face and let a drop or two plop on her cheeks, on her closed eyelids. She drew in a deep sensuous breath.

She saw that the main street had been suddenly emptied, as everyone scurried inside, and doors banged shut, and windows slammed down. You'd have thought they were all spun-sugar Christmas tree ornaments, so afraid were they of a drop of rain. A nice little summer shower.

Rob was just locking up his store to go home for supper. Mercy, was it that late? When he saw her, his face lighted up as if from a glow inside him. He waited for her in the deepening twilight.

"Here's your mail, Roxy." He held out a wrapped cylinder of newspaper, addressed to her in Mrs. Pfaab's handwriting.

She glanced at it with a marked lack of interest. She knew what she would find, a village newspaper from Naomi forwarded by Mrs. Pfaab, telling all about the last church baked-goods sale. At the moment she was in no mood to read about another village baked-goods sale. She took the brown-paper package and tucked it under her arm. She must remember to send Mrs. Pfaab the postage.

"Do you want to stand here under the canopy till the rain stops?" asked Rob.

"No, I like a little rain, don't you?" She laughed. "I was all shriveled up with the drought. Now I can feel my petals uncurl."

He chuckled and took her arm. They set off toward home through the delicate drizzle. Something about their aloneness together on a dusky village street deserted by sensible people who fled indoors at the first sprinkle, something about the admiring look in his eyes and the feel of a man's hand under her elbow guiding her, went to her head. She felt elated, infused with joy.

She threw back her head and sang softly "Sweet Betsy from Pike," because the song was associated with a merry period of her life, and for these few moments she was light of heart.

"You have a gift, did you know it, Roxy, for being happy? For making other people happy?"

She smiled straight up into his face. She was overflowing with felicity. Surely it was all right to let him share her joy. She sang the second verse. He joined in with a shy bass rumble. Unconsciously she went into a slight suggestion of her stage routine. She pursed her lips and fluttered her lashes and smiled roguishly upward.

He caught her hand in his and held it tight against him, as if to capture and hold the singer as well as the song, as if to capture and hold on to this moment in his life. The sudden current that went through her from his warm, hard handclasp alarmed her. She tried to pull her hand away; he would not let it go.

He said hoarsely, "I was a headstrong young fool to dash off in a huff just because you wanted your little stage fling. I know now—"

Oh, he mustn't go on. She must keep him from putting it into words. Everything would still be all right if he didn't put it into words.

"We're all headstrong when we're very young, Rob. I guess that's part of being young," she said tremulously.

His longing gaze was unnerving. It was hard to be stern with the man who had given you your first kiss and taught you the ways of love and admired you and healed your pride.

Suddenly Rob's image was blurred by drops on her lashes that were not rain. She felt a wave of sadness for their lost youth, hers and Rob's. But it *was* lost. Most wisdom came too late.

She moved away from him and sang "Flee as a Bird" in a

[319]

mournful little voice. And Rob went on looking at her across the space that separated them, with the old look, drinking her up, willing her to answer his look.

They turned the corner and heard a gate bang shut. Avis, bent against the light rain, was coming toward them, holding one umbrella over her head, while she carried another in her hand. Over her arm hung a mackintosh.

A wave of tender contrition went through Roxana. How like Avis to come out in the rain just to keep her sister from getting wet. Good, dutiful, anxious little Avis. Her heart contracted. Hurt Avis twice? I almost ruined her life once with my carelessness. Wound her again? Never!

But it was a little difficult to maintain her mood of loving remorse when Avis recognized them and said it was certainly a pity people couldn't remember to carry an umbrella or mackintosh when they started out for long walks in the country, so she wouldn't have to leave her rolls just when it was time to put them into the oven. She held out the umbrella, which Rob opened for Roxana. She draped the mackintosh around Roxana's damp shoulders. Avis' tone implied that there was something self-indulgent about a grown woman taking long walks in the country.

"You'd better hurry on in, too, Rob. You've got the Town Council meeting after supper, you remember. Your coat's all wet. I'll have to press it. You'd better put on your other shoes, and I'll stuff newspapers in these and dry them back of the stove."

It was plain what Avis thought of the pair of them: they were a wool-gathering sister and a husband who required a deal of looking after. Meekly Rob and Roxana followed her into the house.

After Rob had gone, the two sisters settled down to sew, under the hanging lamp in the dining room. Roxana was making impatient and none-too-smooth darns on Rob's socks. She might be able to trim hats and design frocks, but she could not put her heart into sock-darning. When she finished a pair, she rolled it into a wad and threw it toward the center of the table.

Avis, across from her, was sorting freshly ironed napkins and laying them out in glossy white piles. Roxana watched in frank amazement as Avis took out white linen cases, like cloth envelopes, from the sideboard. Each case had the word "Napkins" embroidered on it in blue, surrounded by sprays of forget-me-nots. With lingering pleasure, Avis caressed her shining napkins and inserted them, a half-dozen at a time, in their various cloth cases. As she looked at Roxana, making her indifferent bumpy darns, a frown creased her fairness.

"Dear," she said rebukingly. "I can see you've never been a real housewife. Now in Eden we take pride— Those darns, for instance; no good housewife here would ever make such queer little bumps. And then to roll them into regular little knots when you're through. See the way I do it? I turn them partway inside out, so Rob pushes his toes into the end of the sock, and then I smooth them out and match them up in pairs. If you really hope to become a part of Eden, if you want the nicest women to approve of you—" She paused delicately.

"What if I don't?"

"Don't what?"

"Don't want to be like the women in Eden? What if I don't care what that old bellwether, Mrs. Murdoch, thinks of me?"

Avis was incredulous and outraged.

"How can you say such a thing, when you were the one—? You broke up our friendship. You've made me a laughing stock. You've even been talked about yourself—your past. Wherever I go, I hear whispering. I only ask a little consideration from you, so you won't be so careless, so stagy, so selfish about your own pleasures."

Her own pleasures! Roxana wondered angrily what they were.

"You mean that the 'nice' women of the town spend their

time gossiping about the stranger in their midst, is that it?" she flared. "Well, let me tell you something, Avis. There are other places besides this miscalled Eden of yours. With more tolerance and culture, and maybe more goodness, too. There are better people than your canonized Mrs. Murdoch. The Starbucks, for instance. They don't carp and criticize. They take people as they are and love them and work with them and try to make them see God. They aren't forever pecking them to pieces."

She stopped for breath. Avis was silent, tucking napkins aimlessly into cases and pulling them out again.

"As for wanting to live the life of Eden, I don't, Avis. Everything in piles like your napkins. In stuffy little embroidered cases, even your feelings."

Avis was crying now. She hurled the pile of napkins on to the table where they slid in every direction.

"You don't understand, Roxy. You never wanted a nice life. You were willing to live any old way. In a shaft house. In a coffin shop. In a tent-show car. Any old way at all, so long as you could have change and excitement. It isn't wrong to like things nice. To want to be respected and looked up to, instead of having a patchy, makeshift existence."

Sobbing, she ran out of the room. Roxana heard her bedroom door shut and the springs protest as Avis flung herself down. She started after Avis. Then she paused. She remembered all the symptoms too clearly. Avis would wait there sobbing, to be coaxed out of her cry, to hear the apologies, and finally to weaken and accept them grudgingly with little sniffs.

"I can't do it, Avis," she whispered sorrowfully. "We're both grown-up. We're both to blame for this. But I can't do the way Pa did with Mother and coax you out of a cry every time you get your feelings hurt."

She went to her own room and shut the door firmly so Avis would know she was not coming.

Later, after she was in bed, she heard Avis' door open

softly. A tide of warm regret flowed over her. Avis was sorry for their quarrel, too. Avis was coming to make amends first, this time. Roxana leaped to her feet to meet her sister halfway, to hold her in her arms, to be the first with the apologies.

But Avis did not come. Roxana stood with her hand on her doorknob and heard her go into the dining room instead. Then she knew. Avis was far more worried about her scattered dinner napkins than she was about her sister's feelings. She was picking up the napkins and piling them in neat stacks; she was inserting them in their embroidered cases and putting them away in the sideboard. The drawer protested as she cautiously closed it. Then Avis tiptoed back to her own room.

Much later Roxana heard Rob come home from his meeting and go to bed. The house settled down to its night stillness. The country quiet seeped in. She lay there wide awake. It was long after midnight when she heard the lonely *whoo-whoo* of a train sweeping through the night. The loneliest sound in the world was that of a far-off train at night.

She shivered. How lonely life was, at best. Her native resiliency was pierced. For the first time she had a knowledge of what it meant to grow old. It was a frightening business. You thought you could share your journey, the solitary journey of each soul toward death. But no matter how close you huddled to another—to a friend, a sister, a husband—trying to cheat your lurking enemy, mortality, you failed. All you could do was walk bravely on alone, little and afraid and beset.

Chapter XXVIII

EVEN THOUGH her eyeballs burned and her arms and legs were weighted with lead, Roxana did not dare be late to breakfast. While she bent over and worked her button-hook back and forth, she could hear Avis' vehement breakfast-getting. These thin partitions! Before that, she had heard Rob and Avis quarreling, or rather, Avis' high-pitched scolding and Rob's placating rumble.

It was like the night before the tent blow-down, with all of them ready to leap at each other's throats. But it seemed unfair for Avis to take out her own inner discord on Rob. Poor Rob! How could he go on like this? A lifetime is so long.

She needed to think, yet she dared not take time to think. She must get out to the kitchen.

Dreading the day ahead, Roxana opened her bedroom door and went out. Civil good mornings were exchanged all around. She noted that Avis' eyes were puffy as if she, too, had not slept but had wept into her pillow. Rob looked distressed, but also resentful over having to feel distressed.

As they sat down to breakfast Roxana thought grimly, So help me, if I use a drop of cream on my oatmeal. But there was no oatmeal. As if to prove something, Avis had outdone herself on her breakfast: golden meaty slices of salt pork, rich cream gravy, crumbling hot biscuits, amber honey. Perversely Roxana could not eat.

Avis' eyes were fixed on her plate as she made her announcement.

"I changed my mind about the Beryl Creek School dedication, Rob. With you a member of the board, one of us ought to go. I've sent word to Mr. Murdoch that I'll take your place on the platform. He'll appreciate it, being president of the school board and all. I've put up a lunch for you to eat at the store, Rob. No need for Roxy to have to fix you a dinner this noon. When I get back tonight, we'll have a good hot meal."

She meant that Roxy wasn't "domestic" and would probably not get a very good dinner for Rob if he were to come home at noon. But Roxana was relieved, for it also meant that Avis had made her peace with Mrs. Murdoch; and best of all, it meant that she would be away all day, and the sisters could thus postpone "having it out." So Avis, too, had dreaded this day at home with her sister.

Rob grunted something about its not making any difference whether either of them went. But Roxana knew that it would. Avis would be a credit to Rob, so fair and pretty and mannerly. Beryl Creek and the Murdochs would approve of her.

After Rob had left for the store, the two sisters ostentatiously busied themselves. Roxana thought Avis was trying to say something. There was a quivering look about her chin, about her lips, about her eyes, as if words hovered, waiting to be spoken.

"Oh, Avis," cried Roxana impulsively, "let's not go on like this."

A buggy came to a stop out in front.

"Whoa there, Prince. Whoa there, Sambo," called out Mr. Murdoch's hearty imperious voice, as he tried to hold in the early-morning spirits of his black team. Mrs. Murdoch was moving over in the buggy and turning back the lap robe hospitably to make a place for Avis beside her.

Avis gave Roxana a startled enigmatic glance, hesitated,

[325]

took another harried look out the window at Mr. Murdoch sawing on the bits of his curveting team, and ran for the door.

"Mr. Murdoch hates to be kept waiting," she called back over her shoulder.

From behind the thick lace curtains Roxana watched Mr. Murdoch cramp the buggy sharply so Avis could leap in, settling her sprigged gray flounces and dolman and bonnet all at once. It was a dowdy bonnet, worn too far back, Roxana noted with her critical milliner's eye, yet somehow it framed Avis' wistful young face sweetly.

As they drove off, she gave a wintry chuckle. They would have a splendid day. Avis would sigh over her sister's ways. Mrs. Murdoch would comfortingly hint that all stage people, even those playing Shakespearean roles, were flighty, and that every family had its gray sheep. She would advise Avis how to "handle" Roxana. Mr. Murdoch would pat Avis' hand in a fatherly way and decide to renew Rob's notes, and everything would be lovely again.

Lovely! The ties were binding Rob tighter and tighter.

She finished the housework. It took so little time if you didn't just revel in each silly chore as if it were a religious ritual. The only trouble with hurrying was that then you were through so soon. How did housewives fill their days, with no sides to learn, no rehearsals to attend, no costumes to mend? She wished she could retrim a hat; her fingers itched to get at Avis' second-best. But she would not dare. Not after Mrs. Murdoch's.

She washed out the tea towels righteously and hung them on the back porch. Now there was nothing left to do. It would be hours before she could go for the afternoon mail. Not that there was the slightest likelihood of her getting any. In all the time she had been here, she had heard only from a couple of ladies at Mrs. Pfaab's and from Naomi Starbuck. She felt a twinge of guilt that she had not yet opened Naomi's paper to read about her precious baked-goods sale.

How her feeling toward post offices had changed. She regarded them with neither hopes nor fears, now that Avis had been found. She had prayed so hard to find Avis. She wondered about throwing your whole heart into praying for something, because when you got it— She must write to Naomi, for Naomi had prayed hard, too. But what was there to tell her?

Noon came. She ate a sandwich, standing beside the kitchen table, as women do when there is no man to cook for. Soon she could go for the mail; anything to get out of this neat, careful, reminding little house. She was hanging up her dishcloth when she heard steps on the front porch. She hurried into the dining room just as Rob opened the front door and came in. Slowly he closed the door and turned to face her, looking oddly set of feature.

"I thought I'd drop by the house to see how you were getting on," he said lamely, watching her.

She stared at him, and she was suddenly filled with uneasiness. Rob never left his store in the middle of the afternoon. And now with his wife gone for the whole day—

He read her startled thoughts.

"Yes, I came because I knew Avis would be away. I had to see you alone. I never get a minute with you. I gather you and Avis had a misunderstanding last night."

"Misunderstanding?" She laughed harshly. "Maybe that's the trouble. We no longer misunderstand each other."

"But what was it about? She just got hysterical when I asked. Was it something serious?"

"Of course it was serious, terribly serious. It was about the way I fold socks and how she stores napkins in her sideboard drawer. That's what our quarrel was about." Her laugh was shrill.

He moved closer. Her uneasiness turned into acute apprehension as she saw the reckless grimness in his face.

"Now you see what I mean, Roxy? I can't go on either. Everything just so. Laid out like . . . like rows in a garden.

No lightness. No fun. No singing in life. Nothing—well, fanciful."

She was sobered, filled with quick pity. He asked so little. A tiny joke, a tender smile, a ballad in the rain. But he *had* to go on. That's what marriage meant—going on.

"But this is the kind of life you wanted, Rob. The reason you left Central—left me—was because I didn't fit into your ideas of a well-ordered life."

He looked driven.

"Maybe I don't know what I like. But I know what I love. I've never gotten over you, never gotten you out of my heart. Don't think I haven't tried."

He came steadily toward her. His eyes were queerly brilliant, his mouth taut. He caught her by the shoulders, held her, made her look at him and listen to him. It seemed to her she had been avoiding his glances for weeks. And now she had to face his hungry, misery-filled eyes.

Her frightened heart beat hard. My sister's husband!

"We've both tried," he was saying, "but it's too much for us. We love each other. We have always loved each other." He said it as if there were no possible other answer.

Had they always? she wondered confusedly. He was her first love, it was true. But so much had happened in between. And now there was Avis! She looked around wildly for some sort of soul-stiffening in this neat little house. At the new pink ribbons Avis had sewed on the newspaper rack, at the tawny grasses Avis had freshly gathered for the vase beside the Rogers group.

"Avis gives you the kind of home, the kind of life you need," she protested. "I couldn't—"

"I need you. Your love. I'm wild for you, Roxy. I think of you all day—and all night." The hands on her shoulders were shaking.

She tried again in a breathless way.

"I'm a gypsy. Gypsies don't—they don't get the wash out

first on Mondays and raise money for the library fund and board the teacher."

"I don't care," he said in stubborn despair. "I want to chuck everything."

"But you can't. People think they can start over, but they can't. Divorce—" She faltered over the dreadful word.

She felt him start. Then he was pleading again, with his eyes, his voice, the hands on her shoulders.

"Nothing matters but you," he said thickly.

"Yes, it does. You've got your store here. You'd lose it and all your years of work. Today Avis will make everything right with the Murdochs. You'll see. She'll completely pacify Mrs. Murdoch and she'll make Mr. Murdoch so happy he'll renew your notes at once."

For an instant his glance flickered. He had not thought of that. Then he pushed the idea from him and drew her closer. She put up her hands against his chest to make a barrier between them.

"It's you I need!" he groaned.

Ah, to be needed! No one in the world but Rob seemed to need her. She was rent with the desire to comfort him, to offer him what peace or joy or oblivion he could find in her love. She weakened, and with her weakening, she was in his arms at last. His mouth sought hers, fierce with longing. But with his first kiss, she knew. Even while she felt her hair loosen and heard a tortoise-shell pin crunch underfoot, she knew this wasn't love. This was mature, experienced, long-denied hunger of the senses; this was what her mother would have called "a temptation of the flesh." But it wasn't love.

Somehow she had to make Rob see it, too.

"There's Avis to think about!" she sighed, trying to push him away. But he did not hear. He was beyond hearing, beyond caring for anything but the rapture in his arms.

"We can't do this, Rob, we can't," she pleaded again.

But he could. Passion knows neither unselfishness nor pity

[329]

nor caution. As well expect a drunken man to take thought of the future.

He picked her up in his arms and started blindly across the room with her. She was too startled to struggle. Rob! This ruthless stranger. Even with her face crushed against his hard-pounding heart, she knew instinctively where his steps were heading. She must fight against this madness that possessed him.

Steps creaked on the back porch. She felt him tauten and come to a stop. Slowly he set her down. They stood there rigid, listening with straining attention. A rap sounded. There is nothing like a rap on the door to shatter a mood. Through the window she saw a wagon out in back.

"It's old man Webb with the butter," she whispered. "He always comes on Thursdays." She was tucking up her hair, sticking pins into it, smoothing her disarray. "I'll take the butter from him. You stay out of sight. He mustn't see you here this time of day."

She walked unsteadily out to the back door and opened it.

"Thank you. I'll give the butter to Mrs. Evans," she told the old man and took the cloth-wrapped chunk. She could feel the dents through the cloth, made by the wooden paddles. She stood inside the kitchen door and watched through the starched scrim curtains until he had climbed back into his wagon and driven off.

"Has he gone?" asked Rob in a queer choked voice.

"Yes; I'd better take the butter right out to the root cellar. You know how strong country butter tastes if you leave it sitting in a warm room."

She gave him no chance to answer. She crossed the level yard to the mound that was the root cellar and went down the four steps. She opened the thick wooden door into the cool little underground dugout where they kept their vegetables and meat and milk. Her hands shook so that she could scarcely place the oval shape on the slatted shelf. She stood there, leaning faintly against the mildew-smelling post that supported the roof.

What have I done! Oh, God, what have I done to my little sister!

Bitter anguish, remorseful anguish, swept over her. It was like the time nine years before when she had returned from her week with the DeForest Company to find Avis gone. And like that time, in the extremity of her despair, she prayed.

I know the flesh is weak; how well I know it. But it was a thousand times worse for me to have damaged my sister's chance of happiness. Everything was all right until I came back to Eden. They were both happy then; Avis was happy; Rob was happy too, he had the look. And then I spoiled it all—me the outlander, with my stagy ways. I had to remind him of the past. I had to flutter my lashes at him and sing ballads and make him sorry for himself. I had to stir up his yearnings—as if everybody didn't have yearnings sometimes. I had to all but ruin their lives.

My little sister!

Standing there in the darkness, smelling the damp cellar-smell, she prayed for knowledge and wisdom and cunning— to rebuild what she had torn down; to restore a crumbling marriage. To give Rob back to Avis. To give the real Avis back to Rob.

Slowly she retraced her steps across the yard to the house, her head down, her eyes on the ground.

Rob was waiting for her inside the door with flushed impatience. But she evaded him swiftly this time. When she spoke, it was no longer a breathless Roxana, fighting her own weakness as well as his desire. It was a sisterly Roxana, infinitely remote and gentle.

"All marriages at some time or other are threatened, Rob. Because all of us, now and then, tire of our bargains." She spoke with bleak honesty, remembering those nights lying beside the sleeping Grover in the big bed at the Windsor when she had felt so caged, when the very walls had pressed in upon her. "Yet the worst thing that could happen to you would be to lose Avis."

He stared at her, silent and rebellious.

"I get tired of places, Rob. I'm vain underneath—always posing. I've been 'touched' by the theater until I'm spoiled for a good, sensible life. I'd always be looking back over my shoulder."

He listened to her with twisted lips. His ardor was not to be so easily deflected.

She turned desperately toward the sideboard.

"Look, Rob, I'll show you what I mean." She picked up a handful of socks she had worked on the night before. "I loathe darning socks. I make horrid little bunches that will hurt your feet when you wear them. All I like is to design extravagant hats that nobody in Eden would be caught dead in."

His mouth tightened. Talk, talk, his expression said.

"You like order." She looked up at him with last-ditch pleading. "Life in neat piles. Like this."

She jerked open the sideboard drawer to show him.

"In embroidered cases—everything in its right case," she said.

She stopped. Something down in the corner of the drawer caught her eye. Wonderingly she reached in and drew out a wooden napkin ring, the little old napkin ring Mr. Evans had carved so long ago. The wooden napkin ring that had "Avis" on one side and a bluebird on the other. "And they have clean napkins every Sunday, Roxy, and Aunt Edna bakes cookies on Fridays, and Uncle Than is going to put up a swing for me."

She gazed back across the years, and her throat tightened unbearably. The adored napkin ring, the cherished napkin ring, worn smooth by a little girl's caresses. The napkin ring that stood for all that the eleven-year-old Avis had so grievously needed—security, order, permanence. Whereas she, Roxana, had never wanted any of them. She looked at Rob

[332]

now from far off. Her fingers clutched the napkin ring like a talisman.

"Remember, Rob, how she loved this napkin ring? How it meant everything she didn't have in the life she lived with me? Surely you, of all people, understand. Because you were so sweet to her then; you even scolded me for neglecting her."

She saw that his own thoughts were going backward, too, to the shy, lonely, needing little girl that was Avis. Reluctantly going backward. He did not want to go back, but he had to. The napkin ring had carried him back.

"I believe, for the first time, Rob, I love my little sister enough to think only of what's best for her, not just what will grease my own conscience. Good heavens, what if I *had* found her earlier? I could never have made a home she'd have been happy in. She needed an Aunt Edna." She added gravely, "She needed a you."

He still stared at her, dazed and bereft. But he would get over this, she knew. He had taken the one romantic misstep of his married life; there would never be another one. He was tidy and proper and well-intentioned and not very strong —stiffened mostly, as Monty would have said, by fear of what people would think—and he was exactly right for Avis.

"Opposites may attract, Rob. But they shouldn't try to live together. Like my father and mother. Like Avis and me. Poor young one! All she asked was an orderly life. And look at what she got. A shaft house with a hundred-foot pit in the middle, her parents' sudden death, and a sister that went off and left her alone, so she had that hideous fright in the coffin shop. It was enough to unbalance a child. Oh, Rob, don't you see?" Tears thickened her voice.

Against his will, Rob was seeing. His mouth worked. He turned and looked out the window, rattling coins in his pocket. He was a kind person, and until Roxana had come back and he had embarked upon this brief, bewildering

[333]

journey away from propriety, he had loved Avis devotedly. He would love her devotedly again.

"Rob, I'm leaving. For all our sakes. Try to make Avis understand, won't you?"

"But how can I? I can't tell her I was here today." Already he was wondering about ways and means.

"Tell her—" She halted. "Tell her there was some mail for me that looked important, and you brought it up. Then if anyone saw you come, it will be all right." She could see him relax a little. She went on with her lie. "Tell her I got word to come back—" She paused to search her thoughts desolately. Word from whom? Come back where? "To come back to the theater. There's an opening for me. Tell her I had to take the first train out, but she can always reach me through Mrs. Pfaab. I'll write to her."

She reached up to her throat. "And give her this hair brooch." She felt heady with generosity. Oh, to give everything she had to Avis! "It was our mother's, and Avis is a great one for holding on to things with sentiment." She thrust it into his hand. "Now help me get off, Rob."

His fingers closed over the brooch. He tried to speak, but he could only follow her helplessly to the doorway of her bedroom and watch her throw things into her telescope.

"What will you do, Roxy? Who will look after you? You haven't any money. Will you be all right?"

"Of course, I'll be all right. Gypsies—and theatrical people—always get along."

"But where are you going? To Denver?"

"Yes, to Denver. There's a train out at four, isn't there?"

"A train, yes; but not to Denver. You'll have to stay here tonight and take the morning train."

She was in a sudden panic.

"I can't do that. I must leave today, now, before Avis gets back. It's the only way to save the love we still have—Avis and I. Before I do any more harm to her life here in Eden—

to her life here with you." She said it openly, her suffering plain in her face.

His glance flinched. "If you take this four o'clock train, you'll have to sit up all night at the junction in order to get a train going to Denver in the morning."

"I don't mind. It's the only way. You do see that, Rob? Help me—please."

He caught the contagion of her haste. He helped her pack, rather better than she was doing it herself. He even went out into the kitchen and fixed some kind of lunch for her; she heard him opening doors to the food safe and rustling wrapping paper.

"I think you can just make it, Roxy," he called over his shoulder.

Presently they were hurrying toward the depot. Roxana was smiling tenderly.

"Always keep the upper hand with Avis, Rob. But love her a lot and laugh at her often, so she won't get all puffed up with her virtues. Yet her virtues are very real. She's worth ten of me."

She caught a fleeting expression of pain and denial on his face.

Hastily she went on, "The world needs you both. Eden needs you both. Already you've made it a better town. It will be a wonderful place to bring up children in. Just remember, don't let her lash out at you. Stop her with a kiss— and spank her when necessary!"

He looked at her in doubt.

"Yes. A woman never forgets a man who's once spanked her," she said teasingly. But a wincing memory stopped her.

At the railroad station they looked down the tapering tracks to the feather of smoke from an approaching train. He had put her ticket to Denver into her hand and he stood looking at her with all the unspoken things of his heart still in his eyes. With a sadness for all that he was losing forever.

(But wasn't there a trace of relief, too, at what he was getting back?)

He helped her up the steps to the back platform of the train and lifted her telescope up after her. The train started. She leaned across the back rail and waved to him, smiling brilliantly. And then Eden and Rob dissolved in her swimming tears.

Anyone watching them saw only a slim and pretty woman who wore her clothes with an air and carried her head with an air and even waved smiling good-bys with an air.

A woman saying good-by to her brother-in-law.

Chapter XXIX

S HE SAT THERE with her head back against the plush seat, breathing like a spent swimmer, while the rushing flatness flowed by the train window. At first her only feeling was relief. *I got away just in time to save Avis' marriage, just in time to save our love for each other.*

She hoped she could mend things between herself and Avis. Maybe Avis, too, was filled with regrets. Roxana remembered her tear-ravaged face this morning and the words trembling on her lips. Maybe Avis, too, wanted to say, "I love you, even if your ways aren't my ways. You are my sister, and I love you."

She would forge a new and better bond between them. As soon as she reached Denver she would look up those new cut-paper patterns that made sewing easy. Not that Avis would ever be an inspired seamstress. But with those patterns and the new lock-stitch sewing machine Rob had bought her, she might achieve a bit of style. In a thousand little ways, she could let Avis know she loved her.

But what was to become of her, Roxana? She was suddenly without goal or purpose. All these years she had been sustained by the dream of finding her sister and of their being together. She had molded her whole life—warped it even—striving toward that goal.

She tried to plan and she could make no plans. She could

almost hear Jay saying, "Whatever you do, don't look back. There's only one place to go, and that's ahead. Takes spunk sometimes. A chicken-gutted gambler never filled an inside straight."

The train swung around in a wide curve to follow the creek. She could look across the prairie toward Eden. The wind flattened the grass with great cat-licks as far as the eye could see. But there was no Eden now; not a tree or a house or a smudge of smoke was left on the horizon to mark the scar.

It was after dark when the train stopped to let her off at the junction, a bleak, wind-harried little frame depot located where two railroad lines crossed each other in a great X. She looked about her. No town, no hotel, no houses. Only the station and the section hands' quarters and a shed behind the waiting room. Rob had been right: it was no place to spend the night. But she had been right too; Eden would have been worse.

She entered the darkened waiting room, with its row of iron-armed seats, a cold stove in the corner sitting on a zinc square, and liver-colored wainscoting made of narrow vertical boards, all around. The only light came from a reflector lamp in the ticket office.

She went up to the barred window to speak to the agent, who was bent over his clicking telegraph key. When she had explained her situation, he pushed back his green eyeshade with a gesture of distress.

"Nobody ever stays here all night, ma'am. We usually close up in about an hour. I batch, or I'd offer you—"

She waved her hand dismissingly.

"I won't mind in the least. I'm in the theatrical business, so I'm used to sitting up all night between trains or stagecoaches. You go right ahead as always."

What she meant was, I had no choice; it was the only way.

Before he left, he brought in a pail of water which he placed in the ladies' cloakroom, a bare little closet with one high window, containing a mirror and a scarred table, and gave her the key to what he delicately referred to as the "coal shed." Then he locked up his ticket office for the night and left the stranded passenger to her vigil.

She ate one of the sandwiches Rob had put up for her. There were two big ones and an apple. She put the second sandwich frugally away and settled herself with her feet up on her telescope and her cloak around her. Those hard iron arms, put there as if to make sure no one could stretch out for a nap. But maybe that was for the best.

I might as well get it straight about Rob, she thought; so I can put him away forever. I never really loved him, not even when I was sixteen and full of the romantic gibberish that passes for love. He cosseted my vanity when Professor Jay wounded it, just as he did in Eden when the rest of the town scoffed. It was easy to feel sympathetic toward him after that, and then we both grew so dreadfully vexed with Avis. You can justify a lot of badness in yourself, if only you can be vexed enough with someone.

She shivered at how close she had come to wrecking Avis' life, and Rob's, and her own.

Everything about Eden had been a mistake. She longed to tell someone about it—Jay—and see his sidewise grin.

"What a ninny you were to think you could suit Eden. You, who always have to live stage center, and who'd hate like poison to accept second billing to a Mrs. Murdoch."

"I wanted to fit in."

"You think you did. But you're stage folk. You make a production out of tying your shoelace. You were acting all the while, and they knew it."

"But those stuffy club programs, and Avis' tidy pigeon-holed life, and their awful hats!"

"I bet you tried to make every one of them over. Well, you found out you couldn't."

"I've wasted my whole life, Jay," she wanted to mourn.

"Maybe not," he would say. "You and I are the kind who

shut our eyes and plug up our ears for fear we'll profit by somebody else's mistakes. We have to do our own living and make our own mistakes. Well, we've done it and we've made them. Maybe now, Roxy, at last, we're ready to follow our hearts."

Hearts. Her own heart chilled. For a moment, while she was living this imaginary conversation with Jay, she had been almost comforted. She had forgotten that everything was over between them. She remembered only how profoundly she needed him.

Jay had seen so much of life; yet underneath he was not completely cynical. As Monty said, in the theater the weak are weaker and the strong are stronger. Jay could be savage and cruel in his rage, but he possessed a strength. He kept his word; he had a goal—that rarest of things in the tent-show world—and he could see life as it was. He was the one person in the world who could look at all her imperfections and still find her—desirable.

Grover had never known her; she had not dared be her true self with him for one instant. With Naomi she could be more nearly honest, but Naomi was always attributing high-minded impulses to her that she did not have. Her life with Avis and Rob had been one long strained subterfuge.

But she had fooled herself the worst of all. Now she was being honest at last; she was through with her illusions. I'm grown-up; I want a grown-up love. I want a life that I can be *me* in.

She stood off and looked at herself. I'm of the stage. Whether it's sleazy and weak, or magnificent and strong, the theater is my life. I may never succeed at it, but I'll be doing what I long to do, and what I'm fitted to do.

She went on and said the sobering words at last. And sleazy and weak, or magnificent and strong, *Jay is my man.* We understand each other; we need each other . . . and we can never have each other.

She put her face down on her arms and wept. For there

was Fifi, and there was Crystal! All the old sickness rushed back over her. A man who would run off and leave a woman, even a cheap little tart like Fifi, without caring whether or not she was in the family way—

But I love him.

The long night wore on. At last she slept, cramped and uncomfortable and cold, but at peace. There is peace in reaching even the bitterest conclusion, if it be an honest one.

Morning came. She stretched and tried to get the knots out of her aching muscles. She ate the dry and crumbling second sandwich, and washed it down with water from the pail.

She thought wearily, I must freshen up. But why? Who cares? No bally to make up for; no man to pretty myself for. I'm the kind of woman who has to have a man to cook for, to preen for, to smile for, even.

Listlessly she reached inside her telescope for a clean handkerchief. She turned over the wrapped newspaper forwarded by Mrs. Pfaab from Naomi. Rob must have put it in when he packed. She looked at it distastefully; she was not yet in a mood to relish a village bazaar or a baked-goods sale. The wrapper was torn, exposing a section of fine print underneath. She peered closer. It did not look like a paper from Naomi. Her eye fastened upon an advertisement for "superior horsehair wigs and the finest stick-fast crepe for beards."

She gave a little gasp. Stage talk. With fumbling fingers she tore off the outer cover to find a second cover underneath. It was addressed to her, not in Naomi's writing, but in Jay's forceful, angular, hurried script. She ripped off that cover, too. Jay had sent her a copy of the *Bill-Poster*: "News of Stock Companies, Traveling Tents, and the Carnival World."

In headlong haste she turned the pages. At last she found an item, heavily marked, under the heading, "News of the Traveling Tents."

[341]

The Great Divide Tent Show (Physic) had bad luck in Dry Creek last month. Fire and tent blow-down. But the fire was doused by the rain, and the tent was repaired, minus lean-to. Sutro the Strong Man was slightly injured rescuing his little daughter. He and his wife, the former Mlle. Fifi, with their child, have rejoined the southern carnival circuit where they were popular during recent years as the Tumbling Tortonis. Good luck to the Sutros (or Tortonis) on the fatback-and-grits circuit.

Jay Withrow, owner of the Great Divide, hired the well-known minstrel pair, Deuces Wild, to fill out the season, which winds up the last week in September in Vasquez Fork. Jay will then go into winter quarters, where he plans to organize a stock company to take out next summer —minus slum and pills. Good luck to the new producer, Jared Withrow.

She sat there holding the paper. Tears washed down her cheeks; her lips crimped into a trembling smile. It was a love letter. From Jay. The only one she had ever had; the only kind he would probably ever write.

It said, "See, my darling? Now you know what I found out that last night that put me in a mood to kill. Fifi and Sutro, trying to work the oldest sucker game in the world on me! I'm not half so good as I ought to be, nor half so bad as I'm painted. But I promise you, no more Fifis in my life—thank God, there never were any Crystals—and no more medicine shows either. I want to go on from here—on and up. I need you to go with me. Come back to me, Roxy. Come back."

The station agent was almost alarmed by the wide-eyed young woman who met him when he came to open up. Maybe that long night alone had been too much for her. She was all high color and teary, shining smiles and tumbling words that he could scarcely make out.

Sure, sure, he soothed her. Vasquez Fork was on the cross line. There was a train that would reach it around noon. Certainly she could get off at Vasquez Fork if she wanted to,

[342]

no matter if her ticket did read Denver. Sure he'd fetch her a pail of fresh water. No need to get in such a flutter though. There was plenty of time.

But she was in a flutter. She was drunk with joy as she went into the cloakroom to freshen up. A man to primp for! A bally even! She was glad she was used to dressing in drafty corners or behind screens or back of stage sets.

She splashed the cold water over herself, and the shock of it took her breath away and made her laugh aloud. Where was her rice powder? And her good petticoat? Her fingers could scarcely tie the tulle bow of her bonnet under her chin. It was the same bonnet she had worn last spring when she went out to interview the owner of the tent show at the end of the carline, who proved to be Jay. It was the same dress with the twenty-six crystal buttons down the front and the postilion tails over the bustle.

As the agent helped her on to the train with her baggage, her face was incandescent with happiness. It was all she could do to keep from throwing a kiss back at him. He shook his head wonderingly.

All the way to Vasquez Fork, Roxana was explosively impatient. Long before they reached the town, she was out on the platform, hanging from the hand rail to crane forward.

There it was! The gaudy old combination car on the siding. It had not changed a bit; the same sign telling the wonders of Dr. Langworthy's remedies, the same stovepipe at a crazy angle, the same calico curtains she had made at the windows. She could scarcely breathe.

She left her baggage on the depot platform and ran along it. It was almost noon. There went the noon whistle. There went the medicine-show band! Thin and brassy, as if the players were walking well apart, and brave as lions with their flaring blasts. With Jay at the head, she knew, leading with his golden cornet. She could pick out his gallant notes now, mellow and pure on the clear September air.

She turned the corner and saw them, well ahead of her, marching up the middle of the immensely wide and dusty main street. Something about the squared shoulders in their mussed red uniforms, with the breeze blowing the tarnished tassels on their caps, and their epaulets swaying in jaunty time to the "Tenth Regiment March," cramped her throat. And made her laugh aloud—and cry a little, too.

She hurried after them through the gathering crowd. They came to a halt and took their places at the crossroads in the heart of the town. Recklessly the band swung into Jay's own version of the "Light Cavalry Overture." At last she could make out Jay himself, leading his band, beating time with his cornet, and looking lean as a tomahawk and tough as rawhide.

Jay, oh, Jay, her heart cried out to him as she put her hand to her ribs and leaned out from the walk a little, her gaze devouring him.

And then Jay turned and saw her. His eyes for one un-shielded moment blazed in incredulous welcome. She heard the cornet notes skip and falter. She saw him leave his men, still trumpeting valiantly, and come straight across the road toward her and up to the walk. With one arm, he scooped her up and led her back to the bally. There she stood, close be-side him in the hard circle of his arm, while the shouting melody picked up and went on with a new note of triumph, while the drumbeats boomed and the brassy high notes shrieked.

Music—music was in the air.

Doors sprang open up and down the street. You let the meat burn, you put down the horse's hoof you were shoeing, you slammed shut your ledgers, you left the half-cut length of dress goods. It wasn't every day you had music at your door. It beckoned you, this magical, distracting music from a gayer, happier world. Come with me, it said; oh, come with me.

THE END

[344]